C000127870

WILDFLOWER

MONIQUE MULLIGAN

PRAISE FOR WILDFLOWER

'*Wildflower* is a beautifully crafted coming-of-age story with a powerful message sure to resonate across generations.' – Sara Foster, *The Hush*

'*Wildflower* is a brave and hugely necessary book. Written with such tenderness, grace and sensitivity, this book is a light in the darkness and a strong voice for the rights of all women to be safe and cherished. A triumph of a novel.' – Tabitha Bird, *The Emporium of Imagination*

'*Wildflower* is a skilfully constructed and captivating novel that weaves together a tender and poignant coming-of-age story with a powerful narrative tracing the aftermath of one woman's escape from an abusive relationship ... a totally engaging and convincing read, it's also an important read.' – Lyn Yeowart, *The Silent Listener*

PRAISE FOR WHEREVER YOU GO

'A deeply affecting, beautifully written and sensitively told story that tugs at the heartstrings. Readers will love the evocative descriptions of food peppered throughout.' – Vanessa Carnevale, *My Life For Yours*

'Unfolding with clear-eyed, soulful understanding and with deep respect for her characters, Mulligan's debut is a novel for those who crave stories about real people grappling with real life. A tender tale crafted with love and steeped in the healing togetherness that comes from sharing great food.' – Kim Kelly, *Her Last Words*

'Monique Mulligan takes us on an emotional rollercoaster in this deeply moving exploration of a marriage in distress. Have tissues ready!' – Lisa Ireland, *The Secret Life of Shirley Sullivan*

For the women in my life – my mother, mother-in-law, stepmother, stepdaughter; my sisters, my best friend, my aunts, my sisterhood. You have an extraordinary capacity for survival.

Microscopic threads bind torn pieces of me.
Stitching my soul, hemming in memories.
New experiences appliquéd over old.

This patchwork me
frays when a snag pulls at the fabric of my Self so
I gather the loose threads and mend the tear (invisible to most)
before it becomes a hole.

PROLOGUE
AUGUST 1999

I left him suddenly, but I imagined that leaving moment for years, in my heart and head, in my dreams and my reality. A secretive escape in the dark of night, perhaps, or a dramatic showdown. Or maybe, a carefully planned, piece-by-piece move. In the end, it took three little words from a concerned policewoman to get me over the line. Three little words I needed – wanted – desperately to hear: *you deserve better*. Later, I scrawled the words on a sticky note and slid the yellow square into my purse. A fake-it-till-I-make-it daily reminder.

Maybe one day I won't have to fake it.

He was not my first, but I thought he would be my last. He moulded me like clay and glazed me with love and affection; he broke me into pieces and glued me back together with apologies and flowers.

You're never the same once you've been broken. There are always pieces missing, even if they're invisible.

Tiny pieces of me. Where do they go?

I had left him before, twice, maybe three times. I always went back. This time was different. There are only so many times you can be burnt and, by now, my heart was ashes. He couldn't have put me back together, even if I'd wanted him to.

When you leave someone, the ending is only the beginning. The morning after it happened, I threw random clothes into a duffel bag and walked out of our rental house for good. Britney Spears was on the car radio singing 'Baby One More Time', her lonely desperation almost driving me back to the front door, almost killing me. I avoided looking in the rear-view mirror. Don't look back, don't go back for anything, I told myself. The night before, as he was handcuffed and led away, the policewoman pressed a business card into my clammy palm.

The only way to save your life is to lose the one you have, she said. To focus on what lies ahead, not on who and what is left behind.

Easy to say, I thought, as my former life faded from sight. Hard to start over with a bag of mismatched clothes, an unreliable car with a cracked windscreen, and a name and address scribbled on the back of a business card.

But not impossible.

My destination was three suburbs away. Not far enough to relax. Close enough for him to find me if he knew where to look. But if there's a room available, you take it, and I had nowhere else to go. I wound through unfamiliar streets, listening to Shania Twain, Pearl Jam and Savage Garden sing about love's wounds. Feeling as though my insides would erupt in a hot, sour mess, like the hailstorm that lashed Sydney while he lashed out at me. The SES were out and about, securing roofs and windows, clearing leaves and branches scattered around the streets. Funny how the clean-up lasts longer than the storm itself.

When I reached the address, I wasn't sure it was the right place. There was no sign. Nothing that made it stand out. The kind of place you wouldn't notice because it blended in with every other house on the street. An ordinary red-brick house, with a well-kept lawn and old rose bushes out the front. But it was the right place, according to the business card. Bryan Adams and Mel C wailed 'When You're Gone' as I turned into the driveway.

Reminders of the storm were everywhere. I moved a fallen branch and drove through a puddle as wide as the driveway to reach the hidden car park. Three other cars were parked there; two were blanketed with drowned blossoms from spreading golden wattles separating the car park from a large backyard. The wind must have whipped those trees into a frenzy to cause so much flower-drop, but still they hung heavy with drooping sprays of bright yellow. I squeezed my eyes shut. I can't stand wattle flowers.

It's hard to avoid wattles when you live in Sydney. They're everywhere. When they're not flowering you can zone them out, pretend they're just another tree, but when they're in bloom you can't miss them. And the smell, that sweet woody-honey fragrance. It makes me sick. I leaned towards my car's hanging tree air freshener and filled my lungs with the fake pine scent he always hated. Could I hold my breath all the way from the car park to the door? Or should I take it as a sign and get the hell away from here? My fingers drummed the steering wheel as I weighed up my options.

I didn't want to be here. I couldn't go back *there*.

My eyes darted back and forth: dashboard, house, cars, wattles. Golden balls of sunshine, that's what we used to call wattle flowers at school. Every year on Wattle Day – the first of August in the seventies – we'd plant baby wattle trees in the school grounds and decorate the classroom with flowers made from scrunched-up yellow crepe paper. One year we made golden wattle pom-poms and draped them from twigs we collected from the bushland behind the school. We'd colour in the Coat of Arms and get told off if we used the wrong colour for our national flower. We'd learn about how the wood, pollen and sap was used by Aboriginals for food, medicine, glues, dyes, even weapons. I reckon it's fascinating how trees and flowers can be used for so many things.

I went to an aromatherapy party once and the consultant said wattle oil had properties that helped relieve stress and depression. Does the bloody opposite for me, I said. Stresses me out like you wouldn't believe. And the pollen gives me hay fever, I don't care what the allergy experts say. That aromatherapy woman thought I was a pain in the arse for not believing her flower essence stuff. I don't blame her. I was a bitch that night.

I don't know how long I sat in that car park behind an ordinary red-brick house, wondering how on earth a women's refuge surrounded by wattles would give me the fresh start I needed. But finally, I forced myself from the car, blocking my nose to keep the pollen out, flinching when I stepped on a wattle twig. Flashing back to a sudden, hard slap on the cheek.

You wouldn't think that seeing and smelling those wattles and hearing a twig snap could take me back to an endless, simmering summer twenty years earlier. To a time when my childhood lost its innocence. But that summer is forever graffitied on my mind. Some things can never be undone. You learn from them if you can. If you can't, you do what you can to get by. Do your best to focus on now, not on what was or what could have been.

That's what I was doing when I pressed the intercom on the safety gate and announced myself in a shaking voice. Pushing away the past to reclaim my life, whatever my life was. Telling myself to be strong when I'd never felt weaker. The front door opened, and two women approached the gate: one in her sixties, one about my age. Hello, the older woman said to me, as she unlocked the gate, I'm Pat. Bye, she said to the younger woman, thanks for coming. See you next time, the one my age said to Pat, smiling politely at me as she squeezed past.

Our eyes met.

Someone gasped. Her. Me. Maybe both of us, I still don't know. But I do know this.

I was staring into a face I'd spent the last twenty years trying to forget.

CHAPTER ONE

1979

Mary Evans has me pinned against a brick wall behind the school canteen. Her hands are gripping my upper arms, fingernails digging in. My hands flail uselessly. Vile words spit from her mouth. Her hot breath smells like rank Vegemite. She pulls my hair. Calls me names: fatty boomba, fat cow, fat dobber. I say nothing. I don't call for help. There's no point. No one wants to get on the wrong side of Mary Evans. Instead, I squeeze my eyes shut, twist my face away from hers, and wait for it to be over.

'Teacher's coming,' someone says.

Mary Evans lets go. 'Don't go dobbing, Jane Kelly,' she hisses, shoving me against the wall again. 'Dobbers wear nappies.' She laughs. 'And dobbers get taught not to be dobbers.'

I wait for her to disappear around the corner before bolting to the girls toilets near the library. My back is throbbing, stinging, aching. I think the skin is grazed, but I can't tell for sure. I push the sleeves of my school dress up, first one, then the other. My arms are red and tender to the touch where Mary Evans squeezed. Looking closer, I see fingerprints on one arm, white crescent moons on the other. Sniffing, I wash my face, avoiding the mirror above the sink. I don't want to see myself through Mary Evans's eyes. I'll cry if I do and I can't do that here, not now. Instead, I hide in a toilet cubicle for exactly 360 seconds until the bell signals the end of lunch.

There are still 5400 seconds until the school year is over.

When the bell rings again, I don't hang around to say goodbye and have a good Christmas. I bolt to the school gate for a head start on Mary Evans. She walks home the same way, and I don't want her to see me cry. Because that's what I do as soon as I stop puffing. I can't hold the tears in anymore, can't hold the relief, the fear, the resentment, the anger anymore. I cry the whole way home because of Mary Evans. She's the prettiest and most popular girl in Year 5 and she hates my guts. If Mary Evans hates you, everyone hates you. And Mary Evans hates me worse than anyone at school for three reasons: I'm fat, ugly and smarter than her.

It started with name calling and the odd shove, kick or punch here and there. Warning everyone not to play with me or they'd catch ugly germs. Threatening kids who dared sit with me at lunch or recess. Not even Trisha Longbottom, who gets picked on because of her name and buck teeth, will play with me now. At first it only happened here and there. Now Mary Evans targets me every day. Sometimes it's just a mean prank, like when she told everyone I wet my pants after she squirted me with the bubbler, or when she told the teacher I fluffed, and the smell was making her sick. It wasn't me, it was Paul Jackson, but the whole class laughed and Mr Thiele made me move seats. Other times she ambushes me, without warning or reason. I don't think there has to be a reason, not for Mary Evans.

Because of Mary Evans I didn't get a single Christmas card this year. Mary Evans got fifty-six and some were from boys.

I don't plan on telling Mum what happened, but as soon as I

see her at the front door, wearing a daisy-patterned pinny over a blue sundress, I burst into tears.

'What's wrong?' Mum asks, taking my face in hers.

'I never want to go to that school again!' I tell her through snotty sobs and hiccups. 'I don't like Mary Evans. She's mean and nasty and ugly on the inside. And Jim called me Jane No Friends!' Mum's lips are like pencil lines, and I know he'll cop a telling-off later.

Jim's my brother. He's thirteen and reckons he's cool because he's in high school. On the way home from school, I told him what happened and because his stupid mates were there, he laughed. I wish I didn't have a brother. My big sister Sal wouldn't have laughed. She's sixteen-going-on-seventeen and she would have set Mary Evans straight. *Sisters stick together*, that's what me and Sal used to say.

We don't stick together much anymore.

Ever since Sal made best friends with Margie Murphy, she's been saying *buzz off, short stuff* to me whenever they want to talk in private. She says I'm too young and immature to hang out with them. Now she's got a boyfriend called Robbie Chapman. They're so lovey-dovey it makes me want to spew. I miss Sal. She's nearly a grown-up, but she was the closest thing to a best friend I've ever had. Now that she's swapped school for a bank job and a boyfriend, she's hardly ever home, and when she is, she's too busy getting ready to go somewhere else.

With *Robbie*. The sister robber. He looks like Greg Brady but has dirty fingernails because he's a third-year apprentice mechanic.

Thinking of Sal makes me sniff. In the kitchen, Mum passes me a tissue and a glass of milk topped with four heaped spoons of Milo. Four! She usually limits us to two flat teaspoons and stirs all the crunchy bits in. 'Blow your nose, love. And then give your face a wash. Back in a tick.'

A line of Christmas cards is strung up on the kitchenette, each one overlapping the next. I count forty before the red-cheeked Santas and smiling snowmen make my throat hurt. Five more cards than yesterday. Swallowing hard, I focus on my drink, scooping and savouring the crunchy, malty chocolate before gulping the ice-cold milk.

The toilet flushes. Mum walks back into the kitchen, drying her hands on her pinny. 'I might pop round the corner and have another chat with Dawn,' she says, more to herself than me. 'You and Mary used to be nice little friends. I'm sure we can sort this out.'

Mary Evans and I haven't been nice little friends since the day she put on a silly accent, pulled her eyes up at the corners, and called Claudia Ng names too awful to say. Everyone laughed but me and Claudia. And after I told Mr Thiele why Claudia was crying, Mary Evans called me a dobber and pushed me into a pole. She's had it in for me ever since.

Dobbers wear nappies!

'Jane? I asked if you wanted to come with me.'

'No!' Mum gives me a sharp look and I nearly burst out crying again. 'Don't talk to Mrs Evans. It's the holidays. I want to forget about it.'

Things got worse for me at school last time Mum talked to Mrs Evans. Mum doesn't know the half of it. I quit telling her about the name calling and pinching and shoving months ago. I'm only ten-going-on-eleven but I know this: being a dobber is the worst thing ever in a schoolyard. You're target practice. And no one sticks up for you. They're too busy protecting themselves. At first, I tried standing up for myself like I did with Claudia Ng. Look where that got me. Now I hide in the library at playtime because Mary Evans wouldn't be seen dead reading a book with more than 500 words.

I'm the loneliest person at my school.

'I'll be okay,' I tell Mum. 'It'll all be forgotten next year.' It won't. Mary Evans never forgets.

Mum huffs. 'I don't like this.' She chews her lip, which means she wants to say something, but instead she pulls me in for a hug. I wince when she accidentally touches the sore spot on my back but stay silent. There'd be no stopping her from going to Mrs Evans's house if she knew. Mum smells of honeysuckle talc and sweat, and I want to stay cocooned in her arms forever, but Dad's car is pulling in out the front and she's already gently pulling away.

'Some new neighbours are moving in next door on Sunday,' she says.

I shrug. *So?*

She smiles. 'You never know, they might have a daughter your age. Now, go change out of that school uniform.'

In the bedroom I share with Sal, I tug the buttons on my checked blue tunic with shaking hands. I'm all in a fluster; I can't stop thinking about what Mum said. More than anything in the world, I want to meet a kindred spirit. Someone who gets me like no one else, someone I can share secrets and make pinky promises with. But I don't expect a kindred spirit to move in next door.

The tunic puddles around my feet; I toss it into the laundry hamper and nudge off my scuffed school shoes, kicking them under my bed – out of sight, out of mind – with a loud sigh. The new neighbour is more likely to be someone like mean old Mr Bowden, who growled at me and Jim every time a ball went over the fence by accident, no matter how much we apologised. And even if a girl my age did move in, there's no guarantee she'd want to be my friend. That would be a dream come true – no, a story come to life. Things like that don't happen for real.

Not to me.

There are three things I pray for every single night. For Mary Evans to leave me alone. For Mum and Dad not to get The

Divorce. And for a friend. So far, only one prayer has been answered. I'm beginning to think I'm wasting my breath on the other two.

Standing in front of the dressing table that's covered with Sal's make-up, I peer into the mirror. I'm pale and tense and trembling like Anne Shirley when she's about to meet Diana Barry for the first time. It's my favourite scene in my favourite book in the whole world – *Anne of Green Gables*. Mum gave it to me for my tenth birthday and I've read it cover-to-cover about twenty times. Anne understands me like no one in real life ever has. And we both like using big words.

Maybe Anne's the only kindred spirit I'll ever know.

Wearing only my undies and a singlet, I drop onto my bed and reach for my dog-eared copy. It falls open to the Anne and Diana meeting scene, probably because it's the last thing I read each night before lights out. I know the words by heart and now, even though I'm probably wasting my time, I repeat them the way I do every night, as if I am Anne and my (imaginary) best friend is gazing bashfully at me across a flowerbed: "'I solemnly swear to be faithful to my bosom friend, Diana Barry, as long as the sun and moon shall endure.'"

No one knows I do this.

'Bo-som. Bo-som. Jane No Friends wants a bosom friend.' Jim is leaning against the door frame, holding my netball, and grinning like a laughing clown in a sideshow alley.

I want to shove the ball down his throat.

'Get out!' My book drops onto the floor as I realise Jim's best friend Smiddy is behind my brother, looking anywhere but at me.

'I'm not in.' My brother inches his toe over the line. 'Your toe is! Get lost! And give me my ball.'

'Make me.' A slow, deliberate bounce. 'Sooky la-la.'

'I hate you!' I lunge for the ball. 'Don't touch my stuff! And don't call me sooky la-la!' Slamming the door in his face, I throw the ball into a corner, then kick my favourite book under the bed, too mad to care. My face is hot, my heart thumping painfully against my ribs.

I can't believe Smiddy saw me in my undies.

But there's one thing I do believe.

I'm Jane No Friends.

CHAPTER TWO

1979

Jim's swinging from the gnarly wattle tree in our front yard when I go outside after Sunday pancakes. Mum reckons the new people are moving in this morning. Jim reckons they'll have a boy his age. And Dad says he doesn't care *as long as they mow the bloody lawn*. I don't know what Sal thinks. She stayed at Margie Murphy's last night.

No one has lived in the rental house next door for months, not since Mr Bowden went to an old peoples home. The front garden is overgrown and weedy, and the house looks like no one loves it. Dad reckons it needs a good wash and a lick of paint. Mr Jones across the road says it lets the whole neighbourhood down. The two of them go on about it every afternoon when they're watering their grass or digging out bindiis.

Ignoring Jim, I wander over to the basketball hoop and bounce my netball one-two-three before aiming for the goal. Jim laughs meanly when I miss. He's been picking on me nonstop since school finished.

'Can't you be nice for once? Is it too much to ask?' I yell. Jim's face is round like a ball. I imagine bouncing it into the ground (hard), hurling the Jim-ball across Australia, no, into outer space. I bounce my real ball three times and aim again. *Goal!*

Jim snorts. 'Lucky shot.'

Before I can bite back, a battered ute pulls up next door. Two men – one with shaggy fair hair and sunnies like mirrors, the other with springy curls like the guy who sings 'Feelin' Groovy' – leap out and start untying ropes on the back of the ute. Butterflies dance in my tummy as the ball thuds to the ground, forgotten. I cross my fingers so hard I think they'll break, and when I hear a crack like a fast slap across the legs, I think I've gone and done it. But it's not my fingers, it's the wattle branch, finally snapped after years of Jim's rough treatment. My brother's flat on his back, still holding the broken branch. Serves him right.

'James Albert Kelly, get in here. *Now!*'

'Busted,' I snigger. Dad said Jim was going the right way for a smacked bum last time he caught him hanging off the wattle.

He shoots daggers at me. The grass sticking out of his dirty-blond hair reminds me of an angry Ginger Meggs. 'Get stuffed. Bloody hurts.'

'See if I care.' I'm ninety-nine per cent sure his pride is bruised more than he is.

Jim snatches up my ball with both hands and hurls it over the fence before I can yell *giveitback*. It *thump-thump-thumps* on the ground next door in time with my heart as my eyes dart towards the men unloading the ute. Are they shouters like Mr Bowden? You can't always tell by looking at people.

'What'd you do that for? Go and get it!'

'*You* get it. Unless you're chicken? *Bock-bock-bock-bock.*' Smirking, my brother heads inside, rubbing his left elbow.

'Drongo.' He knows there's no way I'll approach the men, strangers.

While Dad gives Jim what-for, I balance on the fence's lower cross post and bounce as high as I dare without getting caught; when my bare toes leave the safety of the bottom rail, and my fingers dig into the splintering wood, my breath sucks in. The men unload box after box from the ute. Then a small table and four chairs. A floor lamp with a paisley patterned drum-shaped lampshade.

'Hi, Jane!' It's Sal. She's holding a pillow and bag under her arm and waving with the other. 'Spying on the new neighbours, stickybeak?'

'Shh!' Gripping the fence posts, I shake my head at her.

She responds by sticking her tongue out playfully before disappearing inside. Despite myself, I giggle. I can't stay cross when she makes that face.

The shaggy-haired man looks my way and I duck, scraping my knees on the rough wood, and count to ten. At breakfast, I asked Mum what she knew about the neighbours. She said I asked too many questions, to *wait and see*. Dad said curiosity killed the cat. I told him Blackie was hit by a car and everyone laughed. Why? It was sad that Blackie died. And then he said too many questions spoilt the answer. He told me it was a proverb. Fibber.

I'm *not* a stickybeak. I'm curious. If people weren't curious, medicines and machines and televisions wouldn't have been invented.

'How else am I supposed to understand stuff if I don't ask questions?' I mutter to myself. 'No one tells me anything.'

The screen door opens. 'Jane! Come and get ready. Time to go. Shoes on.'

Sundays never change in our family – Nan and Pop's for a roast lunch, Saturday night leftovers for dinner.

Fifteen minutes later, Dad manoeuvres our wagon around the ute partially blocking our driveway, muttering under his breath. At the same time, an orange Valiant parks behind the ute. It must be the rest of the family! I'm in the middle seat – I push myself up on my arms, twist around to see out the window. I gasp – I think, I hope, it's a girl – but before I can be sure, Dad accelerates

down the road. 'Sit down!' he growls at me. 'Get that seatbelt on
now.'

When we return home, the ute and Valiant are gone. As we cruise
past the rental house, where boxes are piled higgledy-piggledy on
next-door's front porch and lawn, Jim lets out a sudden gasp.

Dad slams on the brakes. 'What the bloody—' he growls,
craning his neck to glare at Jim. 'Thought I'd hit something!'

Jim points. 'Check out that Harley, Dad.' He sounds like he's
seen Superman.

In the golden afternoon light, the motorbike glows like a
shimmery machine from outer space. My mouth drops open.
What kind of father rides a motorbike? Our dad drives a white
Holden Kingswood HQ. Dad reckons it's the bee's knees. Me and
Jim reckon it's boring. When I grow up, I'm getting a Gemini. A
yellow one.

'Hmph,' Dad mutters and turns into our driveway. 'That's all
we need. A bloody—'

'Don't judge a book by its cover, Trev,' Mum says.

Dad grunts. 'Sometimes covers tell you all you need to know.'

Me and Jim make a run for it as soon as we get out of the car.
I reckon he wants to know who's moved in as much as me,
mostly because of that totally rad motorbike. He wants one when
he's eighteen, but Mum said over her dead body, so maybe having
one next door is the next best thing.

'Where do you two think you're going?'

'To look at—' we say.

'Not now you're not. You've got Sunday jobs to do.'

The no-nonsense voice. It's pointless to argue – unless you're
Jim. 'But Mu-u-um ...'

'Dog poo duty, Jim. And don't give me that look, or you can
do it for the rest of the week. Jane, bath. And mind you don't add
too much bubble bath like last time.'

'Yes, Mum.' I say it sugar sweet. That's what me and Jim do. When one of us argues, the other act likes butter wouldn't melt.

Jim glowers at me, and I try not to laugh. I don't want Mum to change her mind. Dog-log duty sucks. Our blue heeler cross is called Turtle, but us kids call him Turdle because his poos are as big as cow pats and reek worse than the bathroom after Dad's been reading in there for twenty minutes.

I bet a million bucks Jim will disappear to the toilet. He does that to get out of jobs. But I don't wait to see. Instead, when everyone's inside, I peek over the back fence into next-door's backyard. I spy the Valiant. More boxes. My netball sitting under the creaking clothesline. The back door opens. The shaggy-haired man comes outside, lifts a box onto his shoulder. *Oof.*

'Oi! Gonna give me a hand here?' he calls. 'Or ya gonna leave it all to me?'

A woman answers but her words are fuzzy. And then, as the man walks in his back door, muttering, Jim bursts out our back door, zipping up his fly, also muttering. I cringe against the fence, knowing he's going to bust me stickybeaking instead of having a bath. Hoping I'm wrong.

I'm right.

'Mu-um!' he yells. 'Dobber.'

'Takes one to know one.'

Poking my tongue at him, I run inside.

Mum has cooked corned beef bubble and squeak for dinner, which doesn't bubble or squeak at all but tastes delicious. Salty and sweet at once. We eat it with fried eggs. It's my second-favourite leftover dinner. My first is spaghetti bolognese. Grabbing my fork, I gobble it down so I can return to my look-out. Dad isn't much for talking at the dinner table, so the only sounds are chewing and our cutlery clinking against plates. But then Mum asks a question that makes me slow down. I think she's asking it for me.

'Have you seen who's moved in yet, Trev?'

'Not yet,' he says, swallowing. 'Single mother, so Laurie reckons.'

Mum's eyebrows lift. 'I see.'

'What's that mean? Single mother?' I ask.

'Means there's only a mum, no dad, dumbo,' Jim says in his hateful know-it-all voice.

'Jim!' Mum's eyes narrow.

'But I saw a man moving boxes and stuff,' I go on. 'I thought *he* was the dad.'

'Well, we don't really know, love,' Mum says. 'I'm sure we'll find out soon.'

'That means it was a kid in the car.' Beside me, Jim mutters *der, Fred*. I aim my foot at his shin but miss. 'I hope it's a girl.'

'Sal hopes it's a bo-oy,' Jim sings. 'Sal wants a *boy*friend.'

'Shut up.' From the pained look on Jim's face, Sal's kick didn't miss. 'You know I've been going with Robbie for nearly a year.'

'Da-ad, Sal kicked—' Jim starts.

'Oi!' Dad points his fork at Sal. 'Watch your mouth.'

'What? He called Jane dumbo and you said nothing. I'm sick of him—'

'Enough!' Dad slams his hand on the table, making me jump. 'He was joking, Sal. Boys will be boys. No harm in a little teasing. And don't kick your brother.'

As far as Dad's concerned, that's the end of it. Jim gets away with murder, and me and Sal don't. It's not fair, but that's life in our house.

Sal is pushing corned beef scraps around her plate. Her face is red, and I know she's trying not to cry. Then she lays down her fork and asks, 'Can I please leave—'

'Finish your dinner. Your Mum went to a lot of trouble,' Dad snaps.

Mum raises her eyebrows. Turdle whines from the back door. Even Jim's eyes flick from side to side. Dad is in one of his dark moods. Snappy, negative, angry. He goes inside himself a bit and sometimes blows his top for no reason. When he's like that, we're supposed to leave him alone, and not make a fuss. Mum says it's not our fault, that it's because of the Vietnam War. We're not allowed to ask questions about the war or talk about it ever.

Sal stuffs the corned beef in her mouth. 'Can I leave the table now?' she asks again. She'll spit out the corned beef when Dad's not looking. Sal wants to be a vegetarian and eat vegetables for ever, but every night Mum puts meat on her plate.

'Me too?' Jim adds.

'Me three?'

Dad grunts at our empty plates and nods. Jim's out of there faster than you can say Flash Gordon. Sal spits the corned beef into her hand and drops it in the bin as she carries her plate to the sink and rinses it. She brushes past while I'm rinsing my plate and hotfoots it to our bedroom. The door doesn't slam, but it doesn't shut quietly either.

'You're too hard on her, Trev,' Mum says quietly. 'She's nearly an adult.'

'Don't you start,' he mutters, pushing back his chair. 'I'm well aware. But while she's under my roof ...' His words fade as he strides away. Seconds later, voices come from the telly in the living room. His plate is still on the table.

With a sigh, Mum takes the plate to the bench. She fills the sink with water and adds a squirt of detergent. I grab a tea towel.

'Off you go, Jane. See if you can get your answer.' Mum takes the towel from me. 'I've been crossing my fingers for you all day. I have a feeling you're in for a summer you'll never forget.'

'Me too!' Within seconds I'm outside, up on my toes, balancing on the fence bottom cross post, like I did this morning. I count to 100, 200, 500. When the balls of my feet ache, I wrestle with Turdle until my netball whizzes past my head and thwacks onto the grass.

I stare at it for a moment. Someone's on the other side of the fence. I want to look, but I'm scared. I turn towards the kitchen window. Mum is watching. She smiles and nods her head. *Go on.* Then she gives me the two-minute sign.

And so, I get back on the fence. And I gasp, because standing near the clothesline is a girl about my age and she's looking right at me, eyes wide, like I know mine must be. The butterflies are leaping in my tummy again and all sorts of thoughts, good and bad and hopeful and scared, are somersaulting in my mind. Mary Evans is in my head: *no one likes you, Jane Kelly.* My heart goes *boom-boom, boom-boom* and I know the girl will tilt her nose in the air like Mary Evans and walk away.

But she grins and waves!

'Hi!' she calls. Then, crossly, 'Coming!' She's gone before I have the chance to ask her name.

Inside, everything looks the same: my house, my bedroom, my family. But it's different. A change for the better has come.

CHAPTER THREE

1979

W hy is it that when you work out the perfect plan someone (or something) comes along to spoil it? You plan a picnic at the beach, and it rains. You plan the perfect way to introduce yourself to the girl next door, but your mum has other ideas.

'Finish your Weet-Bix and get dressed, you two. We're going shopping.'

Spoon frozen midway to my mouth, I wait for Mum to laugh lightly. *Just jokes.* She doesn't. Me and Jim explode like firecrackers.

'Not fair!' Jim whines.

'You said we could make scones!'

'It's the first day of the school holidays! You promised!'

'Me and Smiddy have plans!'

Mum fixes pin-sharp eyes on me. 'I said we might make scones later.' She turns to Jim. 'Not fair is children starving in Africa.' Her pointer finger is an exclamation mark. 'You've got six weeks of holidays. A few hours' wait to see Smiddy won't kill you.'

What about me? She knows I'm busting to meet the girl. I

have it all worked out. Mum will help me make her famous scones and I'll take them over as a welcome gift. That's how people welcome new neighbours on telly. Last night, as I wrote my plan in my notepad of lists and ideas, I thought long and hard about a meatloaf or casserole because the mum would probably appreciate not having to cook dinner. I reckon the girl would prefer dessert. Kids always do. And then, after I give them the scones, I'll ask the girl over to play netball or something. Simple. Perfect.

'Good things come to those who wait,' Mum adds, making me cringe. I reckon parents have a list of sayings they trot out when it suits them. *Money doesn't grow on trees, hay is for horses, you'll live.*

'Why can't I stay at home by myself?' Jim presses. 'Smiddy's allowed.'

'Me too!'

Huffing, Mum switches off the telly. 'Because I said so.' She squints at us, all no-nonsense. 'Right. Bowls to the kitchen. You've got ten minutes to finish up, get dressed and be at the back door. I want to be at the shops by nine.'

As far as Mum's concerned, that's that.

'This sucks eggs,' Jim bursts out as we follow her to the kitchen, bowls in hand.

Mum swings around so fast I nearly run up the back of her. 'What did you say? Nothing? You sure? Good.'

You'd think that was the end of it, but it never is with mums.

'You kids seem to forget I've only got the car one day a week and to do that, I have to get up before sunrise to drive Dad to the quarry,' Mum says, washing the bowls and spoons with uncharacteristic roughness. The dishes crash together in the rinsing sink. Me and Jim raise our eyebrows at each other, inch our feet towards the door. She's on a roll now.

'How else do you think I get things done? You think bills pay themselves? You think the groceries appear in the kitchen? And Christmas cookies are baked by elves? No! It might be holidays

for you, but not for me. There's a lot of Christmas prep to do…'
She swings around and glares at us. 'Why are you two standing
there? Didn't I tell you to get ready?'

Ten minutes later, Mum is looking for her keys (at the bottom
of her handbag, as usual) and we're shifting from foot to foot,
trying desperately to hide our impatience.

'It won't take long. We'll be back in about twenty minutes,' I
whisper.

Jim snorts. 'Yeah, right.' His face is screwed up like a used
tissue, he's so mad.

An hour later, I reluctantly admit he's right. For once. In
Mum-speak, shopping is one word for many things: bank,
butcher, fruit shop, post office, putting money on lay-bys at
Waltons.

The whole time, I rehearse what I'll say when I finally meet
the girl.

At home, Jim disappears into the dunny while me and Mum
unpack the groceries. Mum makes us sandwiches – Vegemite and
cheese for Jim, peanut butter for me, salad for her. Jim scoffs his
down in three bites and then scoots off to find Smiddy.

'Can we make scones now, please?' As the day wears on,
impatience is getting the better of me, but I manage to hold it
back. Wrong tone of voice and my perfect plan will be nothing
but a crumpled sheet of paper.

'Of course.' Mum smiles as I whoosh out a breath. 'Let me get
the kettle on, love. I'm dying for a coffee. You get out the mixing
bowl, the special one.'

Opening a cupboard, I carefully lift out my great-
grandmother's old mixing bowl. Mum reckons it's full of love
and makes cakes taste better. She spoons instant coffee and sugar
into a mug and calls out the scone ingredients, one by one. I pull
them out of the pantry and fridge: self-raising flour, baking

powder, salt, milk, cream. We're making enough for our dessert too. It was my idea. Dad will appreciate a couple of scones with jam and cream after a hard day's work.

'The scone cutter is in the drawer.' Mum points to the odds-and-ends drawer while pouring milk and cream into a small saucepan. This is plonked on the smallest hotplate, the heat as low as it can go.

'We only want to take the chill out,' Mum says, stirring. 'You want the milk and cream to be at room temperature. That's what Nan taught me, and her scones were always the best. They won first prize at the Royal Easter Show, you know. Three years running.'

I'm impressed. Nan's a good cook, but a prize-winning one? Wait 'til I tell the girl next door.

Mum sips her coffee and watches as I pour the milk-cream mix into the flour. 'Now fold it with a knife. Like this.'

She helps me tip the mix onto a floured board. I dig my fingers into the sticky dough, watching it ooze between my fingers.

'That's enough,' Mum says. 'You don't want to go at it like a bull at a gate. Scones need a gentle touch.'

I do everything she says. I want the scones to be perfect.

While the scones bake, I pace around the kitchen, stopping every few seconds to stare into the oven. What if they burn? I check the timer. Ten minutes. I hear Mum sigh from the kitchen sink, where she's washing the dishes.

'Catch, love.' She tosses me a tea towel. 'Dry these dishes while you wait. Watching the oven won't make the scones bake any faster. And they'll need to cool a bit before you take them over.'

I dry the dishes in silence. I can't speak. My stomach is churning. I'm sweating and not only because the kitchen is stinking hot from the oven. Mary Evans is back in my head. Laughing. Sneering. Singing. *Nobody likes you. Everybody hates you*
…

What if the girl next door is the same as Mary Evans? What if she hates my guts too?

I think I'm going to throw up and I run to the toilet. Nothing comes up except spit.

Half an hour later, Mum says I can take the scones next door. She's packed six of them in a tea towel-lined basket, with two small jars. One filled with Nan's homemade strawberry jam. Another with whipped cream. The welcome card I hand-lettered last night is tucked down the side. Mum tucks the edges of the blue-and-white towel around the scones and hands me the basket. The buttery smell tickles my nose and I lick my lips. My mouth is dry. My stomach gurgles.

'Off you go.'

I don't move. Now that the time is here, I can't do it. I'd rather give up now than give the girl the chance to hate me.

Mum nudges me. 'Jane?'

I swallow. 'Will you come with me?'

Mum looks like she's about to say yes, but then the phone rings. It's Nan. 'Give me a sec, Ma,' she says into the receiver. I watch it dangle down the wall, swaying from side to side as Mum comes to me. Nudges me to the front door. 'You can do it, Jane. You're a big girl.'

I feel her eyes on my back, hear her words push me on. When I reach the fence, I look back. Mum nods, like she did yesterday. Go on. When I look back again, she's gone. I take sixty-four steps to the girl's front door.

I knock at the door. Three little taps. The screen door rattles. Muffled voices. Footsteps. My heart thumps, faster, faster. If I do a runner, they'll blame a kid playing games. My foot twitches. I'll feed the scones to Turdle. Mum won't know.

The door opens. The girl and I stare at each other through the screen door. She's the first one to speak.

'Hello?'

'I made you scones.' I hold them towards her, hands shaking. From deep within the house comes the muffled sound of a woman – her mother, I guess – singing 'Knock on Wood' along with the radio. Sal loves that song. 'Um, thanks?' *Fanks*. I wonder why it sounds like a question, but then she opens the screen door and takes the basket, giving me a swift glimpse of a dark room before the wooden door is pulled close to her back, blocking my view. It's almost as if she doesn't want me to see inside, but why? It's only a house.

I bite my lip until I remember the lines I rehearsed earlier. I'm such a ning-nong. I did it all out of order. Taking a breath, I rush the forgotten words out. 'I'm Jane Kelly. I live next door. Welcome to our street.'

The girl looks up from peeking under the tea towel. She's still standing between the screen and the wooden door. 'I'm Acacia. Acacia Miller.' Her voice is soft, with a sing-song sound that reminds me of a bird. 'I'm called after the wattle tree.'

'Acacia?' I've never heard of a person being called after a tree before. I roll the unfamiliar name around my tongue: A-cay-sha. I'd imagined her a Jessica, Crystal or Diana. A-cay-sha. It's the most beautiful name I've ever heard, better than anything I could have dreamed up. Mum always says fancy names are a waste of time because of the spelling and that's why she called us kids Sally, James and Jane. I reckon she lost her imagination when she married Dad and had us kids. How would she have time for daydreaming and imagining when she's looking after us?

'I'm called after a girl in a book,' I tell Acacia. 'It's called *Jane Eyre*. Have you read it? I haven't yet but I'm going to when I'm a teenager because Mum says it's the best story in the world. Do you like reading? It's my favourite thing. What's your favourite b—'

I stop babbling. Acacia is distracted. The singing has stopped. Her mother is calling. *A-cay-sha. Where are you?*

Acacia replies, 'Coming, Mum,' as she leans against the heavy door. Her mouth opens to form a word: *goodbye, seeya, thanks.* Unless I do something now, she'll say the word and close the door on the question I'm burning to ask.

I close my eyes and see Mary Evans, arms crossed across her chest, sneering, jeering. My eyes snap open. I'm not going to let Mary Evans be the boss of me when she's not even here. It's probably a big fat no but I ask my question anyway.

'Do you want to come outside and play?'

Seconds pass. I don't know how many. It feels like infinity.

'Cool,' she says.

CHAPTER FOUR

POLLINATION

She pretended not to know me. If I'd called out to her (hey, remember me?), I reckon she would have fobbed me off with something like oh, I didn't recognise you, it's been so long, you've changed so much. That's bull. She recognised me all right. Everything about her reaction was a dead giveaway: eyes wide, nostrils flaring, the sharp intake of breath. A mirror image of my own.

A million questions wanted to burst out, *bang-bang-bang-bang* like hailstones on the roof. What are you doing here? Where have you been the last twenty years? And what happened after that day? But I didn't get to ask any of them. While I was getting my head around the fact that it was *her*, she bolted.

I still can't believe she did that. The rain had started bucketing; she called out something about running late for an appointment. It was probably true, but it felt like a betrayal, treating me like a stranger on the day I needed a familiar face more than anything.

The whole encounter lasted seconds, yet in that short time I'd forgotten what brought me to that red-brick house. My heart thumped as her feet thumped down the wet driveway towards the car park and wattles that only moments before had reminded me of times long buried. Coincidence or fate? I still don't know what to believe.

I wanted to go after her, but the older woman, Pat, was already ushering me inside the refuge, locking the door, offering me a seat. A small part of me was aware of her saying this is your safe place. She must have said the same reassuring words a thousand times before, to a thousand women like me. The words barely sank through my dense cotton wool mind. All I could think about was *her* and why she ran away like that.

Maybe I was wrong. Maybe it wasn't her. Maybe I really was crazy, like he said.

In that moment, I was on the edge of my seat and the edge of myself.

I heard my name called. Did I have any questions, Pat wanted to know. Her eyes were kind. Motherly. No one had looked at me that way for years.

Only about a million questions, I thought, but I asked one. The words tumbled into the room: Who was that leaving now?

One of our volunteers. I'll introduce you next time she's in. Pat told me the woman's name. The given name ticked my memory box, but the surname was unfamiliar. I tested it on my tongue to see if that would bring a taste of the past, but I couldn't dredge anything up. No, the girl I knew had a different surname. Must have married, taken on her husband's name. Not surprising after twenty years.

Pat said, remind you of someone you know? Bless her warm heart, Pat was a perceptive woman. Always watching people, looking for cues and clues. You'd have to be good at that in a job like hers. Managing a women's refuge can't be easy. You'd need some sort of outlet, some way to push aside all the darkness and shame women like me bring into the place. My eyes roamed the room, landing on a crochet blanket draped over a worn sofa. That's what Pat did to relax, I found out later. Made granny blankets for people who came to the refuge, one rainbow square at a time. Mum used to make them too. Rainbow hugs.

Pat gave me an expectant look. I nodded. Yes, she looked like someone I used to know, I told her before the phone rang, saving me from explaining further. I wandered over to a window while I waited. Looked out at the car park, at the golden wattles that tugged my memory where it didn't like to go.

I wasn't crazy, whatever *he* tried to make me believe. And I wasn't imagining things. Surname aside, I recognised her, and she recognised me. Her eleven-year-old face was imprinted into my memory, into me. Was it the same for her? Was that why she ran? Was two decades not enough to put the past behind us?

By the time Pat finished up her call, I'd come to a decision. One day, when the volunteer was rostered on, when I was stronger, I would approach her. Ask if we could have a cuppa or something. After that, who knew? First things first, as Mum always said. Pat was motioning me down the hall, down to my next step: a room of my own. A place to rest.

I'm writing my story to help me make sense of what happened. Before I forget it or tell myself it wasn't that bad. I'm writing it for me, to prove that I have a voice, even if no one ever hears it. Maybe by getting the words on paper, by making my scars visible, my story will help someone else.

Life still has many lessons to teach me. But as I followed Pat down the hall, I remembered something my mum told me. Your past is always part of you, but you choose how it shapes your future.

CHAPTER FIVE

1979

We neighbourhood kids are playing cricket in the cul-de-sac when Acacia finally emerges. Waving, she leans against the new brick letterbox that replaced the one Mr Bowden backed into and watches the game from the sidelines. It's my turn to bat and Jim's to bowl; he launches the tennis ball at me like a rocket. Smiddy tells Jim to take it easy, but on the next bowl I whack the ball straight into Smiddy's hands. *Out!*

'Sorry, Jane,' he whispers as I walk past. Smiddy's nice. Too nice to be best friends with my brother.

'Don't worry about it.' My insides are fizzing with nervous excitement. A soft drink all shaken up and ready to bubble over. I offer Acacia the cricket bat. 'Wanna turn?' She grins and, taking the bat, skips up to the stumps, brushing her milk-white hair from her face.

Of course, Jim goes easy on her and bowls underarm, but she swings wide and hits the stumps first go.

'Out for a duck!' Jim and his mates run around with their arms raised high, victory slapping hands together until the rumble of a car drowns them out.

Everyone scatters to the kerb as Robbie Chapman cruises past in his canary yellow panel van, AC/DC screaming through the open window, Sal beside him looking straight ahead. Robbie parks out the front of our house, then swaggers around and opens the passenger door for Sal. The boys groan because until he leaves, the game is suspended. Robbie went off his nut one time when a ball hit the bonnet and left a dent the size of a flea.

'That's my sister's boyfriend, Robbie. He's obsessed with three things: himself, my sister Sal, and his car,' I tell Acacia, who snorts with laughter. 'He washes, waxes and polishes his car every Saturday and no one else is allowed to touch it.'

My sister dashes past us like we're invisible. The screen door slams behind her. I continue, 'Sal's usually really friendly, but I reckon she's running late. Mum picks up Dad from work on Mondays, and it's Sal's job to keep an eye on us. Except mostly she keeps her eyes on Robbie.'

Acacia laughs again. 'Wanna drink?' She points at the side of our house, where the boys are drinking from the hose and squirting water at each other. We stand back until they slope off towards Robbie's car – they love it almost as much as he does – and take our turn. Acacia slurps the cold water and wets her face. Grinning, she splashes water at my feet; I giggle and try to wrestle the hose from her until we're both soaked to the skin. I've never had so much fun with someone who isn't family.

We leap aside when Mum backs the station wagon down the driveway, honking the horn in warning. She stops, leans out of the window to say hello. 'Look at the state of you, Jane Kelly,' she adds, but there's a smile in her voice. 'Turn off that hose now, no more wasting water. Turn it off properly, hang that hose up or your dad will have a fit. And don't you be going inside until you're dry. I've just mopped the kitchen floor.'

'Yes, Mum.'

'I'll be back in half an hour. Sal's in charge. Bye, girls.' She honks the horn again, *bye*, and reverses down the driveway, and onto the road.

'That's my mum,' I tell Acacia, even though it's obvious. 'She's a bit of a neat freak but she's also the best cook in the world.'

Acacia nods and looks towards her house. I follow her gaze, hoping I haven't offended her already. Does she think her mum's the best cook in the world?

As soon as Mum's gone, the boys jump on their bikes and race around the cul-de-sac, doing wheelies. *Look, no hands!* They're showing off in front of Sal, who's changed from her work clothes into the rainbow crocheted bikini Dad says is too small. They think she's watching them as she lies on a stripey beach towel, covered in coconut suntan oil, and pretends to read *Dolly* magazine. But she's really making love eyes at Robbie. He's helping one of the boys to reattach a bike chain and keeps checking to see if Sal's looking. The way she pretends to ignore him, hiding behind her pink Polaroids and turning the pages of her upside-down magazine, makes me giggle.

'What's so funny?' my new neighbour asks.

'Nothing. Just watching the boys show off.'

I turn my attention towards Acacia, soaking up every detail of her. She's sprawled beside me on the scratchy grass, sucking on a buttercup stem, skinny arms outstretched. Her eyes are the caramel colour of Mum's school fete toffees. Her skin is pale like a ghost; freckles dot her face and blue lines snake under the skin on her skinny arms. Her thin hair hangs past her shoulders but needs a good brush. Her faded brown T-shirt and pink terry-towelling shorts hang on her, like she's been given bigger clothes to grow into. As she lifts her arms and stretches, I see bony ribs.

Everything about her is the opposite of me. My eyes are blue, like Sal's jeans, and my skin is sun golden. My light brown hair is brushed into a ponytail, fastened with bobbles and clips to keep it out of my face. My clothes are a bit tight – Mum says I'm in a growing stage – and you can only feel my ribs if you press hard. Apparently, I take after Dad's side of the family.

Acacia catches me staring; my cheeks feel hot, and I know

they're red as Dad's tomatoes. One time Mary Evans called me *stare bear* and when I told Mum, she explained about *being discreet*, which means don't get caught. I don't mean to stare at people. Everyone knows staring is rude. But no one seems to understand that when I watch people, I'm collecting details for the stories I want to write one day. And sometimes I get so caught up in looking and thinking, I forget to look away.

Faking interest in a scab on my knee, I wait for Acacia to sneer like Mary Evans: *Well? What are you looking at, stare bear? What are ya?*

She doesn't.

'How old are you?' she asks, her hand blocking the sun's hot glare. Her nails are grimy and chewed all the way down, like mine used to be before Mum painted stuff on them that tasted disgusting.

'Ten-and-three-quarters.' I slap a fly away from my mouth.

'Me too.' And then we work out we were born on the exact same day in January. Birthday twins! We both agree it's a very strange coincidence.

'Where did you live before here?' I wonder what it's like to live somewhere other than Penrith, in the valley of the Blue Mountains, far away from the beach. Mum says it's hotter than anywhere else in Sydney in summer, like an oven. When I grow up, I reckon I'll move somewhere cooler, like Parramatta. It's got the biggest shopping centre in Australia!

'Stanmore.'

'Where's that?'

'I dunno. In the city, somewhere.' She goes quiet as Robbie wanders past and drops on the grass next to Sal. He leans in for a kiss and Sal jerks away: *Don't.* Probably embarrassed in front of us kids. 'Did they have a fight or something?'

'What? I don't know.' I don't want to talk about Sal and Robbie.

'Hmm.' Sal turns her back on Robbie, shaking off his fingers as they trail up and down her neck. 'Yep, they had a fight. For sure.'

I think she might be right. Thirty seconds ago, Sal was pouting like a goldfish. Now she's leaning against her boyfriend's chest, all smiles.

'Anyway,' I press on, bored with Sal and Robbie's fighting-not-fighting. 'Did you live in a flat? With a garden on the roof? Where did you go to school? Do you miss it?' I don't know anyone who lives in a flat, but Sal and Margie Murphy reckon they're moving into one when they're eighteen. Maybe they'll move to Stanmore.

Her eyes flick back to mine. 'Nah. I mean, it was a flat, no garden. Small. And Stanmore's super busy, not like this.' Sitting up, she hugs her knees and looks towards her house, before plucking a stem of white clover from a patch Dad missed. 'I went to Stanmore Public School, and I hated it.'

'Why? Were the kids mean?'

'Something like that.' *Somefink*. A pause, then, 'Do you always ask so many questions?' *Arks*.

'Yep,' Jim butts in on his way to the tap. 'Reckons she's a girl reporter on telly.'

'Rack off!' Under my breath, 'No one asked for your opinion.'

Acacia watches as he slurps from the hose, then dribbles water down his front. *Show off.* 'Must be nice to have a brother.'

'*Pfft*. You can have him. Are you an only—'

'Wanna make flower necklaces?'

We thread clover flowers into a chain, pinching the stems and splitting them enough to push the next stem through. Her fingers are quicker than mine, as if making flower necklaces was something she did a lot. She doesn't talk while she threads, which makes me nervous. It's like she's gone inside herself. Have my questions annoyed her?

Acacia is the first person I've met who's lived *in* the city. We only go into the city on special occasions, like Christmas to see the big tree in Martin Place and the windows at David Jones. There are thousands of cars and people and tall buildings everywhere, and my ears hurt from all the competing noises: sirens, shouting, talking, beeping. Penrith hasn't got any tall buildings and where we live, it's mostly quiet. Mum says it's like a big country town. Our neighbourhood is one of those places where everyone says hello when you walk past. There's a street party on New Year's Eve and regular barbecues at each other's houses. All the kids play together after school – in the street, backyards, the park down the road – until it's dark and our mums call us in. It's how it's always been. Is it like that in the city?

I want to ask this and more. I want to fast-forward the getting-to-know-you stuff, but then I remember that every time I skip to the end of a book to find out the ending, it ruins the rest of the story. So, I swallow the bubbling questions. I don't want to scare her off. This is my one and only chance to have a next-door best friend. Acacia must like me. I couldn't bear it if she didn't want to be my friend because I ask too many questions.

'Finished!' She holds out her clover chain for my approval, grinning. She has tiny dimples like Shirley Temple in the old movies Nan likes to watch. Nan says Shirley Temple is adorable. I wish I had dimples instead of chubby cheeks. The only person who calls me adorable is Great-Nan and she's blind as a bat.

'Me too,' I say, pushing the last stem through. 'Fit for a princess, right?'

We tiptoe on the grass, pretending to be princesses with posh voices until Acacia steps on a rogue bindii, says a rude word and hops around clutching her foot. We collapse in laughter in a sweaty heap. And then we sit on the kerb crunching sweet-sour green apples; Acacia talks my ears off, and I talk hers off. The boys have dinky races, and Sal flutters her eyelashes at Robbie, and everyone leaves me and Acacia alone.

Around us, the day fades to a dull gold. Dad, home now, waters the front garden, beer in one hand, hose in the other. The mozzies bite our bare legs, and we slap the insects away without missing a beat. The milko toots his cow-horn as the truck rolls along the road. Boys barely older than Jim leave milk bottles at front doors with a clink-clunk before hopping on the back of the truck. A shiny motorbike thunders up the road and down Acacia's driveway. Food smells drift from houses: mashed potatoes, chops, sausages, eggs. Mothers sing the evening dinner time song. One by one the neighbourhood kids disappear inside until only me and Acacia are left in the cul-de-sac; Jim's already ditched his bike on the lawn and gone inside. Later, I find out Sal set the table for me, so I could linger 'til the last minute.

'Dinner's ready,' Mum calls from the house.

I don't budge. What if my new friend disappears on a puff of wind?

'Jane!' The last warning.

I stand, brushing dirt and grass from my legs. 'Better go inside or Mum will go nuts. See you tomorrow?' I hold my breath.

'Sure. See ya.'

When I wave from the verandah, Acacia hasn't moved. It occurs to me that no one called her inside, but Dad calls my name, and he sounds grumpy, so I leave the thought outside with my new friend on the kerb.

'Sorry I'm late, Dad. I've been making friends with Acacia from next door. She's ten-and-three-quarters like me and our birthday's the same day so we're birthday twins, and she likes reading too. She's read the Narnia books and The Famous Five ones, but she hasn't read *Anne of Green Gables* so I might lend her mine ...'

'Less talking, more eating,' Dad says. But he gives me a wide smile I haven't seen for yonks. 'Tell me about it after dinner, Puddin'.' Will we snuggle in his armchair tonight, like we used to? I miss those feel-safe snuggles, the way he'd wiggle my chin, pinch my nose, then pat my head.

Mum squeezes my hand gently. 'I'm happy for you, darling. Now, pass your plate. It's your favourite. Apricot chicken.'

Later that night, my mind replays the afternoon over and over. I feel like Anne, walking home after she first met Diana. My cup of happiness is full. I've found a kindred spirit and I'm the happiest girl in Penrith, Australia, the world. I won't be lonely anymore. As sleep tickles my eyelids, I make a solemn vow that nothing will separate me and Acacia, so long as the sun and moon exist.

Not even Mary Evans.

CHAPTER SIX

1979

For the next two days, Mum's too busy with Christmas preparations to take us anywhere. It's our favourite time of the year and she prepares for weeks: the pudding is already hanging in the darkest part of the pantry, spiced honey-gingerbread biscuits and rum balls are in the freezer ready to box up for the neighbours, and there's a huge ham leg in the fridge that Dad's not allowed to touch until Christmas Eve. This week she's making buttery shortbread made from my great-grandmother's recipe, and her world-famous rocky road.

And so, me and Jim are free to scoot outside after our morning chores are done. Jim meets up with his mates; I hang out with Acacia. We're best friends now. Kindred spirits. It's only been a few days, but I can't imagine my life without Acacia. I was gobsmacked when she said she was lonely until she met me. We hang out from first thing in the morning through to dinner and we never get sick of each other.

It's stinking hot, though. The sun is a flaming fireball that bakes the earth dry, leaving our gardens blistered and crisp, like the towels we sling over the clothesline. One day the air is an oven, sucking moisture from our skin; the next, it's so muggy it feels like our skin is melting away with the sweat. Each night at the end of Channel 9 News, Brian Henderson talks about heatwaves and droughts and record highs, and Mum and Dad say they can't remember a summer like it. It's a blur of same-old days; one cloudless, boiling, blue-sky day after another. Get up, eat, play, eat, play, eat, sleep. Repeat.

Not that we neighbourhood kids mind. Most afternoons we set up a sprinkler on someone's front lawn and run barefoot under shooting water-beads. The littlest kids on the street strip down to undies or go nudie-rudie, but the rest of us have wet cozzies or T-shirts and shorts glued to our skin. We play sprinkler games with whoever is about – sitting on the squirter for the count of ten or leaping and star-jumping through the spray. If we're lucky, the late afternoon wind blows goosebumps onto our damp skin. Other times, we have water fights using buckets of water, foam car-wash sponges, and the best weapon of all – the garden hose. We've all learnt the hard way that when you're in someone's backyard, you don't wet the washing that's drying on the line. It's not worth the lecture.

At night, we sleep in suffocating bedrooms, with wonky ceiling fans and wet face cloths for cooling. Some nights Mum hangs damp sheets over the fan to cool the air, but I wish she wouldn't. It makes me feel sticky.

When Acacia's not home, I drive Mum bonkers. She threatens to give me more chores, so I learn to busy myself: play with Turdle, read library books on a picnic blanket under the wattle, write stories about two brave girls having adventures. But as soon as I hear the telltale rumble of the Valiant, I start counting down the seconds before I can go over. Mum says to give them at least ten minutes to settle in. Six hundred seconds.

'But Acacia turns up here all the time even when we've just come home,' I whine to Mum the first time she makes me wait. *Hold your horses.* 'You don't mind, so I'm sure her mum won't.'

'I *don't* mind,' she says. Then quietly, 'Most of the time. But that doesn't mean *her* mother likes it.'

'How do you know what her mum likes? You haven't even met her yet.' None of us has, it occurs to me. I haven't even seen her out the front of her house. 'You should go and say hello like a good neighbour. She might be shy about being here.'

Mum's look could cut steel. 'Ten minutes.'

Strangely, I rarely make it to Acacia's front porch before she opens the door and slides outside.

Acacia is different from the rest of us westies. At first, I notice little things, like her wearing the same too-small or too-big outfit days in a row, even if they're dirty. The way she sometimes smells like she hasn't bathed. And the way she drops her *g*s and swaps *th* for *f* – *somefink*, *fings* and *Penriff*.

Acacia holds herself in. It's hard to explain. It's as if she only shows the outside of herself, the parts she wants people to see. The more time I spend with her, the more obvious it is that some topics are off limits. Like living in the flat at Stanmore. Her old school. Her family. If she forgets to hold herself in, she changes the subject quick as a blink. She probably thinks I don't notice, but I do. And like that first day, she goes quiet sometimes. Disappears inside herself, like the sun going behind a cloud, like Dad does. Like she's off with the fairies. I've got a gut feeling Acacia's not in fairyland. But wherever she goes, she always comes back.

I worry that I've upset her, but she always says no, I haven't.

'Maybe she's embarrassed about being poor and coming from a broken home,' Sal says when I bring it up.

'That doesn't make sense,' I say. 'The house next door isn't broken, it's just a bit shabby on the outside.

I try to explain it to Mum while I'm having a bath. 'It's like Acacia knows things the rest of us kids don't. Not everyday stuff you learn from encyclopaedias and school. Stuff about people and how life works. I notice things, but she *knows* things.'

'What do you mean?'

'Well ...' I scratch my head, trying to think of an example. I know Acacia is different, the same way I know we were meant to be best friends. Two lonely people drawn together; two people who are always on the outside looking in. 'She could tell Sal and Robbie had a fight the other day just by looking at them.' I heard Sal tell Margie Murphy that Robbie talked to a girl at the petrol station.

'Maybe she's an old soul.' Mum says it to herself more than me.

'What's that mean, Mum? Can you pass the shampoo? Please?'

Mum hands me a near-empty bottle of No More Tears. 'It means ...' she pauses, like she's trying to work out the best way to explain, 'it's when someone seems older than they really are, not in the way they look, but in ... in the way they act. It's someone who sees the world a bit differently, who thinks very deeply and maybe doesn't relate to people of their own age as well as older people. That's what it means.'

I rub shampoo into my hair and mull this over. Mum's explanation sort of makes sense, because Acacia does have a way about her that makes her seem older sometimes. But Mum doesn't really understand Acacia like I do.

'Acacia gets on with me, and we're the same age,' I point out.

'That's true. But you were the one who said she was a bit different. And from what I've seen of her, I think I know what you mean.'

'I s'pose.' I dip down in the water, letting my hair flow around me like a mermaid. When I sit up, Mum's still there.

'I'm glad you girls are friends,' she says, passing me the conditioner. 'I think it will be good for her.'

'And me!' I smear apple-scented conditioner into my hair. Mum helps me stroke and spread the gloppy mess through to the ends. 'Acacia has never had a best friend before either. I think she was meant to move to Penrith so we could find each other.'

'Maybe so.' Mum's quiet. What's she thinking? 'Well, love, it's time to rinse your hair and get out of the bath. Don't forget to brush your teeth.'

The other thing is that Acacia never invites anyone over to her house. Not even me, her best friend. I've no idea what it looks like inside. Is it tidy like mine? Or messy like Smiddy's since his mum got a job at Franklins? I'm dying to go over, to check out Acacia's bedroom, but every time I bring it up, she says *not today*. Changes the subject. And I know it's only been a few days, but I still haven't seen Acacia's mum. She never comes outside. I haven't even seen her hang out the washing.

'Why don't you ask her why she never invites you to hers?' Sal says later that evening. 'Instead of sooking about it.'

'I'm *not* sooking. I'm pondering. There's a difference.'

She rolls her eyes as if pleading for help from heaven. 'You and your big words. I reckon you think too much.'

'She'll invite you over when she's ready,' Mum interrupts, shooting Sal a look. 'Give her time. Maybe they still haven't unpacked, and they've got boxes everywhere. It's only been a week.'

'It doesn't take that long to unpack a house, Mum,' I say. 'It's a few boxes. You could do that in two hours.'

I take Sal's advice and ask Acacia the next day. 'Why don't you ever invite me to yours?'

We're doing handstands when I ask, so Acacia doesn't answer straight away. But she stays up so long I suspect she's trying to get out of answering.

'Well? Why don't you?'

Acacia flips over and brushes grass from her hands. 'My house is nothing interesting. Really truly.'

'I'd still like to see it, see your room,' I push. 'And meet your mum.'

'Not today.'

'Why not today?' I wait, but no answer comes. 'Doesn't your mum like friends coming over? Does she get headaches or something? Or is your room a pigsty? I don't care if it is.'

Acacia gives me a hard look. It reminds me of Mary Evans. I haven't thought about her all week. She's gone somewhere on holiday. I wish she was gone for good.

I don't want to think about that girl.

'Sorry,' I blurt out. If only there was a spell to banish stupidity.

Acacia gazes towards her house. Says nothing. She's gone inside herself again. She'll walk away, I know it. Then her face softens, and her eyes meet mine. 'No worries. Let's do handstands. Come on.' She's up on her feet in an instant, and then her hands go down and her legs heave skyward. 'One-two-three upsy daisy!'

I'm so relieved she hasn't walked away that I don't hesitate to do what she wants. 'Up-two-three together, down together, back, side, knees together,' I call out. But my heart's not in it and within seconds I collapse onto the grass, wrists aching from holding my weight up.

We've been best friends for three days and I know two things about Acacia's home life: one, she only lives with her mum; two, it's private. I pretend it's okay that Acacia holds herself back, but it's not. Inside I'm hurt, and even a bit mad at her. Best friends are supposed to trust each other. To tell each other everything. To stick together. Mary Evans springs into my thoughts again, her voice so clear it's like she's right beside me. *I'll bet a hundred bucks she's putting up with you until someone better comes along.* I hate how that girl buzzes in my head like a pesky fly.

'I think Acacia's hiding something,' I tell Mum after dinner.

'Don't invent a problem when there isn't one,' she says, scooping vanilla ice cream on top of canned two fruits. The only reason we're having dessert on a weeknight is because Dad's in one of his black moods again and she's pretending everything's hunky-dory.

'What's wrong, Mum? Why have you been crying?' I pop a glacé cherry in my mouth.

'Get your mitts out, miss.' She sniffs. Blows her nose into a hanky. 'I'm fine. A bit of a cold coming on. Here you go, eat your dessert.'

I'm not inventing problems. Acacia's hiding something, for sure. And I'm not imagining Mum's red eyes either. She hasn't got a cold; I heard her arguing with Dad before. They've been doing that a lot lately, speaking in hushed voices, arguing when they think we're asleep, sending us from the room when things get tense. The Divorce has never seemed closer.

When will parents figure out that when they don't give kids a straight answer, it makes kids want to know the truth even more? Parents try to protect kids from grown-up things – they whisper about anything serious, talk about things behind closed doors. But they can't hide everything, and we can't stay little children forever.

'I know more than you think,' I mutter when she leaves the room.

CHAPTER SEVEN

1979

S hane Watters is pointing at us, laughing. He's Jim's second-best friend but I can't figure out what Jim sees in him. He has squinty eyes and he's a bully. Worse than Mary Evans. In Year 6, he was one of the tough boys who dunked younger boys' heads in the dunnies and stole their lunch money. Jim used to keep his distance, but when they were put in the same Year 7 class they started hanging out. Jim reckons Shane's not all that bad, a bit of a joker like Paul Hogan. I can't see the resemblance. And I hate the way Jim acts tough whenever Shane's around.

Me and Acacia are playing hopscotch in the shade, talking about everything and nothing, minding our business. When the boys mosey over, Jim two steps behind, I grit my teeth so hard I think they'll crack. They're up to something.

'Oi, stick insect,' Shane says to Acacia. 'You the new girl? I've heard about you.' A pause. 'And your mum.'

Lips tight, she folds her arms across her chest. Shane breaks into snorting laughter and nudges my brother.

'Chubba!' I hate it when Shane calls me that. I've told him to stop a million times and he doesn't listen. Mum reckons it's better to ignore him. She says bullies always want you to react and the more you do, the worse they get because they think it's entertaining. I don't know what's so entertaining about hurting someone's feelings and making them cry, but I've learnt the hard way that it's true.

'Hey.' Suddenly self-conscious, I cross my arms like my friend.

Shane smirks. 'Told ya,' he says to Jim. I have no idea what he's talking about, and I don't care.

'Come on,' I whisper to Acacia. 'Let's go somewhere else.'

But Shane blocks our way, greasy eyes sliding up and down our bodies. My skin crawls like it's covered in ants. 'Told ya,' he repeats, nudging Jim again. My brother, kicking the ground like he'd rather be somewhere else, snaps to attention. A soldier called to battle.

'Told him *what?*' The words slip out accidentally.

'You're boobless. Boob. Less.' Shane bites the word in two like he's tasting it. 'Hey, Chubba, you're supposed to be smart. You know what these numbers mean upside-down on a calculator? Five-five-three-seven-eight-nought-one-eight.'

'It's nought-*nought*-eight, actually.' *Boobless.* Everyone knows that old trick. I roll my eyes. 'Can you leave us alone now?' I direct this to Jim. *Do something.*

Jim looks towards the road, avoiding my hot gaze, his jaw working. Then, 'Shane-o, let's play frisbee. Girls are boring.'

'In a minute.' Shane grabs my brother. A long look passes between them before Shane turns back to us, releasing Jim.

'Admit it. You're both as flat as a tack.' He dissolves into laughter, whacking Jim on the back. Jim laughs too, but it's only a mouth laugh. My jaw clenches harder. I'm not flat as a tack. Tiny lumps are sprouting on my chest, not that it's any of their business. Mum nags in my head: *Ignore them and they'll go away.*

We skirt around the boys, but Shane follows us until we're cornered, unable to move, motioning for Jim to catch up. Each time we try to move, they block our escape, smirking, snickering, sneering the whole time.

'Are you two lezzos?' I don't know what a lezzo is, but it doesn't sound flattering when Shane says it.

'Ignore him,' I hiss to Acacia, holding back tears that threaten to expose me for the sooky baby I am. I also want to kick Shane in the shins. To show Acacia that I can stand up to bullies, that I've got her back. A true best friend.

Acacia squeezes my hand as we stare him out.

'Come on, Shane.' Jim pulls on Shane's T-shirt. 'Frisbee.' His eyes meet mine briefly.

Shane shakes him off. 'You *are*. Le-zzos. Boob-less le-zzos.' He jabs at my chest. Hard.

'Rack off, Shane.' Batting his hand away like it's a pesky fly, I breathe deep and do the only thing a girl my age can do. Aim for the shins, grab Acacia's hand and bolt to the house.

Shane's parting shot follows like a bad smell. 'Gonna dob, are ya? Dob-dob-dobber!'

For the first time in my life, I give someone the rude finger. Then, from the safety of the verandah, 'I'd rather be a lezzo and a dobber than a … a dickhead!'

Beside me, Acacia bursts out laughing. The words 'Me too!' echo in my ears as we go in search of Mum.

Shane's mother is having a cuppa with Mum. I forgot she was visiting. Telling on your brother is one thing but dobbing in front of someone else is another. But they're waiting, eyebrows twitching, so I spill out the story.

'Girls, girls, girls.' Mrs Watters shakes her head, as if she's disappointed in us and not her bully son. She pushes her hair away from her face, exposing big ears that dwarf tiny gold sleepers. Her ears wobble. 'The boys are just teasing. That's what boys do. And maybe he likes you ...' She sounds as unconvinced as she looks.

The idea of Shane Watters liking me is more revolting than a liverwurst sandwich. 'Ew, that's disgusting!'

'No need for that, is there?' She looks at Mum for confirmation. 'Boys will be boys.'

Mum sucks in a breath. 'Actually, I think we—'

'What? They're being jerks!' My hands are on my hip, voice shrill. 'Why do grown-ups always say that?' I want to shove the words down Mrs Watters' throat, into the pit they rose from. 'So, if I was being mean to Shane, you'd say girls will be girls, or she likes you, and that's it?'

Mrs Watters gives me the stink-eye, but I don't care. 'They don't mean anything by it, Jane. You need to ignore them instead of name-calling. And nobody likes a dobber, do they?'

'That's not fair! I told you, he called us lez—'

Mum clears her throat. 'Jane! That's enough.' Then, softly, 'I'll have a word with Jim later.' Her eyes beg me to trust her. 'Why don't you and Acacia go and play somewhere away from the boys?'

'They keep following us!'

'Well ... you can go to your room for a while. Once they've found something else to do, you can go back outside.' Her face tells me not to push it.

I forget the boys as soon as we get to my room. It's the first time Acacia has seen it and I watch her eyes flick over the Princess Leia and kitten posters on the wall. I wish I'd had time to straighten the pink chenille coverlet, and hide my beloved teddy bear Wally, the dusty fairy figurines on my bedside table, and the Barbie dolls piled in a white cane basket. I view the room through my friend's eyes.

My side looks childish compared to Sal's, where posters of John Travolta, David Cassidy and Andy Gibb paper the walls, and the dressing table is cluttered with make-up: lidless lipsticks, the bottle of Charlie that Sal got for her sweet sixteen, mascara and palettes of eyeshadows in shades of blue. Acacia's eyes linger over Sal's prized record collection and the near-toppling pile of *Dolly* magazines, before moving to my collection of Enid Blyton, Trixie Belden and Nancy Drew books.

'I like Princess Leia too,' she says, after a moment. 'She's so…'

'Beautiful?'

'Brave.'

I nod, remembering the time I dressed up as Princess Leia for a school fancy-dress day. Mary Evans poked and prodded my hair until it fell out of the buns Mum spent ages twisting and pinning. Princess Leia would never have let Mary Evans pull her hair.

I know three different words for brave: courageous, fearless, plucky. Without Acacia by my side, I'm none of those things.

'Your room is so nice.' Acacia moves to the bookshelf for a closer look. 'You've got so much stuff. So many books!'

I stuff Wally under my pillow in one swift swipe. 'You can borrow one. But no folding down the pages, okay? Only monsters do that. And boys.'

She selects *Anne of Green Gables* which makes my insides flutter. What if I need to read it? But I haven't picked it up since meeting Acacia. I haven't needed to. 'Pinky promise,' she says. After linking her little finger with mine, she moves over to Sal's vinyls. 'These yours?'

'Sal's.'

'Can I look?'

'Okay. Wait, I've got a better idea – let's put one on and dance!'

'This one!' Acacia holds up Sal's favourite: *ABBA: Greatest Hits Volume 2.* Sal saved up for ages to buy it the day it came out and played it over and over until Mum begged her to stop.

'Yes! And let's dress up in Sal's clothes and pretend we're going to a disco!' It's too hot to dance, and I shouldn't be touching Sal's stuff, but I don't care. I'm tired of having to control myself all the time. I want to feel brave and powerful for a while, if only in the comfort of my room.

And so, we stuff my sister's bras with socks and try on her going-out dresses. We spray our bodies head-to-toe with Charlie, and colour our lips with Pink Frost lipstick, pouting at each other in the mirror. And then I lower the needle on Sal's portable record player, and we dance and sing and sing and dance. I've never experienced anything like this with someone my age before. It feels like girl power.

We only get through 'Dancing Queen' and 'Does Your Mother Know' before Mum walks in. For a split second, a wistful expression tickles her features, like she wants to dress up and dance too, like she wishes she were young and free. But then she shakes her head and finds her Mum voice.

'What on earth are you girls doing? Why are you wearing your sister's clothes? She'll be home in half an hour!'

'Don't tell her!'

Mum gives me a should-know-better look. 'I won't. But you will.'

As we change clothes and tidy up, Acacia casually asks, 'Do you even know what a lezzo is?'

'Not really. Do you?'

'Mmm. Kind of.' I wait for her to tell me, but her head is cocked sideways. In an instant, she's on my bed, peering out the window. Watching. A quietness settles over her; she's chewing her bottom lip.

'What's up?' I join her, see what she sees. Mum is outside, hanging clothes on the line. We watch silently as Mum squints at the sun and wipes her forehead on her pinny. Pats Turdle, then reaches into the basket for one of Dad's work shirts. Shake,

shake. A pillowcase. Shake, shake. *Snap!* As if she senses us watching, she glances our way. Waves.

'Your mum's nice.'

'Thanks.'

Acacia bounces off the bed, snatches up the book I lent her. 'Gotta go.' At the door, she pauses. 'Jim's okay too. He just hasn't figured himself out yet.'

CHAPTER EIGHT

FERTILISATION

To be honest, I was distracted by questions and answers, and the volunteer slid from my mind faster than she skidded into it. Pat gave me the grand tour: this is your room, you share the bathroom, here's the lounge room, the kitchen, please keep it clean, no smoking inside, no drugs. There was a room full of clothes and toiletries and she said take what you need. I didn't know what I needed so I grabbed the closest things: toothbrush, soap, tampons. In the kitchen, Pat made cups of sweet tea and told me how everything worked, how I could stay for three months, how staff would help with paperwork and finding my own place and a new job and stuff, and not to worry about security; there were alarms and procedures. Trying to reassure me, but the second she said alarms I started looking over my shoulder.

And then Pat took me back to my room, and I told her it was nice, thank you, and it was nice, like a nanna hug. A single bed with a hand-made blue-and-white patchwork quilt. A painted white chest of drawers for my clothes, and a faded floral armchair with a reading lamp next to it. A welcome pack on a scratched side table. Pictures on the wall: motivational quotes, a rosy beach sunset. The window overlooked a garden with a high brick wall instead of a wooden fence. The wall had jasmine growing over it. No sign of the wattles. There was even a sprig of jasmine in an old Vegemite jar on the bedside table. Doilies on every surface. No mirror, which was a relief. I didn't want to see my face.

It's very nice, a bit like a motel, I told Pat again.

How are you feeling, she wanted to know as she prepared to leave me by myself. Not trusting my feelings – can you ever? – I gave the automatic, easy response: *Good*. She must have heard that in a thousand voices, but she smiled and left me to settle in.

I sorted my clothes into drawers smelling of mothballs and shoved the empty duffel bag under my bed. Put my dog-eared copy of *The Notebook* onto the side table. Sat in the musty but comfy armchair and read the welcome pack, all ten pages, front and back. I sat in my nice motel-like room and cried like a little kid missing their mum. I was scared shitless. What the hell was I supposed to do now? Then I washed my face and went to find Pat. I still needed to buy food and I didn't know how to get to the nearest shops.

It was still raining lightly as I jogged across the car park. Only three cars remained, one of them mine. A puddle where her car had been parked. All other trace of her gone, but the absence of proof failed to wipe our short encounter from my mind. Nor her expression when we came face to face; shocked, confused, surprised.

Scared.

Not *like* me. *Of* me.

Of what me being here means for her.

This time, I had to force her from my mind. Her needs, her fears – they were the least of my mounting problems. I scanned the directions Pat gave me, over and over, until the words stopped swimming. Turn left, right at the T intersection, left, right, left, right onto the highway, straight ahead to a once-familiar shopping centre. As a teenager, I caught the train to that dodgy old centre on Thursdays, earning sixteen bucks a week serving customers at the Chinese takeaway. Best spring rolls I've had were from that shop. I wondered if was still there, the takeaway. Maybe I'd buy a spring roll, for old time's sake.

And then I wondered, what if she was there?

What if *he* was there?

The thought almost sent me back to my room. The likelihood of running into him was slim to none, but I would have starved rather than take the risk. It took Pat, worried about me sitting in an unmoving car, to convince me to risk it anyway. You've got to start somewhere, she said.

Three false starts before my car spluttered to life. On the car radio, a newsreader was giving an update about a massive earthquake in Turkey. Thousands of people dead, hundreds of thousands homeless. Sometimes after an earthquake, aftershocks continue for days, weeks, years. But this is something else I know: the aftershocks of life-quakes never fully subside. They ebb and flow, they ease and shrink. The tiniest tremor will set them off.

CHAPTER NINE

1979

S al is getting ready for a date with Robbie. She's in her underwear at her dressing table, putting on make-up, pulling fish lips in the mirror. When she catches me watching, her mouth puckers like a cat's bum. I'm supposed to confess about using her stuff, but I'm not sure I can, even if it is the right thing to do. Sal's been in a mood since Dad asked what time she'd be home tonight and where she was going.

'Stop interrogating me,' she'd snapped, which got him going. They've been like this the whole time Sal and Robbie have been going together.

Back when Sal first got asked out by Robbie, Dad said Sal was too young. But he started going out with Mum when she was sixteen, so Mum said he didn't have a leg to stand on.

'I know what boys are like,' he'd grumbled.

Last night Dad went outside in his jocks to remind Sal about her curfew. She was mortified.

'He's really getting my goat,' she told Mum at breakfast.

But Sal does weird things I don't understand and Dad's probably thinking the same. Like, why does Sal have to take so long to say goodbye to Robbie when they've been hanging out all evening? Why is her bed empty and her handbag gone sometimes when I wake up at night? Why do they talk on the phone and go *you hang up, no, you hang up* over and over for five whole minutes, maybe ten? One time Dad grabbed the phone from her hand and slammed it down. '*I'll* bloody well hang up if you won't.' Me and Jim killed ourselves laughing, but Sal was hopping mad.

No one's ever admitted it, but Sal is Dad's favourite daughter – he calls her *Princess* and me *Puddin'* so it's obvious – and he was never going to accept Sal having a boyfriend without a fuss. But Dad's going to have to get used to it eventually. That's what Mum said to Nan on the phone this morning.

'All these arguments are doing my head in,' she'd said. 'It's exhausting. No, I'm fine, Ma. Just tired.'

'What?' Sal says to me now, her voice snippy.

'Nothing.' I pick up one of her magazines. It falls open to a picture of a boy and girl kissing and I drop it faster than a hot potato.

Jim reckons Sal and Robbie pash in the car. When he told me, he licked his hand and made this disgusting wet *mmm* noise right in my ear. I had to stick my fingers in my ears and squeeze my eyes shut. I do the same thing whenever I see people kissing on the telly or at the movies – it looks like they're swallowing each other. I can't imagine someone's tongue in my mouth, flicking in and out like a snake's tongue. I hope Sal and Robbie don't do that. And I'm glad Mum and Dad are too old for that sort of stuff. The idea makes me shudder although I suppose it's better than them getting The Divorce.

Sal's lipstick clatters onto the dressing table. She stands, walks to the wardrobe, and opens it. She turns to me, a confused expression on her face, and my conscience pricks like a pin in a pincushion.

'Have you been touching my stuff?'

I avoid the question by asking one that's been bugging me all afternoon.

'Sal? Why do grown-ups always say *boys will be boys?*'

'I don't know.' She drapes a hot pink jumpsuit against herself and looks in the mirror. Then she sits on the side of my bed. I can't remember the last time she did that – the last time she'd really wanted to talk to *me*. 'But it pees me off.'

'Me too!'

'I reckon it's something people say to give boys a free pass for bad behaviour.'

'What, like free parking in Monopoly?'

'Kinda.' She half laughs. 'It drives me crazy how boys get away with stuff because they're boys, but girls are always expected to do better. Double standards, I reckon. *Everyone* should do better.'

'Yeah! That's *exactly* what I tried to tell Mrs Watters.' I tell her what Shane called me. Her eyebrows shoot up; she half laughs, half coughs and I pound her on the back, once, twice.

'Good on you for trying,' she says after a minute. 'But that woman thinks the sun shines out of her son's bum. Tell you what, Shane creeps me out and he's only thirteen. He's always staring at me.' She looks at the clock, then stands and pulls her jumpsuit on. With her hair flicked out, she looks like Agnetha from ABBA. 'I don't know why it's like this, why there are different rules for boys and girls. It's just how it is.'

'Why does it have to be?'

She chews her lip. 'Maybe it doesn't. Maybe it's up to us, up to us girls, to make it different.'

'What do you mean?'

'I mean, like when we have kids, if we have boys, we have to teach them different. Like, if they do something wrong, they can't get away with it because they're boys. We should treat our kids the same.'

Robbie's panel van pulls up outside. A door slams. Sal zips up her jumpsuit, fluffs her hair, pulls on white strappy heels. 'I've got to go.'

As she spritzes herself with Charlie, I know what to do. 'Sal?'

'What?' She's halfway through the door.

'Me and Acacia tried on your lipstick and your clothes and played your records. Sorry. But it was because—'

'Bleedin' heck.' Sal gives me a dirty look. 'I knew it.'

'Sorry, Sal.' I look at the floor.

She sighs. Looks at her watch. On cue, there's a loud knock-knock-knock at the front door. 'You can listen to my records if you're really, really careful. But don't touch my clothes and make-up, okay? Deal?'

'Pinky promise.'

I think about girls making things different for a long time after she's gone.

CHAPTER TEN

1979

A woman I've never seen before is walking towards us. It's late Thursday afternoon and the wind breathes hot and heavy on our skin, even in the shade. Acacia and I are gulping down the single cones with hundreds and thousands we bought from the Mr Whippy van, when I notice her. I try not to stare but I can't help it. The closer she gets, the more she looks like a TV star, like Jill from *Charlie's Angels*; her hair is blonde and flicks out to the sides underneath her floppy straw hat. She's beautiful.

The woman waves and I wave back. Is she lost? Then she calls out: *A-cay-sha*. My friend is so busy licking up melting ice cream rivers on her hand, she doesn't react. I bump her with my elbow.

'Ow! What was that for?' She has a frothy cream moustache on her upper lip. I probably do too.

I point at the woman. 'Do you know her?'

Beside me, Acacia sighs. 'That's my mum.'

'*She's* your mum?' My ice cream is forgotten and now I stare openly. The woman is wearing a white singlet top, a paisley gypsy skirt, and oversized, brown-tinted sunglasses. A tinkling sound, faint at first but louder with every step closer, comes from tiny silver bells on her skirt and the thin silver bangles on both wrists. Large gold-hooped earrings dangle from her ears and pale blue eyeshadow shimmers on her eyelids. She's the youngest and prettiest mum I've ever seen and, for a guilty second, I wish she was mine.

Acacia wipes her milk moustache on her T-shirt and gets to her feet. 'Mum, what are you doing out here?'

'Nice to see you too,' Acacia's mum said to my friend. There's a small, fuzzy tattoo on her back shoulder. A rose. I've never seen a tattoo on a woman before. 'Need you to come home. Uncle Daryl's comin' over soon.'

Biting the pointy end of my cone, I suck out ice cream till it slurps. Is Uncle Daryl the man who turns up most evenings, roaring up the street on his too-loud Harley? The man who fixes his shaggy hair in the side mirror, hikes up his jeans, and walks into Acacia's house without knocking?

Acacia winces. 'Again?' she mutters. Something about her tone makes me curious. Doesn't she like her uncle?

'What's that?' her mother says, eyes squinty, and I realise that all mums get the same look on their face sometimes, like the White Witch in Narnia. She looked prettier before.

'Nothing,' Acacia mutters, gazing past her towards the wattle on our verge.

'Better be nothing.' And then, as if she's just noticed me even though she waved at me two minutes ago, Acacia's mother smiles and she's beautiful again. Her frosted pink lips make me self-conscious; I wipe my mouth, then swipe my sticky hands on my shorts. 'So, you're Acacia's new friend, the one she rabbits on about all the time.'

My eyebrows lift. She does? I peek at my friend, but she's still looking at the wattle.

'Hi, Mrs Miller. I'm Jane Kelly from next door.' I start to hold out my hand, then remember my sticky fingers.

'Hi, Jane Kelly from next door,' she says from under her floppy hat. Up close, her voice is wobbly and raspy. She smells like smokes, strong fruity perfume, and something stronger I can't work out. 'You made the scones.'

'Yes, Mrs Miller. Well, Mum helped. I hope you—'

'Call me Rose. I don't go for that missus stuff.'

Mum will have something to say about that. We're not allowed to call grown-ups by their real names until we're eighteen and we're invited. Sal reckons it's a dumb rule because she's allowed to use first names at work, and I agree. It's confusing having different rules for different places and people.

Rose turns back to Acacia. 'Let's go.' She swishes away, thongs slapping against her feet, the bells on her skirt tinkling. 'We're going late-night shopping.'

Acacia doesn't budge. Her face is sulky; her lips are pressed together but moving like she wants to argue. Whether it's about having to go home early, or the man coming over, I'm not sure. Maybe both.

'I'm not askin', I'm tellin', Acacia!'

My friend looks skyward and breathes in, hard. Her hair is haloed around her head in the afternoon sun, like an angel. 'Coming!' Then, quietly, she mutters to me, 'Gotta go. See ya.' She bolts after her mother without a backwards glance.

Their front door thumps shut, closing me out.

'I met Acacia's mum today,' I say at dinner, my mouth bulging with half-chewed chicken.

'Don't talk with your mouth full, Jane,' Mum says, without looking up. Her fork clinks against her plate as she brings a bite-sized piece of the meat to her mouth and chews daintily.

'Sorry.' There are at least five ways Mum and Rose are different. One, Mum smells different to Rose. Soapy and sweet. Of bleach when she's been cleaning. Of Avon Topaz, the everyday perfume she dabs on her wrist and neck. Youth Dew on special occasions. And you can only smell her hug-close, not from a few metres away like Rose. Two, Mum would never wear a skirt with bells, or bug-eye sunnies. She likes pants with tunics, sometimes shorts and homemade crocheted tops when it's a scorcher, and she saves dresses for going out. Three, Mum doesn't wear make-up, except for lipstick and mascara on special occasions. Four, her hair has been short and flicked for so long I can't imagine it long now, even though I've seen black-and-white pictures of her as little girl with long, thick plaits. And five, she's old. Thirty-eight on her last birthday. Rose looks barely older than Sal.

Mum is like most other mums I know. She cooks our meat-and-veg dinners every night and washes up straight after, bakes her own biscuits and cakes from scratch – never packet mixes – and keeps the house in tip-top shape, the way Dad likes it. She makes clothes for us on the rattly sewing machine she bought with her own money when she was eighteen. And she doesn't have a job except looking after us. Mum left school when she was fifteen and turned into a dressmaker, but she had to stop when she got married to do housework and look after babies. I asked her why she had to stop working and she said it was the way things were in the olden days.

'I'm not going to stop working if I get married and have kids,' I told Mum.

'Things are changing for women,' she said. 'They have more choices now. You'll see.'

I don't think Rose has a job either. Who would look after Acacia if she did? Acacia hasn't said much about her mum at all. Whenever I've asked, she's shut me down, but to be fair, we have much more interesting things to talk about than our mums.

'Sal,' I say when I've finished eating. 'Acacia's mum has got those sunglasses you want for Christmas, you know, the big ones. And she's really pretty and her hair is like—'

'Shane's dad says she's a lush,' Jim says, leaning forward on his elbows.

My parents and I react at the same time. 'Elbows off.' That's

Mum. 'And—'

'Mind your mouth, lad.' That's Dad.

'What's a lush?' From my parents' expressions, I shouldn't have asked, but curiosity gets the better of me. 'What? What is it?'

Sal kicks me under the table and shakes her head. *Shhh.*

Later, Jim tells me a lush is the same as a drunk.

'Like Uncle Nev,' he says. That's Mum's uncle. He drinks so much beer his hands shake, he smells funny, and he talks in a blurry voice. Uncle Nev lives with Nan and Pop because he can't hold down a job or look after himself even though he's a grown man. That's what Dad says to Mum every Sunday. He thinks we don't hear him, but all of us kids know about Uncle Nev. And we all know we're not allowed to talk about it to anyone else, because it's family business. 'That's what Acacia's mum is.'

Rose isn't anything like Uncle Nev. No way.

'Liar!'

'It's true. Shane's dad works at the bottle-o.'

'So?'

Jim smirks. 'So, he should know, unlike you, dummy. He says she comes in every day.' My brother walks away, laughing.

'You think you're smart because you're older!' I yell after him. 'She's not the same as Uncle Nev. And mums don't get drunk!'

Mum calms me down, I'm so mad. She tells Dad to take Jim out the front for a serious talk and takes me to the swing chair on the back verandah for the same. It's a warm, muggy evening filled with the hum of flies, mozzies and crickets, far-off voices, the occasional splash in a pool. I sip the lemonade she hands me and gaze towards Acacia's house. The motorbike man – Daryl – roared up on his Harley before Mum called us for dinner, but the Valiant is gone and the house is silent and dark.

'Is it true, Mum? What they said about Acacia's mum?'

Mum takes her time answering. 'I don't know, love. I don't know her mum. But it's none of my business, and it's certainly none of yours.'

'Why did Shane's dad say that then?'

Mum slaps at a mosquito, then gets up to turn on the bug zapper. 'Because some people like to spread gossip and rumours. They point out what's wrong with other people, so they feel good about themselves.'

I nod. 'That's what Mary Evans does.' I finish my lemonade and calculate my chances for a top up. Slim to none, but I'll try. 'She talks about girls behind their backs all the time.'

'What do you do when she does that?'

'I walk away.' I don't always. Sometimes I listen and say nothing because if I walk away, she'll turn on me. But I feel bad for the other girls, her so-called friends, afterwards.

'Good idea.'

'I'll bet Acacia's mum would be sad if she knew people were saying that stuff about her.' Tipping my glass up, I suck on what's left of the ice cubes.

'I think so too.'

'I'd be really mad if someone talked like that about you.'

'I'm glad.' Mum hugs me close. We watch Turdle sniff around a tree before lifting his hind leg. 'And if you ask me, it's better to be curious about ideas than people.'

The two of us talk until the orange-red sun makes the Blue Mountains glow. I count how many mozzies sizzle against the bug zapper but lose track after twenty-nine. The screen door at the front creaks open, then shut. I hear Dad in the kitchen. Ice clinks into a glass. A tap runs. Turdle runs around the side of the house and settles himself at our feet, panting. Mum shifts in the swing chair when telly sounds come from the living room, and I know our time is almost up. I don't want to let her go.

'I love you, Mum. I'll never let anyone say bad things about you.' I count to ten. 'May I have another glass of lemonade, please?'

She laughs. Gets up, switches off the bug zapper and collects our glasses. 'Nice try.'

CHAPTER ELEVEN

1979

Our first argument lasts less than ten seconds.

'Where's your dad?'

Me and Acacia are lying on my trampoline when I blurt this out. It's been on my mind for days, this mystery of Acacia's dad. Everyone knows you need a mother and a father to make a baby – it's all explained in a picture book at the library. Even if Acacia's dad doesn't live with her, he still exists.

She says, 'I don't have one.'

I say, 'Everyone does.'

And she says, 'Well, *I* don't! And I'm sick of you talking about it.'

Then, without even saying goodbye, she jumps off the trampoline and runs home. Her screen door slams, like a sharp warning. At first, I'm upset; tears sting my eyelids, and the familiar fear of loneliness dries my throat. Seconds after the door-slap, I'm heading to her front door. I've got to apologise, beg her forgiveness, promise *I won't do it again*. But as I pass our kitchen window, I hear Jim shouting at someone, probably Mum – *not fair!* Two little words that freeze me to the spot and stick on my tongue. It's not fair for her to run off like that. Not fair that she doesn't tell me stuff about her life. Earlier, I told her my suspicions that Sal's sneaking out to see Robbie after her curfew and Jim has a crush on Margie Murphy; Acacia told me nothing.

'I'm sick of it,' I tell Turdle. 'She can say sorry to me for once.' He licks my hand, stares at me with glassy amber eyes. Follows me to the trampoline and leaps up beside me, turning round and round before curling up beside me. His breath is hot and stinky, but I don't care because unlike some people, he sticks around, no matter what. And he's always happy to see me. 'I love you, Turdle. Don't ever leave me.' I stroke his belly until the angry feelings go away. Dad says you're never alone if you have a dog.

'Mum, do you know where Acacia's dad is?' I ask later, washing my hands. Tiny soap bubbles float before my eyes, carefree and cheerful for their seconds-long life until they go *pop!* I wish I could float on the breeze without a care in the world.

Mum looks up from the thick book she's reading, pushes her reading glasses onto her head. 'No, love, I don't. Have you asked Acacia?'

'Yeah, of course.' I tell her what happened.

Mum shakes her head. 'Maybe you need to keep your nose to yourself until she wants to tell you. You haven't known each other for long.'

'We're best friends!'

At least, I hope so. My throat feels dry again and I gulp a cup of water.

'Well, maybe she's sensitive about it.' Dad calls from the living room: *Barb, your show's about to start.* Mum snaps her book shut and pushes her chair back. Flicks on the new orange electric kettle Dad bought last week, reaches for the brown-and-orange tea canister. Two cups from the cupboard. 'Enough questions. It's nearly bedtime. And no more water, or you'll be up and down like a yo-yo.'

Sensitive about what? Two possibilities occur to me later. Either Acacia's real dad is dead, or her parents got The Divorce, which is almost as bad. The Divorce has happened to some kids at school, like Mary Evans and Trisha Longbottom. Trisha only sees her dad at McDonalds every second weekend. She says it's not that bad because she gets a Happy Meal every time, but I reckon she's fibbing. Not about the Happy Meal, but about The Divorce not being bad. It sounds like the worst thing in the world because of all the fighting and not seeing your dad much. Mary Evans hasn't seen her dad since he walked out to get The Divorce a few months back. He moved to Perth, and she says it's good riddance to bad rubbish. I reckon she's fibbing too. I reckon she misses him like crazy, but she doesn't want to admit it.

Maybe that's what happened to Acacia.

Maybe she doesn't want to admit she misses her dad.

I forget about Acacia's mystery dad when Sal tells me something much more interesting later that night. Turns out that Uncle Daryl is not Acacia's real uncle. He's Rose's *boy*friend.

'I didn't know mums could have boyfriends.' I'm still confused about the uncle thing.

Sal laughs. 'Course she can, silly,' she says, pulling back her sheet. In the moonlight, I notice that she's wearing a boob tube and denim shorts, not a nightie. She didn't see Robbie tonight because he had his work Christmas party. 'Rose isn't married. She can do what she wants.'

'Does that mean she and Acacia's dad got The Divorce?'

'I don't know,' Sal sounds impatient. 'Maybe she never got married.'

'What? But how— I thought you had to be married to—' I scratch my head. None of this makes sense. 'Why does Rose call him Uncle Daryl if he's not an uncle?'

'Out of respect?' Sal huffs. 'Don't ask so many questions. You'll understand when you get older. I'm going to sleep.'

Yeah, right, I think. The room smells like freshly spritzed Charlie perfume. Sal only wears that for Robbie.

Desperate to prove my suspicion about Sal sneaking out at night, I force my eyes to stay open by mulling over this new information about Rose's boyfriend. I met Daryl for the first time this afternoon and he's super nice. Me and Acacia were out the front; he called Acacia over and gave her a crumpled ball of paper. A two dollar note! 'Get yourself a treat from Mr Whippy,' he said, ruffling her hair like Dad does with me sometimes. Then he took off his sunnies and grinned at me: 'Hey, cutie-patootie, I'm Daryl but everyone calls me Daz.' He's so handsome! Dazzling Daz! He could be on telly with his teeth as white as snow, hair as black as night, eyes as blue as the ocean. He's ten times better looking than David Cassidy.

'Are you awake, Sal?'

She groans. 'No. Go to sleep.'

'Will Daryl still be called uncle if he gets married to Rose?'

My sister groans again. *'If* they get married, he'll be Acacia's stepfather. She'll probably call him Dad.'

I think this over. 'Are stepfathers wicked? Because stepmothers always are in stories, you know.'

'Honestly, you're such a weirdo.' Sal throws a stuffed toy at me. 'I don't know where you get this stuff from. He's not in a story, is he? Course he won't be wicked. Now go to sleep!'

In the middle of the night, I get up for the loo. Sal's bed is empty. But in the morning, she's in the bed opposite mine, snoring lightly. Her boob tube and shorts are neatly folded over the chair at the dressing table.

CHAPTER TWELVE

SEEDS

There was an old pressure cooker in the refuge kitchen, but no one used it. I found it in the back of a cupboard full of stained saucepans, unloved and unwanted. Mum used to have one like it. It took anywhere from five to thirty minutes to reach pressure and I was always scared it would explode the way it hissed and steamed. Whenever she used it, I refused to stay in the kitchen. She tried to reassure me, but I didn't want to take the risk; the lid rattled and hummed like it was desperate to break free.

I used to think *he* was like a pressure cooker. He'd let his anger build up, up, up for hours, days, weeks until the button would pop. He'd steam hot words and blistering accusations until he was spent, and I was ugly crying like a kid, convinced it was all my fault.

At first, I thought it was normal. All couples argue, right? Everyone gets angry when they reckon something's not right. But the night we ended the police officer said anger and violence weren't the same. The second is a response to the first; it's a choice, that's what she said. And it's never okay. She took my hands and made me look her in the eyes when she said that: *violence is never okay.*

Now I wonder how I thought he was like a pressure cooker at all. After he lost his job, he'd go from calm to explosive in minutes, more like an instant kettle. It happened before I saw the anger boiling; I was still wondering how he knew exactly which buttons to press. Sometimes it took less than a minute. A blink. A flicker.

Snap!

Ten seconds. That's all it took the first time I left.

That was the night he punched a hole in the wall right next to my head.

CHAPTER THIRTEEN

1979

I don't see Acacia until after Dad's work Christmas party. She's waiting under our wattle tree when we get home and my stomach tightens, remembering the ten-second argument. But she runs straight up to our car, all smiles, as if she didn't flounce off like a peacock last night. Like it never happened.

'Where ya been?' She waves a two-dollar note. 'Wanna go to the milk bar?'

I give Mum a pleading look. 'Please, Mum?'

'Get changed out of those good clothes first,' Mum says, after a quick look at Dad. She looks worn out, like she always does after being with too many people. 'And try to stay in the shade.'

It's a ten-minute walk to the milk bar, fifteen if you dawdle. Acacia wants to know all about the party, so I tell her about the picnic at Warragamba Dam with a jumping castle and fairy floss and a present from Santa for each kid and a Nativity scene with real animals.

'What's a Nativity scene?'

'You know, a stable with baby Jesus in a manger,' I explain. She looks blank. 'They're in shopping centres, so people don't forget what Christmas means.'

'Oh, yeah, those things. I thought Christmas was Santa's job.'

'Yeah, but Jesus is real and Santa's not.'

'I don't know about that,' she says. 'The Jesus part, I mean. But I would have liked to see the animals.'

'It was so funny. A hen pecked a duck, the donkey kicked over the manger, a calf did a poo, and a sheep sat on baby Jesus!'

Acacia laughs so hard I need to whack her on the back. That's when I know everything's alright between us. No need to apologise or talk about what happened.

In the milk bar it takes twenty minutes of *umm*-ing and *ahh*-ing before we make our choices. It's one thing when you have twenty cents, another when you have two dollars to share. The milk bar is like Ali Baba's cave, a treasure trove of sweets: musk sticks, caramel buds, chocolate freckles, licorice sticks. Redskins, fizzoes, jaffas, milkos. Coke bottles, spearmint leaves, jelly snakes, all-day suckers. We leave, clutching white paper bags bulging with sweet treasures: cobbers for me; a mixed bag for Acacia.

And then I nearly start another argument.

'Are your mum and Daryl getting married?' The question spits out like hot potato.

'Why would they do *that?*'

'Because they're boyfriend and girlfriend.' I pop another cobber in my mouth and wait, but my friend says nothing. She pokes around in her paper bag, finds a spearmint leaf. 'Sal says if they get married, he'll be your stepfather and you'll have to call him Dad.'

Her face reddens. 'He's *not* her boyfriend and they're not getting married. And I'll *never, ever* call him Dad!'

'But Sal said …'

'Sal doesn't know diddlysquat. I told you, Daryl's just … a *friend* of my mum's. That's all.' Acacia's glare dares me to argue.

Mind your business.

I don't. I wait 'til I've swallowed my cobber before continuing.

'Well, anyway, Sal reckons he's a hunk.' I pause. 'He is kind of handsome, don't you reckon?'

She squints at me. '*I* don't think so.'

'It was nice of him to give you two dollars for no reason.'

That glare again. *Back off.*

Wiping my face on my T-shirt, I change the subject. 'It's stinkin' hot. My cobbers are melting.'

'Should of got icy poles, like I said.'

'Yeah, but we've got Zooper Doopers in the freezer and they're free. I'll ask Mum for some when we get home.' We're at the park now. The playground is empty; the swings dangle limply in the hot, still air. They look as drained as I feel. The metal slide shimmers, but I know from experience it will be scorching hot. 'I'm getting a drink from the bubbler.' The water gushes out warm, before slowing to a cold trickle; I splash it on my face, my arms. Acacia puts her mouth on the bubbler, and I wonder if her mum ever told her about germs.

Back at home, Acacia waits outside while I get Zooper Doopers. I find Mum in the kitchen with a familiar white-haired old woman. It's Mrs Bubel from down the road, nursing a cuppa in one of Mum's good Royal Albert teacups. Her knobbly fingers are covered with so many rings it's a wonder she can lift the teacup at all, and when she does her hand wobbles so much, I think she's going to drop it.

Mrs Bubel stops talking mid-sentence when she spots me. I see myself through her eyes: red-faced, sweaty, messy. An expression of disapproval comes and goes, fast as a mouse scuttling across the floor. My hands move to smooth down my hair. I stare at the intruder in her floral tunic and pastel blue pants that look too warm for the weather, a spotted headscarf tied under her chin. Her talcum-powder-sweat smell wrinkles my nose.

'Good afternoon, Jane,' she says, peering over her teacup. There's the faintest trace of an accent in her voice. Mrs Bubel came from Poland on a ship after the war. Not the one Dad went to. The Second World War. She reminds me of the old ladies who trill hymns at church – not that we go much, only for Christmas and Easter, and christenings and weddings – except the church ladies are nice. They give me cordial and biscuits. Mrs Bubel gives us kids nothing but grief. Always snapping about one thing or the other. *Off my driveway! Mitts off my flowers!*

Mum stretches out her arms and I sink into them, breathing in her musky Mum-smell. She gives me a gentle poke.

'Hello, Mrs Bubel,' I mutter against Mum's dress. 'Mum, can we have—'

'Jane. You know it's rude to interrupt.' Mum's a stickler for manners when old people visit. 'Have a glass of water, you're all sweaty.' She nudges me towards the tap and turns back to her visitor.

Mrs Bubel raves on and on and on about the people next door to her and how their tree is hanging over the fence, how she's threatened to call the council, and how the man next door is quite rude, if you ask me. I count to a hundred and she's still going. And then, with a pause so teeny I can't get a word in, she goes, 'So, what is she like, Barbara?'

'She?'

'The one next door. I've seen her young one running around with your Jane.' *Chain.* 'Too skinny, the girl. All bones! And that knotty hair needs a good washing and brushing. No one cares for her, I am thinking.'

I grit my teeth. She doesn't know what she's talking about and she's old enough to know about minding her business.

'I can't really say,' Mum says in the voice she uses when she doesn't want to say. 'We haven't met yet.'

'Jonathan at the pub says she likes her grog. Says she comes down the pub a few nights a week with her fancy man. And she has the tattoo, a rose right here on her shoulder.' Mrs Bubel raises her eyebrows and gives Mum a meaningful look. 'She's not married, you know. Living off the benefits.'

'We don't know that.' Mum's pointer finger taps once against the table.

'Barbara, Barbara. She doesn't work, does she?' Mrs Bubel tuts. 'Mind you, women should be home with the kids, but it's a shame we have to fund these unfortunates, these single mothers. It's a disgrace, I am thinking. They shouldn't be allowed to keep their children if—'

'Well, of course, *we* don't work so we're not paying tax, are we? You don't. I don't,' Mum breaks in. An edge to her voice sounds alarm bells. Her face is flat, but her finger is tapping faster on the table. 'Although that's changing soon. I'm getting a job now that the kids are older.'

My mouth falls open. Mum working? *No way.*

'Oy, why you are so defensive, dear?' Mrs Bubel sits back in her chair, shaking her head slightly, as if Mum is a naughty child. 'You know what I mean. Children need two parents. The mother at home with the children and the father at the work. That's the proper way. None of this unmarried mother business with the men in and out of the house—'

'Oh, I'm not sure I do know what you mean, Mrs Bubel,' Mum butts in. 'There's a lot you're saying that I don't understand. And I don't think it's Christian to be gossiping about others, do you?' The two women face off across the kitchen table; I look on with interest, glad they seem to have forgotten I'm there. It's like they're playing the stare game. Who will blink first?

Mrs Bubel plonks her teacup, then stands, her chair scraping hard against the lino. 'Oy-yoy-yoy,' she mutters, her face red. 'I am surprised—'

'Oh dear, look at the time!' Mum claps her hand to her mouth in fake surprise as she points at the wall clock. 'Doesn't time fly when you're having fun? Goodness, I've got to start the dinner, or it won't be ready on time. And you know what men are like when they're kept waiting for their dinner.'

Mrs Bubel nods vigorously. 'Yes, yes, Barbara, you are right. Mr Bubel likes the dinner on time, five-thirty on the dot, making no mistake. One time, he—'

Mum slips her pinny on. 'I can imagine. Do give my regards to Mr Bubel, won't you? I hope he's feeling better after that nasty fall off the ladder.'

I stifle a giggle. Everyone knows Mr Bubel fell off the ladder because he was perving at the lady next door to theirs. She was getting a suntan without her bikini top on. At least that's what Mr Jones told Dad.

Mum propels Mrs Bubel to the front door, all the while keeping up polite chatter about Mr Bubel's health and *goodness me, can you remember a summer like this?* By the time the old woman waddles down the path and turns to wave, she seems to have forgotten she's been turfed out of our house for gossiping. I gaze at Mum, impressed. How did she do that? I would have given the old gossip a mouthful.

My mother notices me watching her. 'Were you listening in again? What have I told you about that?' Then, quietly, almost to herself, 'Sometimes you have to nip things in the bud.'

She walks back to the kitchen and starts collecting the teacups; they clink and clank together and I know she's upset.

'I only came to ask for Zooper Doopers.'

She takes two from the freezer without a word. Snip, snip. Plastic tips fall into the sink; she fishes them out and passes me the frozen tubes. 'Jane? Best not to mention this to Acacia.'

I nod, but I'm confused. Grown-ups keep changing the rules. One minute it's rude to interrupt, then it's not. One minute you should mind your business, the next you should speak up. Will I ever figure it out?

CHAPTER FOURTEEN

1979

L ater, Acacia and I lie on sun-crisp towels under the wattle, drying off after a spontaneous sprinkler run. My wet clothes are clammy against my skin; I didn't bother to change into my cozzie. Around us the street is alive with late Saturday afternoon activity. Up and down the street, men are emerging from houses to mow lawns, trim edges and wash cars. Cooking smells drift from houses, tickling, teasing. Next door, KISS belts out 'I Was Made for Loving You' and the grass stays overgrown and spotted with weeds, the Valiant dusty and dry.

Acacia went quiet when Daryl's motorbike roared up the street.

'Can you believe it's only three days to Christmas?' I ask, breaking the silence between us. 'That's about …' I do the maths in my head, 'two hundred thousand seconds.' I wait for her to look impressed, but she's staring at her house. The music is thumping louder, all wailing guitars and slurred, screaming words.

'Dad reckons he never wants to hear another Christmas carol, but I love them, even the ones about sleigh rides and snowmen,' I continue, brushing stray grass clippings from my legs. 'Do you? Dad reckons they're silly because Australian Christmases are hot.'

True, songs like 'I'm Dreaming of a White Christmas' are like a hot smack in the face when you walk out of the air-conditioned shops into boiling heat. But one day, I'm going to wake up on Christmas Day to frosted windows and a carrot-nosed snowman in the garden.

Her eyes slowly come around to meet mine. 'They're okay, I s'pose.'

'What do you do on Christmas?' I ask, squinting at Acacia from under my hand. She shrugs. 'Dad's taking us to see the big tree in the city tomorrow night. Did you know it's twenty metres high? And Mum said we'll see the displays in the David Jones windows. Have you been? One year there was a real miniature train winding its way through snowy hills, past sleighs and toboggans and reindeer. It's so cool!'

'Haven't seen it.'

'No way!'

That shrug again. 'Don't do much at Christmas. Another day really.'

'Is not! How can you say that? It's the best time of the year!' Irritated, I roll onto my back and stare at the popcorn clouds. I thought every kid in the world loved Christmas – I've never met a kid who doesn't.

In our house, Christmas is special. At the beginning of December, Dad brings home a real pine tree; I love breathing in the sharp piney tang and fiddling with the spiky needles that snap in my fingers. Us kids help Mum decorate it while Dad supervises, which means he sits around telling us what to do and eating gingerbread. It's the most wonderful time of the year: trees twinkling in living room windows, Advent calendars, carols at Warragamba Dam, trips into the city, Dad's big work party. On Christmas Day: presents, church, Nan and Pop's for lunch. We used to go to Grandma and Granddad's for dinner, but they moved up near Port Macquarie a few months back, so we're having a holiday and second Christmas with them after Boxing Day. I love every minute of this crazy, busy time.

'Well, what do you want for Christmas?' I ask a few minutes later. Mum has a tradition, a four-gift rule: something we need, something to wear, something to read, something we want. Choosing the one thing we want is the hardest of all – it changes daily in the weeks before the big day, depending on the ads on telly. 'Me and Jim are crossing fingers for a Slip 'n' Slide. Mum said she'd tell Santa. As if I still believe in Santa!' I don't tell her I only found out the truth about Santa last Christmas, when I busted Mum and Dad sneaking presents under the tree. I cried buckets at the time, but now I'm older I admire the way parents keep up the act.

'Dunno. Haven't really thought about it. Mum usually forg—' She swats a fly from her nose.

'Well, what are you going to give your mum?'

'Dunno. Make her a card, maybe. I told you, Christmas is no big deal for us.'

I stare at her crossly, but she avoids my eyes. After a moment, I try another tack. 'Is your tree up?' I haven't seen lights twinkling in her front window.

'Not yet.'

'Can I come and see it when you do? Or can I help? I love decorating Chrissy trees.' A glimmer of possibility ripples through me and I sit up straight. 'We could—'

'Depends. I'll let you know.' She points at a frog in the clouds and then I spy a whale, and the glimmer is gone like a star in the daytime.

As we cloud watch, an idea blooms: the perfect way to show Acacia how magical the festive season can be.

'Wait here,' I tell her.

Dad's watering the back garden, beer can in one hand, hose in the other. The lawn mower is tipped up on its side, drying after being hosed down. Mum's pulling out weeds from the tomato patch, nudging Turdle away with her elbow. Everything must be spick and span before Christmas, even the garden.

'Can Acacia come with us to the big tree tomorrow?' I ask them. 'No room in the car, Puddin',' Dad says, then burps. *No room at the inn.*

'But Sal's going to a barbecue with Robbie,' I press. Dad scowls at the mention of Robbie. 'So, there is room.'

'That's right, Trev,' Mum says, sitting back on her heels.

I pull on his sleeve. 'Dad? Can she? Pretty please with a cherry on top?'

Mum gives him a blink-and-you'll-miss-it nod.

'Fine, Pud. If her mum says it's okay. Mind you don't talk my ears off though. And none of your silly giggling. You'll do my head in.' He hoses my feet, laughing when I squeal from the cold shock. 'What? There's grass all over them.'

The next day, we all pile into the station wagon about 6 p.m. The hour-long drive into the city is endless and uncomfortable; it's one of those evenings where the heat doesn't let up a whisker. Dad makes us wind down all the windows to let in air that blasts our faces and sucks sweat from our pores. The car seat sticks to our bums; salty rivers run down our legs and our T-shirts are glued to our backs. We eat ham and salad sandwiches and hide the crusts under the front seat; we play 'I Spy' and whistle the 'Colonel Bogey March' until Dad tells us to zip it or forget about mixed gelato cones from the ice cream van. Somehow, we're all still smiling when we get to Martin Place and join the crowd marvelling at the giant, glittering tree.

Acacia has a goofy grin glued to her face, except one time when she thinks I'm not looking. Her eyes linger on Mum; her expression is a mix of sad, jealous and wishful. It's almost as if she wishes Mum was her mum ... but that can't be right. Rose is so cool. And then she sees me watching and her lips morph into a smile.

Later, I walk her home. Daryl's motorbike is in the driveway. I hear the telly blaring over the top of the insect summer song as we walk towards her house. We stand at the bottom of the steps; I feel like I should say something important, but I don't know what. I think Acacia feels the same. Like, if we say something, the night will end, the magic spell will be broken. I chew my lip and look around me; tiny moths zip around the dusty outdoor light bulb, a black Christmas beetle is lying on its back, legs waggling helplessly.

'Poor thing.' Acacia kneels and flips it over. Crouching together, we watch it scurry away.

There are footsteps behind us. 'That you, Acacia?' Rose's words, behind the screen door, are mashed together. *ThashyouAcaaaysha.*

Acacia's face flattens. 'Yeah, Mum, it's me. I'll be a sec.' Her voice is as flat as her face. Like she's hiding her happiness behind a mask.

'S'late.' That's all Rose says before she pads away. No *how was your night* or *did you have a good time?* I hear a fridge door slam, the sound of a can popping, the creak of a sofa. A man's laugh, low and throaty.

My friend makes no move to go in, but Mum is waiting for me on our verandah.

'Better go,' I say.

'Yeah.' Acacia stands up. For a second, I think she's going to hug me. But instead, she leans in, so close I can smell the peppermint from the double choc-mint gelato she'd eaten earlier. 'Thank you,' she whispers into my ear. 'That was the best night ever.'

And then her face goes blank again.

I tell Mum about it when she comes in to say goodnight. 'Mum? I think Acacia was really happy we invited her.'

'Me too,' Mum says, opening the window, letting in outside air barely cooler than the bedroom. 'It's stuffy in here.' She turns on the ceiling fan. 'It was good of you to ask her.'

'Did you see the way Acacia was watching us? I was watching her watching us, and one time, she looked like she was ... jealous. Of our family.'

Mum sits on the side of the bed. 'Maybe she is a bit, Janey. She hasn't got any brothers or sisters.'

'Or a dad.'

'Yes, that too.'

'Mum? She was looking at you too. And she looked ... sad. No, more than sad. Like she ... like she wished ... no, it doesn't matter. I'm probably imagining things.'

Mum reaches down to pick up the clothes I threw onto the floor. 'These will have to get washed,' she says, sniffing them.

'Mum? You know how sometimes we try to hide our feelings from our face? Like, we pretend we're okay when we're not, or we don't care when we do?' My mother nods and stifles a yawn. The clock radio says 11:00. I'm not sleepy at all. 'Acacia hides her happy face from her mum. Why would she do that?' Something niggles at the back of my mind.

Mum is still for a moment. Then she lifts my chin, so our eyes met. Her eyes look wet. 'I don't know. I think she ...' Mum pauses, like she's choosing her words. 'I think she's happy to have a caring friend like you. Now, it's very late and I need my beauty sleep.' She looks worn out from days of Christmas preparations. There will be more to do tomorrow.

As she closes the door, I hear her say to herself, 'Poor little mite.'

I don't think she's talking about me.

Overhead, the ceiling fan squeaks as it stirs the air. My body is coated in a light sweat and I strip down to my undies, wriggling around like Turdle to find a cool spot on the bed and my pillow.

Left alone with my thoughts, I realise what was niggling at me before. Acacia's not the only one who hides her feelings. We all do it. Mum does it when she's sad about Dad. He does it so he doesn't have to think about the war. I do it to get through the school day. And to protect Mum. She's got enough to worry about. But why does Acacia do it? I haven't figured that out yet.

Before I fall asleep, I create a memory picture in my mind – Acacia and me standing side by side under a glittering tree that dwarfs us. I can't help feeling that although I'm turning eleven in twenty-eight days and I should feel bigger, the world is becoming bigger and stranger and newer faster than me.

CHAPTER FIFTEEN

1979

M um's not joking about getting a job. She tells Dad after breakfast on Christmas Eve, while they're having a cuppa on the back verandah. I'm at the kitchen table, making cards for Nan and Pop, and I can hear every word. It doesn't go well.

'Trev,' Mum starts. 'I'm applying for a part-time job in the new year. I've been thinking about it for a while. We'd have a bit extra coming in, and you wouldn't have to do so much overtime.'

Dad splutters his coffee and then he's blustering like a bull at a gate. 'A job? What do you want to do that for? I bring in enough. Bloody hell, Barb, people will think I can't provide for my family. No, no, you don't need to worry yourself about that.'

Mum's voice sounds soothing. 'You're a wonderful provider, of course you are, Trev. But all this extra work you're taking on, it's affecting your mood, affecting us. Even the kids are picking up on it.'

Too right.

'I can manage,' Dad snaps, his voice rising. 'Nothing wrong with working hard. Kids need an example, or they'll grow up lazy buggers.'

'Exactly, that's why—'

Dad cuts her off. 'You've got enough to do, Barb, what with the house and the kids. No, I'm not having it.'

Now Mum's voice gets louder. 'I beg your pardon. Do I not have any say in this? All I'm hearing is your voice.'

My stomach feels hot and crampy. Another argument. Anything sets them off: work, the war we're not allowed to mention, our behaviour. I hope Dad backs off, for all our sakes.

He doesn't. 'You're my *wife*. And your job is in the house. Not out there doing God knows what for other people.'

I hold my breath, waiting for Mum's next move.

'Geez, Trev. You're bloody unreasonable and stuck in the past. I'm going inside. But this conversation isn't over.'

I snatch up a texta and start colouring just as Mum pushes through the fly streamers.

She makes a strangled sort of noise before sweeping past. A door slams. Dad walks in a second later and scowls when he sees me.

'Women,' he mutters, striding across the room. 'Don't listen when you want them to and all ears when you don't.' The bedroom door creaks open. Low voices drift from my parents' room, but I can't make them out.

Sometimes I get the shivers when something bad is going to happen, like I'm cold but it's not cold.

I've got the shivers now. Under the table, I cross my fingers and toes and scrunch my eyes shut.

Please don't let us get The Divorce.

'Acacia? Hello?'

Where is she? Acacia promised to help us make White Christmas today.

Idly, I poke my finger through a hole in the screen door before knocking louder; when no response comes, I wander out to the back yard. She's not there. The only sign of life is the flapping of clothes, forgotten and faded on the clothesline; the only sign of the Valiant is a wet oil stain on the concrete driveway. Out the front, an overflowing rubbish bin balances on the kerb. The friendly garbos in navy singlets are due any minute – I can hear the truck down the street. Dad's left a couple of beers for the garbos next to our bin, but the only beer cans next to Rose's bin are crushed, empty.

I peer through Acacia's front window in hope the house will whisper its secrets, but the curtains are closed from prying eyes. *You'll get nothing from us*, they seem to say. In the wattle tree behind me a tiding of magpies breaks into its morning song. Like a bunch of busybodies gossiping about things they don't want me to know.

Frustrated, I trudge home. The birds quiet when I pass, reminding me of the times at school I'd walk into a room and know Mary Evans was talking behind my back.

'What's wrong, love?' Mum asks when I shuffle into our kitchen. 'You look like you've been sucking a lemon.'

I give her the hairy eyeball. 'Acacia's not home. She promised to help.'

'Maybe she and her mum have things to do. It is Christmas tomorrow,' Mum says reasonably. It makes sense. After all, Jim and Dad have gone last-minute Christmas shopping today. But when you're a kid, a promise means everything.

'Yeah, well, she *promised*. And they don't *do* much at Christmas. I told you already, remember?' Mum gives me her change-your-attitude look; her fingers twitch around the handle of the wooden spoon she's drying. She's never smacked my bum with a wooden spoon, but I know kids whose parents do. 'Sorry, Mum. I really wanted Acacia to have a good Christmas.' I snuggle against her chest and let the familiar thump-thump of her heart calm me.

She strokes my face. 'I know, love. Me too.' A moment later, she pushes my hair behind my ears with a *tsk*. 'Right. How about you start the White Christmas anyway? And I'll start another batch of honey-gingerbread biscuits since you lot have eaten them all. Come on, let's get a move on, love. Christmas Day will be here before we know it.'

'Are you really going to get a job, Mum?'

She hands me a dog-eared, grease-stained recipe card. 'Yes. I'd like to.'

'What kind?' I imagine her working in an office. She's a good organiser.

'I don't know yet. Something that helps people in need.'

I mull this over. Helping people is good, but if Mum has a job, it will change the way we do things at home. I like our life the way it is. But I'm starting to realise that's not the way life is. It does its own thing, and you deal with it. Still, I ask: 'What about us? Who will look after us?'

She sighs. 'How about we worry about that when we have to? Are you going to get the ingredients for that,' she points at the recipe, 'or will I do it myself?'

'I'll do it. But Mum, what about Dad?'

'Let me handle him, okay.' It's not a question. She taps the recipe with her wooden spoon.

I set to work measuring ingredients: copha, puffed rice, white chocolate, glacé cherries, almonds, sultanas, coconut and vanilla essence. At the kitchen table, Mum hums 'Silent Night' with the radio while she creams sugar and butter in the special bowl before adding honey and egg, flour, ginger, cinnamon and baking soda. No Christmas is complete without her honey-gingerbread biscuits. She's already made about four batches but we've gutsed them all. After she kneads the dough, she breaks off a small piece and gives it to me, winking, before wrapping the dough and placing it in the fridge to cool while we finish mixing the White Christmas.

Later, I clear a space on the kitchen table. Helping Mum with the last-minute cooking is my favourite part of Christmas preparation, and I'll never tell Acacia this, but in this moment I'm glad to have Mum to myself. Mum rolls the gingerbread between sheets of greaseproof paper and then I press out star and Christmas tree shapes. As the biscuits bake, the house fills with a warm spicy perfume that makes me lick my lips in anticipation. I hover while the biscuits cool on the tray, desperate for a taste. When my teeth cut through the crunchy outside into the warm, soft middle, my tongue disco-dances.

This is one thing that never changes.

When Acacia turns up a few hours later, I surprise myself by giving her the cold shoulder. It makes no sense; earlier, I felt guilty for being glad she wasn't there, and now I desperately want my friend to know she's let me down. How can you feel glad and guilty at the same time? My feelings seesaw one way, then the other. I'm being a 'Mary, Mary Quite Contrary' and I don't want to feel like any kind of Mary at all. And so, I pick at a stray stem of blowfly grass while Acacia kicks at a stone with her bare foot, probably waiting for me to jump with joy. I'm not going to, even though I feel her eyes piercing me.

'Wanna play hopscotch?'

I shrug. Her broken promise is heavy between us, as smothering as the hot, muggy air with its gathering grey clouds. 'S'pose.' And then, arms crossed, 'I was looking for you. You said you were coming over to make White Christmas.'

'Sorry, Jane,' she says, her head bent, voice soft. She won't meet my eyes. 'I wanted to. Had to go somewhere with Mum, but …' Finally, Acacia looks at me, eyes begging me to understand. Shrugs her shoulders: *you know what mums are like.*

Biting my lip, I nod stiffly and feign interest in a long, brown wattle seed pod with six knobbly seed-bumps. I know the seeds inside are black, like I know mums have a habit of making plans that are more important than ours. But this was meant to be special. Did she even try to talk her mum into letting her stay? I want to say this, to make her see, but I don't. My friend is peering at her own seed pod, turning it over in her hand, holding it up to the sun. The light glitters on a single wet tear tracing down the side of her face and my breath catches at the sight of a crack in her mask.

How is it that moments with our mothers can be so different?

My seed pod snaps between my fingers. I crush it, let it fall to the ground, let go of my sulkiness in a flutter of brown and black confetti. I've never seen Acacia this fragile, like she'll shatter if I press too hard.

'Don't worry about it,' I offer, scrambling to my feet. Us kids are in this together. 'Hey, maybe Mum will let you taste the White Christmas.' Something sweet will make her sadness, whatever it is, go away.

You can't be sad at Christmas. It's the rule, isn't it?

I return triumphantly with two squares of the sweet slice and hand one to Acacia. There's no trace of the tear stain on her cheek now, only a dirty smudge. A lone magpie is watching us from a high branch in the wattle, head cocked, beak quivering, and I eat my piece fast in case he decides to swoop and snatch. Acacia seems unconcerned. As she nibbles the sweet, the heat of her fingers melts the white chocolate, and a grin spreads across her face, all the way to her eyes.

'Yum!' She licks her fingers. 'That was worth waiting all my life for,' she tells me. 'None for you,' she tells the bird, before turning to me, her grin warm as the sun on my skin, sweet like the honey in Mum's gingerbread. The bird chatters something. As if it's a child, protesting.

'Next year you can help us make it,' I promise.

Acacia points at the hopscotch outline I've chalked on the driveway. 'Are we going to play hopscotch?'

'Can't. I'm going out.'

The cloud swallows the sun, a breeze rustles the leaves. A black seed lifts, then falls. The magpie flies away.

'Where ...' she fiddles with a seed pod, 'So, where are you going?'

I think about being vague, like Acacia so often is. But I can't do it. 'Lynda and Terry's. They've been Mum and Dad's friends since forever. They live in Fairfield, and they've got a two-storey house and an inground pool so they're rich. We always go to theirs on Christmas Eve for a pool party.' My voice brightens. 'It's so cool. And sometimes all of the kids put on a show for the grown-ups and it's so much fun.'

'Cool.' Her voice says the opposite.

'Yeah. And Terry always dresses up as Santa, but everyone knows it's him because he's skinny and Santa's not. One year he shoved a pillow up his top, and it fell out while he was handing out presents.'

A small, sad smile follows my laughter. 'Well, see you.' She is already turning away, giving me the back of her head. Her hair glows as the sun pushes through the clouds. The bird is back.

'Yeah, see you,' I say to her back, to the bird. Five steps later, I stop. 'Happy Christmas for tomorrow.'

She turns to look at me. 'Yeah. Happy Christmas.' Our eyes meet for the briefest of seconds; hers look bright and shiny, almost as if they are filled with ... no, it's the sun.

She is staring into the depths of the wattle tree again. Its branches spread like a mother's arms. I wonder if she wants to disappear into its leafy hug, like I do sometimes. Her mouth is moving. I think she's talking to the bird. For a second, I'm almost angry again, this time not at Acacia, but at her mother. Why doesn't Acacia have anything to look forward to at Christmas? It seems unfair that our family does the same thing every year and Acacia does ... what *does* she do? I can't picture anything. The curtains are closed on her day-to-day life.

When we leave an hour later, she's still out the front, under the wattle, all by herself. Up on my knees, I wave at her from the back window of the station wagon; waving back, she grows smaller and smaller until we turn the corner and she's gone.

Dad swerves to avoid a magpie that dive bombs our car. *Bloody maggie!* A flash of black and white spins up and away. The bird is alive, unhurt. A lucky miss, but a sudden shiver runs through me. Mum says a cool change is blowing in, but I have that bad feeling deep in my tummy again, like a different kind of change is coming.

CHAPTER SIXTEEN

SCATTERING

That first night in the refuge, I ate dinner in my bedroom. A two-minute noodle omelette – home brand noodles, eggs, grated cheese, a small tin of tuna. I found the recipe in a tattered *That's Life* magazine in the communal lounge room. The front cover shouted, 'My CHEATING EX got my mum PREGNANT!' over the smaller 'Nifty noodles' coverline. I didn't read the article. Didn't finish the omelette either. It felt like cardboard in my mouth, tasted like dust.

My mind drifted to *him*. Was he eating alone, like me? I pictured him on the floral sofa in front of the telly, watching a sitcom, eating takeaway, drinking beer without a care in the world. I thought of the good times on that second-hand sofa – drinking cheap wine, eating cheesy pizza, making love.

I nearly packed my bag for home, then and there.

But Pat knocked on the door and said, you alright love? *Fine, thanks.* She said, do you want to meet the others? *No, thanks.* Her footsteps faded away as I sat on my sagging single mattress. Forced myself to remember the first time he threw his dinner at the wall. The steak was fucken overcooked, he said.

I read somewhere that, on average, domestic violence victims leave about seven times before they finally call it quits. The first time I left, after he punched the wall, I went back to him within hours. Drove around the suburban streets aimlessly, nowhere to go, music turned all the way up to drown out the screaming in my head. Parked near a playground a few blocks from home, I replayed the scene over and over, this time with me saying all the right things, him listening, both being reasonable. And then I drove home. He was drunk, passed out, snoring, his mouth gaping open, like the hole in the wall. The next day he said sorry, and I said it's okay.

The hole in the wall stayed a hole. I never asked him to fix it; he never offered. I saw it every day, that jagged reminder of what he was capable of.

I learnt to live with it.

After I went back, I started moving through my days in an endless fog of nothingness. I'd drive somewhere, my body tethered to a car seat, but I wasn't in that car. I'd walk somewhere, one foot in front of the other, but I wasn't in my body. Life happened to me. I moved on autopilot. Like I was on one of those moving walkways at airports, glacially slow, but they get you there in the end. How did I drive from one place to another, through traffic lights, down busy roads, and not crash into anyone? How did I live like the walking dead, moving through life seeing but not seeing, feeling but not feeling, hearing but not hearing? I did that for so long; how did I stay alive?

Autopilot is the friend that carries you to the end of another day.

Yeah, I know it's normal to do things without thinking, like turn off the tap, get dressed, put something in the bin. Everyone does it, right? Life can be mind-numbingly predictable sometimes and brains get spaced out with information overload. But this was different. Because most people, they go through their little routines and eventually the on-switch is flicked, and they start thinking and feeling again. When the only thing you're thinking about is protecting yourself, there's no room for thinking and feeling. For overthinking and worrying yourself sick.

I did what I had to do.

I didn't even know I was doing it.

Staying in that fuzzy underworld was easier than facing the reality.

I tiptoed around moods, crossing my fingers and holding my breath so I didn't say the wrong words or look the wrong way or do the wrong thing. Some call it walking on eggshells, but it was more like walking on broken glass or hot coals and trying to be invisible at the same time. And sometimes I felt like a fortune teller peering into a cloudy crystal ball. I'd think I knew what was coming and I was doing things right and then, *BAM!* Sideswiped with words or threatened with a fist. I saved my tears for the shower. And after a while, I barely cried at all.

Over time, I stopped trusting my thoughts, ideas, judgements. They only got me into trouble. He liked it that way, me going along with what he wanted and thought. Wanna watch a movie? *Whatever you want to do.* Wanna have sex? *Alright.* Time to stop the bloody queue jumpers! *Hmmm.* By the time I left him for good, I didn't know what I wanted. The first time Pat made me a cuppa, she asked, one sugar or two? Either way, I said. You must have a preference, she said, and I shrugged. *I don't care.*

The first night in the refuge, I scratched my legs until they bled, knowing I'd have to relive this cycle the next day. Eating alone. Questioning myself. A song clashing in my head: 'Should I Stay or Should I Go?'

Staring at the duffel bag under my bed.

If I went home, the pattern would return. One day fine, one day black.

If I stayed, I'd have to wake up from sleepwalking through my days. And that freaked the hell out of me.

Because when I was awake, I felt everything. All the shame and guilt and fear.

It follows you wherever you go.

CHAPTER SEVENTEEN

1979

The rise and fall of magpies carolling in a gum tree. Bing Crosby and friends sing Merry Christmas. Sitting cross-legged near the Christmas tree in our pyjamas, with bed-hair and sleep-crusted eyes. Dad in a Santa hat, handing out presents. Eyes bright, fingers clutching, waiting for Mum to take the photo that always looks like one of us has a tree growing from our head. The rip-curl of paper, squeals: 'Slip 'n' Slide! You little ripper!' Mum finger-raking torn paper into a pile of festive Autumn leaves. The smell of coffee, bitter-black, from the percolator. The sizzle of eggs frying in a pan. The crunch of crisp bacon against our teeth. Skolling soft drink – for breakfast! – straight from glass Tarax bottles we had home delivered. Fizz-burps of contentment. This is Christmas morning at the Kelly house.

It's the same every year and I don't ever want it to change. But it's bound to. Last night Sal asked if Robbie could come over for breakfast, but Dad said *no, it's family time*. And she said *fine, I'm going to Robbie's family for dinner*, and they didn't talk to each other the rest of the drive home from Lynda and Terry's. They're okay now, Sal and Dad. Sal's all smiles because she got the new Michael Jackson record. She let me use her brand new Cutex

Pink Whisper polish and did my hair in braids without complaining. Dad's dancing with Mum and singing along to carols instead of wearing his I'm-only-putting-up-with-this-for-one-more-day face. His voice is deep and smooth like caramel. Last night I was gobsmacked when I heard he used to be the lead singer in a band with Terry, way back when he was about Robbie's age. It's hard to imagine Dad as anything but Dad.

Mum says *Not today* to test the Slip 'n' Slide, so after breakfast Jim and Dad start setting up Jim's Scalextric set in the living room, Sal disappears upstairs to listen to her record, and I read the Enid Blyton book Sal gave me. Five adventurous kids are rowing across to an island, and 'Don't Stop 'Til You Get Enough' is on its third repeat, when Mum slips out the front door without a word. Dad and Jim are too busy with the Scalextric to notice, but the sneaky way she tiptoes past makes me wonder what she's up to. Tossing the book aside, I follow. She's heading next door, carrying something bulky, but it's cradled against her chest, and I can't see what it is.

'Mum? Where are you going?'

She doesn't answer, so I run barefoot across the lawn, stopping only when the sharp spike of a bindii digs into my big toe. By the time I pull it out, Mum's striding back around the fence, arms empty, thongs slip-slapping against her feet.

'Mum. What were you doing? What did you take next door?'

She shakes her head. 'Nothing, Jane.'

'It wasn't nothing, you were carrying something.' An idea dawns. 'Was it a present?' When Mum breathes in sharply, I know I'm on the right track. 'For Acacia? And Rose? What was it? Why did you give them presents?'

An exasperated huff. 'It was only a few things I thought they might like, that's all. It's no big deal.' She takes me by the shoulders gently and makes me look at her. 'You're not to say anything to anyone. Not even Acacia. I don't want a fuss.'

Later, when we drive past Acacia's house, a bulging

99

pillowcase-sack is propped up against their front door. I smile to myself. Santa, disguised as Mum, hasn't passed them by after all. I wish I could see Acacia's face when she opens the door.

Merry Christmas, I whisper-think. Maybe in a magical Christmas way, Acacia hears.

Of course, I forget Acacia as soon as we arrive at Nan and Pop's. The whole extended family on Mum's side is over for Christmas lunch, cramming into the small but neat weatherboard house in Blacktown. All up, there are seventeen of us. Pop has set up trestle tables outside, covering them with mismatched tablecloths from Nan's linen cupboard. Nan's made roast turkey with garlic and onion stuffing, crisp baked potatoes and piles of mushy boiled vegetables, including brussels sprouts; she cooks the same thing every year, no matter how hot it is. I hate sprouts and push them away, but Dad says *clear your plates or no presents*. Sometimes it's best not to call his bluff, so I drown the sprouts with rich brown gravy and pretend they're sausages. It works if I squeeze my eyes tight and chew fast.

After lunch, the women clean up and talk about their kids and husbands who never lift a finger in the house; the men unbutton their good shirts and lounge on webbed fold-out chairs. They smoke, drink beer and crack nuts from their shells; they talk about cricket, the bushfires in the mountains and someone called Malcolm Fraser. Inside it smells like food and pine; outside it smells like a mix of bushfire and tobacco, beer and pongy armpits. We kids swig soft drink from cans in the shade, counting down until we're allowed in the above-ground pool. Nan insists we wait 3600 seconds after lunch: *you'll get cramps and drown*. One by one, we ask *is it time yet*; the women shoo us outside and the men tell us to stop our whinging. Finally, sixty minutes to the second, Pop says the magic words: *Pool time!*

As we race to the rickety ladder, throwing beach towels over the clothesline, he shouts the same words as every year: 'Stick your feet in the bucket first. No grass in my clean pool!' We make whirlpools and play Marco Polo and sharks and mermaids, squealing and splashing in delight, until someone calls: *Present time!*

'No drips in my house,' Nan says, standing guard at the door while we dry ourselves with scratchy towels and compare pruney fingers and goosebumps. Ash from the unseen bushfire dances like black snowflakes and smudges our skin.

'Wipe that off,' she says. Nan has a no-nonsense manner she got from the Second World War, but she has a good heart. If you ever need a tissue or a Butter Menthol, she'll dig one out from her handbag before you can say please.

'No wet bottoms on my couch,' Nan calls out as we charge to the living room, towels tucked around our waists or slung over our shoulders. 'On the floor, you lot. Adults get the chairs, not kids. Jim! Get down. Yes, you. You're not too big to feel the back of my hand, young man.'

I could be an actor; I know her lines so well.

Nan and Pop's tiny living room is dominated by a real Christmas tree so big it touches the ceiling; underneath, brightly wrapped presents spill out in all directions. The space is too squishy for seventeen people, so the last ones inside sit in the hall. I was busting for the loo so that's where I sit, but I like it better out here where it smells like Christmas pudding instead of pine needles, sweat and chlorine. As usual, Pop plays Santa, handing out presents one-by-one; the rest of us are elves, passing gifts down the assembly line to their rightful owners. I'm dying to test my new rollerskates from Nan and Pop – white boots with pink wheels! – but Nan wants to sing Christmas carols. She backs down when everyone cracks up at Uncle Nev's horrible drone; I escape out the front and practise skating up and down the even path, with Dad and Pop cheering me on.

'It looks a lot easier on telly,' I tell them. My throat hurts from trying not to cry after grazing both knees on the concrete. Inside, stinging Dettol and skin-coloured plasters are applied with a *there, there*. My scabs-to-be are battle wounds or badges of honour, depending on who's listening.

And then it's afternoon tea time. Homemade fruit-and-nut-filled mince pies. Nan's buttery shortbread. Rich plum pudding with a real fire on it. Warm globs of custard poured from an old jug Nan says came all the way from England. Melting Neapolitan ice cream scooped straight from a tub, slathered with Cottee's strawberry or chocolate topping or a sweet river of both. A treasure chest of Quality Street chocolates and toffees, individually twist-wrapped in all the colours of the rainbow. Us kids can eat and drink as much as we want – chocolate, lollies, soft drink, cake – and we cram it in like it's our last day on earth. We stir our ice cream into a beige soup, and no one tells us to stop. Dad doesn't even raise an eyebrow when Robbie arrives in his panel van to whisk Sal away, or flinch when Nan says *what a lovely couple* and something about wedding bells.

One by one, my aunts and uncles and cousins leave for other rellies' houses but we Kellys hang around like the bushfire smoke. We play Mastermind and Monopoly with Nan and Pop and the Italians from next door and nibble *zeppoli* – fluffy deep-fried balls of dough sprinkled with icing sugar. The sun's fire is fading when Mum finally says time to go.

Pop presses five-dollar notes into mine and Jim's hands – 'Spending money for your holiday' – and Nan fills Mum's arms with brown and orange Tupperware containers of leftovers.

'I need those tins back, mind.' As I watch my nan and Mum talk, something new occurs to me. To me, Mum is simply *Mum*; to others, she is someone's child, sister, wife, neighbour, friend. If she can be all those things to different people, why can't she dream of more? Why can't she get a job helping other people and still be a mum?

On the drive home, sun-tired and full-bellied, me and Jim

don't bicker at each other, not even once, which Mum says is a Christmas miracle. We don't even argue about what to watch on telly while Mum and Dad drink shandies out the back, or when Mum says *bedtime*. In my room, I replay the day in my head. There are two things I hope never change about Christmas Day in our family: one, that it will always be a big deal and two, that we'll always put our differences aside for the day.

I'm almost asleep when a loud noise startles me. It's not Sal coming home. It's voices rising and falling next door; one high and sharp like lightning; the other, low and rumbling like thunder. Rose and Daryl. I sit up and strain my ears against the flyscreen, but whatever they're saying is suddenly drowned out by the throbbing rev of Daryl's motorbike and Turdle barking. A squeal of tyres on the road, a door slams, and it's quiet on our street again.

CHAPTER EIGHTEEN

1979

On Boxing Day, our street rings with the sounds of neighbourhood kids showing off new bikes, footies and skateboards. Of men yelling, 'Come on!' and 'Howzat' and 'Bloody oath, Hogg!' from their living rooms. Of Sal and her friends having a pool party for Margie Murphy's seventeenth birthday, listening to thumping rock music and doing bombies in the Murphy's backyard pool. We younger kids aren't invited. We run from house to house, calling anyone home out to play; our parents let us roam free, while they close the curtains to block out the heat and sink into chairs in the coolest parts of the house with belly-deep sighs.

But of Acacia and Rose, there's no sign. No answer when I rap at their front door. No car in the driveway.

No bulging pillowcase at the front door. Only a magpie, poking for grubs, giving me the side eye.

Where are they? My stomach twists with disappointment. I hope they come home soon. Mum says we're leaving first thing in the morning for Lake Cathie.

I find Mum in her bedroom, sorting holiday clothes for her

and Dad into neat piles. Dad is in the living room watching the Australia v Pakistan Test Match on telly.

'Mum, do we have to go?'

'You know better than to ask that, Jane Kelly. And it's only for a few days.' She opens a drawer; her lips move as she counts two pairs of shorts and three T-shirts for Dad. When she looks at me, her forehead creases. 'Why don't you leave her a note if she's not home by dinner? And you can send her a postcard from Lake Cathie. She'd like that. Yes? Good. Now choof off. Unless you want me to give you something to do. Like packing your bag.'

Shaking my head, I wander out to the wattle tree with my new skates. My fingers fumble with the laces. A lot can happen in a few days. What if Acacia finds a new best friend while I'm gone? What if Mary Evans swoops in? She's back from her holiday, I saw her out the front of her house yesterday. What if Acacia is only putting up with me until someone better comes along?

I couldn't bear it if that happened again.

I stand up and hold onto the tree, legs wobbling until I find my balance. I can't shake the uneasy feeling that something bad will happen while I'm away. And I'm confused. I thought I wasn't worried about Mary Evans anymore, that my friendship with Acacia was strong and true. But all this time, Mary Evans has been lurking underneath my skin, like a monster under the bed. Will I ever be free of her?

Get lost!

I skate slowly around the cul-de-sac. Soon, I feel my confidence rising and the wheels roll faster, faster, and I imagine Acacia skating beside me. But a moment later, in my haste to move off the road when Daryl's motorbike flies past, I'm sprawled on the hot, scratchy grass like a winded beetle. No damage done. No one has noticed except a magpie, peering down at me from the wattle tree with red-brown eyes. I think it's the same one as yesterday. I don't think it likes me. A soft white-and-black blob lands on the grass next to me, missing my head by centimetres.

'That's not funny!' The bird cocks its head sideways, chattering as I scramble up and away. Out of range.

Next door, Daryl is whistling as he lets himself into the Millers' house. The front door bangs shut behind him, reminding me of the slamming door I heard last night, of Rose and Daryl's voices, rising and falling, high and low. Does Rose know he's in her house?

'Oi, Jane! Dad's going to set up the Slip 'n' Slide!' Jim yells. Smiddy and a few other boys from the neighbourhood have dumped their bikes and skateboards on our lawn, jostling and hooting, waiting for the fun to begin.

'Jane! Come give us a hand,' Dad calls.

By the time I whip off my skates and run over to help unfold the plastic slide, my neighbours are forgotten.

'Bloody kids interrupting the cricket.' There's no grumble in his words, rather a twinkle in his eye. He's been feasting nonstop on hunks of leftover leg ham and Mum's potato salad and drinking beer all afternoon. Dad's a different person when he's relaxed. I wish he was like this all the time.

He turns on the tap; within seconds, our front lawn is a water paradise. A tidal wave of kids from our street, slipping and sliding down the green plastic, laughing and squealing as we catapult across the water-slick lawn and pull ourselves up, coated in dirt and grass heads. No one tells us to quieten down; no one wants to stop sliding despite grass rash on our legs, sore bellies from throwing ourselves on the mat and sunburnt skin. When Dad good-naturedly turns off the tap because *you've wasted enough bloody water*, that's when I notice my tingling, itchy skin, the fresh scabs on my knees rubbed raw. And something else: Acacia still isn't home.

I wait in the shade of the wattle tree; the magpie is long gone, scared off. Music blasts from next door as a game of cricket starts in the cul-de-sac: *Howzat!* I don't join in. Dad winds the hose into the reel, muttering when it kinks. When he straightens up, his eyes flick towards the music, his mouth forms a grimace. He catches me watching, sighs.

'Taking the dog for a walk. Want to join us? Better than moping around,' he offers, shrugging when I shake my head.

I want to walk with Dad, but I don't. Acacia will be home any minute now. But she's still not home when Dad and Turdle return, when the cricket game ends, or when Mum says it's time to pack for our holiday. Where is she? I feel like a twig about to snap; I'm holding back tears, and I don't know whether they're sad, angry, worried or frustrated tears. All of them, I suppose. And I take it out on Mum even though it's not her fault. Why do we do that? Take out our frustrations on the ones we love most?

'I'm busy. Why can't we pack in the morning?' I whine. Jim, of course, is playing the angel again. 'It'll take me five minutes to pack. Three hundred seconds. You can time me.'

'Your dad wants to leave first thing, that's why,' Mum says, passing me my suitcase.

'Why do you always have to do what Dad wants?' The words snap out.

Mum crosses her arms. 'I'm not in the mood for arguing. Just do what you're told. The quicker you get it done, the quicker you can go outside.'

She hands me a handwritten list: four tops, two pairs of shorts, my good dress, one set of pyjamas, socks, undies, cozzies, sneakers, thongs, hairbrush, elastics, bobby pins. What about books? What kind of a holiday is it without books?

'I can't wait 'til I'm a grown-up and I can do what I want when I want,' I mutter, wiping my nose on the back of my hand.

'Trust me, it's not all it's cracked up to be,' Mum says. Her hand goes up when I open my mouth. 'Before you say another word, don't. I know you're upset about Acacia being out, but you keep on going this way and there'll be no trifle or telly tonight.'

It's too much. 'You don't know anything about how I feel!' The words fall out in a messy sob.

Mum lets out a deep breath and sits on my bed. Pats a spot beside her. 'Why don't you tell me?'

Sniffing, I glance at her kind, expectant face. She pats the spot again. *Come on.* And then, with my hands twisting in my lap, and an uneasy feeling deep in my belly, I begin.

CHAPTER NINETEEN

1979

The next day we drive up north, with Turdle and our bags in the back, boogie boards and fishing rods on the roof. Dad is in one of his dark moods, the storm-building kind that crushes holiday excitement and puts us all on edge. It went downhill fast after breakfast. He started barking orders like an Army sergeant. He can't handle being late. We were right on his (too early!) schedule until Turdle did a runner to the park and jumped into the duck pond. Dad was fuming by the time he dragged our sopping wet dog back to the car, but when he stepped in fresh dog poo, he blew his top like a soft drink that was all shook up. I reckon the whole neighbourhood is awake because of his yelling and blustering.

Mum takes charge. She herds us into the car quick smart, gets us settled: *windows down, seatbelts on, no fighting!* Dad says nothing when he gets in the car, but the way he sits heavily in his seat and grips the steering wheel means his mood is coming for the ride. Wedged between Sal and Jim, Turdle panting hotly near my ear, I wonder how many hours, minutes, seconds of the drive Dad's dark mood will last. Five hours is a long time to be stuck in a car with a bad mood and a stinky dog.

'Which way will you drive?' Mum's voice is blurred by the hot wind blasting our faces.

'Wisemans Ferry,' Dad grunts. He pushes in a cassette, presses play. Supertramp's 'Bloody Well Right' fills the car, and he turns the volume up, up, up.

Mum turns her head towards the window. We kids listen in silence as Supertramp belts out songs none of us like, over and over as bushland and bone-dry pastures flash by. Sal is buried in the new *Dolly* magazine. Jim draws tattoos on his leg with a texta he smuggled into the car. I'm too wound up to read *Bridge to Terabithia*.

I shift in my seat, thinking about Dad. I love him to the moon and back, but his dark moods unsettle me. Sometimes they brew and brew like billowing storm clouds but blow away; other times they gust out of him like a sudden squall. When he loses his temper, he yells a lot. He gets louder and louder and stomps and slams. When Dad's in a dark mood, whether he yells or not, it freaks me out. I don't like sharing the same space as an angry person. I wish I was back at home, hanging out with Acacia. But she's still not home. I didn't get to say goodbye.

The car veers sharply to the left, knocking us kids together like bowling pins.

'Oi! Stay on *your* side of the road!' Dad shakes his fist at an old man wearing a straw hat before muttering, 'Silly old bugger.'

I glance at Mum; she's still staring out the window, her body tilted away from Dad. She's so strong. She knows how to handle him, but I can tell it wears her down. And here's what I don't get: how can something that happened before I was born still affect Dad? Mum says some things are best left in the past. So why does the past bother Dad in the present?

Mum fumbles in her bag, dabs at her eyes with a tissue. Does she ever secretly wish she married someone else, someone who didn't get dark moods? I suppose that would wish us kids away, so she gets on with things. I know she loves him, and I don't think she wants a different husband, any more than I want a different dad. But I'll bet she wishes he behaved differently sometimes.

I do.

'I'm sick of this music,' Sal whispers to herself.

Me too.

The Supertramp music seems to soothe Dad; he taps his fingers on the steering wheel and hums along. When he's played both sides, he flips the cassette back to Side A and starts it again, turning down the volume. By the time we reach the Wisemans Ferry crossing, the mood in the car feels lighter. The anticipation of seeing Grandma and Granddad slowly returns. Less than four hours to go.

The music stops mid-song.

'Reckon we should stop in Singleton for ice cream?' Dad says to Mum.

I hold my breath and whoosh it out when she turns to him: yes. His hand snakes across to her shoulder and he pats it gently before fixing his eyes back on the road. Dad has found his way out of the dark again. I'll bet they're holding hands. I hope so.

It's like a switch has flicked; in the back seat, we relax into normal. Me and Jim play noughts and crosses, Spotto and I Spy, like we did with Acacia on the way to the city. (Was it really only three days ago? It feels like weeks since I've seen her.) We tell stupid jokes that make us laugh hysterically until that moment when things go too far – when we're tired and bored and cranky but don't know it yet – and the bickering starts. Mum reckons she can tell the second it's going to happen.

'Pinch bug!' A beetle-shaped VW passes, and Jim pinches my upper arm.

'Ow! Not so hard!' I pinch him back, digging in my barely-there nails.

Mum twists around to face us. 'That's enough, you two. Jim, don't be so rough with your sister.'

'But it was a pinch bug, that's what you do. And she pinched me back. With her nails.'

'I said, don't be so rough,' she repeats, voice firmer. Dad gives her a sideways glance but says nothing. She faces the front.

I wait three seconds. *Sucked in*, I mouth at my brother.

He rubs his right cheek slowly, middle finger upright: *Up yours.*

I elbow him.

He elbows back.

'Get out of my space.'

'You get out of mine.'

Without turning, Mum says, 'I guess you two don't want ice cream, after all.'

'We do!'

'Then behave.'

At Singleton we eat ice cream cones in a big park. Dad and Jim take Turdle for a walk and Sal calls Robbie from the public phone. I stay with Mum, who's still quiet and staring off into the distance.

'Are you okay, Mum?'

'Of course, love. We're on holiday, aren't we? What's there to be sad about?' She sounds like she's trying to convince herself and won't meet my eyes. I scan the park for Dad; he and Jim are at the far end, playing fetch with Turdle.

'Mum? Why does Dad get in his moods?'

'We all get in moods, love.'

'You know what I mean. The dark moods.'

Mum sighs deeply. 'Look, love ...' Dad's walking towards us with Jim and Turdle. She starts talking quickly. 'Your dad has seen and experienced things we'll never really understand. Bad things.'

'Why doesn't he talk about them? Or let it go? That's what you tell us to do.'

'It's complicated. Right now, he can't. Not to me, not to anyone. The memories make him too sad and ... angry ... and all kinds of feelings.' Dad and Jim stop at the toilet block, taking turns to go while the other holds Turdle's lead. Mum continues, 'Instead, he boxes the bad things away in his mind, but sometimes they get out. These moods are his way of trying to deal with the bad things when he remembers them. Okay?'

I nod, but it's not okay, not really. 'I wish there was no such thing as war or bad people or bad things.'

'Me too. But we can't change what has happened to us before, only what happens next.' She stands and brushes grass from her skirt, signalling the end of the conversation. 'Up you get. Do you need to wee? You sure? Go anyway. I don't want to stop five minutes down the road because you've changed your mind.' But before we move, she leans down and whispers, 'Dad loves us very much, you know. Don't forget that.'

Back in the car, we head north again. I open my book and start reading. The air starts to smell salty, and I catch glimpses of the ocean in the distance. Dad says he'll take us to the beach later.

Jim elbows me again, knocking my book from my hands. 'Move.

You're in my space.'

I elbow him back. Later can't come soon enough.

CHAPTER TWENTY

DORMANT

I kept to myself the first few days at the refuge. Barely left my room, except to eat and drink, use the bathroom, going through the motions like a zombie. I didn't feel safe out there, only in my room. And I reckon I cried an ocean in that safe house prison.

I was like a mad woman's breakfast, all over the place. One minute crying, why me, why did this happen to me? How could I let it happen? Freaking out, having panic attacks because I heard a motorbike, convinced he'd tracked me down. The next, missing him like crazy, thinking what happened wasn't that serious after all. When you share a bed with someone for years, it's hard getting used to a single bed. I told myself I'd rather be with him than be alone.

I didn't see the volunteer in those early days. She'd been rostered on one day, but a line was drawn through her name on the roster I found outside Pat's office, another woman's name scribbled above. I wondered briefly if she'd changed her plans because of me. Her name wasn't listed for any shifts for the next two weeks. Would she ever come back? But to be honest, I wasn't thinking much about her one way or another. If it wasn't for Pat checking in on me, I wouldn't have stayed at the refuge at all.

She was nice, Pat. Nanna nice, like my room.

It was Pat who introduced me to the other residents. Come on, love, she said after a couple of days, it's time you met the others. Five women, four kids. She told me their names, but I didn't take much notice and forgot them almost immediately. Best to keep them at arm's length, that's what I told myself. No one stays for long, what's the point of getting personal?

One of the women – in her thirties, I reckon – had blotchy yellow-green bruises splattered on her upper arm and face. Didn't even try to hide them, not even from her daughter. Another one had twin baby boys. Looked like the life had been drained out of her. Jumped like a scared cat every time someone moved. Pat said she was sleeping in her car 'til a place came up here. There was one girl, maybe seventeen, with a black eye and a fat lip. Kept disappearing outside and reappearing in a fug of weedy smoke. And one woman wearing a headscarf, sitting at the dining table with her two kids, talking in a language I didn't understand.

The woman with the bruises saw me looking. She'll go back, she said, pointing at the woman with the scarf, she don't have a choice unless she wants to kip down at the train station. I forgot I didn't want to know, couldn't help myself: What do you mean, she doesn't have a choice? The bruise-woman said: Bet you a tenner she's on a spouse visa, no rights without her bloke, can't get Social Security or nothing.

Pat and I had a cuppa at the table while the other women watched Friends and talked between themselves: Ya call the cops? Nah. What's the point? They don't do anything. If you don't got bruises or broken bones, how're you supposed to prove anything? Too right. Really? Cops arrested mine. How'd that work out for ya? Made it worse.

The first and only time I called the cops, my ex denied it all. That time, they believed him, and he made me wish I'd never called. My next-door neighbour called the cops this time because she couldn't stand by any longer, that's what she said. He denied it all again, but this time they believed me. Arrested him. Sent a police liaison officer to talk to me. She's the one who fixed me up to come to the refuge. The one who helped me pack. Told me I deserved better.

Pat said, see love, you're not alone.

And I was thinking, yeah right, I have nothing in common with them. They're proper battered women. My ex only hit me twice before I came here. No, three times. But the first time didn't count because it was an accident. I mean, I got in the way. If I hadn't moved when I did … It's not the same as if he deliberately belted me or something. The second, well, it was more of a shove as he walked past me. He didn't mean to. He apologised afterwards and he meant it. He was practically in tears. The next time, I gave him lip, so he slapped my face. And the last time … I wasn't ready to think about that right then.

Mostly, it was yelling and put-downs that I copped.

And most times I thought I deserved it.

As I looked at the other women, I thought, this is not the right place for me, I shouldn't be here, I shouldn't have let the police arrest my ex, they should have just talked to him, he's reasonable when he calms down, and my bruises are only on the inside.

I thought, these women need the refuge more than me. I'm taking valuable resources from someone who needs it.

The weight of it all – the stories, the responsibility, my decision – was crushing. I couldn't breathe. Pat led me outside, under the patio where a lone smoker in a puffer jacket stared at nothing and no one. Trying, like the rest of us, to hide her shame in silence.

I said to Pat, I don't belong here, it's a mistake.

And she said, he's still in your house. Where else will you go?

It was weeks before I accepted what Pat was trying to show me.

Us women, she said, we've travelled different roads to get here, but underneath there's no discrimination. We're all haunted by the same old story.

CHAPTER TWENTY-ONE

1979

I t's mid-afternoon when we arrive at Lake Cathie. The long
drive was worth it. Grandma and Granddad live in an old but
tidy cottage across the road from the beach. By standing on the
picket fence, I can see the white-capped waves rolling in, one
after the other. I'm itching to run straight into that sparkling
water and wash the sweat off me, but Mum says *soon*. Inside, the
house is small and neat, like Grandma, with three bedrooms and
a sleep-out out the back. Jim gets the small spare room because
he's a boy; Sal and I don't care because we like the sunny sleep-
out better. We can hear waves crashing on the beach, smell salt
on the air, and feel the sea breeze tickle our skin through the big
windows.

Grandma has cans of soft drink, sandwiches and ice-cold
sliced watermelon waiting for us. We polish it all off, wiping
watermelon juice on the backs of our hands, then pull on our
cozzies. We cart boogie boards and towels across the road and
throw them in a messy pile on the hot sand. Then we leap into
the water, squealing, splashing and yahooing, all of us, even
Grandma. It's cold, but only for a millisecond. After a while, Dad
and us kids grab the boogie boards and paddle out deeper,

waiting for the perfect wave to shoot us towards the shore. He makes me stay close to him and I remember what Mum said earlier in the park.

'I love you, Dad!' I shout the words into the wind and the waves, and I think he doesn't hear me.

But he grins and says, 'I love you too, Janey.' He points at a wave rolling towards us. It's perfect. 'Ready ... set ... go!'

Later, while I'm making a sandcastle, I look up to see Mum and Dad hugging, holding hands, talking. Their words are drowned in the wind and waves and screeching seagulls, but what I see is enough.

We cram as much as possible into our three-and-a-half days: a belated Christmas dinner with Grandma and Granddad; fishing off the bridge and swimming in the saltwater lake; sculpting sand-mermaids with seaweed hair and sandcastles decorated with shells; boogie-boarding and beachcombing. We visit Fantasy Glades and King Neptune's Park, stroll along the Port Macquarie foreshore, and eat ice creams every day. There's no sign of Dad's dark mood. It's like he's a different person: relaxed, happy, fun to be around.

'If we lived here,' I tell Mum, 'He'd be like that always.'

'You can't run away from the dark moods that easily,' she says. 'Eventually they catch up.' But I spot her looking at the real estate noticeboard next to the milk bar later that day.

Being here hasn't helped Sal's mood much; she's up and down like a rollercoaster at Luna Park. She misses Robbie, but she's a total sad sack about it. I miss Acacia, but apart from sending her a postcard, I've been too busy to think about her much. Sal says she'll die if she doesn't talk to Robbie every day and *none of you understand anything about being in love*. She rings him from the public phone at the milk bar after dinner every night because Granddad says long-distance phone calls are for emergencies, not for calling boys. She sends him love letters every morning. They're sprayed with Charlie perfume and on the back, she writes SWALK: Sealed With a Loving Kiss. We'll be home before he gets them, but Sal says *leave me alone*. And last night she cried for hours because Robbie didn't say he missed her.

Having a boyfriend is hard work.

It's the last night of our holiday and me, Dad, Granddad and Jim are walking down to the lake to see the prawners. Granddad says his mates go down there every night. We're like the Famous Five – four, really, because Granddad said Turdle wasn't allowed – going on an adventure, using torches and the light of the rising moon to guide the way. At the lake, which is still and pitted with night-black puddles and pools, the men put on headlamps and tell us to stay close and *do what I say*.

'The lake is in between tides,' Granddad says, 'and some of the pools are deeper than they look.'

'And they're full of night sharks and sharp-toothed eel-snakes,' Jim whispers.

I don't believe him, but I stick close to Dad anyway.

And then I trip over a bucket someone left on the edge of a lakepool. One minute I'm holding Dad's hand, the next I'm in the water, tangled up in a prawning net. I hear Jim laughing and Dad shouting and men swearing – *Get the eff out!* – and I want to tell the men to stop shouting, *it was an accident*, but my feet can't find the sandy bottom and my arms are waving and my head goes under one, two, three times and I can't breathe. I'm going to drown; I'm going to die …

Dad hauls me out and dumps me on the sand. I cough up salty water; I vomit, and my throat burns with acid. Jim's stopped laughing now. He's kneeling next to me and Granddad's on the other side, patting my back.

'I dropped my torch,' I sniff, then burst into snotty, gulping sobs when Granddad says *it's gone, love*. It's too much.

The prawners don't care that I nearly drowned. They're too busy untangling their net and swearing.

Dad helps me up. 'Come on, love, let's get you home.'

'Good idea, go on, get lost.' A squashed beer can lands at my feet. 'Yeah, take the little bitch back home, before she friggin' scares away the whole bloody catch,' the other man says.

Dad straightens up to his full six-foot-three height. 'You wanna say that to my face?' he calls to the prawners. His voice is throaty and low, daring them to say yes.

'Trev …' Granddad begins. 'They're pissed as farts …' He reaches for Dad's arm, but Dad shakes him off.

'Wait here,' he says to us. The light from his headlamp bobs up and down as he makes his way towards the two men and gets right up in their faces. It's too dark to see what he's doing or hear what he's saying, but there's no mistaking the tone: *don't mess with me*.

A mumbled response.

Dad punches the man in the face. There's no mistaking what I heard.

Jim's gasp is piercing. My hands clap over my ears. His arms go around me and he says *don't look* and Granddad says *wait here* and footsteps thump and there's another thump and more yelling and swearing worse than I've ever heard and I think Dad said some of those words and he goes *there's more where that came from, mate*. I'm scared stiff and freezing cold and I'm going to be sick, and I want them to stop it.

But no one listens to me.

Stop it!

'Trevor. Trev! That's enough!' Granddad yells. 'There are kids here, son. They don't need to be seeing this.'

And then Granddad's back, pulling us up, pushing us towards Dad. 'Let's get the kids home. Now.'

Dad doesn't say a word. He strides ahead, like he can't bear to be near us. I run to him, try to hold his hand, the same one he punched the men with. It doesn't feel different. How can a hand feel the same when it's used for love and pain? Dad yanks his hand away and walks faster. I start to cry again, and Granddad says *there, there* and holds my hand the rest of the way.

Dad disappears out to the backyard. He sits in the dark with Granddad and Mum for a long time. They're still outside when I get out of the bath; still outside when Grandma tucks me into bed. The sleep-out windows are open; low voices nudge me towards sleep. I wake from an unsettling dream about a girl with no voice when the door opens. Dad sits heavily on the edge of my bed.

'I'm sorry, Janey,' he says. His hand feels for mine, squeezes tight. 'So sorry.'

I'm not a hundred per cent sure, but I think he's crying.

CHAPTER TWENTY-TWO

1979

We leave Lake Cathie after Sunday lunch and arrive home early evening. We're all hot, sweaty, and sick to death of each other; the car stinks of dog. Turdle makes a run for it as soon as Dad opens the boot. We kids want to do the same, but Dad puts his foot down: no one's going anywhere or coming over. Turdle needs a walk, the garden needs watering, our bags need unpacking. Me and Jim aren't impressed, but Sal has a meltdown.

'Why? I've already told Robbie he could come over,' Sal says, as we follow Dad into the house with our bags.

'Well, now you can tell him not to.'

'But I haven't seen him all week!'

'Four days. One more night won't kill you. And no, you're not going to his. You'll see him at the New Year's party tomorrow.' Dad fills a glass with water from the kitchen tap and gulps it down. There's a purple bruise under his left eye. At breakfast this morning, no one said a word about it. It's like last night didn't happen; if it wasn't for the bruise, I might have imagined the whole thing. 'I don't want anyone over tonight, no comings and goings. It's been a long day.'

'This su—' Sal makes a strangled noise. 'Why does it always have to be what *you* want?' She swings around. 'Mum, can you talk to him?'

'You heard your father. Not tonight, Sal.'

That strangled noise again. 'You're ruining my life!' Sal barrels past me so fast she knocks me into the wall with her overnight bag.

'Watch where you're going! That hurt!'

Our bedroom door slams. Dad's face is red, he's puffed up like a balloon. He takes a step towards the hall.

'Let her go, Trev,' Mum says quietly. 'We'll deal with it when she's calmed down.' Her hand reaches for his, squeezes.

The balloon deflates. After a moment, Dad strides out the back door, the screen door banging behind him.

Mum turns to me. 'Jane, why don't you take Turdle for a walk.' It's not a question. Mum ducks into the laundry and comes back with the lead.

'I don't want to be anywhere near Sal right now,' I tell Turdle as he yanks me down the driveway. Dogs are better than people when it comes to listening. They don't try to tell you what's what or put their own two cents in. 'Or Dad. You'd think he'd be happy to have a break from us for a bit.'

As we reach Acacia's driveway, I dither by the kerb, checking my thongs for non-existent pieces of gravel. Maybe Acacia will see me. But the Valiant isn't there. A horrifying thought leapfrogs into my mind. What if Rose and Acacia moved out while we were gone? The thought makes me want to run to the front window, try to peek inside and look for a clue, anything to tell me they haven't moved. But Turdle's straining at the lead, so I force my feet onward, force myself around the duck pond three times. Tell myself to breathe.

When Rose's Valiant rumbles past me on the way home, I want to kick myself for leaping to the worst possibility. Acacia is waving from the back seat. I start to run; Turdle gallops beside me, tongue hanging out. My friend is already inside by the time we reach the end of the driveway; I climb onto the side fence and call her name, over and over, louder and louder – 'Acacia ... Acacia' – and right when I'm about to give up, her back door opens and there she is.

'Jane! You're back!' She drags a milk crate to her side of the fence and stands on it. Our faces are almost touching. 'I missed you!'

No one – apart from Mum and Dad – has ever said that to me before. I feel like crying and laughing at the same time. 'I missed you too. I've got so much to tell you.'

'Me too! Look,' she points at a familiar-looking magpie perched on her clothesline. 'He's my friend now. I've been feeding him devon.' The magpie makes a begging noise, and she flaps her hand at him, giggling. 'Don't be greedy, George.' She keeps talking to the bird in a sing-song voice. *Aren't you a good bird? Yes, you are.*

'You're more interested in that bird than me,' I grumble.

She swings back to me. 'Are you jealous of *George?*' Her tone makes me feel like a wriggling worm. Bird food.

'Yeah, right. As if I'd be jealous of a *bird.*'

'Are too. You hear that, G—' Her lips thin into a red line as a familiar, throaty growl gets louder and louder, closer and closer. Daryl parks behind the Valiant, takes off his helmet, runs his fingers through his hair.

Noticing us, he waves. 'Hey, girls.'

I wave back but Acacia doesn't. Her lips stay in that tight line as he struts to the back door, calling, 'Rose? What's for dinner?'

I clear my throat. 'Did you get my postc—'

'A-cay-sha ...'

'Shit,' Acacia mutters. It's the first time I've heard her swear. She doesn't move.

Behind me, I hear the back door open. 'Oi, you!' my brother yells. 'Dinner.'

The door shuts. I roll my eyes at Acacia. 'Me too.'

'A-cay-sha!'

She swears again, louder this time. 'I'm coming!' Jumping off the milk crate, she runs off.

'See you tomorrow?' I call out. The only answer is the thud of the back door and up-and-down voices from the inside of her house. I hope she's not in trouble. When I look at the clothesline, her new best friend is gone.

'Oi!' Jim yells.

'Shit,' I mutter under my breath. It feels good.

Inside, the oily smell of fish and chips fills the kitchen. Two paper-wrapped parcels rest on the kitchen bench, a bottle of ginger beer beside them.

'Nice of you to join us. Wash your hands,' Mum says shortly, unwrapping a parcel and scooping hot chips and fish cocktails onto plates. 'We're having a picnic in front of the telly tonight.'

I sneak a steaming chip, flapping my hand in front of my mouth. 'Where's Sal?'

'She's not hungry,' Mum says.

My eyes flick to Dad. 'More for me,' he says after a beat, popping a crunchy chip in his mouth.

In the living room, we wrap strips of paper around the fish, dip chips into tomato sauce and slurp ice-cold ginger beer, eyes glued to the box the whole time. Dad does his Donald Duck voice during *The Wonderful World of Disney*, and we all crack up, even Sal, who crept in with a plate of cold chips when *Countdown* started. I lean back against Dad's legs. When I was little, I thought ours was the happiest, most perfect family in the world. Now that I'm nearly eleven, I see things differently; no family is perfect or happy all the time, not even ours. But in this moment, we're perfectly happy together.

It's short-lived. That night, I catch Sal sneaking out of the house to meet Robbie.

'Don't dob,' she says, giving me a pleading look. 'Please, Jane. I miss him so much.'

Mary Evan's voice drifts into my head for the first time in ages.

Dobbers wear nappies.

'I promise,' I hear myself say.

The bitter-sweet scent of Charlie lingers when she's gone.

CHAPTER TWENTY-THREE

1979

Sal's sleeping like a log the next morning. She doesn't move when Mum knocks on the door at 7 a.m. – *breakfast is ready* – and rolls over to face the wall with a grunt when I give her a gentle shake. The clothes she was wearing last night are scrunched up in a ball under her bed; her cork wedges are on top of her sheet. I put them in the wardrobe before slipping out to the kitchen.

Mum hands me a plate of crispy bacon, fried eggs and toast. There's a glass of orange juice already poured in the cup with my name on it.

'Eat up,' she says, winking. 'It's the last breakfast you're getting all year.'

I groan. That joke stopped being funny when I was seven.

'Where's your sister?' Dad says, looking up from the sports pages.

'Asleep.' It was 2 a.m. when Sal crept back into our room. It's hard to sleep when you're weighed down with secrets and worries. I listened to her undress and settle onto her bed. She was snoring within minutes.

'Tell her breakfast is ready.'

'Leave her be, Trev,' Mum says. 'She's on holidays.'

'You don't see me sleeping the best part of the day away,' he grumbles. 'And won't you need help with the cooking for the party tonight?'

'You could help,' she says, kissing him on the head, handing him a mug of coffee.

Dad coughs and turns the page, blowing on the hot drink. 'I'll give her another hour, that's it.'

But Sal stumbles into the kitchen a few minutes later, holding her head. 'Why do you have to crash and bang everything?' she says to Mum, her voice sleep-fuzzy. To the rest of us, she adds, 'And must you bellow across the table? Haven't you ever heard of inside voices?'

My parents exchange looks. 'Someone got out of bed on the wrong side,' Dad says. 'You'll want to sweeten up if you want Robbie to come around later.'

'Why? He takes me as I am. Unlike *some* people. Besides, there's no rush. I'll see him tonight, like you said.' Avoiding my raised eyebrows, she slides a rasher of bacon onto her fork. 'Want this bacon, Jim?'

Dad's eyebrows twitch. 'You've changed your tune.'

'More coffee, Trev?'

Dad nods. Mum fills his cup, stirs in two heaped sugars. Probably wants to sweeten *him* up. We eat in heavy silence until Daryl starts revving his Harley right outside the window.

'Bloody long-haired tossers and their big bikes compensating for something,' Dad mutters. Now his pointer finger is twitching.

'Trev. Little ears.' Mum nods at me. Jim and Sal snigger.

'What's so funny?' I ask.

'Nothing,' Mum says, giving Jim and Sal the stink-eye.

'It means Daryl's got a little w—' Jim begins, his voice rising over the revving noise.

'James Albert Kelly! What did I say?' Mum slams a plate on the bench, making us jump. Dad goes to peer out the window; I feel him bristling from the table. The revving gets louder.

'Jeez Louise, give it a rest!' Dad yells, rapping on the glass.

'Little what? Why can't someone tell me?' I insist. 'I'm not a little kid anymore. You can tell me stuff.' I look meaningfully at Sal. Guilt reddens her cheeks; she mouths *thank you*. I scowl, torn between feeling smug about knowing something my parents don't and irritated about the secrets they keep.

'Enough, Jane,' Dad growls. 'Some things you don't need to know. Leave it at that.' He lets out a *hmph* when Daryl guns his bike down the road, then says to Mum, 'If he does this every morning, I'll bloody throttle him.'

'Trev!'

'I bloody will.'

By the time breakfast is over, two things have occurred to me. One, Dad doesn't like Daryl because Daryl has a shiny motorbike and sunglasses, while he has a boring station wagon. Two, he's jealous because he's old and Daryl's not. And Daryl's a spunk and Dad is … just *Dad*.

After breakfast, Dad mows the lawn and trims the edges, Jim washes Turdle, Sal takes charge of the dirty washing, and Mum makes me go grocery shopping with her. When we get back, us girls get to work making salads for tonight's street party. The kitchen sings with the sounds of chopping, slicing and dicing for three-bean, curried rice and Waldorf salads. I don't like any of them, but no one will make me eat my veggies tonight.

Outside, Dad and Jim wash the car while Turdle rolls in the wet grass. The earlier tension is gradually replaced with a sense of excitement as our family prepares for the second biggest night of the year after Christmas. None of us kids complain about doing chores, even though we don't finish until lunchtime. The party, down at the Murphy's house, will make up for it. Tonight, we can guzzle soft drinks until our stomachs fizz – even Coke – and no one will say *that's enough*. We can eat what we like, when we like. Best of all, we can stay up 'til after midnight.

'Off you go,' Mum finally says. Sal and Jim are out the door in a flash, but Mum stops me before I get too far. 'Check if Acacia's mum knows about the party.'

'I will.' I pause, fiddling with the fly streamers. Someone would have mentioned it, I'm sure. The whole street is invited. 'Mum, I can't wait. It's going to be the best night ever!'

I skip the sixty-four steps to Acacia's front door, noticing that Daryl's motorbike is back in the driveway. As I lift my hand to knock, the door swings open. Rose stands there, blurred by the dusty screen separating us. Behind her, the house looks like a dark cave. I blink at her just-woke-up appearance – the tangled hair, the sleepy face. She's wearing a tight singlet and a pair of black undies. Mum would never answer the door like that – she never walks around the house in her undies. And she certainly doesn't wear black ones. Hers are the colour of milky tea.

'Mu-um—' Acacia pushes in front of her mother, covering her mum's bare legs.

Ignoring her, Rose squints at me. 'Jane, isn't it? You're up nice and early, love,' she says, voice sleep-thick. She yawns. Through the screen, her breath smells like sour fruit.

'Um … Hi, Mrs … Rose. I came to see if Acacia could play. I didn't mean to um … to wake you.'

'Nah,' she said, rubbing her eyes. 'Was already awake, sort of. Acacia can come over soon, she's got some things to do first, haven't you, love?'

'I've already done them.' Acacia squeezes out the door, nudges me towards the steps. 'Let's go.'

As Rose edges the door shut, I remember what Mum said. 'Mum says are you coming to the street party tonight?'

Rose coughs. 'Party? Never heard nothing about a party.'

'For New Year's Eve,' I explain. 'It happens every year. The whole street is invited to the Murphy's house at Number 26,' I point down the road, 'because they've got a pool, see, and there's a barbecue and we all bring salads and desserts to share ...'

'We got no invite.' Rose scratches her head.

'I don't think there is an invitation, a proper one, or anything. Everyone just knows about it, that's all. Will you come?' Acacia shifts next to me, her restlessness leaking into me.

'Rose? Where are ya, babe? Get your skinny arse in here.'

'Hold your horses, Daz!' She yawns, then looks down. 'I'll think about it. Jeez. Look at me standing here in my knickers. Sorry 'bout that, love. Sight for sore eyes, eh?' Acacia groans, pulls on my arm, but Rose is still talking. 'Hey, that was real kind of your mum to leave us those Christmas goodies. Say thanks for me.' She pauses. 'Nah, don't worry, I'll say thanks when I see her.'

'Rose? What's keeping ya?'

She shakes her head. 'Men. Always wanting something from us women, aren't they?' To Daryl, her voice shrill, 'Told ya, I'm coming.'

'So's bloody Christmas!'

'Oh, for Pete's sake,' she mutters, shooing us off like pesky flies.

The door closes.

Me and Acacia are free to spend the last afternoon of 1979 doing what we want. We eat orange-flavoured Sunny Boys and catch up on each other's news – I tell her about Lake Cathie, and she tells me all about George. We play frisbee with the boys until I accidentally throw the disc into the wattle tree. And when Mum's not looking, Jim nicks detergent from the kitchen and squirts it on the Slip 'n' Slide; all the neighbourhood kids come over to our house to slide until one-by-one our parents say it's time to get ready for the party.

Later, we follow a trail of music, laughter and barbecuing meat and onions down the road to the Murphy's house, where Jim and Sal are already waiting. I want Acacia to walk down with us, but Mum says no, *I think they've already left.* The first thing I do is search for my friend, pushing through the tangle of people in the backyard, peering into the pool where heads bob like apples, and back out the front where kids run and squeal. There's no sign of her.

'What if she doesn't come?'

'Don't worry, love, I'm sure she'll be here soon.' Mum squeezes her three salads onto the already loaded table, pats my head – 'Off you go' – then moves off to chat with our neighbours.

I'm piling a paper plate with food – cheese-and-pineapple sticks, tiny red and green pickled onions, cabanossi chunks, a near-burnt sausage, a hearty handful of plain chips – when I spot her. Not Acacia. Someone who makes my stomach clench so hard I think I'm going to vomit the chips I ate.

Mary Evans is standing near the pool, drying herself with a striped towel. As if she knows I'm staring, she lifts her head. Her eyes narrow. A cold shiver tickles my skin.

That's when I know she still hates my guts.

CHAPTER TWENTY-FOUR

HEAT

When someone asks me why I finally left him for good, I tell them the short version. It goes something like this: we met, fell head over heels and got married too fast, too young. Our wedding song was 'Always' by Bon Jovi ... ironic, I know. In the beginning, life was good. Most of the time. Then he lost his job in the recession we had to have. His moods got darker. He grew more withdrawn. Blamed everyone but himself. Including me. Especially me.

He started drinking and shouting and blaming and ... I never knew what each day would bring. Put up with it for years. Why? I loved him. Made vows, you know? You don't just walk away from vows. You see things through. Work things out. That's what I told myself every single day because, ever since I was a kid, I vowed never to be a divorce statistic. Even when I knew things were spinning out of control, I couldn't summon the guts to say to him, this relationship is over. Couldn't bring myself to leave him for good, despite increasingly imagining life without him. Like I said, I loved him. But after the police took him away, I made my move.

That's the version I told Pat. What I didn't tell her, or anyone else who asked, was that before I left for good, I was dying from the inside out. A flower wilting in the heat. I wanted an end to everything. When you're in a state of permanent agitation, it's hard to see things clearly, so you go with whatever is easiest.

The day before I left, I was driving across the freeway bridge on my way to work and a swan dropped dead onto my windscreen. Literally dropped from the sky and cracked the glass. I'm not kidding. I pulled onto the shoulder, got out and lifted the body off my car. It was heavy, I wasn't expecting that, and my mind was going, *oh my god a swan fell on my car and it's dead I'm going to need a new windscreen what the eff do I do with this swan?* No one else pulled over. Places to go, people to see. And so, I left the swan in the dry grass beside the road and said a little prayer over it. It seemed the right thing to do. And then I got in my car and went to work and made up some reason for being late because my boss wasn't going to believe a swan did a death dive on my car. The rest of the day I was trying to think of a good reason I had a cracked windscreen, knowing no reason would be good enough, the truth would be worse, and somehow, I'd pay for it.

On the way home, I crossed the bridge again and a thought dropped into my head: drive off the bridge. Death dive into the river like the swan into my car.

I could end it all.

Right now.

I was driving onto the bridge, working out the moves. Slam on the accelerator. Jerk the wheel to the left. Bang! And then I'd be flying, flying, falling, falling.

I wouldn't be living my horrible, shitty life anymore.

I wouldn't *be*.

I would be free.

And my foot was hovering, my hands were shaking, and my heart was thumping, and I felt my foot press down. My head was going: *I'm tired, I'm done, can't do this anymore, will it hurt?* When

135

your foot is one push away from death, questions are like arrows launched in a battle you barely know you're fighting. Will I feel myself die? Will it happen instantaneously like the swan, or will I scream silently while I drown?

What if it doesn't work?

I didn't do it. Obviously. Some tail-gating jerk beeped his horn, and I gave him the finger.

But I wouldn't have gone through with it anyway.

I wouldn't.

After you get that close to ending it, the first thing you feel is shame. It's like standing under a shower and too-hot water washes over you and it burns, and you scream and shout and cry. That day, when a hot flash of shame washed over me, I pulled over and screamed and pounded the steering wheel with my hands until there was nothing left. Then I went home.

I don't tell anyone this part of the story because I'm embarrassed. I'm not the kind of person who runs away from things. I stick it out. Those thoughts on the bridge, they were not like me at all. But that is what I was reduced to, and that is why I finally left.

No one knows about this.

No one knows that's the day I decided to live.

CHAPTER TWENTY-FIVE

1979

I'm playing with Margie Murphy's tabby cat and avoiding Mary Evans, when Acacia walks through the gate. Rose and Daryl aren't far behind; Rose is carrying a plate of devon sandwiches and Daryl has a case of beer cradled in his arms. They seem nervous, like they don't know where to go or who to talk to, so I lead them through the side gate to the backyard. Mrs Murphy rushes over to welcome them, and within minutes Rose and Daryl are swallowed up in a sea of laughing adults.

I turn to Acacia. Her fine hair is brushed straight; it glows in the golden evening light. She's wearing a white dress like one I had before I grew out of it. Is it mine? She looks like an angel without wings. 'I thought you weren't coming.'

'Yeah, thought we'd ne—' Her words trail off.

'Hey.' Mary Evans butts me out of the way like I don't exist. My heart lurches. This is it. The moment Mary Evans will steal my best friend from under my nose. The bad thing I knew was coming. 'So, you're the new girl Shane Watters was telling me about. Alicia, right? I'm Mary. Mary Evans.'

Acacia doesn't know about the bullying. It's one secret I haven't told her, for two reasons – I didn't want her to think I was weak, and I didn't want to mention *that girl's* name. For all Acacia knows, Mary Evans is a perfectly nice person. A potential friend.

'It's Acacia.' My friend shifts so she's standing next to me. 'Like the wattle.'

'Yeah, right.' Mary Evans looks directly at her. 'Anyway, you wanna hang out with Shane and me and the older kids,' she waves her hand towards the Murphy's sunroom where lights are flashing and disco music is playing, 'instead of out here? Margie's gonna teach us the Nutbush City Limits dance.'

My stomach clenches again. It's clear I'm not invited, but what's not clear is what I'll do if Acacia follows Mary Evans. She loves dancing. I'm not going to stop her if that's what she wants.

'No, thanks. Jane and I have stuff to do.'

'Oh yeah? Like what?' Her nose wrinkles at my name, like I'm an icky slug. 'Writing stupid stories and reading boring books? No, I know, counting down the seconds until the New Year.' She fake laughs. 'Just jokes.'

Mary Evans wouldn't know a joke if it bit her on the bum.

'Something like that,' I say.

She rolls her eyes at Acacia and mouths *what a drag*. 'Well, if you change your mind and want to hang out with the cool people …'

'Already am,' Acacia says, earning her a death stare that nearly makes me laugh. A few weeks ago, a look like that would have buried me.

'See ya.' Using a fake nice voice is strangely liberating. Why haven't I done it before?

I know why.

Before Acacia I didn't have a voice.

Mary Evans flounces towards Shane Watters and two other girls I recognise from Year 6 and says something, gesturing wildly; they turn to look at us, their dislike reaching towards us like tentacles. I don't care. Neither does Acacia, it seems. She grabs two soft drink cans from an esky. 'Let's go somewhere it smells sweeter,' she says loudly.

We collapse onto the grass out the front, laughing until our bellies hurt. But when the laughter fades, the ginormous realisation of what we've done sinks in.

'She'll hate you now,' I say, popping open my can.

Acacia has a long swig from hers, then burps. 'I don't care. I don't like her, either.'

'Why?' I'm glad, but curious. 'I mean, you don't know her.'

'I don't need to. She's a bully.'

My mouth drops open. How does Acacia know this about someone she's just met? The question is on the tip of my tongue, but I don't have to ask. Acacia lies back on the grass and continues, 'I know her type. See them coming a mile off. I reckon I can read people.'

Read people? How? And what type? I want Acacia to tell me what to look for, how to protect myself from being bullied by people like Mary Evans ever again. It's one thing standing up to a bully when you've got a friend by your side, another when you're on your own. Strength comes in numbers, but what if you don't have the numbers?

Instead, on the last night of the year, while the younger kids run wild around us and our parents are too busy socialising to care, I spill my guts about Mary Evans. The words pour out of me like hot, sour vomit. Acacia listens but doesn't seem surprised. I am. Not by what happened to me, but by how telling what happened makes me feel. I'm free to be me, lighter inside; Mary Evans isn't squashing me anymore.

'I didn't want you to think I was weak,' I confess. 'People keep telling me to stand up to her, to tell her to stop.' I pause, watching Sal and Robbie leave the party, walking hand-in-hand down the street towards the park. 'Or they ask what I did to encourage her.'

'That's stupid. She's the bully. She should stop. That's what I reckon,' Acacia says.

Me too.

'You could have gone to learn that dance though,' I say after a while. 'I wouldn't blame you.'

'What, without you? Why would I do that?' She shakes her head. 'Besides, I already know it. Mum taught me. Here, I'll show you.'

Humming the music, she leads me through the line dance's side steps and kicks. Before long others join in, even Jim and Smiddy. The sun sets and distant magpies warble as we sing and dance and kick and step. The only person who isn't smiling is Mary Evans. She watches from the verandah, arms crossed, her mouth a hard line.

In the distance, a kookaburra laughs.

Later, we sit in the shadows, watching the action out the back. Two men hoist a squealing woman into the pool. She's fully dressed, and the men roar with laughter when she comes up dripping, gasping. Near the patio, women huddle in a circle, screeching, cackling with laughter. Piled-high plates of dessert wobble in their hands, but none of them are eating. Most have chucked off their high heels. Voices grow blurred and loud. Dance moves look wonky, like they've forgotten the steps.

Mum is off to one side with Mrs Evans, who looks upset. Dad is by the barbecue with men who clutch beer cans, hairy chests and bellies sticking out from unbuttoned shirts. Some have towels wrapped around their waists. Others wear tiny, tight Speedos that look like undies. Jim and his mates sneak around, collecting cigarette butts and draining the dregs from beer cans and plastic cups. When my brother sees me watching, he presses his fingers to his lips: *Shhh!* My sister and her boyfriend are nowhere to be seen.

I thought Rose didn't know anyone on our street, but she must do the way she smiles and dances and tosses her flat-as-an-ironing board hair. Her voice carries over quiet parts of the music; she calls the men *darling* and *honey*, touches their arms. The men seem to like it, but the women give her dirty looks.

I watch Acacia watch her mother. Her face is hard to read. I still want to know how she reads people.

Daryl is dancing, flexing his muscles under his tight white T-shirt, pretending he's Rod Stewart singing 'Do Ya Think I'm Sexy?' The women think Daryl's a total spunk, giggling and cooing and fluttering their lashes when he pays them attention. I reckon a few are jealous of Rose from the sideways looks and sneaky whispers. One even said in a loud voice *what does he see in her?* They don't think she's good enough, and they talk about her almost in front of her face, but I don't think Rose cares.

I can see why they like Daryl, though. His smile makes you feel like you're the only one that matters. When Acacia is in the loo, he walks past me to pull a beer from the melting ice in one of the eskies.

'G'day, cute stuff,' he says, winking. That smile.

My cheeks feel warm, like the time Smiddy smiled at me playing cricket. 'Hi, Daryl.'

But his eyes are on Rose, whose hand is on my dad's arm. She's laughing so hard her boobs look like they'll pop from the tight animal-print dress she's wearing. After a long swig from his can, he swaggers over, hips swinging like the Fonz. Stands right behind her. Pulls her close. He's smiling, but his eyes are on my dad. *She's mine. Hands off.* Even I get the message.

A new song starts: Blondie singing 'Heart of Glass'. Now Rose is dancing, eyes closed, hips swaying, leaning into Daryl. His hands move up and over her hips, his mouth is whispering a trail up her neck. Her blood-red lips mouth the lyrics. It's like they're on stage, performing for applause, the party entertainment. But I'm the only one watching. I can't tear my eyes away.

I want to feel like Rose one day.

When Acacia comes back, I ask *do you want to dance?* A stiff shake of the head. She's in a sulk. I wonder why at first, and I want to ask her, but I know she won't tell. So, I watch her watching them dance, Daryl's hand resting on Rose's bum in front of everyone, and I think I know. Just imagining Mum and Dad dancing the same way makes me shudder from top to toe.

'Let's go find the others,' she says, walking away without waiting for me to follow.

I follow but pause after a few steps for one last look. Rose and Daryl have stopped dancing and are talking to Mr Murphy. Daryl has one hand on his hip, the other clutching Rose's wrist, pulling her close.

As if he feels me watching, his eyes meet mine. Again, he smiles.

CHAPTER TWENTY-SIX

1979

old on. Hold on! I repeat the phrase in my head like it's the ten times table as I explode into Margie Murphy's house, busting for a wee, hands pressed between my legs. I don't know why I waited until the last possible moment to go – maybe it's a fear of missing out. This time, I've pushed it too far, and I nearly cry with relief when I find the toilet unoccupied. A girl in my class wet her pants in Year 3 and still gets teased about it. If it happened to me, I'd refuse to go to school ever again.

On my way outside, a strange shuffling and grunting noise stops me near the laundry. Poking my head around the doorway, I reel back in shock. Daryl is pressing Rose against the sink. His hand is cupping her neck, thumb pressing against her throat. My body prickles all over; I'm hot and cold all at once. What are they doing?

'Don't make me do this. You always make me do this,' he hiss-whispers against her ear, sending a shudder all the way to my toes.

I should leave, pretend I didn't see a thing. I should join Acacia outside, before Mary Evans pounces on her again. It's none of my business what Daryl and Rose are doing. But I'm frozen to the spot. What does he mean? *Don't make me do this.* What did Rose do?

'I saw you flirting. You got something going on with that old guy next door?'

Rose gasps.

Or maybe I do.

Daryl must have heard something – the gasp or maybe my heart thumping, I don't know. He turns towards the door, gaping at me like a kangaroo caught in headlights. And then his mouth twists into a smirk. The kind Mum always tells Jim to wipe off his face. His hand drops away from Rose's throat, down to her wrist; it happens so fast that I think I imagined his grip on her throat until Rose reaches up and rubs the spot. Her face looks like the colour has been squeezed from it. She refuses to look at me, stares at the wall before her gaze flicks down to her dress, which has ridden up her thighs. She tugs it down, as if making it longer will hide her. Daryl's eyes burn into my brain like he's a mind controller, and I don't like the feel of that at all … but I can't move.

'Well, hey there,' he drawls. 'Caught us sneaking an early New Year's kiss, didn't ya. Sorry about that.' That's what he says out loud. He's smiling, but it no longer feels good. He's daring me: *Tell me you saw otherwise.* I can see it in his eyes, that *dare you* look.

My heart thumps like a drum, but I say nothing.

He says, 'Come on, Rose. Let's get you outside.' He pulls her to the doorway, and she trips on the tiles.

Legs trembling, I shrink against the wall as Daryl pushes Rose around me. If there was ever a time to have the power of invisibility, it would be now.

Daryl stops. Bends so he's in my face. And then he winks, like he did at the esky. 'Don't tell anyone you sprung us kissing, short stuff. Rose would be embarrassed.' Spittle lands on my cheek.

Even when Daryl is out of sight, I still can't make my feet move. That wasn't a kiss. It *wasn't*. It looked nothing like any kiss

I'd ever seen on telly. Kisses are supposed to be soft and loving. Or gross, like the eat-her-face ones that I can't watch.

That's not what I saw.

At least, I don't think so. How would I know about kissing? I'm a kid. *Practically a baby*, Sal would laugh. *Everyone knows what's on telly is made up*. Maybe I got it wrong. Dad always calls me a dreamer and Mr Thiele at school says I have the wildest imagination of anyone in Year 5.

You're doing it again. Letting your imagination get away with you.

My head is a jumble. It can't be real. I must have got it wrong.

Daryl's nice. Handsome. He wouldn't hurt Rose.

Would he?

I didn't think Dad would hurt someone with his own hands, but he did. People surprise you, even when you think you know them.

'Jane? What are you doing here?' Acacia says, coming to stand beside me. 'I've been looking for you everywhere. It's nearly time for the countdown!'

Her voice thaws my feet and I follow her outside. We stand arm-in-arm under coloured party lights with our neighbours and chant *10, 9, 8 ... 3, 2, 1,* Happy New Year! My eyes meet Daryl's across the patio. He gives me another slow wink before pulling Rose to him, pressing his lips, slowly, deliberately, to her neck. *Don't tell.* And I know, without a doubt, I did not imagine what I saw in Margie Murphy's laundry.

We leave the party straight after the singing of 'Auld Lang Syne' because Jim spewed all over Mrs Murphy's good shoes and started cackling like a hyena.

'But Mum—' I can't leave Acacia after what I saw.

Mum grabs my hand. *Now!* I drag my feet down the road, battling the urge to yawn. Mum's hissing something at Jim while he sways left-right, trying to keep up with her businesslike stride.

'Get to bed,' she orders Jim when the front door is unlocked. 'Your dad and I will talk to you in morning.'

He's in Big Trouble. What have I missed?

Jim clutches his stomach and moans. Then he bolts to the toilet. Seconds later, there's a retching-heaving sound, followed by piteous moans. He sounds like a sick kitten. Probably ate too much party food.

'What happened?' I ask. 'Why is Jim spew—'

'That means you too.'

'What? What did I do?'

'Bed!'

'That's so unfair!'

Outraged, I throw myself on my bed, fully dressed. I'm still stewing when Sal creeps in, reeking of Robbie's aftershave. While she's getting changed, she tells me Jim and Shane got sprung nicking beers from the eskies and that's why he's in Big Trouble.

'He got totally smashed,' she finishes.

'Smashed?'

'Drunk.' Sal reaches over me and opens the window.

'*Drunk?*'

'Yep.'

'But he's thirteen!'

'You *can* get drunk when you're thirteen.'

I think this over. Then, 'Sal, have you been drunk?'

She's quiet. 'It's been a big night. Let's get some sleep.' She rolls over and that's that.

I lie awake long after Sal's breathing slows. Long after the hum of voices from Mum and Dad's room switch to Dad's wall-rumbling snoring. Long after the music down the road fades. The lightness I felt earlier is gone; my mind is weighed down with worry, fear, secrets. I desperately want to sleep. I count a hundred sheep. Two hundred. A thousand.

Every time I shut my eyes, Daryl squeezes Rose's throat.

CHAPTER TWENTY-SEVEN

FIRE

H is hands are on me, grasping, squeezing. His breath, hot and rancid against my ear. Foul words forced from gritted teeth like he's in pain. He's squeezing me from my body, out through my mouth. I close my mouth, to keep me in, but I can't breathe. My eyes close, part terrified, part resigned: I'm going to die. This is the day what's left of me will disappear for good. A loosening, a relaxing of his grip. I appeal to him: stop! It doesn't work. He's stronger and angrier and more scared than me and I think he doesn't know what he's doing or saying any more. My back rubs against the bricks. Hail pelts on the carport roof. Water drips on my face. The darkness rises. I wait for nothingness, but it doesn't come. Instead, a howl, a release. He slumps against the wall. I run away from one storm, into another.

This is the flashback, the waking nightmare that still makes my heart race, my skin sweat, my breath come in heavy pants. It turns up like a surprise visitor, unwelcome and rude, triggered by something as simple as a smell or a sound. The Revlon Fire & Ice perfume I wore for him. Chris Isaak singing 'Baby Did a Bad, Bad

Thing'. A yellow ute with a Triple M sticker peeling off the back window.

At first, when these jumbled memories came, I wanted to run, run, run like hell was snapping at my heels. Away from my memories, my problems, myself. But running away solves nothing; your problems catch up sooner or later. It was Pat who gave me the idea of turning running into some sort of physical therapy; you wouldn't have thought it to look at her, but she ran the City to Surf every year until her knees gave out.

I think I laughed in her face when she suggested it. Me? Take up running? She had no clue how much I'd always despised and avoided strenuous exercise. At high school, I used every excuse to get out of PE: periods, headaches, stomach aches, heartaches. In my twenties, anxiety stripped the weight from me, so I didn't bother with exercise, ate what I wanted. Back then, I didn't know – didn't care – that exercise was as much for the mind as the body.

One day, after a flashback caught me off-guard, I went for a walk in the park with a volunteer and had a crazy urge to break into a jog. The next day, I pulled on some loose track pants and a looser T-shirt from the Lifeline op shop and went for a jog around the oval across the road, looking over my shoulder every few seconds. My lungs and legs were burning in less than a minute; I had to walk out a stitch that stabbed at my ribs, panting and half-sobbing, before I started jogging again. I hated every stinking second of that five-minute run. Cried like a baby in my room afterwards. But the next day I went back to the oval. And the next day, and the next, until I couldn't imagine a day without a run.

The more I ran, the less anxious I felt. It was as if I left all the flashbacks, what-ifs and what-nexts behind at the refuge, and later, in my new home. They couldn't keep up with me, and even if they could, there was no room for them in my head. Instead of focusing on what he was doing or what I *should* be doing, instead of trying to control everything I couldn't, my brain focused on other things. The little things, like the slap-slap rhythm of my feet and the burn in my legs. The beat of my heart. The dip in the pavement. Birds singing. Barking dogs. Kids playing. And now when I go running, I don't see danger everywhere I go, don't look over my shoulder every few steps.

Unless it's dark.

I never did thank Pat for putting the idea in my head. But this is what I learnt from giving it a go. I don't need to run away from my problems; I need to run so I can deal with them. And when I run, I'm pushing back on everything that scares and worries the hell out of me, even the flashbacks that pop up out of the blue.

I'm running back to myself.

CHAPTER TWENTY-EIGHT

1980

O n the first day of 1980, I don't wake until nearly lunchtime. No one cares. It's as if no one noticed I was missing, as if they'd gone about their business without giving me a second thought. Sal's already out with Robbie. Mum and Dad are like bears with sore heads. When I stumble into the kitchen and pour myself a bowl of cornflakes, Dad's giving Jim the *I'm disappointed in you* lecture. Then Mum says the same thing all over again, but with more words, like *embarrassed* and *mortified*. Jim is grounded until further notice, and, after they've left the room, he looks so miserable I can't help feeling sorry for him.

I'm rinsing my bowl, minding my business, when he elbows me out of the way, knocking me against the bench.

'Watch it! That hurt!' I elbow him back.

'You're in my way!' Jim turns on me, eyes fury-black, like it's my fault I was at the sink first. Fine spittle lands on my cheek, reminding me of Daryl, making me flinch, step back. I wipe my cheek as my brother slams out of the room. Down the hall, his bedroom door thuds shut.

I'm not putting up with this.

'Mu-um!' I find her out the back, hanging out our beach

towels, still wet from the night before. Turdle rushes over when he sees me, but I push him away – *don't Turdle* – before launching into my story.

'Sort yourselves out,' she says shortly. 'You kids need to learn to fight your own battles.'

'But—'

'No buts.'

'Fine. I'm going to see if Acacia can come over.' I hope Daryl's not there.

'After lunch.'

'But I just had breakfast!'

'And is it my fault you got up so late?' She picks up the washing basket. 'I said after lunch, and that's that.'

'And when's lunch?'

'Don't give your mum lip,' Dad says, coming out of his shed. 'Or you'll be grounded next.'

'What? This is the worst first day of the year ever,' I burst out. 'You're all mean!'

'Go to your room.' I look to Mum, but she keeps pegging towels.

In my room, I stare at the circling ceiling fan until my eyes blur. I try reading – *Five Run Away Together* seems fitting – but the words blur like the fan going round-round-round. At Sal's dressing table, I sift through the make-up in her toiletries bag, smell her perfume, try on her lip gloss. None of it makes me feel better.

None of it makes me forget what I saw last night.

Sal's *Dolly* magazine collection catches my eye. Choosing one, I turn the pages roughly. Why does she read boring articles about clothes and boys and make-up? How are they supposed to solve everyday problems? 'Be Assertive – Make The First Move With Guys', 'Fun Things To Do With Your Guy'. Who cares? I'd rather read some- thing with useful articles like 'How To Deal With Idiot Brothers' or 'What To Do When Your Parents Are Mean'. As

I toss the magazine aside, a dog-eared booklet falls to the floor. I snatch it up. Drop it like a hot potato when I read the title: 'Dating, Relating and Sex'.

Why is Sal reading stuff about s-e-x? Does Mum know?

Probably not. There's a lot Mum doesn't know about Sal, I think, remembering the way my sister snuck out the night before last. It seems so long ago. So … last year.

Like what happened last night.

My thoughts tumble like autumn leaves kicked up by a cheeky wind as my mind drifts again to the memory. I've been shoving it away since I woke up, but it's persistent. Rose, pressed hard up against the sink. Daryl's hand around her neck, pressing, squeezing. My eyes are open, but I can see it clear as the day outside. My legs start to tremble; my hands rub at my throat. And then I hear Jim in the hallway, talking to Mum and Dad.

Anger prickles my skin. What's wrong with people? Why do they blame others? Take out their anger on others? Why did Daryl say, 'Don't make me do this' when Rose wasn't making him *do* anything? She was the one pushed against the sink. Why did Jim act like it was my fault when he smashed into me because *he* was in a foul mood? I didn't ask to get bumped into like a wall with no feelings.

I wish I was an only child.

If I had a boat like The Famous Five, I'd escape to an island with no one to bother me, no one to be mean to me or anyone. Except Acacia. She's invited, but only her, not even Sal. And after the two of us row out to an island and have a picnic with ginger beer and sandwiches in a sandy cove, I'll ask her straight out: *Have you seen Daryl be mean to Rose? Is that why you don't like him?* And then I'll tell her what I saw.

Maybe.

It occurs to me that Daryl is two people in one body: Nice Daryl and Mean Daryl. Until last night, he was Nice Daryl. The spunk who makes women melt into puddles with a single smile.

The deadset legend with a Harley. The boys on our street would trade everything they owned for a dink on the back. The only ones who don't give two hoots about Daryl's charming smile and motorbike are old men like Dad and Mr Jones.

And Acacia.

That's the other confusing thing about Daryl. He's nice to Acacia. Gives her treats: a white paper bag filled with two-cent sweets from the milk bar, a yellow hula hoop. But the hula hoop is still on the front lawn at hers, untouched. She gave the sweets to me, saying she wasn't hungry. Ungrateful, I thought then.

Acacia has never said outright that she can't stand Daryl. But it's in the way her eyes screw up when he rides into their driveway. The tone she uses when she says his name. The angry way she says he's just a *friend*. Now, more than ever, I want to know why. I want to know if she's seen Mean Daryl too.

Standing, stretching, I decide to ask her … if I'm ever let out of this stuffy room. Seconds later, I snort and slump onto the bed. What's the point? I know Acacia. She'll change the subject, or tell me I'm making too much of it, turning what I saw into something it wasn't. Or she'll snap *mind your beeswax!* then go quiet.

Maybe I am inventing problems that aren't there.

'Jane! Lunch is ready.'

The smell of reheated sausages reaches my nose, makes me nauseous. They remind me of the party last night. I don't move. I'm still mad at my entire family.

'Jane!'

Huffing, I head to the kitchen. Deep down, I'm grateful for the distraction. I don't want to think about Daryl and what I think he did anymore because it breaks my heart. And as Mum plonks a sausage on a piece of buttered white bread and passes it to me, I realise I don't want to talk about it yet. Not with anyone, even Acacia.

And I'm pretty sure now that I got it wrong.

My mind is still switching between Nice Daryl and Mean Daryl when Acacia knocks on our front door. I've got a thumping headache from thinking about it too much, but I don't tell Mum because she'll make me have another lie down. We run out to the trampoline, Turdle at our heels, and bounce up and down until we're all puffed out and lying flat on our backs looking at clouds. That's when I blurt out what I want to know.

'Do you like Daryl?' It's the easiest question to start with.

'Mmm,' she says, pointing. 'That one looks like a frog.'

'Why don't you like him?' I hold my breath.

'Never said I didn't. I said "Mmm".'

Sal hates it when I fuss with details. She calls it being pedantic. I call it being correct. But now Acacia is being pedantic, and I want to scream. It's another way to avoid answering a question she doesn't want to answer.

'It's obvious. You act differently when he's around. Admit it.' I want to know what she knows about Daryl. To know that I was right about last night, that I didn't make it up.

She refuses to look at me and the feeling of confusion returns. My head thumps harder. No, I *don't* want to know. I want her to tell me I'm wrong, that Daryl is *alright, really,* she simply doesn't want to share him with her mum. I want to like Daryl again because thinking of him as Mean Daryl hurts my head. My mind is as jumbled as the white elephant stalls at the school fete, and there's only one thing I'm certain of: Daryl will never charm me again.

'Some people you just don't like,' Acacia says quietly. 'Can't like everyone. He gives me the creeps, like that Mary Evans. That's all.'

'But has he done anyth—'

'I don't want to talk about *him* anymore!' She slides off the trampo- line, shoots me a dirty look. Starts walking. 'I'm going h—'

'Don't go! I'm sorry!'

Thirty painful seconds pass before she turns around. 'Don't worry about it.'

Later, me and Acacia picnic in the shade of the wattle, a picnic blanket protecting our bare legs from the dry, brittle grass. We eat leftover party food and make New Year's wishes on fairy clocks picked from her front lawn. George watches from above, diving down occasionally to snatch the scraps Acacia throws him. Beside us, Turdle snores deeply, tired from a game of fetch. I'm exhausted too – my head from thinking, my body from lack of sleep and too much sunshine.

'What did you wish for?'

Acacia blows the last remaining seed heads from her fairy clock. Her hand clenches around the dandelion stalk. The seeds dance on the warm summer breath before drifting away to fairyland. If they make it there, our wishes will come true.

'It's a secret,' she says.

'I'll tell you my wish if you tell me yours.' Mine is a no-brainer: best friends forever.

She furrows her brow. 'I told you, it's a secret.' The stalk falls to her lap, bruised and bent.

We fall silent. I pat Turdle, scratch the back of his neck; he puts his head in my lap, his wet nose on my knee. Acacia shreds grass between her fingers, flicking the ragged bits into the air like confetti. A bike whizzes past. In the distance, a lawnmower coughs to life.

'Sal says fairy clocks tell you how many children you'll have,' I say, hoping to bring her back from wherever she's gone. 'You blow the clock and the number of seeds left are how many kids you'll have.'

'Really? Cool.' She turns to me, smiles. Mum says smiles are only real if the person's eyes crinkle, but Acacia jumps up to pick more fairy clocks before I can be sure. 'You go first.'

'Let's go together.'

Dandelion seeds scatter, rising on the wind. I count the remaining seed heads: one-two-three.

'I'm going to have three kids.' A boy and a girl, a boy first to protect his little sister. Will my third baby be a boy or a girl? I glance at Acacia's dandelion head. It's empty.

'Let's do another wish,' she says, after a moment. She crawls over the grass towards another fairy clock, ignoring the yellow dandelion flowers we call wet-your-beds, and plucking a seed head between two thin fingers. When she crawls back, her knees have grass bits stuck to them, and little dents, like someone has pressed too hard with a pen.

She takes a deep breath. A puff of air.

Seeds scatter.

CHAPTER TWENTY-NINE

1980

The first week of January, me and Jim have vacation swimming lessons. Every morning we walk with Mum to Penrith pool for our half-hour lesson, then walk home, hair dripping, soggy towels wrapped around our waists. Around 3 p.m. we walk back for Jim's lesson, joined by Acacia, Smiddy, and whoever else is free on our street. The afternoons are the best. The mums spread towels on the grassed area and gasbag; we kids have *who can hold your breath the longest* competitions, do bombies when the lifeguards are distracted by girls in bikinis, and teach Acacia to swim. When we're done swimming, me and Acacia hurdle over towels and kids and race to the kiosk – she always wins. We stand in line clutching our twenty cent pieces, rattails of hair dripping down our backs, and buy Redskins and Milkos, twisting the candy into unicorn horns.

On Friday night, Dad meets us there after work. He joins us kids in the pool, splashing and dunking and playing pool tag, then cooks sausages on the barbecue behind the fifty-metre pool. As we eat, I watch him smiling and joking with the other parents, one arm draped over Mum's shoulders. He hasn't had a dark mood since we got back from Lake Cathie.

'I like your dad,' Acacia tells me. Then, softly, 'I wish he was my dad.'

Rose and Daryl are here too, all touchy-feely like teenagers. Rose in a tiny, ruffly bikini that shows the tattoo on her shoulder. Daryl in tight cozzies, showing off his nearly hairless chest. There's a tattoo on his shoulder too. A curling viper. At one point, I notice Daryl studying me. He winks, making me shiver, whisking me back to the New Year's party. *Don't tell.* I look away. Everyone thinks he's the ant's pants. Even Mum. When Daryl called her *the delightful Mrs Kelly*, a silly smile spread across her face until Jim asked why she had hairy armpits. Mum nearly died of embarrassment.

I still don't know what to believe about Daryl. And I still haven't told anyone what I saw.

The biggest surprise about the week is seeing kids from school at the pools. When I first saw them, I thought they'd ignore me, like at school. They didn't – instead, they mucked about with me and Acacia, in the pool, on the climbing equipment. The only dark spot was this afternoon when Mary Evans turned up. The girls buzzed around her like worker bees. She pretended me and Acacia didn't exist.

'I reckon this week was the best week of the whole summer,' I tell Mum that night. 'Except for Mary Evans.'

And Mean Daryl.

Mum kisses my forehead, then says something I don't quite understand. 'Well, love, the skies aren't always blue and sometimes you can't see the sun for the clouds.'

Much later, I realise she doesn't mean clouds in the sky.

I don't need to tell anyone about the two Daryls. The following week, everyone on our street sees Mean Daryl for themselves. It happens late one afternoon. Me and Acacia are under our tree, while the neighbourhood kids play cricket in the cul-de-sac. We're supposed to be fielding but instead we're talking about Sal. I'm worried about her. She snuck out again last night.

'She always says the same thing. "You'll understand when you're in love",' I tell my friend, mimicking Sal's voice, 'but this time she also said she'd give me two bucks if I keep my mouth shut. Two bucks!'

'Did you take it?'

'Of course! It's two bucks. I can buy two hundred fizzoes with that.'

The cricket ball lands on the grass next to us. Acacia lobs it to Jim. 'And your parents have no idea?'

'Nup. They haven't said a word.'

'You know, if you get two bucks every time Sal sneaks out, you'll be rich!'

'I didn't think of that. Still, I don't know why she bothers. I mean, she sees Robbie pretty much every day, so why does she have to sneak out at night? It's weird.'

'Maybe they're ki—'

'Don't say it! Gross!'

'Sal and Robbie sitting in a tree, k-i-double-s-i-n-g.'

I cover my ears. 'La-la-la, can't hear you.'

Acacia cracks up. 'I'm *never* going to be in love,' she says when she's stopped laughing.

'How do you know?'

'I just do.' She picks at a scab on her knee.

How can she possibly know what will happen in her future?

That's when the storm comes out of nowhere. A shouting, screaming, swearing storm. My head whips towards Acacia's house. The storm is coming from inside, as if someone has turned the telly all the way up. My skin goosebumps. The boys stop playing cricket. Mum, then Dad, come outside and look next door. Mum says something to Dad. He shakes his head. Across the road, Mr Jones starts watering his grass; from the corner of my eye, I spy George sitting on the fence. I think he's listening too.

Moments later, Daryl slams out of the house. At his bike, there's a pause. Then, a roar. *Fucken bird!* A thump on the fence. George flaps away. *Teach you to fucken shit on my bike!* A moment later, another roar. The kids scatter to the kerb as if they are marbles and Daryl's the shooter. And then, Dad says *just a tiff* and Mum goes back inside. Mr Jones waters a different garden bed, muttering *language!* The cricket game resumes. Acacia runs off. *George, come back!*

The next afternoon, when the tell-tale *bom-bom-bom-bom* of Daryl's bike beats him around the corner, Acacia avoids going home. She's still sitting under the wattle tree by the time we finish dinner, batting away the mozzies on her legs and arms.

As the days go on, I dread saying goodbye because I know what will happen. I never know when Rose and Daryl will fight, only that they will. Sometimes, the fights happen soon after Daryl gets home. Other times, it's late at night, when I'm in bed, window open to let in the barely cool air. The cricket-song will be drowned out by booming shouts and ear-splitting shrieks. Curses, crashing, slamming, so loud that I muffle the sound with my pillow.

What does Acacia do when they fight? Where does she go? Do her eyes squeeze shut, and her hands fly to her ears to block out the sound?

There's a pattern. They have a blue; he clears off, ending the argument as fast as it starts. A door slams. Daryl shoots out the driveway on the Harley, leaving wiggly skid marks on the road. Turdle barks: *good riddance*. Rose hides inside and Acacia acts like nothing happened. War and peace.

I'm always relieved when Daryl takes off – for two reasons: one, things go back to normal; two, now that everyone knows about Mean Daryl, it's one less thing to keep to myself.

One evening, an argument blows up while we're eating

dinner. They are standing on the other side of the fence, and their shouts blast through our open kitchen window. My eyes dart between Mum and Dad. What will they do?

Mum puts her fork down, hard. 'I can't listen to this, Trev. We should do—'

'Don't interfere. It's none of our business.' He starts eating again. A few seconds pass, then we kids do the same.

Mum closes the window.

If we kids argue in public or private, you can bet a grown-up will step in. *Stop it! Sort it out nicely!* But when grown-up couples argue in public, it's ignored. Everyone in our street knows what's going on at Acacia's house, but no one does a thing. No one says *Put a lid on it!* to Rose or Daryl. Instead, they stickybeak. The women twitch their curtains or blinds – even Mum. They casually stroll out to check their letterboxes or have a chat over the fence. And the men are no better. They have a good look and listen while they water the garden, wash the car, or dig out weeds in the lawn. And then they stand in little groups, pretending not to look and listen, collecting gossip while pretending to mind their business.

This afternoon, Daryl stormed out of the house yelling *wish I never set eyes on you and that little bitch.* Dad was across the road talking to Mr Jones. Surely, they'd do something? They shook their heads and kept right on talking. Like it didn't happen.

'We should say something,' Mum tells Dad later. I'm supposed to be in bed, but I shrink back against the wall, strain my ears to listen.

'Barb, I've told you. What goes on in someone's house is their business. It's the way things are. Like an unspoken code.'

'What a load of codswallop,' Mum says. 'If it's outside, disrupting the neighbourhood, it's our business.'

People on our street were curious at first: *what's that noise?*

What's going on over there? Now they get on with things, and Rose and Daryl's fights are part of life on our street. They come; they go. Ignore them, show no interest, and they go away. It's like a show on telly: The Rose and Daz Show. If you don't like it, change the channel.

I'm curious too. I want to know *what happened* and *who started it?* The same things Mum wants to know when she catches me and Jim arguing. Although, those questions aren't really the right ones. They never help us work things out; they make us more determined to be heard, to be right.

Me and Acacia also pretend nothing happened, but the questions lurk under my skin. One day, I blurt, 'Does it bother you when your mum and Daryl fight?'

'Don't your parents ever argue?' she shoots back. Answering questions with questions is another way she avoids talking about things. 'Anyway, why are you so obsessed with my life?'

'I'm not!'

'Could of fooled me.'

'It's just that—'

'Everyone fights sometimes,' she says. 'No one's family is perfect.'

'But Rose and Da—'

'I know. I know.' She crosses her arms over her body like she's hugging herself. 'I can't believe your mum said we could share a birthday party! I've never had one before.' The subject is closed.

Acacia pretends she's not bothered by what's going on, but later that day there's proof that she does. I'm waiting for Acacia, eyes trained on George. I'm worried he'll swoop. Mum says magpies only swoop in spring, but you never can tell. I hear yelling. A minute later, maybe two, my friend slides out the door. Her eyes are all red and her nose is running; she's wearing a cardigan in the middle of summer.

'What's wrong?' I hesitate, then drape my arm around her. She jerks away like I've hurt her. 'Nothing.'

'But you're crying. What happened?'

'I said, *nothing*. And I'm *not* crying. Must be hay fever from the wattles, that's all.'

My eyes flick to the wattle tree. The flowers disappeared months ago.

CHAPTER THIRTY

1980

I'm cooking dinner tonight. I offered, expecting Mum to say no. But she didn't, so now I'm in the kitchen, wearing her apron, cooking a feast: scrambled eggs, fish fingers, baked beans, mixed frozen veggies. Lime jelly with custard for dessert. Mum's helping. She's getting in the way, so I've asked her to set the table. The fish fingers are ready, a bit dark on one side, but a dollop of tomato sauce will hide that; the veggies are draining in the colander and the baked beans are warming up in a saucepan.

While Mum watches, I crack fourteen eggs into a frypan, add a chunk of butter and move the pan onto the stove. Stirring quickly, my mind wanders around an idea I've been working on for days. It goes like this: I think anger is contagious. Like a bad germ that infects people, like a cold or the flu. If laughter is contagious, if someone's smile makes you smile back, if a big open-mouthed yawn is catching, then it makes sense that anger works the same. It must be contagious because my family is arguing more than ever since the fights started next door.

'Keep stirring,' Mum says.

Over the past three days, I've counted five arguments between Dad and Sal, seven between Mum and Jim, and three between

Mum and Dad. I haven't counted the arguments I've had with Jim. They never last long, and everyone makes up eventually, but I'm sure it's getting worse. I don't think anyone in the street can hear us – Acacia hasn't said anything – and there's no swearing or yelling or really bad name calling. Calling your brother an obnoxious imbecile doesn't count. Does it?

'They're done, love. Quick, take them off the heat. Here, let me help.' Mum rests the frypan on a trivet next to the stove. 'Why don't you start serving the rest of the food?'

She's taking over, but I don't mind. I'm tired after all that cooking. I don't know how she does it day after day, week after week, year after year.

'Dinner's ready!' I bellow the words into the hallway, then turn to Mum. 'I can't wait for them to taste my feast!' Behind my back, I cross my fingers.

No arguments tonight.

Dad's first to the table and Jim scoots in a few seconds later. Sal keeps us waiting a minute longer. She's been faffing about in the bathroom since Robbie dropped her off, having an early shower. When they're all settled, I bring their plates one-by-one, and wait for the congratulations.

But Dad's not looking at his dinner, he's looking at Sal. 'Any particular reason you're wearing a scarf in the middle of a heatwave?'

Now everyone's looking at Sal. Her cheeks are as red as the polka dots on her scarf. 'It's fashionable,' she says.

'In Paris, maybe.' Dad crosses his arms. 'But we're in Penrith. Take it off.'

'Why?'

'Because I asked you to.' He gives her a look that would shrivel me like a walnut, but she stares him down.

'Why should I? I can wear a scarf if I want to.'

'Sal …' Mum reaches for Sal's hand, pats it. 'Trev, leave it. She's right. Come on, look at this lovely dinner Jane made us.' She forks up a mouthful of scrambled eggs. 'Delicious.' She gazes at Dad while she chews.

Dad opens his mouth, then closes it. 'Pass the salt,' he says, stabbing at a fish finger. His fork screeches against the plate and I wince. It reminds me of chalk on a blackboard. He peers at the fish finger then pops the whole thing in his mouth.

Jim pushes his fish fingers aside. 'I'm not eating these. They're burnt.'

'Are not!' I glare at him. 'They're dark brown, not black!'

Pushing her plate away, Sal stands up. She hasn't even touched her food. 'Fine,' she says to Dad, her voice trembly. She yanks the scarf off, drops it next to her plate. 'Happy now?'

I gasp. There's a dark red circle on my sister's neck, bruising her pale skin. The first thing I think of is Daryl pressing on Rose's neck. Did Robbie do that to Sal?

Across the table, Jim bursts out laughing. 'A hickey. Sal's got a hickey!'

'Drop dead, Jim!'

'Sal!' Mum shakes her head. Dad stares at Sal, breathing deep, his brow furrowed, lips pressed tight. As if he wants to say something but is holding it in.

'What's a hickey?'

'Nothing,' Sal snaps.

'It's a looove bite,' Jim crows. 'Robbie's been sucking her neck as well as her face.'

'Shut your face, Jim!' She snatches up her scarf and heads for the door, kicking the leg of his chair as she passes. Like an afterthought, she adds, 'I'm taking Turdle for a walk.'

'Sally Anne Kelly, get back here and finish the dinner your sister made,' Dad calls out. 'There's no need to get hys—'

'Not. Hungry.' The screen door slams.

'She's gotta come back some time,' Dad mumbles and eats another fish finger.

Mum sighs, heavily. She looks at her plate as if she's not hungry either.

I don't blame her. It doesn't look like much of a feast now: overcooked fish fingers, gluggy baked beans and cold scrambled eggs. But after a minute, Mum picks up her fork and starts eating, and so do I.

'Eat your dinner,' she tells Jim. 'No complaints. Children are starving in—'

'Africa. As if we could forget,' my brother mumbles.

Things are strained with Sal and Dad, but I reckon they're worse with Mum and Jim. Mum says it's growing pains; all I know is that since Jim turned thirteen, he's grown into a deadset pain. It's like aliens abducted the real Jim, swapping him for a croaky-voiced, stinky stranger who looks and sounds like my brother. These days Jim picks on me and Sal nonstop, and argues with Mum over the stupidest of things, like why she said *hello* or *where are you going*.

'You don't understand me,' he'll yell. He's like a stuck record. 'You can't tell me what to do.'

He'd never dare say that to Dad, not in a billion years. No, he sucks up to Dad and saves his bad attitude for Mum, his meanness for Sal and me. And Dad lets it go. Whenever me or Sal complain about Jim's behaviour, Dad says *boys will be boys* and *don't be so sensitive*. It drives me and Sal nuts the way Jim gets away with stuff. I don't know how Mum feels. But I do know that she doesn't like him hanging out with Shane Watters.

'That boy's a bad influence, a bad egg,' she tells Dad now. Two minutes ago, Jim took off out the front because Shane was hollering for him. It's almost dark; the streetlights are coming on. 'I don't like Jim hanging around with him, getting up to God-knows-what.'

'Leave them be,' Dad says. I know what his next four words will be.

'Yes, yes.' Mum sounds weary. 'Boys will be boys.'

. . .

I'm playing Uno with Mum when Sal comes home. I hear her out the back, talking to Turdle. Mum looks at the clock, sighs. I sigh too, but on the inside. I'm relieved my sister is home, but nervous too. I don't want her to argue with Dad again. He's watching telly with Jim. They've been laughing like nothing's wrong, although Dad's wandered into the kitchen a couple of times: *she home yet?*

'Uno.' Mum slaps down a Draw Four. 'Yellow.'

'Mu-um! That's so unfair.' I pick up four cards: two Draw Fours, a Draw Two, a Skip. A hundred and forty points.

'I know. But it's funny when you do it, isn't it, love?' She stands and lays down a yellow Skip, then kisses the top of my head. 'I'm going to talk with your sister. Pack those cards up and go have your bath. And wash your hair. It's full of grass seeds.'

By the time I'm done, towel wrapped on my head, Mum and Dad are out on the back verandah, talking in low voices. I listen from the laundry. They're not talking about Sal, but about Mum looking for a job. I thought she'd forgotten about that. So did Dad, it sounds like.

'Things have changed, Trev. I want to do this for me. Jane's about to start her last year of primary school, and I'm only thinking school hours, besides.'

'What about the housework? And the dinners?'

'It'll be fine, love. It'll all get done.' I hope that doesn't mean more chores for us.

'It's not necessary.'

'It is for *me*.'

Dad doesn't say anything for a while after that. A chair creaks. Mum's voice moves closer. 'Trev. Go to talk to your daughter, okay?' I freeze, thinking she means me, but she adds, 'I'm going in to see what the others are up to. Jane should be out of the bath now.'

Dad says something, but I don't wait to hear. I bolt back to the bathroom and grab my toothbrush. As I brush, I remind myself of what Acacia said: *no one's family is perfect.* I say it over and over to push away another thought that's been lurking for weeks.

I think we might get The Divorce.

'Mum? Are we going to get The Divorce?' The question explodes the next morning, after Jim yells *you're not the boss of me* for about the millionth time this year.

Mum is at the dining table, making a skirt for Sal, and I shout the question above the clatter of the sewing machine. She lifts her foot from the pedal and looks up at me, a surprised expression on her face.

'What? Where on earth did that come from?'

'Well, Sal and Dad and you and Jim keep arguing. And sometimes I hear you and Dad arguing about us kids and stuff.' I sniff. *It's obvious*, I think. Who would want to live in a house with kids who talk back and slam doors? 'That's how The Divorce starts, everybody knows that. And Dad has his dark moods, and you want to get a job—'

Mum comes to me, pulls me close. Her skin smells like a comforting mix of salt and Lux soap, and I breathe in deep. 'Now, love. You're not to worry about that. Dad and I are not getting a divorce. Goodness me. Goodness.' She bends down, wipes away a tear I didn't even know was on my cheek. 'The heat's making us all a bit tetchy, that's all, love.'

'But Sal and Jim—'

'Are teenagers and their moods are always all over the place. Up and down like rollercoasters. You'll see. We Kellys will get through this little storm cloud. And the next. They'll blow away, one by one. No matter what, we love each other … even when we don't like each other. Even when someone's being a big pain in the you-know-what.'

That makes me laugh, despite my tears, and then Mum hugs me tight. 'You're squashing me!'

She laughs, loosens her hold. 'There's *nothing* to worry about, Jane, nothing at all.' There's a knock at the door. It's Acacia. Mum lets go. 'Off you go. And don't worry about a thing.'

I want to believe her. Most of the time we feel like a proper family, laughing and eating and talking. And all families argue. Disagreements are normal when people live together – you can't all think the same way. Even the *Brady Bunch* kids on telly argue, and they're not even real, they're made-up characters. It's probably like this at Smiddy's house. And Margie Murphy's house. Up and down like roller-coasters, like Mum said.

She's probably right. But it feels like our family is falling apart this summer, worn down by the heat and humidity. I stop in the middle of the lawn and peer up at the endless blue sky. There's not a single cloud. I hold out my arms, wishing the skies would open and rain would wash away the bad tempers once and for all. What was that Mum said earlier?

Little storm clouds.

I look at my friend, waiting under the wattle tree. She's twirling like a ballerina to whatever music is in her head. Do Rose and Daryl's arguments blow over fast? Acacia stops twirling when raised voices drift across from her house. Her forehead wrinkles as she strains to hear. She catches me watching, waves.

'Let's go to the park,' she calls, heading in that direction without waiting for an answer. I follow, without asking questions.

Deep down I know they're not normal, the arguments next door. They might be normal for Rose and Daryl, for Acacia. They might be what the people in our street expect to hear, day after day. But they're not little storm clouds, easily blown away.

CHAPTER THIRTY-ONE

ASHES

B reaking away from him left me in pieces: broken woman, broken life. One minute I had a house, a job, a husband – shitty as they all were – and the next, I had nothing but a handful of clothes and a single room in a place I didn't want to belong.

Those first few weeks, I had no idea how to stitch myself, my life, back together. Honestly, I didn't even want to, didn't care if I did or not. Pat tried to help me, but I was hard work. It wasn't easy to break the silence when I'd been living in it for so long. Not easy to trust. To believe I deserved better, when somewhere out there was an absent volunteer who knew the truth of me.

If I were Pat, I'd have shown myself the door and bolted it shut behind me. But Pat was a one-in-a-million woman. A warrior angel. Strong of spirit, always fighting evil. She persisted when others wouldn't have. Shouldn't have. First, she told me her story: how she'd risen above her rock bottom, left her abusive husband (six tries), gone to university, and built a new life helping other women. Then, she listened to my story, drawing me out of my room and my tough-as-nails shell in painful but loving steps.

Not once did she ask the question everyone asks (in their

head or out loud) when they hear stories of abuse. Why didn't you leave?

Not once did she judge.

I told her about the time my hand curled around a knife handle, how I imagined myself slashing him. I'd read about a woman who did that to her husband. Stabbed him in the chest. It was all over the media. *Wife stabs husband! Good family man!* Photos of a laughing husband, a respected footy coach and businessman, arms around his wife. But when I looked closely at the photo, when I looked at the woman's eyes, it was obvious she was broken. The truth of him came out in the trial, but the damage was done. She was the one people pointed at, whispered about.

Pat didn't flinch when I told her about the knife. Didn't look at me like I was an attempted (in my head) murderer. Just offered me another cuppa.

And Pat never asked why I stayed with him, but I told her anyway. I said to her, same as most women: money, fear, shame, isolation. But when it came down to it, I stayed because of love, despite everything he did. Love is what I held on to, what kept me going. The other women in the refuge thought I should've hated him, and sometimes I did. But I could never bring myself to hate him with every ounce of me. Still can't. Because once, I loved him more than anything. And by the time I saw him for what he was, it was too late. I was dying inside, but I lived on hope that he would change, taking each day at a time.

All Pat said to that was what do you want to happen next?

Day after day, she encouraged me to work through my anger and pain. You will survive and you will thrive, she said after one intense heart to heart. Once you leave all this behind.

I stared at my fake-it-till-you-make it sticky note for a long time that night.

· · ·

In group sessions I learnt that women were killed or broken by their partners every day. And I knew from experience, that instead of understanding and support and change, abused women were judged constantly. Even by other women. As if you asked for a punch in the wall, a smack in the face, a fist in the belly. Or words that slash like a knife.

What did you do?

Why don't you leave?

Where are your bruises?

Everyone argues. Shut up and deal with it.

She's so argumentative, she always goes for the bad guys, she brings it on herself.

I've said these things myself. Hypocrite, right?

The only time I told a so-called friend about a fight with him, she said you're making too much of it. She said fighting was a sign of a healthy relationship, of passion.

Is it?

What would have happened if she'd said, like Pat, what do you want to happen next?

CHAPTER THIRTY-TWO

1980

Daryl lives next door now, even though he and Rose aren't married. He moved in when we were at Lake Cathie. Margie Murphy told Sal, and Sal told me this morning before she left for work. I told Mum while I was eating breakfast, but she already knew.

'I thought you had to be married first,' I say, smearing a thick layer of strawberry jam over my toast.

Mum shrugs. 'The world is changing.'

'So, do we still call it the Millers' house? Or is it Daryl's too?' I don't even know his last name.

The phone rings. Mum turns away to answer it.

'Hi, Ma,' she says, waving me off. *Go outside and play.* 'No, I haven't heard back about that job. Yes, it's the right thing to do. It's the right thing for *me*, Ma.' She throws me an irritated look – *are you still here?*

I grab two apples from the bowl on the bench and wander outside. Acacia is already out the front, talking to George. I swear, she talks to him more than me. She takes an apple and bites into it greedily, like she's had no breakfast. Juice dribbles down her chin. I nibble off pieces of skin and toss them to George. He gobbles them up. Squawks for more.

I finish my apple, then ask, 'Now that Daryl lives with you, are you like, you know, a family?'

Her face twists in revulsion. 'No. He's not *my* family. Daz,' she spits out his name like she's bitten a worm, 'he won't last. They *never* do.'

'What do you mean, *they* never do?'

She looks around as if to make sure no one is listening. 'Boyfriends,' she says. 'Mum's boyfriends. They come and go. Like wildflowers. You'll see.'

Boyfriends? Plural?

Standing, Acacia tosses her apple core into the garden bed for George, who pecks at it as if unsure what to do with it. 'Let's play Narnia. I'll be Lucy and you can be Mr Tumnus.'

It's my turn to be Lucy, but she's already waiting at the tree we pretend is a wardrobe.

'Come on, Jane. I'm ready,' she calls. 'But it's too hot to be winter in Narnia!'

'Just *pretend*, Jane.' Then, so quietly that the words nearly blow away on the wind: 'That's what *I* do.'

Rose appears next to us, in a jingle of bells like the White Witch in the forest, making me shiver. 'Acacia?'

Acacia's face goes blank.

'Been calling you and calling you,' Rose says. Up close, her words melt together, and she has the same strange smell I noticed the first time I met her.

Leaping up, Acacia rests her hand on her mother's back, as if she's trying to herd her home. 'Sorry, Mum, didn't hear you. We were playing Narnia.'

Rose's eyes narrow. That White Witch face again. Beautiful but cold. 'Yeah, you did. You were ignoring me. As usual. Now, come on. Need you in the house.' To me, she flashes a toothy smile. A gold filling winks at me. 'See you, kiddo. Acacia can come back later, after she's done her jobs. *If* she does them properly.' She gives Acacia a little push. The tiny bells on her skirt jingle again.

'See ya.' Acacia's voice sounds happier than her face shows. When Rose gives her arm an impatient tug, my friend turns away from me and doesn't look back.

I don't get it. What did Acacia do wrong? Angry and confused, I search for Mum. She's in the laundry, putting on a load of washing. She wrinkles her forehead at me when I stomp in, smacking aside the fly streamers that twine around my head and arms as if on purpose.

'What's got your goat?' she says.

'Not what, who.'

Closing the lid, she twists the knob, then faces me, hands on hips. 'Have you and Acacia had a fight?'

'No!' I karate-chop a rogue fly. 'It's Acacia's mum. She's mean.'

'I see.' She heads to the kitchen, talking over her shoulder as she walks. 'I was about to have a cuppa, read my magazine, but ... want a Milo while you tell me about it?'

While Mum bustles around, I reach across the table for her *Australian Women's Weekly*. It's open to an article called 'Your party face'. There are pictures of women with their hair tizzied up and jewel-coloured make-up around their eyes. One woman has emerald eyeshadow painted all the way to her eyebrows and green satin ruffles around her neck. She looks like a frill-necked lizard going to a party. Like Rose. *All tarted up.* Does Mum want to look like that? Like Rose? I hope not – I like Mum the way she is. Just because someone looks pretty on the outside doesn't mean they're nice.

'So, tell me what happened.' Mum sets a glass and a shortbread biscuit in front of me. The malted topping wobbles.

The milk is so cold there's condensation on the glass; I trace a J in it before blurting out the story.

'Why is she so mean?' I finish. '*You're* never mean.' She laughs. 'That's not what you said yesterday.'

'Well, you did make me eat brussels sprouts and you know they make me spew.' She doesn't need to know I fed two to Turdle. Jim gave him three.

'They're good for you. And I know you kids fed them to the dog. He was tooting like nobody's business last night.' She sits forward, taking my hands in hers. 'You know, Jane, parents aren't perfect. Rose is having a hard time.' A meaningful look. 'Sometimes we judge others without knowing what they're going through.'

My stomach prickles. 'Yeah, I guess.' I toy with my biscuit, no longer hungry. Crumbs speckle the table; I use my pointer finger to push them into a neat pile. 'Mum. Why do they fight so loud? Rose and Daryl. Why do they fight all the time?'

Mum looks down, as if she's searching for the right words. 'Well, Jane … some people have loud voices, that's all. And when they get heated up … sometimes their voices do as well. And sometimes men think they have to shout to be a man.' She pauses. 'But I don't know why Rose and Daryl fight. And it's not really our business, is it? It's private, between them.'

'Even if we can hear it?' I remember what Mum said to Dad about the fights disrupting the neighbourhood.

'Well, no, I mean, yes. I mean, they shouldn't be arguing in public about private things. But we don't need to know what led to them arguing and all the ins-and-outs of—' She runs her fingers through her hair. 'Look, Jane, sometimes adults disagree on things. Even when they love each other. And it's up to them to sort it out.'

'But you and Dad don't fight. Not like that. You have discussions. That's what you said.'

'We're not perfect, Jane. We argue, of course we do. Some people might call that a fight. It's just that we're quieter about it.'

'I *hate* hearing them fight.'

'Me too.'

'I'm worried about Acacia. She never talks about it.'

'Of course. She's your friend, after all.'

'My *best* friend.'

'Silly me. How could I forget that most important part?'

Despite myself, I giggle. And then I clamber onto Mum's lap like a little girl. *I miss this.* Relaxing into her, sucking the ends of my hair, I think of something else. 'Mum, Acacia said something about Rose having lots of boyfriends. Before Daryl.'

She pushes my hair behind my ears. 'Well, some people do that. We're all different. Not everyone wants to get married and settle down like me and Dad. And for some people life doesn't turn out that way.'

Frustration needles me. Everything I thought I knew about life is being challenged every single day. I'm constantly playing catch-up. 'Why is everything changing? Why can't it stay the same? Sal's got Robbie and she's always arguing with Dad, and he's always grumpy, and Jim's being rude to you all the time, and …' I burst into tears.

'Life is like that,' Mum says when my sobs ease. 'The only constant thing is change. And it hardly ever turns out the way you think it will when you're young.' Her voice sounds far away and she's staring out the window.

'What are you thinking about, Mum?' When no answer comes, I poke her in the side.

She gives a little start. 'Ah, nothing for you to worry about, love. Just … Mum things.' She shifts in her seat. 'Up you get. You're getting so big I'll have to sit on *your* lap soon.' She pauses. 'And go easy on your dad. I know he's a bit of a grump sometimes, but he's working on it. He's been trying really hard.'

Later, when Acacia comes back over, her eyes are puffy-red. She pretends nothing is wrong, as usual.

'Did you get in trouble?' I ask, shooting a dark look at her house. I'm still mad at Rose.

'Nah, not really.'

'Is your mum still cranky?'

'Nah.'

'But you've been cry—'

A dirty look. 'No, I haven't,' she says, hands on hips. 'And I came over to play Narnia, not Twenty Questions.' Her eyebrows arch like sideways question marks. 'Maybe I should go home.'

Her threat hovers between us before I respond the way she knows I will, the way I always do. 'No! Please don't.'

CHAPTER THIRTY-THREE

1980

I'm standing on Acacia's verandah, waiting for someone to answer the door. Mum's taking me and Jim to see *The Muppet Movie* at Panthers, and she said we can invite a friend each. Thank goodness Smiddy is back from holidays, and I don't have to put up with Shane Watters. I count to ten, knock again on my friend's screen door: three short, sharp raps, a pause on the fourth, then two slower ones. One-two-three, four ... five, six. It's the same knock-pattern Dad does, and so far, I've had three goes without a response. Frustrated, I knock harder, louder. They're home. The curtains are open, the living room window is open. The telly is on, turned up full bore to one of those talk shows Nan likes. The Valiant is parked down the driveway in its usual spot, Daryl's motorcycle behind it.

'Hello!' I knock on the living room window, cup my hands to call through the fly screen, 'Acacia?'

Nothing.

My hand hovers, poised to knock the second there's a lull in the telly noise. I imagine Mum saying, *perhaps they're busy, or asleep, darling.* And then I imagine Jim saying *they're hiding from you*. Dad made me and Jim do that last time the Jehovah's Witnesses came knocking.

'I didn't want to talk to them,' he said when I asked why.

Acacia wouldn't do that to me.

Would she?

I wipe sweat from my forehead and count to ten again. It's hot, hot, hot like the song and there's no end in sight. Last night the newsreader said Sydney was expecting a record run of temperatures soaring past thirty-five degrees.

'We're heading for another night with a minimum of more than twenty-four,' the newsreader said in a serious voice as our fans rattled and whirred fast as they could, whispering *sorry-sorry-sorry*. Dad shook his head, *bloody summer, bloody heatwave, that's all we need* as the news faded to an ad. Laughing people swigging ice-cold, refreshing soft drink from dripping bottles. *When you want to feel refreshed ... Coke is it.*

And Mum said, like she does any time the weather is mentioned. 'It'll be hotter out here than in the city.' It's always either hotter or colder.

The same ad is blaring from Acacia's telly now. I'd give anything for an ice-cold Coke now, but Mum says it rots your teeth. I think that's another white lie parents tell; all the teenagers on the ad have sparkling white teeth. I sing the jingle under my breath, then knock. Wait.

I'm about to give up when I hear angry voices. Daryl and Rose. They're close – in the living room, not far from the window, their words as clear as if I'm in the room.

'I said I was sorry, Daz. How many times do I have to say it?'

I should leave. It's none of my business. But like that other time, I'm frozen to the spot. Then, despite knowing it's wrong, I peek through the window. There they are, maybe two, three metres away. I can see everything.

'Didn't mean it. Can tell by the way you said it, can't I. Can't even cook a friggin' fried egg without burning it. Useless cow.'

It's one thing to hear their fighting from a distance, another to hear it up close. Every part of my body is tense and tight, except my heart, which is pounding so loud they're going to bust me, for sure. But I still don't move.

'That's what you are,' he says. 'A. Useless. Cow. Go on, say it.'

'I'm not.' Her voice wobbles.

A sharp sound. A slap?

'Say it, bitch. Say it!'

Silence. *Say the words*, I think. Even if you don't mean them.

Daryl grabs her hair and twists her face to his. 'Say it.'

'I'm a … a useless cow.'

He lets her go and she falls to the ground. Now I can't see her, only Daryl, and he just –

I stifle a gasp – he just kicked her! The words keep coming, like lava spilling from an angry volcano.

'See what you made me do, Rose? Hmm? A man shouldn't have to eat shit like that for brekky. Work hard to bring in some dough, provide for you and your bloody kid, I deserve better.'

Acacia! Where is she? What is she doing while this is going on? Watching, like me?

Is she okay?

Daryl stretches his arms over his head, turns towards the window. I duck low, just in time. 'Going to work. I'll grab some Maccas on the way. You can make it up to me later.'

The back door slams. Seconds later, Daryl's motorbike roars awake. I push myself down, praying that Daryl won't come after me too. Gulp great breaths of relief when he rides past without glancing at the verandah. Pull myself up. I need to get home. I need to wash my face, my eyes. Scrub that scene away.

And then the front door opens and there she is. My friend. Safe. 'Fall off your bike and die!' she yells at Daryl's back.

Can you blame her? I don't, but I gasp anyway. She whips around. 'Jane? What are you doing there?' Her voice is wary. Almost unfriendly.

'I c-c-came over to invite you to the movies …'

Those eyes. Hot coals, hotter than the sun on my arms. She knows what I heard and saw. Maybe she'll finally talk to me about it.

'Acacia, I—'

'Can't come,' she says, after a long moment. That hot look again. 'Got stuff to do. Another time, maybe.'

In Year 5, Mr Thiele had a game called 'One Word' – he called out an object and we had to come up with one word to describe it. I was the best in my class at this game.

'Lemon,' he said once.

'Yellow!' Mary Evans, always the queen of the obvious, didn't bother to put her hand up and wait.

'Zesty,' I said. Mr Thiele clapped; Mary Evans looked like she sucked a lemon.

If I played that game right now, if someone said, 'One word for how you're feeling', I'd be stuffed. Because as I walk home, I feel everything and nothing all at once. Scared. Confused. Worried. But most of all, I feel alone. Like there is no one I can talk to about what I've heard. Dad always says, 'What goes on in other people's houses is their business, not ours.'

Mary Evans comes into my vision, her sucked-lemon mouth sneering sour words: *Dobbers wear nappies!*

Acacia is my best friend. How can I ignore something like this?

Mum doesn't notice anything is up.

'We're running late,' she says, ushering me, Jim and Smiddy to the car, without even asking *where's Acacia*. I open my mouth to tell her but she's running back inside to find her keys.

Throughout the movie my body twitches like a sleeping dog. Mum gives me a funny look and rests her hand on my tapping leg. Comfort is instant, but the second she lifts her hand, the twitching resumes. Trapped in the theatre, while a bunch of Muppets sing silly songs and the kids around me laugh and crunch popcorn, I think about Acacia and how little I know of her life. How small my view of her world – and life – seems now.

'What's wrong, Jane? You love the Muppets,' Mum says during intermission. 'You've been squirming like a fluff in a bottle.'

'Fart,' Jim corrects her. 'It's *fart* in a bottle.'

Ignoring him, she pulls me aside. 'Do you feel all right?'

I want to tell Mum the truth. What happened next door. That Daryl and Rose's fighting is far, far worse than shouting. Mum will say all the right things. She'll realise that something needs to be done. She'll make it happen, make sure Acacia and Rose are safe. Won't she?

Don't tell!

The words I want to say, the words I should say, dry up in my mouth.

'I'm fine … I'm hungry. Can we get choc tops?'

Acacia isn't waiting out the front when I get home. I'm relieved – I don't want to see her and pretend everything is fine. I need time to figure out whether to say something or keep myself to myself. But that evening, while we're watching *The Odd Couple* on the telly, I summon up the guts to ask Mum, 'If someone is doing something wrong, you should tell someone, right?'

'Yeah, if you want to be a dobber,' Jim says. 'Wait for the ad break, dumbo.'

'Bug off, Jim. I'm not asking you. Mum?'

Before answering, she looks at Dad, who nods meaningfully at the telly. 'Wait a sec, Jane.' I count thirty seconds and then the *Life. Be in it* ad comes on. 'Well, it depends. There's a difference between dobbing on someone to get attention or get them in trouble and telling someone if you think another person needs help.'

'So, if you're worried about someone you should tell someone else, right?'

'Well, yes. If you think they're not safe or can't handle it themselves.'

I breathe out. *Finally.* Those are the words I needed to hear. 'I'm worried about the fighting next door. I heard Daryl—'

Dad cuts in. 'Jane. That's different. We don't interfere with that sort of business. Whatever's going on there, it's for them to sort out. It's not our business. I've told you this before.'

I knew it. 'But what if someone gets hurt? Or is getting hurt?'

'Jane, I'm telling you, whatever's happening there is none of your – our – business. What goes on in another's home is their personal business. Stay out of it.'

My throat narrows, squashes a scream. 'You've just said the opposite of Mum! I saw Daryl—'

The ad break is over. Oscar and fuss-budget Felix are back to arguing about the state of the apartment. Dad settles back in his chair. I know what I'm supposed to do, but I can't. My mouth has a will of its own.

'So, we ignore it? You don't ignore it when we, me and Jim, fight. You tell us to stop it!'

Dad's eyebrows merge into one. 'That's different. You lot are *my* business. And there's no need to get hysterical.'

'Well, Acacia's my business. She's *my* best friend!'

He stands abruptly and I flinch. Dad's never hit me before, but the movement reminds me of Daryl. 'Enough! That's enough of your cheek! Take yourself off to your room, young lady.' He glares at Mum who is shaking her head. 'No, don't give me that look, Barb.' To me, 'Go!'

I don't go to my room. Instead, I bolt outdoors to the trampoline. No one stops me. Turdle follows, panting; he rests his front paws on the trampoline frame, whining when I ignore him and curl into a tight ball. My cheeks are hot with tears, my mind boils with unfairness, my fist thumps the mat.

I don't know what to do.

I'm angry at everyone. Mum. Dad. Jim. Mostly, I'm mad at Daryl. And Rose. I don't understand why she would have a boyfriend like him. Doesn't she care about her daughter?

Eventually, the anger fades, the tears dry up. The mozzies are biting, but I ignore them and pat the mat, once, twice. Turdle leaps up beside me. Licks my salty face and I laugh despite the scream that's still stuck in my throat. The day is dying, and the sky is a dull purple, with a thick red line tracing the Blue Mountains. Somewhere, someone is cooking a late barbecue, and the smell of flame-grilled meat tickles my nose. A lone star glints in the sky. I stroke Turdle's belly; as his chest rises and falls under my hand, the bad feelings drain away.

I must have dozed off because the next thing, a faint banging noise from next door jolts me upright. Wiping away snot and tears with the back of my hand, I jump down from the trampoline and run to the fence. Rose is standing at the bottom of her back steps, smoking. A faint orange light glows from the end of her cigarette. She looks up at the sky and puffs out a mouthful of smoke; the outside light switches on and the screen door opens again. Acacia jumps down the steps and hugs her mother. Holding onto her daughter with one hand, Rose stubs out her cigarette, then hugs my best friend back. I watch them talk, hearing only murmurs that drift away with the balmy breeze, and the slapping of mozzies on their arms and legs.

I'm so caught up with watching that I don't hear Mum until she's right beside me, whispering, 'Jane. Love. What are you doing out here? The mozzies will eat you alive. Come inside.' Her arms wrap around my waist, and I lean back against her, sniffing, closing my eyes to stop the return of tears. When I open them again, Acacia and Rose have gone inside.

CHAPTER THIRTY-FOUR

1980

After a record nine days of temperatures above thirty-five, a southerly buster and a weak cool change puts a spring in our steps. Rose and Daryl's fights all but disappear. There are fewer arguments at home. Neighbours smile and say *nice weather* when they stroll past with their kids or dogs, instead of sighing *hot, isn't it*. Even Turdle has a bounce in his walk after days of lying around, tongue lolling, moving only to snap at flies.

Despite the southerly taking the sting out of the heat, Dad and Mr Jones are all doom and gloom, complaining about the lack of rain every afternoon at watering time. Sometimes me and Acacia hide behind a bush and listen, clapping our hands over our mouths to stifle our giggles. The conversation is always the same.

Dad: 'Forecasters are predicting a bad drought this year, Jonesy.'

Mr Jones: 'Too right.'

'Reckon it'll be worse than in the sixties.'

'That right?'

'Yep, that's what they reckon.' A pause. 'Shame after all that rain the year before last. The river flooding, and all.'

'Right-o.' And then they ramble on and on about cricket and politics and other boring stuff.

Me and Acacia pinky promise we'll never be as boring as them when we grow up.

Even better than the cool change is the news that Daryl is gone.

'Where's he gone?' I quiz Acacia.

'Don't know. Don't care.'

'He's gone out west for work,' Mum tells Dad at dinner. 'Rose told me. He'll be gone for a week.' Rose and Mum have started talking to each other over the fence. I'm hoping Mum's good influence will rub off on Rose.

'What kind of job does he do that makes him go away?' I want to know.

'Mind your beeswax,' Mum says.

With Daryl away, Acacia smiles brighter and walks lighter, like when we first met. She seems taller, as if invisible worry-weights have lifted from her skinny shoulders. And she's easier to be around. Not as jittery, like she's always waiting for something to happen. I suppose she could say the same about me. I want Daryl to stay away and never come back, even if that's unfair to Rose. I've decided she probably loves him despite his bad temper. Mum says some people can't see for looking and I reckon Rose is one of those people.

One afternoon, when Daryl's been away a few days, Dad and Mr Jones start talking about him instead of the weather. I'm on my own – Acacia's gone shopping with Rose and Jim's somewhere with Smiddy – when I hear his name mentioned. Dumping my scooter on our lawn, I sneak across the road to listen.

'Bludger could've mowed the bleedin' lawn before he nicked off,' Dad says. 'Letting the whole neighbourhood down, that house.'

'More ways than one, I'd say,' Mr Jones agrees. 'Not much chop, is he?'

'Too bloody right. Although it could be 'Nam messed his head. God knows, it messed with mine.'

'War does that to a man.'

They clear their throats and stand in silence for a moment. A twig is poking into my back. I want to move, but I don't want to give myself away.

Mr Jones speaks first. 'Still and all, life goes on. And I'll tell you something for nothing, Trev. If he were my son, I'd give him what-for. His foul language and shouting, you know. Doesn't do to have the ladies hearing such stuff. Needs to tone it down, he does. And they need to keep themselves to themselves, if you get my drift.'

'Too right.' Dad looks around, like he's making sure no one is listening. I burrow deeper into the bush, ignoring the twig. 'Speaking of ladies, Jonesy ... the missus is on at me about getting a part-time job.'

Mr Jones makes an old-man noise, like he's hawking up spit. 'You don't say. Modern women, eh? Want it all, don't they? Next thing they'll be wanting equal pay. Equal pay! What's the world coming too, eh.' Another old-man noise. 'Still, the extra money wouldn't hurt, I s'pose.'

'Hmm. You could be—' Dad stops talking. His hairy feet get closer and closer ... and then he's staring into my face. Definitely not smiling. 'What have I told you about eavesdropping?'

'I was ... looking for—' I'm hopeless at coming up with excuses on the spot.

'You were listening. I know what you were up to. Go on, get back home before I give your big ears something to listen to.'

I slink home, like a guilty dog with its tail between its legs.

. . .

The cool change is brief as the dawn. Summer's heat returns with a vengeance, punishing us unfairly with hot north-westerly winds. Bushfires are all people seem to talk about, day and night.

Mum says it's natural for people to be worried because Sydney is surrounded by bush. 'No rain and hot winds make the bush a fireball waiting to happen,' she says when I ask, and then goes on and on about the bushfires in 1977.

By now, the summer holidays have lost their spark. Me and Acacia are bored with the same old games. The sprinkler has lost its appeal, the Slip 'n' Slide is leaking, and there are only so many times you can hand clap *a sailor went to sea, sea, sea.*

With six days until our eleventh birthdays, I'm convinced it's time we expanded our horizons. Convincing Mum is another matter. It's all about getting her in the right mood. Acacia doesn't have the same problem. She doesn't even bother to tell Rose what she's doing most of the time.

'Mum, can we walk to the library? By ourselves?' I ask. Me and Mum walk there every week. It's about a twenty-minute walk, a bit further up the road from my primary school. A lot further than the milk bar. If Mum says yes, it will be the longest distance she's let me walk without her supervision. Ever. 'Please?'

Before I came inside, I wished on a fairy clock for luck.

Mum looks up from tapping on her old typewriter. I didn't know she owned one until it appeared on the kitchen table a couple of weeks ago, a stack of paper beside it. She types letters on it when Dad's at work, and packs it in a case before he gets home. If that typewriter were mine, I wouldn't write letters. I'd write a book for the library. But when I asked if I could type up my ideas, she said *no, I need it.*

'The library? Please?' I say again.

Mum stretches her arms. 'Well, I suppose so. But you'll have to walk straight there and come straight back,' she says. 'No going elsewhere. I'll be timing you.'

Squealing with joy, I throw my arms around Mum's waist.

Acacia gives me a thumbs-up. I reckon she reads books to escape, like I do. The difference, although she's never admitted it, is that I escape into a different world, but I reckon she escapes from her world. It sounds the same, but it's not.

'Pinky promise.' I link fingers with Mum, then Acacia. 'Come on, let's get the books to return.'

'Wait.' Mum holds her hand up. 'Have you got your own library card yet?' she asks Acacia. 'Remember what the librarian said?'

Acacia shakes her head.

'She can borrow them on my card like last time, Mum,' I butt in.

Mum nods slowly. 'Okay … one last time. Love, you really need your own card. Your mum just needs to sign the form.'

'I'll ask her again.'

She won't. The first time Mum asked about the card Acacia told her Rose hadn't had time to get to the library; the next time she slapped her forehead and said she'd forgotten to ask. I don't know why Mum is making a big deal of a little thing. We share books anyway – split the pile and swap books halfway through the week. Does it matter if Acacia uses my card?

All the same, I do wonder why Rose doesn't do things mothers are supposed to do. Like fill out forms. She doesn't even hang out the washing – Acacia does it. One time I spied over the fence as my friend heaved an overflowing clothes basket into a laundry trolley, then wheeled it, wobbling and squeaking, to the clothesline. Balancing on tiptoes on a faded milk crate, she pegged the washing on the line, wobbling when the wind whip-slapped clothes into her face. She forgot to give the clothes a good shake, so the finished result was a scrunched-up mess.

The walk to and from the library is nothing special and super cool at once. I pinch myself hard several times, convinced I'm sleepwalking, but I'm not, I'm really doing this thing. Growing up, step by step.

But Acacia is less enthusiastic. 'Stop going on about it,' she says, staring down the road. 'I'm used to doing things on my own. Sometimes,' she turns to me, 'I stay home all by myself. Even at night.'

My mouth drops open. 'Really? All by yourself?'

'Mum doesn't mind. She trusts me.'

'But ... at night?'

'Yeah.' She shifts her books to her other arm, squinting at me. 'It's no biggie.'

'But you're only *ten*.'

'So?' Narrowed eyes cut deep. 'Are you having a go at my mum?'

'No!' My head is shaking no but what I mean is *yes, no, not exactly*. I reckon it's not very responsible of Rose to leave her daughter home alone, that's all. Especially at night. But I can't say that to Acacia, so I backtrack. Fast. 'I'm just ... surprised. My mum would never let me do that.'

'Ri-i-ight.' She strides off.

CHAPTER THIRTY-FIVE

RAIN

Time passed in a blur. Adjusting to new routines, the chores roster and the revolving door of women and children coming and going. Counselling. Job seeking – I quit my other job so he wouldn't find me. And paperwork, so much paperwork. Pat and the team of staff and volunteers were great, but they couldn't lift the crushing weight of overwhelm. They couldn't carry my emotional baggage or give me definitive answers about the next steps. All they could do was point me in the right direction. And listen when I lost the plot.

I looked for that volunteer every day, mentally prepared myself for a cuppa and a long overdue chat. Knowing she was out there, fully aware of my childhood shame, was hard. I wanted to get it over with. But she never turned up and wasn't rostered on. Pat was cagey when I asked – *she's busy with personal matters* – but later, in the communal lounge, she filled us all in. The volunteer's mother had terminal breast cancer, and she wouldn't be in for a while. The news made some of the staff and volunteers cry – the dying woman was well known to them. I didn't know whether to cry with sympathy – I'd lost my own mother to that horrible disease a few years earlier – or sigh with relief that my shame would remain buried a little longer. As much as I wanted to do the right thing, to bridge that twenty-year gap, I didn't want to see my hypocrisy reflected in the volunteer's face.

How could she see anything else?

In the end, I put her out of my mind, trusting that our paths would cross again when the time was right. It took me a while to appreciate what I'd found in the meantime: a community. A place I belonged, where I wasn't alone, except in the dark hours of the night. A place to gain the strength I needed to piece myself back together, one stitch at a time.

You want to know how to spot women like me?

Most people can't, not unless they know what to look for. I mean, it's not like some radar goes *ping* when abused women walk into a room. And yeah, I'm obviously a westie, always have been, even when I lived in Glebe for a while – you can take the westie out of the west, but you can't take the westie out of the girl – but women like me, they're not all westies or bogans, alcos or junkies. You might not think that but loads do.

Just like some people reckon women with more money and education and privilege, they attract the good guys, the decent ones. Or they'd be smart enough to get themselves out of an effed-up relationship because they'd see it coming a mile off and run for cover.

I used to think that too.

It's bullshit.

It only took a week or so at the refuge to realise that abused women came from all over. The western suburbs, the North Shore, out in the sticks. Mothers, sisters, daughters, friends, lovers, employees, bosses. Broke addicts and alcos, rich socialites whose husbands thought their million-dollar salaries entitled them to control their wives, or somewhere in between. Some were university educated, others didn't finish high school. All ages, all income levels. Different on the outside, but not so much inside.

Look around. Any woman wherever you are right now could be a victim. How would you know? Seriously, unless people can see the bruises, unless they know the body language or excuses, unless they see abuse with their own eyes, they wouldn't have the foggiest.

I learnt how to hide it. Most of us do. Who wants to see the shocked gasps, sympathetic smiles, and misperceptions and judgements written on people's faces? And so, we pull poker faces better than politicians peddling their lies. Like Meryl Streep playing Lindy Chamberlain in *Evil Angels* – I never knew what Meryl/Lindy was thinking or feeling. (Meryl was ripped off. Should have got an Oscar.)

I reckon sometimes I could have won an Oscar too. But I didn't care about some fancy gold statue or the glory of fame. I never wanted to be on the front cover of a magazine or on telly. When I was still with him, when it all fell apart, I simply wanted to make it through another day unnoticed.

But here's the most important thing about women like me.

Scars don't have to be visible to exist.

CHAPTER THIRTY-SIX

1980

I watch her walk away. *What happened?* The distance between us stretches: ten, twenty, fifty metres. An Olympic swimming pool. A fly buzzes dangerously close to my lips, snaps me into action. 'Wait!'

Acacia walks faster.

'Acacia, wait!'

'Leave me alone!'

No!

'Acacia!' I start jogging, break into a run, my mind moving as fast as my feet – *party will be cancelled, Jane No Friends forever, nobody likes you everybody hates you.* I'm puffing and panting by the time I snatch the back of her singlet top, realising belatedly that we've reached the wattle tree in front of my house.

She swings around, glaring. 'What?'

'I— I— I didn't me— mean to upset … you.' I bend over to catch my breath, gulping deep breaths that threaten to turn into sobs. Sweat drips down my face and I pull my T-shirt up, rub my burning cheeks. Any other time, I'd splash cold water on my face, straight from the hose. When I look up, Acacia is staring at the tree, at George, who is making a chattering noise, as if he's talking directly to her.

'I'm sorry. I wasn't having a go at your mum. Really, I wasn't.' *Party will be cancelled, Jane No Friends forever, nobody likes you everybody hates you!*

George chatters again. Her face softens and she sighs, deeply. Scratches her head so hard I think she'll split her scalp. Peers at her nails. 'I know. It's just …' She pauses, like she's searching for words so she can open her heart at last. 'I … I'm sick of … I'm … I'm tired.'

'Did you have a bad sleep?' I blurt, knowing instantly that it's a stupid question. Rose and Daryl were fighting last night. So loud, Sal told me to close the window at 1 a.m. and we tossed and turned on sweat-soaked sheets while the fan did its best.

'Something like that.' She slumps to the ground, books on her lap. George flaps down beside her, so close she could touch him.

We sit in silence, a little further away from each other than usual. I'm not sure what to say, whether things are alright between us. A car rumbles past. It's the Valiant, with Rose in the driver's seat. But she's not coming home, she's leaving. Without a wave, a glance, a word for the girl slumped beside me. We watch until the car is out of sight, and then I say – crossing my fingers, my toes – 'Do you want to come inside and read for a bit?'

We've made up, but the unsettled feeling is glued to my gut, even when we're sprawled on the living room floor, kicking our legs, and leafing through our new library books. And then Mum walks past with her typewriter case and stops short, giving me a funny look.

'Jane, why are you scratching your head? Come here, let me see …' Setting the typewriter down, she rifles her fingers roughly through my hair and sighs heavily.

'What's wrong, Mum?'

'Nits, Jane, that's what's wrong. Nits.' She crouches next to Acacia. 'Let me check...' She runs her fingers through Acacia's hair, probably more gently than with mine. 'You've got nits too. Your mum needs to get the nit shampoo onto it. Today.' She stands up, dusts off her hands. 'Off you go, love.'

'What? No way!'

Mum glares at me. 'Sorry love,' she says to my friend. 'You can come back over once the nits are gone.'

I wait for Acacia to say *mum's not home*, but she doesn't. Without a word she slopes out of the house, like Turdle does whenever Dad yells at him for digging in the veggie patch. The screen door thuds shut behind her.

'As for you,' Mum continues, 'bathroom. Quick-smart.'

In the bathroom, she half-fills the tub with lukewarm water. No bubbles. Mum wastes no time when it comes to nits. She almost died of embarrassment last time the nit nurse sent us home from school.

'I don't want a bath. It's daytime.' I cross my arms.

'Get in, wet your hair and wait for me. And wipe that sulky look off your face.' She shuffles through bottles in the cupboard under the sink. I do as I'm told.

'Out you get,' she says, after rubbing my head – *too hard!* – with nit shampoo, 'and put your dressing gown on.'

'It's too hot!'

'Just do it.'

She stomps out the front and hollers for Jim, who glowers at me. As if it's *my* fault. Sour-faced, we sit in front of the telly while Mum strips our beds and throws the sheets in the laundry. Stinking lice treatment drips down our necks from under the towels on our heads. Cupboard doors bang. The washing machine lid clatters. Footsteps stomp backwards, forwards. Water on, off. Finally, Mum reappears with a towel on her own head.

'Time to rinse. You first, Jane.'

Moments later, the tedious combing process begins. Mum fusses over nits and knots, pulling extra hard on purpose.

'That hurts!'

'You're infested! There's a nit farm in there.'

Jim thinks that's hilarious. He only has a few nits.

When Sal gets home from work, she keeps her distance from us. 'You're probably infested too.' Jim pretends to flick a bug across the room.

'What? Mum! Tell him to shut up.' She swings around to face us, jabbing her finger towards us. 'I'll never forgive you if Robbie has nits too.'

'They're probably having a pash-fest in his hair,' Jim snorts, 'just like youse two in the car.'

'Get stuffed, you little—'

He pretends to flick another bug.

'Be quiet, the lot of you. Sal, sit still.' Sal gives us the death look while Mum inspects her hair. 'It looks fine,' Mum says after a minute, 'but you might want to treat it, just in case.'

'Great. Now my hair's going to stink, thanks to you,' Sal says to me and Jim. 'And I'm supposed to be going out with Robbie later.'

'Poor Sal. She'll have to keep her lips to herself,' Jim whispers.

Mum cracks a smile for the first time since I scratched my head, but I can't do the same. Instead, tears rise. If Rose doesn't fix Acacia's hair, I'll probably never see my best friend again.

Party will be cancelled, Jane No Friends forever, nobody likes you everybody hates you!

My mind flashes to Acacia challenging me: *are you having a go at my mum?* The way she looked, I thought I'd lost her for good. I've got to make it up to her.

'Can't you fix Acacia's hair?' I plead with Mum. She's chopping carrots and potatoes, the knife moving so fast it blurs my eyes.

'No, love. I've got enough on my hands already. Dinner won't cook itself, you know. It's up to Rose.'

'But she's not even home! She went out.'

'She came home not five minutes ago.'

'But what if she doesn't know how? Rose isn't very good with responsible things!' My mouth wobbles. Mum fills a saucepan with water. Adds the potatoes, salt. 'If she doesn't do it, I won't ever be able to play with her again and I won't have a best friend anymore and it will be *all your fault*!'

Mum opens her mouth to say something, but before she can, Sal yells, 'Mu-um? Where's the nit shampoo?'

Two days later, Acacia is waiting for me out the front. She's talking to George, who is perched on top of her letterbox, begging. He flies to the wattle tree when I approach, watching from a distance. When she faces me, my hand claps over my mouth. Her fine hair is cropped into a messy pixie cut, almost as short as a boy's. Without her flyaway tangles, she looks even more skinny and frail, like a twig that will snap if you bend it too hard.

'What … what happened to your hair?' Tears sting my eyes as I squeeze the words out. I already know the answer. That's how Rose fixes nits.

She gives a short laugh; the kind people do when something isn't funny, but they pretend it is. When she answers, she's looking across at George, not me. Her hand floats to her head, fingers her hair. As if she's just remembered. 'Oh, Mum cut it short to get rid of the nits. She doesn't want them to catch me again. Because of her long hair, you know.'

In that moment, I want to scream. To cry. To yell at Mum, *it's all your fault! Look what you made Rose do!* But in my heart, I know it's not Mum's fault at all, and my head swings around to Acacia's house, fists curling into balls.

'Don't be mad, Jane.' A light touch on my shoulder. 'It's much easier to look after like this. And so much cooler on my head.' Acacia's voice cracks. Like it's glass.

My hands soften. Now I want to hug my friend, hug her tight, but I'm scared she'll break, and I'll cry.

'I think you look … like a …' I look towards the wattle tree for inspiration, 'like a wild pixie in an enchanted forest.'

She smiles, a little wobbly at the edges.

Of course, I should have remembered Acacia doesn't break easily. She barely flinches when Jim and Shane Watters start to bully her. Behind them, waiting at the kerb, is Shane's girlfriend. Mary Evans. Watching, egging them on. Letting the boys do her dirty work.

Not that Shane Watters needs encouragement.

'Ha ha! Check it out. She wants to be a boy.' Shane reaches out and ruffles what's left of Acacia's hair.

She jerks away. 'Don't touch me.'

He laughs. 'You want to be a boy.' He looks at Jim, nods. Your turn. 'Why do you want to be a boy? Is it 'cause you're too … ugly to be a girl?' Jim adds. He doesn't look at me. Maybe he knows I want to deck him.

Leave her alone, I shout inside.

But I don't say it out loud. I'm not making myself a target.

'Good one!' Shane high fives my brother and looks towards Mary Evans for approval. Thumbs up.

Still, I do nothing.

Acacia lifts her chin. 'I like short hair and you can all get nicked.' She gives them the rude finger and my stomach lurches as she walks away. George swoops from the tree to follow her, missing Shane's head by millimetres.

He ducks, swearing. Any other time, I'd laugh.

Instead, shame eats at me. I've failed her. For not standing up to the bullies. For protecting myself at Acacia's expense. Saying nothing makes me as guilty as them – it makes me part of the problem. I thought heartache came from sadness, but now I know it also comes from guilt and shame.

Shane turns on me. 'Gonna follow your lezzo friend, chubba?'

I open my mouth.

'James Albert Kelly, get inside now. Shane Watters, Mary Evans, your mothers will be hearing about this from me. Get yourself home. Now!'

Mum is standing two metres from us. Eyes blazing, hands on hips she stands like a Valkyrie in one of Dad's Marvel comics; the force of her fury pushes Jim inside without her lifting a hand. I follow them in, stand in the hallway, listening.

'I did not raise you to be a bully, James Albert Kelly.' A deathly silent pause. 'How dare you talk to Acacia Miller like that? And your sister. How *dare* you?'

Her words pierce me. They're arrows aimed at my brother, but they're meant for me too, because I did nothing. Mum continues the lecture, using expected phrases like *will apologise today or spend the rest of the holidays in your room, poor example and disappointed in you.* But the phrase that scores itself into my memory is one I've never heard before.

'I didn't raise you to be a sheep!'

Once, when we drove across the Blue Mountains and down onto the plains, a flock of sheep blocked our way, scattering into the ditches in sheepish panic. Each time the road was almost clear, a random sheep ran in front of the car. Then another and another and another. All following a leader with no direction. Dad thumped the steering wheel and swore. Us kids laughed and laughed. *You're baa-aad, Dad.*

I'm not laughing now. I'm a sheep as much as my brother. He barrels blindly past; his cheeks are as red and wet as mine. He slams into his room with his guilt, leaving me in the hallway with mine.

For a moment, I'm at a loss. What now? When I hear a soft whimpering, I follow the sound to the living room. The sight of

Mum sitting on the sofa, head in hands, freezes me in place. Mum looks up and her watery eyes lock with mine. Then she holds out her arms and I snuggle into them, rest my head on her shoulder.

'That poor girl,' she whispers, her mouth close to my hair. 'That poor, poor girl.'

CHAPTER THIRTY-SEVEN

1980

I wake suddenly, dragged from sleep by low voices outside my bedroom. The door creaks open, clicks shut. Creeping footsteps, the sigh of a mattress. My sister is a shadow in silvery moonlight, sitting on the edge of her bed, breathing hard. It's 11 p.m.

'What...' Propping myself up, I fumble for the bedside lamp, squint into the shock of light. 'What's going on?'

'Turn it off!' she hisses. A *click* plunges the room into darkness. My eyes blink to adjust, slowly making out a strip of light under the door. I hear the splash of wee in the toilet.

'What—'

'Shhh!'

I wait. The toilet flushes.

'Nearly got busted,' she whispers when the hall light flicks off. 'Dad sprung me near the front door. Must have fallen asleep in front of the telly.'

I muffle a gasp under my sheet. 'What did you do?' With Daryl still away, and all quiet next door, it's Sal who worries me most lately. She sneaks out every night now as soon as Mum and Dad are asleep. It's only a matter of time before she gets caught, and if

– no, *when* – she is, she'll be in for it. Mum will flip her lid, for sure. Dad's been in a dark mood for a few days – more like a little black cloud than a storm. I don't even want to think about how he'll react.

'Told him I couldn't sleep, and I was getting a drink of milk. Thank goodness he didn't notice my clothes.' She sighs. 'Robbie's waiting down the road. But I can't risk it again tonight.'

I push myself up on one elbow. 'What do you do out there, you and Robbie?'

'Go for a drive. Talk. That's all.'

'What about? What's so important you can't talk about it in the daytime?'

'First of all, we can't because we're at work, silly. And second, we talk about … everything. Our day, our dreams … stuff like that.'

'Do you … kiss?' I don't want to know the answer, yet at the same time, I do.

'Sometimes.'

I can't help shuddering. 'Yuck. That's disgusting.'

A soft laugh. 'Jane, you're such a baby.'

'Am not!'

'Are too.'

'You are!'

Sal laughs again. 'We are in love, you know. You kiss when you're in love. You'll understand one day. You'll want to kiss someone too, to be with them all the time.'

'Never!'

'I used to say that when I was your age. But things change when you grow up.' She goes quiet. The ceiling fan chops the air, squeaking in protest.

'I don't think you should sneak out anymore,' I say, to break the silence. 'You'll get caught.'

'I won't.'

'You might. Look what nearly happened.'

'Are you going to tell?' Suddenly the air in the room feels thick.

'No!'

'Well, then, nothing to worry about, is there.' The bed squeaks and she's up, tiptoeing around the room, shrugging off her dress, hanging it over the chair with a sigh. A cloud of Charlie drifts over, mixes with the honey perfume of frangipani coming through the window. After a few moments, the bed squeaks again and the sheets rustle. 'We're going to get married, you know,' she says dreamily. 'When Robbie's finished his apprenticeship. We've got it all worked out.'

Staring at the black emptiness of the ceiling, I try to imagine my sister married to Robbie Chapman. I can't. In my mind, she is just Sal, my big sister. Not a wife, and maybe one day, a mother. If they get married, they'll have to do *It*. How *It* works precisely, I'm not sure; all I know is that it involves *being in the nuddy* and *rude bits*. Shuddering again, I roll over and will myself to sleep.

In the morning, I head next door after my chores are done. I've offered to walk Turdle before it gets too hot, but the truth is, the dog's an excuse to get me out of the house, away from Shane Watters. His mum has a hair appointment and she dropped Shane off without asking our mum, despite what happened yesterday. Mum has been banging the kitchen cupboards and clomping around since Shane arrived. I don't blame her. The house feels less comfortable with that boy in it. Like we must stay on guard.

A sound freezes my hand midway to Acacia's front door. Deep in the house, someone is crying. Is it Acacia? Rose? Turdle nudges his wet nose against my hand – *walkies?* – but I push him away. The trembling, shuddering sound breaks through the sticky air again. Someone is crying like their heart is breaking. Why? What's wrong? Misery leaks from inside the house, creeps under my skin. An unwelcome thought occurs to me, making me shiver. Is Daryl inside the house?

Every single night since Daryl went away, I've asked God for one thing. For Daryl to never, ever come back. And every time I hear a motorbike, any motorbike, I feel my body tense. But I didn't hear one this morning.

The dusty screen tickles my nose as I peer through the door, mouth open to call my friend, hand raised to knock …

'Jane!' I pull my head away at the sound of Mum's voice. She's at the fence, looking even less happy than five minutes ago, and I drag Turdle home with difficulty. Mum huffs. 'What were you doing over there? I thought you were taking the dog for a walk.'

'I was, but—'

'Well, get on with it, instead of poking your nose into someone's business. I saw you peeking through that door.' Heading back to the house, she calls over her shoulder, 'If Acacia's not home, there's no need for you to be loitering.'

'They *are* home,' I say to her back. 'I can see their car.'

At the duck pond, Turdle sniffs here and there, yanking at the lead like he wants to break free. My feet move where he wants to go, like a robot set to automatic. My mind is another story, crowded with thoughts of my friend, moving where it wants to go, to questions with no answers.

At home, I'm refilling Turdle's water bowl when a sharp, smoky smell wrinkles my nose. It's coming from the direction of the incinerator Dad uses to burn leaves and garden clippings. But that's not the culprit. Shane Watters and Jim are sitting on a pile of bricks smoking cigarettes. Shane looks like an expert – his eyes close as he inhales and open as he puffs out a hazy smoke cloud. My brother, sunburnt and freckled, his hair sticking up like a cockatoo, looks like a try-hard, coughing and spluttering as he inhales.

There's always someone smoking at barbecues and family gatherings, but I can't stand the stink of it. Dad smoked a pack a day until he went cold turkey. Ever since then, at every opportunity, Mum drums this into us kids: smoking turns your lungs into lumps of coal. How long has Jim been doing this? Are his lungs already black?

Shane reaches for something at his feet. A magazine. I can't make out the cover, but I hear the pages turning, the boys snickering. And then Shane holds the magazine up so the centre unfolds.

'You're dead meat, Jim.' My brother jumps like a startled kangaroo. 'Looking at dirty magazines and smoking. Mum's going kill you.'

Shane drops the magazine, leaps up, grabs my arm and pushes his face into mine. His breath smells sour, and I wrench away, wincing.

'Don't tell anyone,' he hisses, twisting my forearm in a stinging Chinese burn until I cry out. 'Or you'll regret it.' A small smile curls on his lower lip. I'm back in Margie Murphy's laundry and Daryl is smiling-not-smiling at me. *Don't tell.*

'Ah, leave her alone, Shane,' Jim says, stomping out his cigarette. 'Let her go.'

Shane laughs and drops my arm, then drags on his smoke, blows foul air into my face. Then he says to Jim, 'Remind Chubba who's boss around here.'

My brother's jaw works, unreadable eyes on me as I rub my throbbing arm. 'Rack off, Jane,' he says quietly. Then, in a harsher tone, 'If you dob, I'll tell Dad that Sal's sneaking out at night.'

I can't let that happen. I promised.

Forcing back tears, I sneak inside without Mum noticing. If she'd stopped me, I would have blabbed everything, promises or not. I'm like a bucket full to the brim; a gentle nudge will spill my secrets out. In the bathroom, I splash cold water on my face, dry it roughly with a scratchy hand towel. My arm is still red and tingling from Shane's grip and I remember Rose, rubbing her neck, avoiding my eyes as she walked by me that night. My stomach heaves, leaving my mouth dry and sour. Sinking onto the cool tiles, I hug my knees to my chest as tears slide down, down.

Who do I protect? My sister or my brother? There are three choices, none of them good. One by one, I tick them off my fingers. If I tell on Sal, she'll never trust me again. Tell on Jim, and he'll tell on Sal to take the heat off him. Or say nothing.

I go for the easiest choice.

At lunch, Mum doesn't notice my puffy eyes, and she's forgotten to cut the crusts off my peanut butter sandwich. When Jim and Shane come in, reeking of smoke, she doesn't bat an eyelid. Watching her rinse dishes, face blank like her mind is anywhere but here, I wonder if she's daydreaming, or thinking of her lists – shopping lists, to-do lists, and whatever other lists mums have. Or upset.

'You okay, Mum?' I ask. *Ask me the same.*

She looks surprised to see me. 'Fine, love.' But when Nan rings a minute later, I hear her say, 'I'm so busy, I can't think for doing.'

While she's on the phone, I concentrate on pulling the crusts off my sandwich. But I feel the boys' eyes on me, burning a promise out of me. *Don't tell. Or else.* Shane wolfs his Vegemite-and-cheese sandwiches like he hasn't eaten in a week, chewing with his mouth open. The wet smacking sound makes me wants to scream, but still, I don't look up.

'Me and Shane are going to the pools this arvo,' Jim tells Mum when she hangs up. Then, as an afterthought, 'That okay?'

'Mm-hmm.'

'Um, I need money? For pool entry?'

Mum takes a one-dollar note from a jar on top of the fridge. 'Here.' Her normal Mum voice is back. 'Take your pocket money if you want snacks. And be home by five-thirty.' She wrinkles her nose. Sniffs the air. 'What's that—'

The boys bolt, leaving their plates for Mum to clear up.

'Stop playing with your food,' Mum snaps, turning her attention to me. 'For goodness' sake, Jane, sit up straight. And eat your crusts; you're a big girl now.'

'Sorry,' I sniff. Ask me the right question, and I'll crack. But I am saying this to her back. She has walked out of the kitchen. I hear the jingling of coins, the front door lock. When she comes back in, she has a straw hat on and keys in her hand. My crusts are in the bin, buried deep like my secrets.

She sighs when she sees me, back at the table, an innocent angel. 'You're always a bit out of sorts when that boy is around,' she says. 'Come on, then. Rose next door is coming over for a cuppa later and I need milk.'

CHAPTER THIRTY-EIGHT

1980

Rose is sitting at our kitchen table. I'm used to seeing her daughter in our house, and while Acacia seems comfortable enough, Rose seems out of place, awkward. Perched on the edge of a chair, her feet are jiggling up and down. Like a nervous runner waiting for a command. *On your marks, get set, GO!* I study her while Mum makes coffee and places four Monte Carlo biscuits on a plate. Her sunnies are pushed high on top of her head, and her hair hangs in two thick plaits over her shoulders, tied with ribbons like a little girl. Her gold hooped earrings catch the light when she moves her head. There are dark bags under her eyes and her bottom lip is swollen, red. A whopper of a yellow-brown bruise peeks out from under one T-shirt sleeve. Her fruity-smoky scent wrinkles my nose. I wonder if Acacia likes it.

My friend gazes at the bruise on her mother's arm. Strokes it gently. I watch as mother and daughter exchange a look that's hidden from me.

'Rose and I want to have a grown-up talk,' Mum says to me and Acacia, setting two of her good cups on the table. She offers the biscuits to Rose, who takes two. 'About your birthday party. Off you go, now. Outside.'

'Can we watch *Skippy*?' I ask, after a quick glance at the clock. 'Please? It's super-hot. And can we have Monte Carlos too?' I want to know why Rose is really visiting. Whether it's about the crying I heard earlier. When we walked to the milk bar, I asked Mum. She said *because I invited her* but I'm a hundred per cent positive there's more to it than that. Answers starting with *because* is how parents pretend that they're answering when they're not.

Mum gives me a stern look. 'No listening in,' she warns, her voice low as she takes two more biscuits from the packet. 'Or the telly will be off, and you'll lose your privileges for the rest of the week. And don't give me that butter-wouldn't-melt face, Jane Kelly. I know you better than you think. Now, shoo. Off you go.'

The whole time *Skippy* is on, I pace the living room. Curiosity is killing me. My body twitches: every part of me wants to sneak out and listen from the hallway. Acacia, on the other hand, is sprawled in Dad's chair, legs dangling over the armrest, completely absorbed in Skippy and Sonny's latest adventure. Like she isn't at all curious about her mum *just visiting*. Like she doesn't have a care in the world.

'Your dad a glassmaker?' she says, reaching towards the coffee table for a biscuit. 'Sit down! I can't see.'

I pull apart my Monte Carlo and lick the jam-and-cream filling while the credits roll, and the ads start. I've given up on Mum and Rose for now, but there's still something bugging me. 'Were you home when I was knocking at your door this morning?'

'No,' she said. Her eyes flick from side to side, her shoulders stiffen. There are crumbs around her mouth. 'Why?'

I narrow my eyes at her, finish my biscuit. *Liar, liar, pants on fire.* 'Yes, you were. I heard you.' Wipe my mouth pointedly, delicately, with my fingertips.

She swallows, wipes her mouth on her sleeve. 'Okay, fine, I was home. But Mum was sick ... headache ... and I had to be quiet, so I couldn't answer the door.' She fixes her eyes on the telly. *Scooby Doo* is starting.

I'm not letting her off that easy. 'I heard crying. Like someone was hurt.' The bruise on Rose's arm leaps into my mind. After a quick glance upwards – a reminder – I ask, 'Is ... is Daryl back?'

From the look on her face, I think she knows what I'm really asking. But her voice is casual. 'Nah, not yet. Tonight, Mum said.'

'Oh.' I think this over. 'But if he's not home ... the crying ... I heard—'

'I *told* you!' She glares at me, then rushes on. 'It was Mum. Being sick. One of those twenty-something-hour tummy bugs. That's *all*.'

Acacia said headache earlier, but her that all sounds like a warning. We watch *Scooby Doo* in uncomfortable silence, the stuffy air pressing down, down. She's sitting stiffly in Dad's chair now, no more dangling legs. Arms folded over her chest, hands rubbing up and down. As if she's cold. Only a metre away, but it feels like a thousand. Like she would rather be anywhere but here with me. And so, when the ads come on, I change the subject, making sure Mum's not in earshot. 'Sal nearly got busted sneaking out last night.' She shrugs. Looks in the direction of our kitchen. 'And I caught Jim and Shane Watters smoking this morning.' Another shrug. 'And looking at a dirty magazine!'

Now I've got her attention. 'Really? What are you going to do?' She peppers me with questions faster than kids chasing an ice cream van.

'I dunno. Jim said he'd dob on Sal if I dob on him. And Shane gave me a Chinese burn and told me to keep my mouth shut. Anyway, they probably wouldn't get in trouble. Boys will be boys, right?'

She stands up, fists clenched, cheeks red. 'Stuff that! I'll give him a bloody Chinese burn! And a kick up the arse!'

She's a pixie taking on an ogre. 'He's twice your size, silly,' I say, lips twitching at the image. Then, giggling, 'And ten times as thick.'

She roars with laughter. 'That's the funniest thing I've heard all day. Shane Watters. A thickhead and a dickhead.'

Before bed, Mum checks my hair for nits *just in case*. Her fingers massage my scalp and I close my eyes briefly, enjoying the sensation that trickles from top to toe.

'All clear,' she says, satisfied. I wonder if Rose checks Acacia's hair every day for weeks after a nit-festation. And I wonder again why Rose really came over.

'Mum? What happened to Rose's lip? Did … Daryl punch her in the mouth? Is that why her lip—' The words fall out higgledy-piggledy, like the thoughts swirling in my head.

Mum's hands still. Then, 'Of course not! Why would you—' She opens the bathroom drawer – *goodness, me!* – takes her time digging out a bobby pin and elastic band. 'Rose has a cold sore. And we were talking about the birthday party.' With expert moves, she plaits my hair, twists the elastic around the ends. Pats my head. 'You're going to need a haircut soon.' She smooths stray side hairs behind my ears, kisses my forehead.

'Mum! I know something was wrong with Rose. And I reckon it has to do with—' If she admits it, if she says *his* name, I can tell her what I know.

'Look, Jane. You know how you need a friend sometimes … and Sal needs a friend sometimes … and Acacia—'

'Yeah,' I cut her off before she rattles off the whole address book. 'Well. Rose needed a friend today. Someone to talk to. And today that was me. Now, it's time for bed.'

'But what did she—'

'Jane Kelly, what Rose and I talked about is for me to know.'

Her knees creak as she stands and moves to the bathroom door. 'And not for you to find out. I saw that look. It's an adult conversation. We talked in confidence and it's not for your ears.'

'Will Rose … will she be okay?' No sooner are the words out than a deep rumble echoes through the front door, rattling the window frames.

Daryl is back.

Mum looks down the hall, towards the sound of an unanswered prayer. 'I hope so, Jane. I really do.'

In bed, I face the open window, listening for the telltale sounds of a fight next door.

When it's all quiet on Acacia's home front, I roll onto my back, relieved, listening to the ceiling fan drone. Still, sleep doesn't come. I can't stop thinking about the secrets I'm keeping. About my sister, my brother, my friend. Her mum. My body itches with dried sweat. Heavy air smothers my skin. I shrug off my short nightie and toss this way, that way, my skin sensitive to every bump in the pillow and fold in the sheets. The cold shiver is back, and I pull on my sheet. Throw it off again.

I feel alone with my secrets, with everything I can't tell. Like I did before Acacia came along. I try to picture what she's doing now that Daryl is back. Is she sleepless, tossing and turning like me? Is her tummy rocking and rolling? It upsets me when I can't picture her at all. I still have no idea what her life is really like. More and more, I get the feeling Acacia wants what I have: a mum who looks after everyone, a dad who mows the lawn, and brothers and sisters who stick up for each other, even when they drive each other crazy. But she never says so.

Thunder rumbles in the distance. Pressing my nose against the fly screen, I sniff the air, hoping for the wet, earthy perfume that promises rain, but only smell dust. When did it last rain? Mum says rain washes everything clean, and in that moment, I wish the sky would pour cats and dogs – that pure water from the sky would wipe away the bad and bring back the good. But it's not that easy to make things better.

You can't wash bad things away. And mums can't fix bumps and bruises with a kiss.

CHAPTER THIRTY-NINE

GERMINATION

Refuges aren't long-term solutions. They're like band-aids over a cut; they've got to come off sooner or later. Whether you rip them with one sharp tug or peel them slowly, your eyes sting either way. Pat gave me plenty of warning, but there was no getting out of it. I had to free up the room for someone else.

It's time to take the next step, Pat said. To be the best you can be.

Whatever that meant.

So, as my time in the refuge neared an end, Pat's question – *what do you want to happen next?* – morphed into a more specific one. Where am I going to live? It was the first thing I thought about every morning, the last thing I worried about at night, until a solution was found.

Moving out of the refuge scared the shit out of me and I was one of the lucky ones. I'd scored a factory job, saved a bit of money. Enough to pay a bond and buy odds and ends. Pat found me a room in a share house with a couple of other single women 'til I got a housing commission. I was on the priority list, but there was a long queue and you had to wait your turn. Complain to the wrong pencil pusher and you'd be bumped down the list a few names, and then a few more for good measure.

On my second-last day at the refuge, Pat took me to the Salvos to buy the essentials: cutlery and crockery for one, bed linen and blankets (faded and reeking of mothballs), two mismatched bath towels and a face cloth. Keep these in your room, she said. We picked up a second-hand mattress and I tried not to think about the stains or the stale smell of sweat and smoke and sex. Or my empty wallet, nothing left until the next payday.

You'll need to collect a few things for when you're on your own, she said. Kitchen stuff. Basic furniture. When you get the call about the housing commission, you'll be moving into an empty shell. Do you want to go back to your old house tomorrow, get a few things?

I'd been at the refuge a couple of weeks when I got up the nerve to return to my old house, carefully choosing a time when he'd be at work. Pat came with me and I'm glad she did because he came home while I was shoving clothes and shoes and books into the jumbo checked storage bags you get from the two-dollar shop. He watched from the doorway while I packed, and he watched from the window while I walked out of the house with Pat and four straining bags. He didn't say a word the whole time I was there, probably cause of Pat. I don't know if that scared me more than if he was holding a gun.

I nearly went back to him that day. There was a moment when he was watching that I looked up and caught his eye and all the good memories flooded back the way they do when you open an old photo album: bushwalking in the Blue Mountains, singing around a campfire, our holiday in Fiji. My skin goose pimpled all over and I thought it was because of love, and then I saw his eyes were cold.

When I told Pat in the car what I nearly did, she nodded, like she expected as much.

I'm glad you didn't, she said. You've survived the storm and come back stronger.

I liked the way she said that. Like she believed in me, even if I didn't.

When Pat asked if I wanted to go back again, I hesitated for the briefest time. Despite it all, I still missed him sometimes. Mostly at night. If he was there, what would I do? I don't know if I'm strong enough, I told her, and she said, here if you need me. That's what netball players say, I told her. Turned out she played wing defence in the Monday night B-grade comps for years.

The next day she drove me to my old house. The whole way I was as stiff as an ironing board. My back didn't touch the car seat until the moment I saw that his car wasn't there.

I was jiggling the key in the lock when the door opened and this man said, *what the fuck are you doing?* When Pat explained, all apologetic and soothing, the man calmed down and told us his family moved in a few weeks earlier. No, there was nothing left behind, he said and then his wife pushed her head under his shoulder. Left the house in a right state, she said, her voice all huffy like it was my fault. Holes in the walls, doors hanging off hinges. Then she gave me the once over like she was trying to figure something out and her voice changed. Did we want her to call and ask the real estate agent where my ex was? I shook my head so hard my neck hurt, and Pat said, no thanks. In the car, I got the shakes and told Pat that it was worse not knowing where he was. Worse knowing that he was out there somewhere.

Keep burning bright, she said, holding my hand.

The shakes calmed down on the outside, but inside I was a wobbly mess. No one would have known from looking at me, not even the girls at the new house. They had no clue I was jumpy as a virgin in Long Bay Prison, but Pat did her hand-patting thing and said, if it's not right, tell me, we don't want you to fail because it's the wrong place.

I'm fine, I said and even though she knew I was lying, she gave me a hug.

When I was finally alone in another new bedroom, that's when the fear rose, scalding my throat with hot, acid spew. It's hard to relax when every knock at the door, every scratch of a branch on a window, every whiff of aftershave like his makes your throat ache and your body shake, no matter where you are.

He'll find me here, I kept thinking. He'll find me and make me pay. It happened to one of the girls in the refuge. Her ex turned up, was bashing on the gate, screaming, *I'm going to fucken kill you!* until the police came. She had to move to another refuge the next day.

But he didn't find me, and I kept my head down while I lived in that house. When the girls had friends over, I made myself scarce. When they had men over, I hid in my room and turned up the volume as far as I dared on my portable telly. They had no idea the whole time I was counting down my escape, imagining my future, wondering if it was safe to hope.

CHAPTER FORTY

1980

The next day, Daryl starts making noise at 6.30 a.m. The lawnmower splutters into life, then rattles and hums, up and down, drowning out the cartoons on telly. Jim turns the volume up a few notches, but it doesn't help. Frustrated, we head to the kitchen, following the smell of crispy bacon and fried eggs.

Mum is standing at the stove, spatula in hand; she looks over in surprise when we plonk ourselves at the table. 'Thought you were watching cartoons.'

'Can't hear the telly,' Jim says, pouring himself a glass of juice.

'Why the bloody hell is he doing that at this time of the morning?' Dad barely lifts his head from the newspaper.

'Language, Trev!' Mum hands him a plate loaded with crispy bacon, buttered toast, and fried eggs. 'You did say their lawn was getting untidy.'

'Doesn't mean I want that racket this early,' he mutters. 'It's not gone seven, yet. People want to eat their brekky in peace.'

'Can't have it both ways. At least he's getting around to it, love.' She pats the shiny patch on his head and gives him another piece of bacon. But I notice she frowns as she looks in next door's direction.

'Hmph.' Setting the newspaper aside, Dad blobs tomato sauce on his eggs.

After breakfast, Mum sends me outside to check the letterbox for catalogues. Already the sun is furious, promising a stinker. Next door, Daryl has finished mowing and is raking grass cuttings into piles out the front. As I watch, he stops, wipes his forehead on his blue singlet, then yanks it over his head and tosses it to the ground.

'Rose, bring me a drink of water, will ya?' he calls.

Seconds later, Rose hands him a glass. He gulps down the drink, and then pulls Rose close, gives her a smoochy kiss, pinches her bum. She wipes her mouth and cheek, smacks his hand away – *Ew, you're all sweaty!* – but she's giggling.

An hour later, the Valiant disappears down the street. Later, Acacia tells me Daryl took them shopping for a new telly and stereo, and an Atari console with three games. And a portable telly for Acacia's room! I'm busting to ask how they got rich suddenly, but I don't; Mum says it's rude to talk about money and how much things cost.

Maybe this is Daryl's way of saying sorry for being mean.

Maybe he's turned over a new leaf.

Acacia is still going on about the new stuff when the Mr Whippy van rolls around the cul-de-sac, down the street. It stops a few houses down from mine and within minutes there's a queue of kids, each one clasping a handful of coins in hot hands. Smiddy's at the front of the queue; my brother is by his side. *Scabber.*

Daryl calls from the fence, 'You girls want an ice cream? My shout.' We look at each other before racing to the fence, where he is holding out a couple of folded one-dollar notes.

'Go nuts,' he says, flashing us a wide grin as Acacia snatches the money with a muttered *fanks.* That smile. I'd forgotten how warm-fuzzy it used to make me feel.

I'm speed-licking my dripping soft serve when Acacia nudges my side. 'Look.'

Daryl is talking over the fence to Dad, who must have come home from work while we were lining up. I nearly drop my ice cream. From where we are under the wattle tree, all I can hear is mate-this and mate-that. I can't get my head around it – I thought Dad didn't like Daryl. Next thing, Rose comes outside, all smiles and perfectly waved hair. She hands each of the men a beer, leans in for a kiss from Daryl. Not just a peck on the cheek either.

'Gross.' Acacia shudders beside me, and I agree … mostly. If kissing in public means they're happy, I guess I can put up with it.

Dad must be uncomfortable though, because he looks away and cracks open his can, taking a big mouthful.

'I'm bored,' Acacia says, licking her fingers. 'Let's go to the park.'

That night, I prick my ears out of habit, listening for shouting and banging next door. All I hear is muted music. I fall asleep, hoping the peace will last. It seems too good to be true, but after a few days, I'm convinced that the peace is real, for Daryl seems like a changed man. Whenever I see him, his smile reaches his eyes; whenever I see him with Rose, they're as lovey-dovey as Sal and Robbie. I come to think that whatever happened was a glitch, a bump in the road.

'It's so good that Rose and Daryl don't fight anymore,' I say to Mum one afternoon.

'Mm-hmm.' Her face is hard to read. I can't decide if she doesn't know what to say or doesn't *want* to say what she thinks.

'What do you mean, Mum? It is good, isn't it?'

'Yes, it's good.' She pauses, then adds, 'It is.' It sounds like a question. As if she's trying to convince herself.

Unconcerned, I wander outside. I don't need any more convincing. Life is good. Out on the trampoline, peering up at puffy white clouds dotting the blue sky, I list the reasons on one hand: one, Acacia is the best friend in the world; two, Mean Daryl is gone for good; three, Mum and Dad aren't getting The Divorce; four, Sal and Robbie are in love; five, Daryl and Dad are mates. I pause, then keep going on the other hand. Six, Shane Watters has gone to his granddad's farm in Bathurst, hopefully never to return. Seven, Dad reckons rain is on the way. Eight, it's my birthday tomorrow. Nine, Acacia and I are having a joint birthday party. Ten … I stop counting, scared to admit what comes into my mind next.

I have a crush on Smiddy.

No one knows about it, not even Acacia.

It started when Smiddy came back from his holidays. He came over to see Jim and when I answered the door, he flashed me a grin that stretched his freckled cheeks wide, revealing the gap between his two top teeth.

'Hey, Jane,' he said, sounding genuinely pleased to see me. 'How ya doing?' A strange fizzy feeling rose in my tummy, a sensation I'd never felt before and couldn't explain.

It happens every time I see Smiddy now, that fizzy feeling. I keep thinking about him, imagining conversations with him. Sometimes, I wonder what it would be like to hold his hand. Would it feel hot and clammy or cool and dry?

Ten. Smiddy's coming to my party.

CHAPTER FORTY-ONE

1980

On the morning of my eleventh birthday, I squint at my image in the bathroom mirror. I've been waiting for this day all summer and now that it's here, I feel different, like I understand more about the world every day I'm alive. But do I *look* different? Older? Wiser? Taller? I can't tell.

'Mum, do I look older?' I ask after opening my presents – strawberry lip balm from Sal, a Kit Kat from Jim, and a shiny red Malvern Star bike with a white basket from Mum and Dad.

'Nah, just dumber,' Jim says, winking.

'Yes.' Mum looks me up and down, smiling. 'You look like a big girl of nine.'

'Mum!'

Laughing, she hands me a plate of creamy scrambled eggs with buttered toast. 'Eat up, love. It'll be party time before you know it.'

'Did you make the cake?' It's a silly question – Mum spends hours making extra-special birthday cakes – but this one is even more important because I'm sharing it with Acacia.

She smiles and opens the fridge. There it is, the Dolly Varden cake Acacia chose from Mum's birthday cake recipe book. With its pink-and-white marshmallow skirt ballooning from the doll's waist, the cake is perfect.

'I love it! Acacia's going to be so happy!'

Acacia has never had a proper birthday cake before. I still can't believe it. A few days ago, when we were looking at the cookbook, dithering over which one to choose, I had a great idea.

'I know! If your mum bakes the doll cake, my mum can bake the fairytale castle cake. Then we'll both have the one we want.'

'Nah, Mum can't bake,' Acacia said. 'Last time she tried she nearly blew up the microwave.'

I try to imagine cooking a cake in anything but an oven but can't. 'Does she buy cakes for your birthday parties?'

'Never had any of those, either.'

'Cakes or parties?'

'Parties.' She didn't seem to care. 'Don't look so sad. You don't miss what you never had.'

That's why I let her choose the cake.

After breakfast, party preparations begin in earnest. Mum and Sal fill the fridge with food: big bowls of salad covered in cling wrap, trays of meat for the barbecue, coconut ice, frog-in-the-pond. Dad says there's enough to feed an army, but all the kids from the street are coming, as well as our extended family. Mum says it's better to have too much food than not enough.

Outside, Dad and Jim get to work. They set up the marquee and drag gear from the shed: camping tables, chairs, two dusty eskies. They hose down the chairs and tables and Turdle, sweep the verandahs, front and back. When I bring them glasses of water, they are blowing up pink and white balloons: Dad's cheeks are puffing like a blowfish, while Jim is tying the balloons together in groups. Every arrangement has a sausage balloon in the middle of two smaller round ones. Dad splutters his water everywhere when he notices.

'Let's hope your nan doesn't see that,' he tells us.

Half an hour before the guests arrive, Daryl comes over with bags of ice from the servo; they fill eskies with ice and soft drinks, then have a beer while Dad cleans the barbie. Mum and Rose carry plates loaded with chocolate crackles, coconut slice and curried egg sandwiches to the trestle table outside, while George supervises from the fence. Inside, me and Acacia make fairy bread.

'Does your mum teach you how to cook?' I ask casually, spreading margarine on white bread. Fairy bread is one of the first things I learnt to cook.

'Nah.' Acacia presses each slice margarine-side-down into a bowl of hundreds and thousands. She's never made fairy bread before. Then she cuts a slice in half. Two rectangles.

'Stop! What are you doing?' She stops cutting, eyes wide. 'Fairy bread is always triangles!'

'*Pfft*,' she scoffs. 'Why? It's going to taste the same, triangles or oblongs.'

'No, it won't! Do it this way.' I cut the bread in triangle quarters and, rolling her eyes, she does the same.

'Mum hates cooking,' she says after a moment, 'so I do most of it when it's just us. I'm really good at two-minute noodles and spaghetti on toast.' She licks hundreds and thousands from her fingers. 'Daryl's always on at her to cook chops and steak and stuff, so she cooks meat-and-veg when he's around.' A laugh. 'Her mashed potatoes are lumpy as my mattress.'

I'm not sure what to make of this, but there's no time to think about it. Smiddy has arrived early, and he has a birthday present for me.

Tossing my hair, like Sal does with Robbie, I try not to look too pleased.

'Mum, I want my hair short like Acacia.' My six-year-old cousin Melissa points at Acacia, who's playing totem tennis with Sal. I can't help rolling my eyes. An hour ago, Melissa was screaming her head off because she didn't win pass the parcel. Acacia won, but she gave the prize, a Fanta yo-yo, to my sooky-baby cousin. Since then, Melissa has followed Acacia around like she's a princess or something.

'You don't need a boy haircut,' my aunt says. 'You've got beautiful long hair, like little girls are supposed to.'

Says who? Half the girls in my class at school have short hair. 'Besides, Daddy likes your long hair. You don't want to make him sad if you cut it all off like a boy, do you?' My aunt smooths Melissa's hair. 'Boys like long hair, darling.'

What the heck? I like my aunt, but I have to say something.

'Acacia hasn't got a *boy* haircut,' I tell Melissa. If my aunt knew the full story about the nits, she'd lock my cousin in a tower, like Rapunzel. 'Who cares what boys think? Girls can have short hair if they want.'

'Yeah,' Melissa echoes. 'Girls can have short hair if they want. I want hair like Acacia. I want hair like Acacia. I want—'

My aunt gives me a filthy glare and I realise how similar she and Mum look. 'I'll thank you to mind your business, Jane,' she says, dragging Melissa away.

Across the table, Mum shakes her head at me. 'What?'

'You know what.'

'But I was sticking up for my friend. And it was true, what I said. Girls *can* have short hair. It's stupid to say girls can only have long hair!'

Standing next to me, she says quietly, 'Maybe so. But there's a time and place for challenging things and now's not it. Agreed?'

I don't agree. One thing I've learnt this summer is that if you don't challenge something unfair when it happens, you might as well not bother. But I don't want time out on my birthday, so I nod.

Turns out, Nan also has a big mouth, but grown-ups call that *speaking your mind.*

The whole afternoon, Rose and Daryl have been nuzzling like

lovebirds every chance they got, not caring that they were in public at a kids' birthday party and too old to be acting like teenagers. I watch Nan watching them, certain she'll disapprove because she's old. She loves to tell us kids what's proper and what's not, but this time she surprises me.

'Aren't you two sweet,' she says to Rose while Acacia and I are opening our presents. 'You look so much in love. I remember those days, before this one here lost all his hair.' Grinning, she pokes Pop with her elbow.

'Oi, watch it, old chook,' Pop retorts.

Rose laughs. 'Yes, Daz here is a keeper. I'm a lucky woman.' As she speaks, her hand drifts to her stomach. Mum has a funny look on her face.

'You'll be wanting to get married, what with a baby coming on,' Nan says.

What baby? Someone moves next to me. Acacia. I glance at her, but she doesn't notice. Her eyes are fixed on Rose's hand, the one cupping, patting, stroking a slightly curved belly.

My friend is shaking. 'You okay?' I whisper, my hand reaching for hers. She shakes it away, eyes fixed on her mother.

Rose nods in Daryl's direction. 'You'll have to tell him that,' she says to Nan while looking at her daughter.

'It's for the best, don't you think? Living in sin's probably not the best thing for little ones, now, is it? Oh, I suppose you all think I'm old-fashioned, but I'm old enough now to say it how I see it. Marriage first, then babies.'

'No!'

Stunned, I swing towards Acacia. So does everyone else at the party. Talking, laughing, eating, playing – it all stops, like a giant hand from above has reached down and flicked the party off. Turdle wanders over, nuzzles my hand, and looks up at me with worried eyes. Across the lawn, Daryl's smile is gone, his face blank.

Acacia's eyes are fixed on her mother in a death-stare; brows knotted, lips narrowed and quivering. She looks fierce and scared at the same time. Her mouth opens and for a split second I think she's going to back down.

She ruins the party instead.

'No! You can't marry him, Mum!' She whirls away from Rose, who is reaching out to her. 'Leave me alone!'

When the last guest is gone, Acacia finally comes out of hiding, acting like nothing happened, like she didn't scare everyone off with her outburst. Silently, she packs her presents into a laundry basket, folds up chairs and throws used paper plates and cups into the bin. I give her the silent treatment. I don't know what that was all about, and I don't want to. It's my birthday party and she behaved like a spoilt brat. Go home, I think. But each time I think the words, I mean them less. And by the time she asks if we can have a slumber party in the marquee, I've forgiven her.

I've never been to a slumber party. Mary Evans had one on her tenth and eleventh birthdays, but I wasn't invited, of course. I heard they stayed up all night and had a midnight feast like in *The Naughtiest Girl in the School*. And they made prank calls to strangers and asked, 'Is Mr Wall there? Is Mrs Wall there?' and when the person said no, they said, 'Well, if there are no walls, how does your roof stay up?'

More than anything, I want to experience a slumber party; looking at Acacia, I can tell that more than anything, she doesn't want to go home. And so, I convince Dad not to take down the marquee and Mum talks to Rose. As the light fades on our eleventh birthdays, we lie on patched blow-up mattresses and watch the stars flicker to life. The air smells of Aeroguard and charred meat. The ripe perfume of Mum's gardenias. Wet dirt and grass from melting ice and the hose. Questions zing back and forth; we whisper over the night sounds of humming crickets, whining mozzies, yowling cats, barking dogs, the soft hoo-hoo of an owl. We talk until our mouths are dry. About school starting soon. What we want to be when we grow up: me, a famous writer; Acacia, a doctor. The only thing we don't mention is Acacia's tantrum.

'When do you think we'll get bras?'

'What's the one place you want to visit one day?'

'What would you do if you won Lotto?'

'Do you believe in God?'

And, over a not-quite-midnight feast of leftover birthday cake, I finally spill the beans about Smiddy: 'I *like* like him.'

Acacia giggled. 'I know. You go all gooey when you see him.'

'I do *not*.'

'Do too.' In the dark, she makes wet kissing sounds. But now that I'm eleven, kissing doesn't seem so revolting after all.

'I'm never having a boyfriend,' Acacia says.

'One day you will.' I feel like a big sister, wise and all-knowing.

'No. Never.'

'Maybe when—'

'Nope.'

'How do you know? People change. Things change. You can't see the future.'

'I know what I know. And I don't like *boys*.'

I feel as if I've missed something important, but what it is I'm not certain.

Listening to her breathing slow and deepen, I wonder again why Acacia always seems to be a step ahead of me when it comes to understanding the world.

CHAPTER FORTY-TWO

1980

'It's not fair!'

'I'll tell you what's not fair. Starving children in Africa, that's what.'

Mum and I face off in the living room, reflecting each other with our crossed arms and lips pressed in white lines. She's being stubborn. She won't let me go to the Nepean River weir for a swim. I glare at her, wishing she would listen, not lecture. When Jim said he was going with his friends earlier, all Mum said was *don't go to the mud baths* and *be back in time for dinner*. Sal and her friends go nearly every weekend in summer because teenagers can do what they want. I'm eleven now and I want what they have – freedom to go further than the streets around our house, further than the library.

The weir is the second most popular swimming spot around, after the pools. It's been popular since the olden days. Dad used to swim there when he was a kid. He got stuck in the mud baths on the other side once. It was life-threatening if you believe his million-times exaggerated version. Thanks to him, Mum never lets us go to that side of the weir.

'Please, Mum?'

'I told you. You're not old enough to go by yourself.' Mum picks a piece of fluff from her blue-and-white flowered blouse. The tag is sticking out behind her neck, but I'm too annoyed to tell her.

'But Jim will be there, so I won't be alone.'

'No means no.'

I hang my head, knowing that Mum's next words will be *one more word and you can stay inside the rest of the day.*

'You're ruining my life,' I mutter when I think she's far enough away.

'What was that?'

'Nothing!'

'Hmph. For a second there, I thought Sal was in the room.'

I stomp outside and swing back and forth on a tree branch as Jim and Smiddy tear down the street on their bikes. *It's because I'm a girl,* I think. *If I were a boy, Mum would have let me go.* A sharp gust of wind makes the branch creak and I drop to the ground before it drops me. Seconds later, George flies into the tree. I call him. Maybe I can tell him my problems, like I suspect Acacia does. He turns his back.

I'm still worked up when Acacia comes over. Straight away, she starts talking to George in a baby voice and he chatters back. I feel like I'm in the schoolyard, invisible Jane No Friends.

'It's so unfair!' I blurt out. They finally stop ignoring me and listen to my tale of woe. 'Girls always get treated differently to boys,' I continue. 'And boys always get to do things girls can't, like go places without having a grown-up around. It's not *fair.*'

'I reckon girls can do anything boys can.' Acacia flicks a clover flower at me. Up in the tree, right above my head, George makes a noise that sounds suspiciously like a laugh.

'No, they can't.' I move out of George's firing range.

'Yes, they can. They can be doctors. And police officers. I reckon they could even be mechanics. I saw a girl mechanic once. I'm thinking of being one instead of a doctor.'

'Yeah, but they can't go to the weir when they're eleven.' She can't argue with that.

Acacia tilts her head, considering. One second. Two. 'Yes, they can.' She stands. 'Come on.'

'What?'

'The weir. Let's go! I've never been and now I'm going to.'

'Are you kidding me? We'll never get away with it.' But I want to. The idea excites and scares the heck out of me at the same time. 'I don't know how to get there.'

'We'll figure it out. Come on!' Her face is shining. 'But ... how ... what ... what will I tell Mum?'

'Tell her we're going for a bike ride to the big park.'

'But ... what about your mum? And what will we eat? And—'

'But, but, but,' she mimics in a high voice. 'Mum's asleep. Don't worry. Ask your mum if we can take some sammidges with us for a picnic at the park. Easy-peasy. If the boys can do it, so can we.'

'Fine. Put your cozzies on under your clothes. I'll get the food.'

The plan works better than expected. Within twenty minutes, Acacia and I are on our bikes, cozzies on, baskets loaded with cheese-and-tomato sandwiches, bottles of lime cordial, Granny Smith apples and old beach towels. We pedal down the street faster than Mum can have second thoughts.

At the milk bar, I pull on my best innocent face. 'Mr Lee, will you help us? We're going to the weir with Jim and Smiddy, but they took off and we don't know the way.'

This strategy works too, like Acacia said it would. 'Straight down to High Street, turn left and go all the way down that road to the river, then turn right along the river and follow the path to the reserve. Can't miss it.'

We follow his directions, legs pumping furiously, round and round, up and down. Hair slaps our faces, sticking to the sweat on our forehead and cheeks; we don't care, just swipe it back with one hand and keep going, ignoring the *are we there yet?* and *how much longer?* thoughts that go round-round with every wheel revolution. I push down lurking thoughts of Mum that get stronger the closer we get to the weir. I can't let her spoil this adventure – I'm going to show her that I can be trusted to go to the weir by myself, that nothing bad will happen.

Finally, we're there. We ditch our bikes, shed our T-shirts and shorts, and run full pelt to the weir. The first leap into the water, the airborne second between the step and the landing, the first rush of sensation as cold water meets hot skin – this is freedom like I've never experienced and probably never will again.

'Jane! Acacia! What are you doing here?' At the sound of Smiddy's voice, I blush and duck my shoulders under the water. The fizzy feeling is back, watered down with guilt.

Before I can answer, Jim asks the same question, but his tone is less friendly.

'Mum said we could,' I fib, crossing my fingers under the water. 'She said you and Smiddy would keep an eye on us.'

The boys exchange glances. 'Liar,' Jim says slowly. 'No way she would've said that without telling me. You're dead meat.'

My body tenses under the water, but I'm pretty sure he won't tell. He knows I've got something on him.

'Don't tell, Jim,' Acacia says, patting his arm. She'd clambered onto the weir beside him during our heated exchange. 'We wanted to have an adventure. Please?' I stare at her. She looks like a younger version of Rose. The hair is different, of course, and her bony body is dripping with river water, but there's something about the way she's tilting her head sideways and talking that is pure Rose.

I have a feeling she knows exactly what she's doing.

Jim reddens. To me, he says, 'You owe me. Big time. And if you get caught, I've got nothing to do with it, 'kay?'

'Thanks, Jim, you're ace,' Acacia says, looking deep into his eyes.

He jumps in the water and swims a few metres away. 'Yeah,

well … fine. But don't hang around too close. You'll cramp my style. And you have to leave when we do.'

Whooping with joy, Acacia swings her arm around, scooping water in a wide arc that peaks in my face. I splash her back, giving as good as I get; we don't stop until our arms tire and our bellies ache from laughing.

'Let's try the mud baths.' I don't know who says it. Her. Me. Maybe both of us.

Across the weir, thick mud squelches between our toes. Acacia's delight is contagious, pushing Dad's mud-sucking story to the furthest corners of my mind. She plonks herself down, laughing, smearing gunky paste over her face and body, her bubbling laughter infectious.

We cover ourselves in cool mud and bask in the sun until the mud dries and cracks on our skin. My mind flashes to a documentary I watched at Nan's: an initiation, a sacred ceremony. That's what this feels like. Clay-covered and laughing, we jump in the water to wash off the mud, before starting all over again.

If only Mum could see us now. There's no danger in this, I'd tell her, only fun.

And then my stomach cramps, way down low. If Mum finds out about this, she'll … freak out. Lecture me for an hour, two hours, eternity. Ground me until the end of the holidays.

Ban me from seeing Acacia ever again.

Hot bile gathers in the back of my throat. Acacia, mud-covered and happy, looks like she doesn't have a care in the world; I care so much about what others think, it makes me feel sick. When she's looking the other way, I spit the burning mouthful into the mud, jump back into the river, wash myself clean.

How do I tell her we made a mistake? She'll think I'm a scaredy-cat. Worse. A baby.

'I'm hungry,' Acacia says.

We head across the weir, back to our bikes and picnic. The cordial is warm, but the sugary sweetness eases the bitter taste in my mouth. I slurp it down, reach into the bicycle basket for a sandwich, squeal at a queasy tickle on my hand, up my arm. The bread falls to the grass as I leap up, swiping at my skin like it's on fire.

Acacia looks puzzled. 'What are you doing?'

'Ants. In my sandwich.'

'Ew.' Acacia inspects the rest of the sandwiches, throws them in a heap on the grass. A hovering crow bravely snatches up a slice of bread with a satisfied caw. In a dead tree behind us, a murder of crows watches.

Shivering, I pull my towel tight around my shoulders. Nan says crows are bad luck. Mum says that's superstitious nonsense, but right now, I believe Nan.

Acacia tosses me an apple. 'Here.' She crunches into her own apple, wincing at the tart bite; the bad-luck crow cocks its head before continuing to tear apart our discarded lunch. Another crow lands nearby but keeps its distance, white eyes fixed on us. For the first time, I wish George was hanging around.

My stomach cramps again. It must be hunger. I gnaw at my apple until only a skinny core remains. Spitting out a seed, I toss my core over my shoulder. Seconds later, it boomerangs onto my back.

'Watch where you're throwing your rubbish, Chubba.'

CHAPTER FORTY-THREE

SEEDLING

There's a scene in the movie *Jerry Maguire* where Tom Cruise is in the car belting out 'Free Fallin'. He's free, he's in a good place, he's moving on. When we were newlyweds, we sang that song at the top our voices every time it came on the car radio, drumming on the steering wheel and dashboard like we were Jerry/Tom Cruise, young and free.

After I moved into the share house, every day felt like free falling. Like I'd jumped from a plane with no parachute. At least at the refuge I had support. Here, I was on my own with four strangers who loved Tom Cruise and his flashy white smile.

I still can't listen to that song.

Not long after I moved in, I started a journal (Pat's idea). Every morning before work I'd write down what I was feeling. No filter, Pat said. Easier than it sounds, I said when she asked how I was going. It took me months to write from my truth. I was petrified someone would find my journal and read it, so I censored everything I wrote. Kept the rest – the unedited, unfiltered truth – deep inside. And before I left for work, I shoved that journal (a cheap exercise book from Kmart) as far under my mattress as my arm could reach.

You can leave a life behind, but when you're a woman like me, paranoia follows you into the new one like a creeping shadow. For a time, it felt like the shadow was stronger than me. Living in that house made me realise I'd come so far but had further to go.

After I left him, I was always looking over my shoulder. Scanning the environment, wherever I was – a room, a shop, wherever – because I wanted to know one thing. Is it safe?

Is *he* there?

It amped up when I first moved out of the refuge – there were no alarms, no padlocked gates to blunt my need to be on red alert every single second. So, I was constantly watching like a cat at the window: tail twitching, nose quivering, back shivering. Jumpy. Itchy. Tingly. Seeing him here, there, everywhere. In the shape of his head, the way he held himself, the unmistakable voice. And before I could think it through, a chill would rush over my body, and I had to get away now.

In those moments, I would have leapt as high as the clouds if someone whispered *boo*.

One time I saw him standing in a random front yard when I was driving to work. A cold, tingly feeling shivered under, over, across my skin. What was he doing there? Whose house was that? How did he know I drove this way? And then I realised it wasn't him because he was in the four-wheel drive behind me, following so close his breath was burning my skin. My mind went into overdrive: turn down here, see if he follows, ohmygod he did, what do I do now? When you see chase scenes in a movie, it kind of looks fun, especially if you're the one who gets to say *follow that car*, but in real life, it's the opposite of fun. You feel like you're one step closer to eternity.

It wasn't him that time.

Or most of the times I saw him. Thought I saw him.

He was everywhere and nowhere at once.

I was good at controlling it. Most people would have missed the cues unless they knew what to look for. Most people didn't see my eyes darting side to side wherever I went. And if they did, they probably wrote me off as one of the many drug-or-alcohol-scrambled nutcases who lived in the area. No one knew their true stories either.

I saw him in the supermarket the other day. He was with another woman (she looked a bit like me, same hair, same shape), pushing a trolley down the cereal aisle towards me. I spotted him first – I could have backed away, but I pushed on. Our eyes met; his eyes were no longer cold. In them, I saw something new: fear. It would have been so easy to expose him. I said hello instead. And as we talked (two minutes, max) I realised that somewhere along the way, I'd stopped missing him. Stopped loving him. I was doing okay.

Free but no longer falling.

The body takes longer to let go.

Even now, there are moments when the iciness freezes my veins; a shiver still runs through every cell in my body.

CHAPTER FORTY-FOUR

1980

S hane Watters. Squinting into the sun, I peer up at him. He's backed up by five or six boys I don't recognise. Some have smokes hanging from their lips. The cold shiver returns. That look in his eyes. My skin bristles as if ants are still crawling over my body. 'Surprised to see you here on your own,' he says to me.

'We're not.' Our eyes make contact. I look away first.

'We're here with Jim,' Acacia says. 'Bugger off.' Standing up, she's tiny compared to him, but strangely unbreakable. How does she do that? Appear strong and fragile at once?

'Looky here. It's the skinhead. Guys, check it out.'

A red-haired boy moves in. 'Are you a boy or a girl?' He high-fives Shane.

Another says, 'No boobs ... no hair ... let's see. Skinhead must be ... a boy.'

Relentless stares. Chortling laughter. Taunting voices: *skinhead, boobless, chubby, ugly.*

Wincing, I huddle under my towel; Acacia, on the other hand, stares them down. She looks like a twig in a storm, all by herself. I know I should back her up, but I don't know if I have it in me.

I'm freaking out. This isn't my aunt making silly comments about girls having long hair. This is Shane Watters.

But I must try or, when I look in the mirror tonight, I won't like what I see. A coward. And so, I heave myself to my feet, wishing my still-damp cozzies weren't clinging to my body.

'Get l—' I start, my voice small and quivering. As if my tongue is tied in a knot.

'Get what? Telling *me* what to do, Chubba?'

'Don't call me that.'

'I'll call you what I like.' His voice is hard. 'You know what I reckon? I reckon you're not supposed to be here at all, Jane Kelly. And I reckon you don't want your mum to find out you've nicked off down here with your skinhead lezzo mate.'

'Get lost, Shane.' Even as the words slip out, my insides lurch. From the corner of my eye, I see the other boys move closer, forming a loose circle around us. A pack of dogs.

'Make me.' He looms over me, pokes me in the shoulder. His hot breath grazes my ear. It stinks of cigarettes and unbrushed teeth.

'Oi, Shane!' He swings around and Acacia knees him in the nuts. 'She told you to get lost, ya dickhead.'

'Shit!' His face crumples in pain; he clutches at his groin, gasping. 'Bitch! You'll pay for that.' In a strangled voice, 'Get their bikes. See how they get home without them.'

'No!' We bolt towards our bikes, but Shane's mates block us, forming a shifting wall of arms and legs, laughing as we dodge and duck and twist and yell. Two boys snatch up the bikes, hold them out of reach.

'Shall we throw the bikes in the river or in the mud?' Recovered now, Shane is back in control. 'What d'you reckon, Chubba? Mud or water? You choose.'

'None,' Acacia spits out, face beet red. 'Leave our bikes alone!'

He ignores her. 'Mud. Or. Water?'

There's no way out. He won't stop until I decide, but my mind is jumbled: *shouldn't have come my new bike Mum was right where's Jim mud or water.* Acacia is yelling and swearing, and Shane keeps saying mud or water and—

'Oi! Put the bikes down.'

Jim. My brother pushes in front of us, puffing heavily, river water puddling around his feet. Hands gently propel us away from the group. Smiddy. We pull our shorts and T-shirts on, eyes fixed on the boys.

'Stay out of it, Jimbo. We're just joking around.'

'No one's laughing. Bugger off away from them, all of you.' My brother's voice rises.

Shane smirks, puffs out his chest. Size-wise, he has the edge, and he knows it. 'You and whose army?'

Jim looks over his shoulder. Another group of boys, puffing and dripping wet, has gathered. 'You heard me,' he addresses Shane's mates. 'Drop the bikes.'

Shane's mates waver, eyes darting up-down-around: *whatdowedo, whatdowedo?*

'Need help?' Smiddy's voice is mild, but they scatter like frightened sheep, bikes thudding to the ground. Acacia races over, wheels her bike to safety. After the briefest hesitation, I follow suit. Shove towels and drink bottles into the basket.

I need to get out of here. Now. I've brought this on us. If I hadn't fussed, hadn't whinged, hadn't gone along with Acacia's crazy idea, this wouldn't be happening. *My fault, my fault*: the words loop endlessly, a scratched record.

But Jim's next words freeze me to the spot.

'Don't mess with my sister. Or her friend. You hear me? Stay away from them.'

'Gonna make me?'

'If I have to.'

Their eyes lock, engaged in a battle I suspect will end their friendship. Fists clench, unclench. Nostrils flare. My eyes close. Can't watch.

'Whatever ya reckon. Just jokes, anyway,' Shane says. My eyes snap open. 'Stupid girls can't take a joke. You know what they're like.'

Jim snorts and in that moment, he looks almost a man, not a thirteen-year-old boy. 'If you think it's funny to bully girls, you're a bigger dickwad than I thought.'

Shane's mouth works like he wants to say something smart but hasn't got the brains. Then his eyes narrow. Jim's lost a second-best friend and gained an enemy.

'You'll keep,' he grunts, casting a filthy glare at the sheep watching from a distance. He walks a few steps towards them, then turns to Acacia. 'Your mother's a moll. Gets what she deserves.'

Acacia lunges for him. Smiddy and I grab her by the arms. She's shaking so hard I think she'll explode. Or is it me shaking? My eyes squeeze tight. *Ignore him, ignore him.*

Raised voices. Threats. A scuffle.

Thump.

Thump.

When I crack open my eyes, Shane is gone. Jim drops to the ground next to me. His right eye is red, swollen. He'll have a shocker of a bruise tonight. He breathes deeply, in-out, in-out, then takes my hand.

'Let's go home,' he says.

CHAPTER FORTY-FIVE

1980

'Where. Have. You. Girls. Been?' Bullets squeeze through gritted teeth.

'At the p—'

'Don't even try to put one over me, Jane Patricia Kelly. Don't even *try*.' Mum barely glances at Acacia. 'Acacia, your mum's looking for you.'

'Sorry, Mrs Kelly. It was my—'

'Mum—' Jim skids to a halt beside us.

Mum holds up her hand. 'Acacia, go home. Jim, I need to talk to your sister.'

'But Mum—' he tries again, as Acacia slinks home, her bike squeaking in protest.

'Later.' She holds the screen door open. 'Inside. Living room.' The door shuts.

Five, four, three, two, one …

'What. Were. You. Thinking?' And she's off, voice rising and fall- ing, like a mighty wave rolling in. There's no stopping her. 'Do you have any idea how worried I was? I've been up and down the street, knocking on doors, looking for you for two hours.

Two hours! You could have been hit by a car. Worse! You could have been kidnapped!'

I'm pretty sure they're both bad outcomes.

Jim shoots me a resigned look. Mouths *I'll be back*. As Mum continues her tirade, I hear his rapid movements: toilet flushing, tap running, freezer opening.

'Were you at the park like you said? No. You were not at the park. And when I checked the milk bar, do you know what I heard? No. I'll tell you what I heard. That nice Mr Lee told me you asked for directions to the weir. The weir! The exact place I said you could not go! But did you listen? No. You did not. You could have drowned!'

I'm trembling. Not with fear, but with all the words that are bursting to get out, burning my throat. On the way home, I'd decided not to tell anyone about Shane Watters, to pretend it never happened and stay out of his way.

I meant to warn Jim not to say anything either, but I didn't have the chance. Now, the more Mum goes on about how scared she was, the more I remember how scared I was. My eyes feel gritty as I hold back tears, words, memories. I want her to stop talking. I've got to get away before everything bursts out.

'I was so worried, Jane.' Her voice cracks.

'Sorry, Mum.' The dam breaks. I bawl, cough, splutter until my nose drips onto my knees. Mum wraps her arms around me, holding me close until the sobs ease, pushing hair back from my face. She thinks I'm crying because I got caught.

I'm not.

'Mum?' Jim comes to stand beside us. He's holding a bag of frozen peas, wrapped in a tea towel, over his eye.

'What, Jim? Can't you see I'm—' She gasps. 'What in God's name happened to your eye?'

'That's what I've been trying to tell you. I got in a fight with Shane. He was bullying Jane and Acacia again.'

Mum looks from Jim to me and back again. 'Let me look.'

After a second, she turns back to me. 'Now, tell me exactly what happened.'

'Shane was mean to us, and he called Acacia a skinhead and told his friends to throw our bikes in the river or the mud and I had to choose—'

'Slow down, Jane.' Mum puts up a hand. 'Breathe.'

I sniff. Take a tissue from the box Mum is holding. Blow once, twice. 'And then Jim stopped him, and Shane said something disgusting about Acacia's mum and it's all my—' Tears grip me once more and I fall into Mum's arms. Her heartbeat, strong and loud against my ear, calms me: *I'm-here, I'm-here, I'm-here.*

After a minute, Mum lets go. 'Look at the state of you; you're exhausted. Go on, wash your face, have a lie down. I'll get to the bottom of this with Jim.'

'But what's going to happen? Will you punish me?'

Her eyes move towards Jim, who's looking at his eye in the reflection of the telly. 'We'll talk about it later.' Then, whispering, 'But I think you've been punished enough.'

I'm too tired to feel relief.

When I wake, the shadows are long and golden light is filtering through a gap in the curtains. Sal's work clothes are draped over her chair and her handbag is lying sideways on her bed, its contents spilling out onto the bedspread. My stomach gurgles. It's seven-thirty. The last thing I ate was the apple that set Shane off. The reminder shivers me into a ball.

'Jane?'

I unfurl like a jack-in-the-box. 'I didn't hear you come in.'

'You were out like a light.' She switches on the light, sits at her dressing table. 'Mum saved you some dinner. Pineapple chicken and rice.'

I'm almost out the door, when Sal says, 'You missed all the drama while you were snoring away.'

'Drama? What drama? Did Dad do his nut?'

'Well, you know how Jim got in a fight with Shane ...'

'I was there.'

'Well, Shane copped a black eye and a fat lip. So, Mrs Watters had words with Mum out on the street, everyone could hear her. Said Jim better stay away from Shane or else.'

'Or else what? Shane was the one—'

'I know, I know. Jim and Acacia told me all about it. Don't worry. Dad sorted Mrs Watters out. Said he'd set the police on Shane if he came near you girls again. Said Shane was banned from playing with Jim. Then Smiddy's parents got involved, said the same. Biggest drama we've had on this street since Rose and Daryl ... well, you know.' Sal riffles through her lipsticks, then chooses a frosted peach one. 'Oh, Dad wants to talk to you after you've eaten.'

Jim's watching telly in the living room. He gives me a little wave when I walk past. The kitchen is dark. I find my dinner in the fridge, covered in alfoil. I don't know how long to heat it for, so I don't bother. At the table, I pick chicken off the bones, but leave the rest. Eating alone isn't much fun. Eating alone when you're upset or worried is worse. Your thoughts get in the way, squeezing your throat, tensing your belly. I push the plate away, counting the results of today's events. Shane Watters and Jim are enemies now. Mum and Mrs Watters too. Dad wants to talk to me, and I'm probably grounded until school starts.

Standing, I empty my dinner into the bin and dump my plate in the sink. I can hear Mum and Dad out the back, their voices floating through the rustling fly streamers. Words I can't make out at first slowly filter in – *bad influence, troublemaker, stay away, not welcome* – and then I'm filled with alarm. I expected consequences, but not losing Acacia.

Turdle spots me first. Tail swinging like a skipping rope, he plants a slobbery kiss on my hand. He follows me all the way to the cane outside chairs, where Mum and Dad are relaxing, having a beer, or in Mum's case, a shandy. They exchange looks, then Mum gets up.

'I'll leave you to it,' she says to Dad. A shoulder squeeze, two little pats, a smile as she passes. I wish she was staying out here. When we're in trouble, Dad doesn't chat. He yells.

'Come here and sit down beside your old Dad.' He pats the chair next to him. He sounds calm, but I'm still wary. I perch on the edge. Wait. If he yells, I'm ready to run.

'Now, your mum said you've had a good telling off already,' he says, brows gathered close, like he's thinking hard. I hold my breath. 'And I don't see the sense in another long lecture. You've been punished enough, seems to me.' My breath whooshes out, but he's not finished. 'You nearly gave your mum a heart attack. I don't ever want to hear her so worked up like she was this afternoon. Ever. You hear me?'

'Yes, Dad.' A tiny voice, squeezed by shame. Turdle nuzzles at my hand. Licks it.

'You will never disappear like that again without your mum or me knowing where you are. Understand? I won't have kids of mine sneaking around behind our backs.'

'Yes, Dad.' Dad is looking at me, like he's trying to decide if he's said enough or there's more to come. 'Sorry, Dad.'

'Well. That's all I'm going to say about it.' He leans back, drains the last of his beer. 'Look, Puddin', a shooting star. Did you see that?'

Moving to the steps, I peer up at the sky. The shooting star is gone, but a million stars gaze down on me, glittering eyes in the sky. Dad and Turdle join me. We sit side by side, watching the stars, the cool end of the day breathing across our skin. Out the front, Sal calls *See ya*. Robbie's panel van putters down the road. In the distance, muffled night noises sing out of tune: traffic, sirens, a car horn blast, a distant train.

'Dad?' I say after a long silence. 'It wasn't Acacia's fault today.

She's not a bad influence. She's a good friend. Please don't ban me from seeing her.'

'Huh? Where'd you get that idea?'

'I heard you and Mum talking about her when I was eating dinner.' His cheeks puff. 'We were talking about Shane Watters, not your Acacia.'

Oh, the relief, how it tingles my body. 'Sorry, Dad.' I snuggle close, breathing his sweaty-salty Dad smell. Pushing away the rogue thought poking, prodding, needling at me: *It's not fair.*

Anyone would say I've been let off lightly. That I'm lucky not to cop a punishment for disobeying Mum. And I am lucky, I know this as Dad's arm rests over my shoulders and Mum brings me a bowl of Neapolitan ice cream. But a tiny seed of resentment has sprouted and won't die. Sal's been sneaking out at night for months. Jim was smoking and looking at dirty magazines with Shane. Why did *I* get caught?

CHAPTER FORTY-SIX

1980

I can't believe it. Dad has busted Sal sneaking out. He's gone ballistic – yelling and carrying on in the middle of the night. Did I jinx her?

I sit up, squinting in the dark. The sound of yelling pulled me out of a dream about climbing the wattle tree and finding a magical land. I was completely out of it, tuckered out after a long day of back-to-school shopping with Mum. It took a few groggy minutes to work out that it wasn't coming from next door, but the other end of our house. The living room.

They're really going hammer and tongs. Pulling on my nightie, I stick my head out the door. Jim's listening from his doorway, wearing nothing but Batman undies. He shifts into the shadow when he sees me and raises his finger to his lips. The words are disjointed: *sneaking out, dare you, how long, curfew*. I creep down the hall, hide in the recess leading to the toilet. Jim follows seconds later, a white singlet now covering his chest.

'I'll tell you something for nothing, I'll give that boy what-for if he noses around here again after curfew.'

'He's not *that* boy,' Sal yells back. 'He's my boyfriend and his name's Robbie and I *love* him.'

'I couldn't care less if his name was John bloody Travolta!' Dad roars. 'You're *my* daughter and my daughter doesn't go sneaking around at night with any boy, whatever his bloody name is.'

'Trev,' Mum cuts in. 'Calm—'

'I will *not* calm down. How can you stand there while your daughter's running around all over town with some hoodlum in a panel van? A panel van, mind you. You know what they're bloody called, don't you?'

Beside me, Jim snorts and whispers, 'Yeah, shaggin' wagon.'

'What's a sh—'

Shhh! He raises his finger to his lips again. 'He's not a hoodlum!'

'He is if he's got a panel van and he's sneaking around with my daughter! You're bloody grounded until you're eighteen, you are, Sal.'

'You can't do that!'

'I can and I will. While you're under my roof—'

'Trevor Francis Kelly, listen to me.' Mum usually saves that voice for us kids. 'You'll wake the neighbours. The Jones's light has already gone on. See? Do you want the whole street thinking we're like you-know-who next door? *Do* you? No. Let's talk about this in the morning. Sal, you go off to bed.'

'You're still bloody grounded,' Dad calls after my sister, who stomps past without seeing me and Jim.

'Oh, Trev ...'

'You're ruining my life!' Sal slams our door so hard the toilet door rattles.

Back in our room, I find Sal lying on top of her sheets, facing the wall, crying.

'What happened, Sal?' I feel for her shoulder in the dark. 'Leave me alone!'

'Geez. Sorry for breathing.' Hurt, I climb onto my bed and

turn my back on her. Sometimes you try to be nice, but you get mean in return.

I hear her sit up. Wait for an apology.

'Did you dob me in?'

'No! It wasn't *me*.' Rolling over, I hiss, 'And it wasn't Jim either. I can't believe—'

She says nothing, and I roll away again. Anger breathes out in waves. Why did she accuse me of dobbing? I kept her secret, even though I disagreed with her actions. All I did was warn her she'd get caught if she kept on with it. Sure, it was unfair that I got busted yesterday. But I didn't dob her in to save my skin. I roll onto my back. Kick the sheet off. Wrench open the window. Why is it so hot in here?

Mum says the truth always comes out in the end. Sal's only got herself to—

'Sorry, Jane,' my sister says in a low, trembly voice. 'It's not your fault I got busted. I … I really needed to talk to him tonight.' She starts to cry again, softly now. Whispering to herself. I think I hear the word *trouble*.

Above me, the ceiling fan hums. Tonight, it's hypnotic, draining my anger away. I fall asleep thinking that growing up is a lot harder than it looks.

The next morning, Dad's in a foul mood, snapping at anyone who looks at him sideways. Even Turdle cops a tongue-lashing when Dad finds a fresh hole in the grass under the clothesline. Jim and I are desperate to escape, but not dumb enough to try. There are only two ways to deal with Dad when he's in a mood like this – one, keep out of his way, and two, do jobs without being asked. Use our initiative. Jim baths Turdle. Mum covers my new school exercise books with brown paper; I write my name on each one in fancy letters and decorate them with stickers, pushing away thoughts of facing Mary Evans in Year 6. The clock is ticking away the summer holidays faster than I want.

Sal refuses to get up. Whenever I go into the bedroom, she fakes sleep. I used to do that when I was in the car, because I wanted Dad to carry me inside. To be close to him. Sal's faking sleep to avoid him. It's driving Dad nuts.

'She up yet?' Dad fills a glass with water, chugs it down. Another glass. He's hot and sweaty from mowing the back lawn. His dirty sock smell wrinkles my nose. Plonking the glass down, wiping his forehead on his singlet, he gives Mum a questioning look. With his sunburnt nose, he reminds me of a laughing clown at the Penrith Show. Except he's not laughing.

'Not yet,' Mum says, looking up from the book covering. He clomps away, swiping the fly streamers roughly.

Outside, the mower roars back into life.

'She up yet?' he asks after trimming the edges.

'She up yet?' he wants to know after sweeping and hosing.

Finally, Dad says *enough is enough*. Thumps on the bedroom door. 'Get yourself out here, Sal. On the double.'

Moments later, the toilet flushes, and Sal appears. She's still in her nightie, hair a sticky-up mess; her face is as sour as the smell hovering around her. Dad sends me outside with the warning: *keep your ears to yourself*.

After lunch, when I ask Sal what happened, she tells me to mind my beeswax. All I can get out of her is that she's not grounded; she's going to the movies with Robbie tonight. I have no idea how she did it. Jim reckons it's special women's magic, whatever that means.

The uncomfortable feeling lingers all afternoon. Sal keeps to herself and bolts the second Robbie's panel van pulls up. Me and Jim stay on our best behaviour, but a few times I hear Mum and Dad bickering. Even Acacia is in a strange, distracted mood when she comes over. Has the atmosphere in our house rubbed off on her? I'm fine, she tells me. I don't believe her, but

I've got too much going on in my own house to ask more questions.

I'm getting a drink of milk after dinner when I hear Mum and Dad arguing about us kids. They think me and Jim are watching telly, and so they're out on the verandah with a beer (Dad) and a shandy (Mum), the way they do most summer nights.

'Stop worrying about that lot next door, Barb. It's settled now. Worry about what's going on in your own home,' Dad says. 'Sal's running around at all hours with that boy and lollygagging the day away, and Jane needs to tame her mouth. You coddle her too much.'

By now, I'm crouching in a dusty corner of the laundry. My mouth pops open. The only thing stopping me from marching out there and setting Dad straight is what might happen if I do.

'Sal's not *running around* with him, as you so delicately put it,' Mum says, an edge to her voice. I imagine her eyes glinting like ice in the fading light. 'Or *that boy*. Robbie's her boyfriend and has been for a year. And Jane is growing up and trying to figure out how things work. She's worried about her friend.'

'Hmph.' A chair creaks.

'Of course, Jim is perfect,' Mum continues, the edge sharper now. 'Never does *any*thing wrong.'

'I never said that.' Now Dad's voice is edgy, like he's getting ready for an argument. For the first time in weeks, I wonder if we'll get The Divorce. It's clear the three of us are too much of a handful.

'You implied it. You might want to have a chat with our son about respecting his sisters. And me. God knows I've tried, but his attitude's getting worse. I don't want him growing up to be like that Shane Watters.'

'He's nothing like that cretin! What are you on about, Barb? You heard what he did for his sister the other day. He's still got a black eye!'

'He's been smoking. I smelt it on him the other day. Found

cigarettes in his room. And a *Playboy* magazine. You should have heard the way he reacted. I didn't tell you at the time because—'

A sigh explodes from him. 'Chrissake, Barb.' The scrape of chair legs on concrete. Heavy footsteps pacing. 'Jim's testing his boundaries. He's being a boy.'

'That's right, boys will be boys. God, I hate that saying. I never want to hear it again.'

A long silence. My feet have pins and needles. I should move … I need to move. But I stay put, hugging myself tight. Mum says silence is golden, that sometimes it's better not to say anything at all. I reckon that when people argue they only stay silent long enough to work out what to say. Half the time they spit out the first words that come to mind, going round and round in circles like tumbleweed on the sand.

Mum starts again. 'So, *girls* can't test their boundaries, is that what you're saying? Sal can't. Jane can't. I can't even say I want a job without you getting your back up.'

'It's not the same.'

'It *is*, Trev. It is.'

The phone rings. I have three seconds to get back in the kitchen and pretend to drink freshly poured milk before Mum rushes in. It's a wrong number. She thumps the receiver down, then gives me a sharp look.

'One of these days,' she says, 'you'll realise that eavesdropping does more harm than good. You never hear the full story.'

CHAPTER FORTY-SEVEN

SAPLING

By the time I moved out of the shared house, I was well and truly ready to be on my own. It took nine months all up to get a housing commission place. Nine months of keeping myself to myself. Nine months of preparing to birth the new you, Pat said. She came up with some weird stuff sometimes, but I got the drift. Moving into your own place is critical to recovery.

When I was little, I thought parents picked babies out of the sky: *I'll have this one, she's cute.* Got that notion teased out of me in the first year of school. You can't choose where you're born. Can't choose your family, or what happens to it. Trying to control every aspect of life is a waste of time and energy. But I told Pat, if I could have chosen where I'd be reborn, I wouldn't have picked a housing commission dump on struggle street. A musty two-up, two-down with paint peeling from grimy walls, cockroaches scuttling underfoot, holes in the walls and cupboard doors dangling from broken hinges. It was worse than I imagined but beggars can't be choosers.

Pat helped me give the place a good top-to-bottom scrub. It was late winter. Cold and pouring rain, but we opened the windows to release stale energy and burnt incense I bought in a two-dollar shop. The sweet, woody smell of Nag Champa filled the house and seeped into my clothes, but it was only ever a cover-up, like spraying Impulse under your arms in a high school changeroom. No matter how often I burnt the incense, I could never completely remove the wet dog smell in the carpet and the cigarette smell layered in the walls. Here's one thing I know about being poor. The sour stink of poverty gets under your skin, no matter how hard you scrub.

Something else got under my skin the day Pat helped me move in. We were cleaning the kitchen, 'Don't Call Me Baby' was on the radio and I was telling her about my ex. You think I'm stupid, falling for a bloke like that, I said, looking away so I didn't see the truth on her face.

No, she said. I think you're strong. You got away. And you will rise stronger than ever, like Scarlett O'Hara.

Turned out *Gone With the Wind* was her favourite movie of all time. Mine too. I used to watch it with Mum. My favourite scene is where Scarlett rises from the ground after losing everything, shakes her fist at the heavens, and vows never to go hungry again. She's like a phoenix rising from the ashes: reborn, battle-scarred, beautiful. When Pat said I would rise strong, I imagined myself as Scarlett. I reckon I was like her when I was little. Wilful and spoilt – until my parents split, leaving Mum on a pension. Everything changed, including me. Anyway, while Pat unpacked another box, I leapt onto the second-hand sofa I found in the Trading Post, shook my fist at the roof and said: As God is my witness, as God is my witness, I'm going to get through this. I don't care if I'm lonely for the rest of my life, but I'll get through this and rebuild my life.

Pat clapped and whooped like a kid at Christmas. Then she said, you'd better get off that soap box before you put a foot through it.

Later, she picked up an old Polaroid photo of me and my mum at the Nepean River. I was about nine, blonde hair in plaits;

Mum's eyes were hiding behind tortoiseshell sunnies. Where's your mum now, she wanted to know. Her eyes teared up when I told her Mum had aggressive breast cancer, no chance by the time they found it. Six months was all she had. Pat gave me the longest hug.

I think she needed it more than me, because straight after, she told me the volunteer's mum died a few weeks earlier. The funeral was still fresh in her mind. It was heartbreaking, she said. Then Cliff Richard's 'The Millennium Prayer' came on the radio. I got goosebumps; she burst into tears. They played that song at the funeral when the coffin slid behind the curtains. Her crying made me cry – look at us, she said after a minute, I think we need a cuppa.

I put the kettle on, found two mugs and a box of home-brand teabags. As the kettle boiled, Pat told me the dead woman was one of her best friends. A long-time supporter of the refuge. It was hard to see her fade away, she said, sniffing at the memory.

I handed her a tissue and asked about the daughter. I hadn't forgotten her, or the day our paths collided again. Maybe now was the time to reach out. Enough time to let the dust settle.

Devastated, Pat said. We all were.

I asked, do you think she'd talk to me?

Pat gave me a curious look. I played it cool. Told Pat we knew each other when we were kids, but lost touch when we were about eleven. That I'd recognised her and wanted to catch up for old time's sake, but the time hadn't been right. That we had things in common – including our mothers, who also knew each other back in those days.

She didn't ask questions. That was the good thing about Pat. She could tell when you didn't want to say any more. Respected your right to hold back, didn't push for details. Instead, she told me about a memorial service at the refuge in a few months, a big deal. You should come, she said, I'll send you the info. Then she drained her cup, turned up the radio, and said it was time we got

259

back to work. Before she left, she gave me a gift wrapped in recycled cellophane: a crocheted blanket. A rainbow hug.

That night, the old feelings returned. Fear. Anxiety. Indignation. How long would it take before he found me, or someone broke in? Would I ever find a pathway out of struggle street? Why did this happen to me? I could see my life unfolding: a dead-end factory job, bills piling up, not enough money to make ends meet. Trapped in poverty. Old before my time.

And then I imagined another life. The one I have now.

Before Pat left, she said words I will never forget: *You have an extraordinary capacity for survival.*

It took me a long time to believe it.

CHAPTER FORTY-EIGHT

1980

'Hurry up!' I bang on the toilet door for the third time in five minutes. Sal's locked herself in and won't come out. From the sounds of it, she's spewing her guts up.

'Go away.'

'I'm busting!'

'Go away!'

When my sister emerges, the same sour smell I noticed this morning surrounds her like an invisible cloud. The toilet smells worse, so bad it makes me gag. I hold my breath the whole time I'm in there. Twenty-three seconds.

I find Sal in the bedroom, curled up on her bed. Her skin is white, like the colour has drained away with all the vomit. She looks wiped out. Same as yesterday. And the day before.

'Are you okay?' I give my forehead a mental slap, bracing myself for a dirty look, a snappy response, but Sal doesn't seem to care. 'Sorry. I mean, want me to get Mum?'

'No!' She softens when I step back. 'I'll be fine, Jane. An icky tummy, that's all. Probably something I ate at lunch. I'll get up in a minute.' Pulling herself to her feet, she says, 'See? I'm fine.'

Her face warps, her hands clap over her mouth and she bolts

from the room. The toilet door slams. The explosion that follows is enough to send me running to the kitchen for help.

'Mum! I think Sal's dying! She's throwing her guts up!' Mum's knife clatters to the bench. 'What?'

'She's spewing again!'

'Again? What do you mean *again?*'

'Nothing.' I have an uneasy feeling, like a storm is coming. 'She said it's a tummy bug, Mum.'

Mum's face whitens. 'Stay here. And peel those potatoes for me.'

It's so warm and muggy my clothes are clinging to my skin, but the cold shiver returns.

By dinner time, the sky is blanketed with swollen grey clouds. Is a storm coming? Rain? Dad says we need a thunderstorm to clear the air, and I wonder if he's talking about the air inside or out. Or both. He strips the meat from his chop bones, licking each one clean with lip-smacking pleasure. Does he even know that Sal might be dying? Surely if he knew, he wouldn't be enjoying himself so much.

How can he not notice something is wrong? Sal hasn't even touched her eggs or salad – she still looks tired, although the colour has come back into her skin. And Mum isn't eating either. She's pushing food around on her plate, watching Sal, who is pretending not to notice. Sighing like her thoughts are too heavy for her to contain. Finally, Dad notices.

'Is something wrong?' He pauses, looks from Mum to Sal. Wipes his mouth with a serviette, steeples his hands together. Waits. 'What?'

'Nothing,' Mum says in a voice that means *something.* Something big. She nods at me and Jim, mouths *little ears.*

'I'm pregnant,' Sal says.

I didn't know silence could be so loud.

'I'm going to have a baby. Robbie's baby.'

Jim spits out his drink, spluttering, choking. I thump his back because Dad's too busy staring at Sal, mouth open, and Mum's watching Dad, twisting a serviette in her fingers. It's as if me and Jim are invisible.

'Pregnant?' Dad's roar nearly knocks me off my seat. 'What the—' He slams his hand on the table, then thrusts his chair back, away from Sal. Finger pointing, trembling. 'I'll kill the bastard. Messing with my daughter. I'll bloody rip his—'

'Trev!'

'Dad!'

Dad stops. Heavy breaths. I count to ten. Twenty.

'I cannot believe a daughter of mine got herself into this mess. I thought you knew better.'

A tear trickles down Sal's cheek. She doesn't wipe it away.

'Trev!'

Dad glares at Mum. 'For Chrissake, Barb. You knew, didn't you.'

'Only today, Trev. But calm down. Calm down.' Again, she nods towards me and Jim.

'Don't bloody tell me to calm down. Our daughter's sixteen and pregnant. How the hell did that ... no, don't bloody answer that ...' he drums his fingers on the table, 'we'll have to ... there are places ... adoption ...'

'No!' Sal is standing now, trembling, tiny as she faces Dad across the table. But her voice doesn't wobble. 'I'm not getting rid of it, Dad.'

How do you get rid of a baby? The conversation has raced ahead of me.

'You can't *have* it. You're *sixteen*. Barely old enough to take care of yourself.'

'I'm nearly seventeen. And Mum was nineteen when I was born.'

'Nearly twenty. And that's different. We were married.'

'Yeah, because Mum was three months' pregnant. I've seen my birth certificate. I've done the maths.'

'No way!'

Three sets of eyes swing to Jim, then me.

'You two.' Dad's voice is tight. 'To your rooms. Now. Take your dinner with you.'

We take our plates but listen from the living room. They're too involved to check up on us. Snippets drift down the hall: *going to get married ... after apprenticeship ... move it forward ... first I've heard ... gimme a break ... reconsider ... harder than you think.*

Sal's next words come through loud and clear. 'Dad. Read my lips. I'm. Not. Getting. Rid. Of. It.'

'Oh, for Chrissake.' Fly streamers rustle. The screen door bangs.

Someone – probably Mum – carries dishes to the sink. Taps are turned on. Running water drowns out most of their words. More fragments: *give him time ... seven months ... his little girl ... not anymore.* When footsteps head our way, we bolt out the front door. Dad is across the road, talking to Mr Jones. He doesn't look our way. I wonder if he's told Mr Jones about Sal.

'I can't believe Dad's princess is up the duff,' Jim says. 'What's up the duff?'

'Bun in the oven. Preggers.'

I can't believe it either. My big sister is going to be a mother. Jim whistles softly. 'This is gonna change everything.'

CHAPTER FORTY-NINE

1980

A few days later, me and Dad are washing the station wagon after dinner. It's the first time I've had him to myself in days. After Sal made her big announcement, me and Jim were packed off to Nan and Pop's for two sleeps, with at least two nagging reminders that *Sal's situation is family business* and no one, not even Nan and Pop, was allowed to hear about it *until we say so*. Our grandparents spoilt us: a trip to the zoo, the movies, soft drinks (even Coke!), unlimited cartoons, just-because presents. I forgot all my back-to-school and family worries until Dad picked us up after work. He didn't say much on the drive home, and I sat with Jim in the back seat, wondering what kind of topsy-turvy mess I was coming home to. Turns out, he used up all his words at work.

Now, as my father covers the car in thick, soapy bubbles, he seems relaxed. He and Sal are talking again and Sal's still having a baby. I saw them hugging earlier and, as I rub down the wheels, my heart swells with relief. If I hadn't heard their argument the other day, I would think it never happened.

'Hey.' Dad aims the hose at my bare feet, causing me to squeal.

Seconds later, a handful of bubbles is flicked towards my face. I lift a dripping sponge, take aim ... and that's when the fight is on.

But it's not a water fight – that stops before it starts. It's coming from next door and I'm so surprised that my sponge drops to the ground. I step away from the car, almost tripping over the bucket. It's happening again. The only warnings: a door slamming like a gunshot, the thump of footsteps and voices coming closer, closer.

'Stupid cow! Lazy bitch. Sit around on your fucken arse all day drinking and—'

'Bugger off, then!'

'Don't call my mum a stupid cow!'

I don't understand. Only days ago, Daryl was all smiles and charm, bringing Rose flowers and presents, mowing the lawn. Now Mean Daryl is back. With all that's been going on, I'd forgotten he existed.

Funny how fast you can forget some things. As if bad memories and feelings are locked into a jack-in-the-box, hidden until someone twists the handle, and *pop*, out they fly. Listening now, I remember all over again: the laundry, that creepy wink, the daily fights we all pretended to ignore. And it's not only Daryl. Rose is giving as good as she gets, or so it sounds from this side of the fence. It's as if someone drove past and flicked a cigarette butt into their house, sparking off a bushfire.

'Stay inside, 'caysha.'

'But—'

'Do what you're told!'

Hands grip my shoulders. 'Inside,' Dad says under his breath.

'But Dad, shouldn't we ...'

Murmuring and talking and voices rising. An explosion of eff-words and c-words that make my ears burn and my stomach cramp. A heavy noise I can't make out. A cry.

My throat feels like it's being squeezed.

Laundry. Fingers. Neck.

Don't tell.

I can't believe I was sucked in by Daryl's charm. He hasn't changed at all. Mum says we are what we hide. We all have good bits and bad bits, but some people are better at hiding the bad bits than others. Like Daryl.

'Now!' Dad twists the hose nozzle and a rush of water on metal drowns out the shouting over the fence. I remember he did that to two fighting tomcats once. Would it work on Rose and Daryl?

Inside, Mum and Sal are watching from the kitchen window, looking as worried as I feel.

'Daryl said the c-word,' I say, and Mum simply nods, like it's not the worst word in the world. 'What do we do?'

'Nothing. We can't do anything now.' She dries her hands on a tea towel, disappears outside without another word.

Sal tries to reassure me. 'They're just yelling, right? That's not so bad. Everybody yells sometimes. Look at what happened here the other day.' She picks up a tea towel and starts drying the dishes, before adding, 'Tell you what though. I'd never let Robbie call me names like that. Wouldn't put up with it in a heartbeat. Not that Robbie would ever. He's too respectful and …' She stops. Pats my hand. 'They'll sort it out. Don't worry.'

But I do worry. Because this is how it started before.

And Acacia is stuck in the middle of it.

When Mum and Dad come back inside, they act like nothing is wrong. Mum spoons vanilla ice cream and canned two fruits into dessert bowls, while Dad washes his hands and grabs a beer from the fridge. Next door, the fight continues.

'Right-o, nearly time for *Mork and Mindy*,' Dad says, looking at the clock. 'It's family time.'

'What about *The Incredible Hulk*? We always watch that, Dad,' Jim moans.

'Which is why we're watching a show the girls like for once.'

I don't want to watch telly. This feels like more than a distraction, like something they cooked up to send us a wordless message: *look at our nice family, spending time together, happy and normal, nothing like next door. Let's hide in our nice family bubble and pretend we're perfect.* My teeth grind every time someone laughs, because, despite my parents' pathetic attempt at a cover-up, our neighbours are still shouting.

Do something, Dad. Tell them to keep it down, like you do when we kids get carried away. His face is blank, eyes glued to the telly.

Do something, Mum. Tell Acacia she can stay here for a while. She swallows but stays put.

My eyes stab into them. Still, my parents do nothing.

I want to throw the telly at the wall.

'Turn up the sound, love, there's a good girl,' Dad says to me.

My eyes blur and, in that instant, I'm more than upset. I'm disap- pointed and scared and worried and furious all at once, and the feel- ings explode. 'You do it!'

Four gasps chase me out of the room, but no one follows. In my room, I pull a pillow around my ears, muffling the raw sounds from next door and canned laughter from the telly.

CHAPTER FIFTY

1980

No one mentions my outburst the next morning. Dad pecks Mum on the cheek before leaving for work. Sal runs around like a chook with its head cut off because she's late for work. Jim's watching telly and now Mum's sorting laundry. I wait for someone to say something, hating the fake way they pretend Rose and Daryl didn't have an hour-long screaming match in front of the whole neighbourhood. I don't know why I'm surprised when Acacia does the same; she could win a Logie award, she's so good at acting.

'So, what's going on at yours?' We're spreadeagled on towels under the wattle tree, watching George peck half-heartedly at a black lawn beetle.

'Nothing much.' She rubs a towel over hair still wet from the sprinkler, causing it to stick up in spikes that shimmer in the sun. 'Why?' Her voice is wary.

'No reason.' I back off, like always. Like everyone does when it comes to Rose and Daryl.

'Hey, you want go for a bike ride?' She leaps up and pulls shorts over her cozzie. When I don't move, her voice turns impatient. 'Come on.'

'Give me a sec to tell Mum.' I'm sick of being dismissed. Of secrets and pretending. But I'm too sluggish from the muggy weather to argue. This weather sucks the life out of everything. Even George looks droopy.

Within minutes, my hair is flapping behind me, and I feel the life come back into me. There's something joyful about being on two wheels. You're so busy staying upright, watching where you're going, you can't help but feel that everything is alright in the world.

Even when it's not.

Dumping our bikes at the park, we race to the swings, wincing at the burning of rubber on bare legs. Our feet drag on the ground as we tear wrappers from icy poles and thrust the already melting treats into our mouths. They disappear in seconds. We start swinging, legs stretching in and out, pumping the swings higher and higher, soaring above the playground.

Acacia jumps off mid-air and heads for the seesaw. I stay put, enjoying the feel of hot air hugging my legs, arms, face. With my eyes closed, I tilt my face towards the sun. I'm flying. Free. Nothing else matters: Sal, the baby, The Divorce, the fighting next door. In this moment, it's me, the swing, and the sun.

A familiar voice snaps my eyes open. Mary Evans is next to the seesaw, talking to Acacia. What does she want? For the last week, as the first day of school looms, I've prayed every night that I'll never see her face again. That she'll disappear in a puff of smoke. Change schools. *Be gone!* I'm breathing hard and fast, not from swinging in the sun, but what I know is coming.

Five days from now I will be in jail and Mary Evans will be my jailer.

My legs stop pumping. Feet drag on the ground. The swing slows to a stop. I glance around for Shane Watters, breathe out when there's no sign of him. Last I heard, they were *going together*.

'Jane, watch this!' Acacia is balancing in the middle of the seesaw, one foot on either side of the pivot. She inches herself away from the midpoint and the board wobbles, teeters, and then lowers to the ground as she moves painstakingly to the end. And then she jumps off, curtseys to Mary Evans. 'Cool, huh? Bet you can't do it.'

Still frozen in my seat, I cringe. Might as well have handed Mary Evans a live hand grenade.

'Do it again.' Mary Evans is up to something. Her crossed arms, the half-smile on her face, they're dead giveaways.

'Don't listen to her,' I call out. Or do I think it? Maybe I do, because neither of them looks my way.

My friend repeats the routine, starting at the end and suddenly, I know what Mary Evans has in mind. I cry out a warning, just as she jumps onto the end, launching my friend skywards. I'm off the swing before Acacia hits the ground.

'Acacia!'

She's curled up like a baby, clutching her foot and making a strange not-quite-crying sound. As if she's trying to stop herself from showing her pain. Her face is pale and screwed up, free of tears. The opposite of me. Mum reckons I carry on like a banshee when I'm hurt.

I turn into a banshee when someone hurts someone I love. Without thinking of the consequences or right or wrongs, I do the one thing Mum told me never to do in anger. I slap Mary Evans across the face.

It feels good for precisely five seconds. Then her hand flies to her cheek, and she stares at me in shock, rubbing the spot as I burst out, 'That's for hurting my friend!' The words keep coming as I kneel next to Acacia. 'What'd you do that for? You could have killed her. What if her ankle's broken, huh? Or her leg? How's she supposed to get home?'

'Shut your face, Jane Kelly.' Mary Evans kneels opposite me, but her eyes are on Acacia's white face. 'It was a joke.'

She sounds scared and something in me goes *aha!* I don't know how it happened, but something has changed between us: I'm not afraid of her anymore. I lean forward, get in her face. 'See anyone laughing?'

Acacia grasps my arm. 'If anyone wants to know, I'm okay. Just a bruise, I think.' She rubs her foot. Winces.

Mary Evans sits back on her heels. Her cheek is pink where I hit her. 'See? She's fine. You're such a drama queen, Jane Kelly.' She stands. 'I'm outta here.'

Faster than Superman, I'm in front of her. 'And you're a bully, Mary Evans.' To my surprise, we're the same height now. I've grown taller this summer and didn't notice. She opens her mouth, but I talk over the top of her, my words like jabbing fingers. 'You're nothing but a bully and I'm sick to death of the way you pick on people. Of the way you treat me! And I'm not putting up with it anymore. It's going to be different from now on.'

Mary Evans looks miserable. Bites her bottom lip. Sniffs. For a second, I think she's going to cry. Or apologise. If she does, I don't know what I'll do. What if she's faking? Her eyes are glassy, but then her face fixes into the defiant stare I know so well. 'Who cares? I'm moving away from this hole anyway. This weekend. Going to a new school and everything.'

There's no sting in her words. It's like she wants me to believe she doesn't care, but she can't quite convince her voice. I'll bet she's not happy about any of it – moving, changing schools, starting over. I wouldn't be.

Maybe she's given up fighting against it. Maybe it's too hard.

Now she's looking at the seesaw, at Acacia.

Anything but me.

I almost feel sorry for her.

Almost. Then I remember the way she shoved me into the brick wall that last day of school, fingernails in my arm, hot breath on my face. And all I feel is relief. At last, Mary Evans will leave me alone. Another prayer answered.

'Good,' I say, but she's already walking away, out of my life. Under my breath, I add, 'I hope I never see your face again.'

'Way to go, Jane,' a small voice says behind me. 'You finally stood up to Mary Evans.'

I swing around to find Acacia sitting up, holding her ankle, still pale, giving me a strange look. Not admiration. Disappointment. And I know why she's looking at me that way.

I avoid her gaze. 'Your foot! Is it okay? Let me see.'

'It's fine ... ouch!'

'Stop your fussing. I need to know if I've got to get help.' Acacia's worn-out thong falls to the ground as I move her foot from side to side, like Mum did for me when I sprained my ankle once. She only flinches when I touch a red spot on the side. It's about as big as a fifty-cent piece. 'Can you stand?'

'Yep.'

'You sure? Can you walk?'

She takes three steps forward, three steps back. 'Yep.'

'Good. Let's go. Mum says you've got to ice a bruise as soon as possible. Do you need to lean on me?'

'I'm all good. Your tongue's blue from the icy pole.' She pokes her tongue out. 'Is mine?'

I nod. Blue tongues are the last thing on my mind. 'Are you going to tell your mum what happened?' I'm still wondering this myself.

'Nah. No need.' She looks towards the road and gestures towards Mary Evans, by now a dot in the distance. 'I think she's a sad person.' She pauses, as if thinking of how to say something important. 'You shouldn't of hit her, you know.'

I hold my hand up. 'She deserved it. She's a bully.' I'm not ready to admit out loud that she's right, that I feel awful. And rightly so. Now I'm the girl who slaps people.

Acacia sighs and I'm positive she's thinking what I'm thinking, and I wish I could rewind and un-slap Mary Evans, anything to wipe that disappointed look from her eyes.

But instead, she goes, 'I'm just saying, she's sad inside.' Acacia stretches her legs and arms; her too-small T-shirt rides up, revealing a black-blue patch about as big as my fist.

I gasp. 'How'd you get that bruise?'

Acacia yanks the T-shirt down. 'Fell over the other day.'

'What? When?'

'Pretty sure I told you what happened.'

Her note of impatience makes me hesitate and I do what comes naturally: scold myself. *There you go again. Asking too many questions.*

And then I stop. Like I said to Mary Evans, things are going to be different from now on. 'No, I don't remember.'

And so, we push our bikes home, and she tells me a story: she was reading a book, walking at the same time, tripped, and landed on something. *That's all. Nothing to worry about.* Her eyes beg: *let it go.*

I've walked into things while reading. Everyone at home calls me the clumsy one – it's a family joke I don't find funny. Why do we laugh when people get hurt? And Acacia isn't clumsy. I don't think for a second that what she says happened is the whole story, or even part of the story. But she wants me to say *I believe you*, and I don't want her to be disappointed in me, so that's what I do.

I let it go.

CHAPTER FIFTY-ONE

ROOTS

True to her word, Pat invited me to her best friend's memorial. Tucked inside the creamy envelope was a personal note on old-fashioned writing paper with wattles around the edge. The message, in Pat's neat cursive, said: *I talked to your old friend. She wants to meet after the memorial.* My hands trembled as I read the words, over and over. The envelope and papers floated to the floor. This was it. I had a month and then it was time to come face-to-face with the one person from my childhood I could never forget, who deserved better than what I gave her. No backing out now.

A week before the memorial, I started to panic. The more I practised what I'd say – in the shower, on the bus, before I went to sleep – the worse I felt. Where would I start? With what happened to me and my family when I was a kid? Would she see this as a fair explanation or a pitiful excuse? How about two simple words: *I'm sorry.* I tried to imagine how she'd react, to write the script line-by-line in my head. It changed every time. I couldn't bring myself to ask Pat, or anyone, for advice, because doing that would mean admitting to what I was back then. Not much of a friend.

That week, I felt more alone than I had in months. I had a freedom I'd never had before. I could do what I wanted when I wanted. I only had to think of myself. No constraints, no complaints, no criticism. I was my own person. But for the first time since I left him, I wished I had a significant other. Someone to hang out with, to talk to about my problems and stuff. Someone to cuddle up with in front of the telly. To make love with. Have a child with – I was still young enough to want that and the urge, disappointed for so many years, was growing by the day. I wanted kids, but it never happened with him. You can't even do that simple thing, he'd sneer when he found me cramped on the lounge, hot water bottle pressed to my belly. And I'd think, what if I'm not the one with the problem? What if it's you? Now, I'm glad we never put a child through the hell of our relationship.

You'd be a shit mother, he said after I burned his dinner one evening. I used to think he was right, but alone with myself the memory made me mad. Made me want to prove him – and myself – wrong. I wanted to give motherhood a try, but there was a hitch.

Would anyone get through the barricades around my heart?

You get a lot of advice from the other women in a refuge: helpful, practical, unwanted. Most of it disappears into the murky fog of anxiety and paperwork and what next. But one piece of advice stuck: *Be careful of blokes. Some of them prey on women like us. We're easy targets, it's written on our foreheads.*

I don't remember the name of the woman who said that. She was there one day, gone the next. But I remember her voice: rough, husky, a heavy smoker's voice. A few of us were having a cuppa under the patio; a thirty-something woman called Shaz, I think, was going on about a guy who'd smiled at her in the line at Social Security, how he'd asked her out and she was thinking of saying yes, and she had his phone number, so did we think she should ring? Her friends were going, yes, ohmygod, that's so sweet. And this other woman, the one with the cigarette voice, took the last drag on her smoke, crushed it in an overflowing ashtray, and told her – *us* – to be careful. The others rolled their eyes and Shaz said she knew what she was doing, thanks very much; the new woman shrugged and went inside. I followed her.

While we were rinsing our mugs, I said something like, is that what it says on my forehead, that I'm an easy target? Playing cool but hoping to God I wasn't like the others out there, laughing and pretending they had their shit sorted when everyone knew they didn't.

And she looked at me and – isn't it funny how you can forget someone's name but always remember what they said – she said, Nah. Your forehead says *fuck off*.

The way she said *fuck* without even thinking or blinking didn't faze me. Once, after the word stopped being a smack on the bum, it was a slap in the face. But it lost that power over me years ago. When a word like that is thrown at you daily – in bed, in anger, in everyday conversation – it's only a word. No, it thrilled me to have that word on my forehead, an invisible yet visible message: *Fuck off.* In the months that followed, I looked in the mirror and repeated those words every morning. And it worked because men stayed away. You know that song, the Paula Abdul one, 'Opposites attract'? Yeah, that wasn't happening, and it was fine with me. In my undercover fantasies, I even toyed with the idea of giving up men forever and batting for the other side.

Although, sometimes, on the long, lonely nights when my bed felt like an endless desert, I wondered, am I invisible? Because I didn't want to be invisible. I just wanted to be left alone. But most of the time I didn't care what men thought. They probably didn't care what I thought either.

I don't know when or why I stopped saying those two words every morning. Maybe I got complacent. Maybe I thought of Mum, standing there with a bar of Sunlight soap. Or maybe, I got cocky, like whatshername-Shaz and her friends. Which led to Sean.

CHAPTER FIFTY-TWO

1980

'B ack in a sec!' I leave Acacia outside while I get an ice pack and go to the toilet. But I forget what I'm supposed to be doing when I see Rose and Mum sitting at our kitchen table. They stop talking when I barge through the door, the way people do when they don't want you to know what they're talking about. Rose looks away, but not before I see her puffy eyes and red cheeks. Are they talking about last night?

'Did you have a nice bike ride?' Mum's face gives nothing away. 'Yep. We went to the park.'

'Do you want something? You look like you want something.'

'Um …' All I want is to know what they're talking about. It's not good judging by the way Rose is fiddling with a Scotch Finger biscuit, breaking it into crumbs instead of eating it.

'I see.' Mum's on to me like a flea on a dog. 'Acacia's outside, isn't she? How about I make you girls a picnic? You can have it at the park.'

'But we've already been to—' Images smack into my mind: seesaw, Mary Evans, *slap!*

'Go again. It won't hurt you.' She spreads VitaWeets with Vegemite and marg, pops them in a Tupperware box, and makes up a bottle of cordial. It only takes a few minutes but there's a growing impatience in her movements. Clearly, I've interrupted something important. 'Off you go.' She hands me the container and bottle, practically pushes me out the door.

Halfway down the road, I realise I'm busting. There's no public toilet at the park.

Acacia rolls her eyes when I tell her. 'I'll wait here.' She plonks herself under a straggly bottlebrush outside Mrs Bubel's house. Rubs her sore ankle.

'The ice pack! I forgot. Sorry! I'll get it now.'

'Don't worry about it,' she says. 'It doesn't matter.'

Guilt needles me. A good friend wouldn't have forgotten. This time, as I race up the front steps, I'm determined not to be distracted by Mum and Rose, no matter what they're talking about. But what I hear, as I sit on the loo, sends my best intentions down the toilet. Clamping my legs together to quieten the flow, I strain to listen.

'When ... leave him? What if ... belts Acacia?' Mum's voice is urgent in a way I've never heard before.

'... never hit her ... hasn't ...won't ... loves her ... like she's his own.'

'... but thump you ... you say he loves ...'

'Yes.' A sobbing sound. '... isn't always like this ... when he's on the turps ... something I do ... sets him off.' A pause. '... thought he *had* changed ... the man I fell for ... told him about the baby ... I hoped.'

'... all think that.' Mum's voice is gentle. '... doesn't always happen that way.'

There's a silence. I finish my wee as quietly as I can. Wipe, pull up my knickers, shorts. Don't flush.

'... *love* me ... my fault ... push his buttons ... fight back.'

'... blame yourself ... not responsible for his actions.' More silence.

When Mum speaks next, it's like she's weighed her words as

carefully as ingredients for a new recipe. 'Acacia wants to protect you. How do you—'

'He won't!'

'You sure?'

'Yes.' Rose is crying properly now. '… *never* hit her … won't let him.'

Mum's chair squeaks on the lino and I'll bet a hundred bucks she's hugging Rose, the way she does with us kids when we're upset. I back out of the house, without the ice pack, my body shaking. I've heard enough. Too much. Things are worse next door than I imagined. Daryl does more than yell and swear and call Acacia's mum bad names.

He hits Rose.

I remember the time his thumb pressed into Rose's neck. The fear on her face, the horror and fear I felt all the way to my bones. I feel that way now.

Does he hit Acacia too?

I think of her reaction when I asked about the bruise on her stomach. First, she stared me down. Then she made up a story, begging with me to believe it, to go along with it.

I think she wanted to believe it too.

Acacia is still waiting under the bottlebrush tree. Mrs Bubel peeks at us from between her blinds and ducks away when I wave.

'Where have you been? I've been waiting and waiting. Thought you fell down the dunny.' She doesn't mention the absent ice pack.

'I was patting Turdle. He was lonely.' I pedal ahead so Acacia can't see my face.

CHAPTER FIFTY-THREE

1980

That night, I'm too hot and bothered to sleep. The open window lets in fresh air and a gentle cool breeze, but it's useless. My skin, body, mind is too worked up by angry noises coming from the front of Acacia's house. So far, they've been at it for ten minutes. My mind wanders and wonders, imagines and spins, questions and answers. The longer I listen, the more convinced I am there's the crack-slap of a hand, the thump of a fist. I imagine what I would say and do. What I think *Rose* should say and do.

Someone, anyone, tell them to SHUT UP!

Slamming the window shut, I pull on my nightie. My lips are dry. I need water. In the kitchen, the smell of fried fish and mashed potato remains. I gulp a glass of water. The sounds from next door are muted only by the telly in our living room. I wonder if Dad has turned it up on purpose, to drown out the noise, to pretend he can't hear. Tiptoeing to the living room, I peer around the doorway to find Dad in his armchair, apparently engrossed in the telly. Part of me wants Mum to look up from her crocheting or knitting, to whisk me back to my room and tell me everything's okay. But she's standing at the window, watching Rose and Daryl through the curtains. The way people do when they're spying but don't want to be caught.

When she sits on the couch with a heavy sigh, I slide into the shadows, yawning. Soon the click-clack of knitting needles turns into a pattern: *one, two, one, two, one, two, one, one, two.* I yawn again, rub my eyes, but as I turn away Mum starts talking about Acacia, and I'm wide awake again.

'Sometimes I wonder if anyone feeds her. Lord knows she eats over here often enough. She's like a stick. I'm scared she'll snap.'

Dad grunts. *One, two, one, two, one, two, one, one, two …*

'Half the time she smells like she hasn't even bathed for days. Or brushed her teeth. And her clothes are too small. I gave her some more of Jane's old things the other day and she couldn't get them on fast enough. And that hair. The way it was hacked off, not a care.'

Another grunt. *One, two, one, two, one, two, one, one, two …*

'And all this fighting … night after night. Listen to it.' Mum sets down her knitting, returns to her curtain spyhole. 'Come here. Look at this.'

Dad doesn't move. 'It's just a domestic, Barb.' He sounds irritated. 'Rose gives as good as she gets. You've heard the language that comes out of her mouth.'

'For Chrissake, Trev. He's hitting her. Rose, I mean. She admitted it today. And I'm worried he's doing the same to Acacia.'

'You don't know the whole story. Daryl went to 'Nam too. Messed him up a bit, I'd say.'

'That doesn't make it okay! How can you make excuses for him?'

'Well … well …' Dad seems lost for words. 'It's still a private matter.'

I shove my hand against my mouth, so I don't scream. Dad always says that. *It's private. Don't interfere.* But it's not right. Why can't he see that? Every bone in my body, every inch of my skin feels the wrongness of this. Why doesn't he?

'It's not good for the little one, living like that. Or for Rose. And now she's pregnant, as if she needs a baby in the mix. We should do something. Tell someone.'

'Barb ...'

'What if he turns on Acacia? For all we know he's already—'

'Stay out of it, Barb. Not our business. What happens in a man's home is his business.' It's the No Arguments voice. Mum ignores it.

'I disagree.'

Dad lets out a heavy, tired sigh. 'Rose needs to sort it out herself, love. She can leave if it's that bad. Kick the bastard to the gutter. Never did understand why women stay.'

'Are you saying she brings it on herself? If you ever did that to me—'

'Don't put words in my mouth. And I would *never*. I'm saying, she doesn't *have* to put up with it. And maybe if she didn't drink so much, she'd look after her daughter better. Maybe Youth and Community Services should get involved.'

I don't know what they are, but it doesn't sound good. Sitting back on my heels, I hug myself tight.

'Trev, that's not the answer. At least, not yet. Rose needs to get away. But I don't think she knows how to help herself. I've tried to help, to talk to her about options. But it's not that easy for a woman, especially when you've got no money, nowhere to go. She's got no family. And now she's expecting. Where would she go?'

Dad says nothing. Mum paces back and forth between the window and the lounge, twisting her fingers together. 'I'm calling the police.'

'Blast it, woman.' Dad slaps the couch. The sound echoes around the walls, making me rear back, almost overbalance. 'You know what'll happen if you call the police. Nothing. If they come out at all, they'll tell the two of them to get their acts together. The police don't deal with this sort of stuff – they leave it to the family to sort out. So, it'll be a waste of time and won't change anything. You know that.'

What? A waste of time? That makes no sense. Police help keep people safe. It's their job.

'Well, it bloody should! God, Trev, these laws, policies, whatever they are, they need to change.'

'Barb, love, you know this stuff happens in some relationships.' A long pause. 'You know I would never ... even when ...'

'I know. I know you wouldn't. But we're not talking about *us*. And just because it happens, doesn't mean this sort of abuse should be ignored.'

'Come on, now. Abuse is a harsh word.' When he walks to the window, I realise that the fight next door is over. 'All this stuff you're reading is putting notions in your head.'

'What else would you call it?' Mum snaps. 'All this stuff I'm reading is waking me up. When we do nothing, we're part of the problem. I want to be part of the solution! I can't believe—'

She breaks off and peers in my direction, like a fox catching scent of a rabbit. I shrink into the shadows, but she closes the distance between us in five fast steps.

'Get back to bed,' she snaps. 'I cannot believe you sometimes.'

Later she comes to lie beside me, removing the pillow from my head, stroking sweaty strands of hair away from my face. I bury myself against her chest, and she pulls me tight. Her face is wet. Like mine.

'Don't ever let a man treat you like you're worthless, Jane,' she whispers against my hair. 'Ever. Don't put up with it.'

CHAPTER FIFTY-FOUR

1980

Acacia is crying.

She's under a knotty tree in her front yard, her body shuddering with sobs. George is lying motionless on the grass in front of her. There's a red gash on his head. Ants crawling, flies buzzing.

'What ... what happened?' I choke the words out, kneeling beside her. I can't believe George is dead. 'How—'

'I don't know.' Her voice wobbles and when she looks at me, her eyes are red and puffy, like she's been crying for hours.

'Did a car ... a cat ...?'

'I don't know!' Standing, she bolts away from me, into her house.

The slap of the screen door feels like a slap on my face.

I don't know what to do. I can't leave George like this. He didn't deserve whatever happened to him. He should be buried. But Acacia needs me more right now.

Or do I need her? Ever since I noticed the bruise on her stomach, she's been keeping me at arm's length, pulling away as I pull closer, making excuses not to hang out. It's like she's run across a rickety suspension bridge, leaving me on the other side, too scared to cross. My eyes move down to George. His neck is at a funny angle. One eye is missing. He must have been dead for a while. I can't look at him anymore. But I have a feeling he would want me to make sure Acacia is okay.

Taking a deep breath, I pull open the screen door, pausing before I step inside for the first time, pushing aside the weirdness of walking into someone's house uninvited. I need to comfort my friend. She might push me away, but I need to try.

'Acacia?' As I step into the kitchen, my hand claps over my mouth. I've never seen anything like it. Blackened saucepans and greasy frypans on the stovetop. Dishes piled up in the sink, spilling onto the dirty orange laminate bench. Cigarette butts overflow from an ashtray. The table is piled with junk mail, rubbish, unwashed cups. The room reeks: rotten bin, stale oil, beer, sour cigarette smoke.

'Acacia?' The living room is no better. Dirty, greasy plates stacked on a coffee table. An empty pizza box on the floor. A baked beans tin stuffed full of more cigarette butts. In front of a new television, there's a raggedy lounge with a spring almost poking through. 'Don't Leave Me This Way' is playing softly on the new stereo. Sal always turns this song up.

My eyes inspect the room. I'm curious as a cat and jumpy as a flea all at once. There's something wrong with the way this house feels. As if the walls are so sad, they can barely hold themselves up. As if the air snaps and crackles with worry: *snap, crackle, pop!* I almost expect Daryl to leap out – *boo!* – even though I heard him leave earlier.

'Jane? What are you doing here?' Acacia is in a doorway, arms crossed. No smile. Her cheeks are still wet, her eyes as puffy as her voice.

'I-I c-came to be with you,' I stammer. 'I'm so sorry about … about George.'

Acacia stares through me like I'm invisible, then her shoulders droop, a sigh leaks out. As if her sadness is squashing her. She looks around the room, and I wonder if she's seeing it through my eyes.

'Cay-sha?' Rose's voice is thick but weak at the same time. From the shuffling sounds, I imagine she's getting out of bed, or at least trying to. 'Cay-sha!'

Acacia glances behind her. When her eyes meet mine again, what I see shocks me: shame.

'Go home, Jane.' The sadness in her voice nearly makes me cry. 'I don't want you here.'

Mum is on her knees, scrubbing the bath. Something must have given my feelings away, for she wipes her forehead and hands on her pinny, then opens her arms wide. I burst into tears and cry for a long time. I can't stop thinking of George's lifeless body, of Acacia's heartbroken face.

'Tell me.' She strokes my cheeks with her thumbs, before kissing my forehead.

The story spills out in sobs and sniffs: *George is dead and Acacia doesn't want to see me and the house is disgusting and no one looks after Acacia and Rose is asleep at lunchtime and everything is different and ...*

The whole time, Mum listens, without telling me I'm wrong or overreacting, and by the time I'm done, I think I'll never have a friend better than her. In the kitchen, she makes me my first-ever cup of tea, in one of her special cups, the one with a gold rim and bright blue cornflowers on the side. The tea is hot, milky and sweet. The best thing I've ever tasted.

'Mum,' I say, between sips of tea, 'when I first met Acacia, I liked thinking about what her life was like and what she was doing when I wasn't there. But now it makes me sad.'

'I know, love. I know.' She looks towards Acacia's house. 'I think Acacia is trying to take care of her mum, to protect her as best she can.'

For the next few hours, I stay close to Mum. One thing I love about her is that she's always the same. But I can't stop thinking of Acacia, living in that sad, dirty house. Listening to her mother cry, comforting her after another fight with Daryl, like she's the mother, not the other way around. I think about the way people talk about Acacia – *that poor child* – and her tangled hair, dirty teeth and too-small clothes.

Being her, being Acacia, must be hard.

And then it hits me. I've got friendship wrong. I thought being a best friend was about trading secrets and fixing each other's problems. But what Acacia has wanted all along is simple: be her friend. Hang out. Play games. Do handstands against a wall. Eat ice blocks and share dreams. Lie around and wish on stars or fairy clocks. Listen, don't fix. *Be*, not do.

I think George figured that out long ago.

We bury George in the garden bed closest to the wattle tree. Acacia wanted to bury him under the tree, his favourite place, but the ground was rock hard. I dig a hole, then Acacia carefully places George in it. He's wrapped in one of her T-shirts, and she tucks it around him as if tucking him into bed for the night. I ask her if she wants to say a prayer; she shakes her head, *no*. We cover him with dirt and scatter flowers on the mound, and then she whispers thank you for being my friend.

Mum brings out fizzy drink and four Monte Carlo biscuits. Acacia chomps into hers like she's starving. 'Thanks,' she says, mouth full.

We chew in silence. I don't know what to say. I don't think she does either.

'Here,' she says after a time, passing me a wattle seed pod. I run my fingers over the dents separating the hidden seeds. 'You can plant the seeds, you know. Mr Jones told me. He said they would grow into beautiful acacias, like me. You can have it.'

She nibbles at her lip, like she's embarrassed. We continue to sit in silence. It feels weirdly awkward, like the first day we met, when we asked *how old are you* and *where did you live before here?* I remember waiting for her to sneer *what are ya* and thinking *I'm plain Jane Kelly, no one special.* That's one thing that hasn't changed. I clutch the seed pod to my heart as if it's a hug.

She breaks the silence first. 'Sorry about this morning. It's just … finding George, that was a shock … and the other stuff … I can't talk about it, you know. It's family stuff. I'm not supposed to. You're the same in your house, you are. There's stuff you don't talk about with other families.'

She's right. I don't talk about Dad's dark moods. I haven't told her about Sal's baby.

Acacia continues, 'And I don't want to. Talk about stuff at my house, I mean. If I don't talk about it, then it doesn't have to be real.' She stares at the flower-covered grave while she talks, as if she's confiding in George instead of me. Maybe it's easier.

'But …' I struggle to find the words, 'but, it is real. I mean, everyone knows about the fighting. We can hear it.'

Acacia chews on her lip, like she's battling to keep the words in. And then, finally, for the first time since we've met, she stops hiding herself. 'I know,' she says hotly. 'I know what everyone thinks of our house. And me. And Mum. And it's … bigger than embarrassing. I hate it. I hate all of it. The fighting. The mess. I never wanted you to see that, you know. Your house is so clean and tidy,' her voice breaks but she goes on, 'and mine is … mine is *shit*! And I hate him. That man. I know it's wrong, but I hate him. I really do. I *hate* him for hurting Mum. For calling her names. For punching her. For knocking her to the ground and saying it's her fault. *Her* fault! And then acting all sorry and buying her flowers and *shit* … and then sometimes I hate *Mum*. For falling for it, for staying with him. For getting drunk all the time. For … for not looking after *me*.'

For the second time in one day, I see my friend cry. I don't know what to say to make her feel better, so I resort to Mum's fix-all: a hug. As she sinks against me and cries her heart out, thin body shuddering, I know this time I've got it right. For now, a hug and a listening ear is the best way to show that she matters.

When the tears finally dry up, Acacia gives me a fierce look.

'I want to kill him,' she whispers. 'I dream about it.'

CHAPTER FIFTY-FIVE

TREE

Sean lived across the road, in a mission brown housing commission the spitting image of mine. I'd seen him around, roughhousing with his blue heeler, mowing the lawn, or fiddling with something under the bonnet of his beat-up station wagon. He was about my age, but he lived with his mum. Her name was Val. I'd seen her a couple of times from a distance, but she hardly ever came outside except to yell at him: *Where's me smokes, Sean? Whatchadoin', Sean?* Two people from the same family couldn't have been more different. Sean was skinny as a string bean and Val was, well, she was the opposite. No nice way to say it.

My next-door neighbour Edna told me Sean was a good bloke for two reasons: one, he quit his factory job and got a Social Security pension to look after his mum, and two, Sean kept his yard neat, unlike most of the people on our street. She stared at my overgrown yard when she said that. And so, I let him mow my lawn when he offered. A man like him was harmless.

Sean didn't want money for doing the lawn, just a beer if I had one. Said he had the lawnmower out anyway and it was no trouble at all. To be honest, it was a relief. I couldn't afford a lawnmower and the one time I borrowed one from next door I had to ask her husband to start it. You would have thought I'd asked for a million bucks, the way he carried on to his wife about missing the footy and bad timing, not realising I could hear him ranting through the screen door. When he came out, he was all smiles, going on about the weather and how good's the rain. Started the mower and went back to his footy, leaving me with it. I never asked to borrow their mower again. The grass could grow up to my armpits for all I cared.

But Sean didn't let that happen. And that's how it started – him mowing the lawn every week or so, me keeping a case of VB in the fridge.

After a while, Sean started doing more stuff in my garden, even though I never asked him to. At first, he'd do it while I was home, and if I said he didn't need to, I'd get to it later, he'd say, nah, don't worry yourself. But sometimes I'd come home from work and see evidence he'd been there – edges trimmed, branches pruned, garden beds weeded – and it creeped me out. It was one thing him coming over when I was home and another to have him invite himself into my space. I didn't say anything though because I still wanted him to do the lawn and stuff. I hadn't gotten around to buying any garden tools. And he was just being friendly. A nice guy. Even Edna next door said how tidy my garden was looking and how nice Sean was to help me out. *Wink-wink.*

I told her no, it's not like that, he's just being friendly, and she laughed and winked again. She didn't believe me, and sometimes, when I worried myself awake at night, I didn't believe me either. She was wrong and I was right. I was wrong and she was right. How could they be the same thing? Turned out, she wasn't wrong, and neither was I. Sean wasn't just being friendly. He wanted payment, of course he did. Everything has its price.

So, one day, he cracked open his beer at mine instead of taking it home like he usually did, and he said, why don't you get yourself one? I don't like beer but I'm partial to a shandy when it's really hot – and it was stinking hot and muggy – so I went inside and got a glass and a can of Schweppes, and we had a drink on the porch. And we were saying how hot it was, and what a pity we were so far from the beach (a day trip by the time you get there and back), and he said, wanna get some fish and chips later?

And I thought, it's only fish and chips, can't hurt. He said he'd go pick it up and what did I want? Couple of fish cocktails and some chips with chicken salt, I said. Then he said, what about I grab a bottle of plonk or something, and we watch *Hey Hey It's Saturday* together? Or maybe I can get a video out, There's *Something About Mary*'s supposed to be a crack-up. And I was nodding, yeah okay, but inside I was screaming NO! You want to come along for the ride, he wanted to know. This time I said no, I might have a shower.

He smiled and I knew, the way you just know, I knew I'd said the wrong thing. Right for him but wrong for me. I wanted to say, I've changed my mind, I don't want to hang out with you. Or better yet, I just remembered I'm supposed to be somewhere. But I couldn't get the words out. It was as if I'd taken a giant leap backwards, unable once more to trust myself. What if I was wrong about him? What if his smile was just a smile? Times like this you just want to phone a friend, but who was I going to call? I thought of getting in the car and not being there when he got back. And go where?

He made his move after the fish and chips. He wiped his mouth on the back of his hand, but his lips were greasy with fat when they came for me and I was thinking the whole time, like it was slow motion, *what do I do what do I do?*

I turned my head, so his lips slid on my cheek and said, no, I don't want that.

And he went, come on. Just a little kiss, that's all. No.

Come on. Show some appreciation. No.

Fucken cocktease leading me on all this time you should be grateful no one else would have you ugly bitch don't expect me to mow your fucken lawn again!

Later, when I'd checked and triple checked the locks, I imagined that woman from the refuge blowing smoke in my face, saying, told you, love, that's what happens when you let down your guard.

I reckon wisdom comes from experience, from trying and failing, from watching and learning. Mistakes are like stepping stones – if you mess up, you take the lesson you need and another step forward. Lucky I'm a fast learner. After Sean tried his worst, I bought a second-hand lawnmower and garden tools from the hardware store. Did my own mowing and weeding from then on, kept myself to myself. A man thought I was an easy target. It was not going to happen again.

I never told anyone about Sean. Too ashamed, embarrassed.

Mad.

The day after he tried it on, a woman at work asked if I was okay. I said my usual: good, right, fine. Or a version of that. I told myself, she doesn't really care, she's asking out of habit. She reminded me too much of that so-called friend at my old work; I told her about the hole in the wall, she said I was overreacting and changed the subject to her new shoes. Until I went to the refuge, it was the last time I talked honestly about my relationship. If anyone asked, I said yeah, we're good, we're happy, he bought me flowers, he's so sweet.

Do people really want to know the truth? Can they handle it?

How many times have you asked someone how they are while you're walking past them? How many times have you stopped to hear the answer? Do you really want to know about their gassy belly from the can of no frills baked beans they ate for dinner?

No. You don't. It's gross. Do you really want to know about the dream they had that was like, so, so weird? No, because that stuff is boring as batshit. Do you really want to know about the fight they had at home that scared them so much they thought they'd rather be dead than keep living their life?

No.

Because then you'd have to do something about it.

We all cover up our truth. Even when we're dying inside, that's what we do.

But it keeps loneliness alive, don't you think?

After Sean, I convinced myself that being alone was infinitely better than getting involved with another man. It wasn't true, of course. You tell yourself whatever you need to make it through. My heart was already whispering for a lover, but I wasn't ready to open it. I was scared, wary, prickly as a rose. So, I reminded myself that some of the loneliest people were in a relationship. Sounds ridiculous, I know. How can you be lonely when you've got someone sharing your house, your bed, your life? But I'd been there, done that, got the T-shirt.

The day before the memorial, the volunteer dominated my thoughts. I wondered if she was a lonely woman now that her mum was gone, despite having a husband. Or if she'd been blessed with a good listener, an equal partner, a decent man. The kind of man who brought flowers because she liked them, not because he was making up for something or wanted something. I hoped she wasn't lonely with him. And either way, I hoped she had friends and family to be there for her while she grieved her mum. She deserved that.

Me too. Yes, I was finally beginning to take in the three little words on that sticky note in my purse. My fake-it-'til-I-make-it reminder. *You deserve better.* A couple of years later, love – real love – came my way, and that gave me the best thing of all. A precious daughter of my own. But on the eve of the memorial, my heart was calling for something I needed even more than a lover or a child: a friend.

Before that door could open, I had something to do. Something long overdue.

CHAPTER FIFTY-SIX

1980

R obbie proposed to Sal today. They had a picnic sitting on the big rock overlooking the Nepean River and Robbie got down on one knee and everything. Sal reckons she cried, it was so romantic, and then she laugh-cried because he used the ring from a Coke can as a joke. Her real ring is simple but pretty, with a tiny diamond chip in the centre of a thin gold band. She looks a bit like a princess with a diamond on her finger and she acts like one too, the way she waves it around.

Dad doesn't say much when Sal and Robbie break the news. Mutters *congratulations*, shakes Robbie's hand, then disappears to clean the barbecue. In the kitchen, Mum tells Sal he's still getting over the shock of his daughter having a baby.

'Don't worry, love,' she says. 'He'll come around.' I reckon she's right. Dad carries on like a pork chop sometimes, and he still gets into his dark moods, but deep down he's a softie.

But Sal keeps glancing outside, a sad and hopeful look on her face. She brightens up when Dad comes looking for the tongs and invites Robbie to have a beer around the barbie. That means Dad's treating Robbie like a man now. Watching them laugh together, Dad flipping chops and Robbie cracking open a Tooheys, I reckon Sal's got nothing to worry about.

'When's the wedding?' I ask when we're all at the table.

'In March,' Sal says, patting her tummy. 'After my birthday and before I start to show. I still want to wear a white dress.'

Dad snorts. Sal gives him a dirty look. 'What's so funny?'

'Goodness, that doesn't give us long.' Mum ignores me and elbows Dad.

'We want something simple. Maybe have the reception here? I don't know. We haven't got it all figured out yet.'

'We'll have to have your parents around for a barbie soon,' Mum says to Robbie. 'How are they feeling about the whole thing?'

'Oh, you know, bit freaked out at first, but once they got over the shock, they were cool,' he says. 'Mum's already started buying baby clothes.'

'Has she really? So have I. Put some on lay-by at Waltons. A few little bits and bobs.' Next thing, they're all going on about cots and prams. Tuning out, I wonder if Sal is having a girl or boy. I hope she has a girl and calls it Jessica. Or Crystal.

With all the talk of marriage and having a baby, Sal seems different. Older. Almost a stranger. Sal but not Sal. As I pluck soggy cheese cubes from my salad, I realise our relationship will change again once she and Robbie get married. There'll be no more sister chats in our room. She'll be too busy being a wife. And once she has her baby, she'll be too busy with nappies and bottles for me. I'll be an aunty at eleven-and-three-quarters, and I'll have my own room, but I'll have to share Sal forever.

'Can I be a bridesmaid? Sal? Can I? Please?' Maybe Smiddy can be a manservant, or whatever you call the groom's men.

Sal laughs. 'Course you can. I want you and Margie to be my bridesmaids. But Margie's older so she gets to be maid of honour, okay?'

'Yes! You're the best, Sal.' I'm going to be a bridesmaid. Mary

Evans is the only girl I know who's been in a wedding, and she was only a flower girl. It's a pity she won't be at school on Monday. I'd give anything to see her face when she heard I was going to be a bridesmaid and an aunty.

Laughing, my sister turns to Mum. 'I thought Robbie's little sister could be flower girl.'

'I thought you were having a simple wedding,' Dad mutters, which earns him dirty looks from Mum *and* Sal. 'What? I was just saying. Gonna be bigger than bloody *Ben-Hur* at this rate.'

'Mum, can I tell Acacia after dinner? That I'm going to be a bridesmaid? And an aunty?'

'Tomorrow, Jane. Don't give me that face. And don't think I didn't see you give Turtle a sausage. What have I told you about feeding the dog at the table? Jim, stop playing with the sauce bottle. Now, Sal, do you think we should have an engagement party? Something simple, family and a few friends. We haven't got long to plan.'

'Crikey.' Dad turns to Robbie. 'See what you're getting yourself into? Weddings, parties, everything.'

The next morning, Mum calls me and Sal into her room. We sit on Mum and Dad's double bed; the flowery coverlet is pulled up tight, the pillows plumped like fat, flowery clouds. Mum's knee joints crack when she squats to open her glory box. As she shuffles through it, I reach for the book on Mum's bedside table, expecting to find one of the romances she borrows from Nan. Instead, the cover has no picture, only black words on a white background: *Scream Quietly or the Neighbours Will Hear*. Mum plucks it from my hand, but I catch the words *wife battering* angled on the bottom right of the cover.

'What's that story about, Mum?'

'Not now,' she says, tucking the book under her pillow. 'Shove up.'

Sitting between us, she hands Sal a small pink jewellery box. Inside the box is a dull gold chain with an oval locket dangling from the middle. The locket has a carved, white silhouette of a woman's face set on a light blue background and looks like it's about a hundred years old. I want to touch it, to trace the sideways face, to open the locket and see if there is anything inside, but Sal doesn't let go.

'Nan gave this to me when I got married, and her mum, your great grandma, gave it to Nan. It's yours now,' Mum tells Sal. 'It's called a cameo. I've been saving it for your wedding. It can be your something blue if you like.'

I've wanted a locket since Mary Evans showed off the heart-shaped one she got for her eleventh birthday, and Mum knows it. I hinted at least fifty times before my birthday.

'Don't worry, love,' Mum pats my knee. 'I've got something special for you too. For your wedding day. But wait until you're at least thirty, or Dad will have a heart attack.'

I giggle. 'What if I don't get married? What if I don't want to?'

'You will,' Sal says.

'If you're not married by thirty, you can have it,' Mum decides. 'Now, girls, listen to me and listen hard. I brought you both in here for another reason.' She swallows. Her eyes are shining, like she's sad. It's on the tip of my tongue to ask why, but she continues, words gushing like water from a tap turned all the way up. As if she must get them out before Dad and Jim come looking for us, or she changes her mind.

'You – that's *both* of you – deserve to be valued. That's how Dad treats me. I want you to remember that if a man, no, anyone, doesn't value you, they don't deserve you. And one day, when you have daughters of your own, you tell them the same thing. Okay?'

Mum has never talked to us like this before.

'Girls. Promise?'

'Promise,' we chorus.

Mum twists the hem of her Sunday dress, like there's more

301

she wants to say, but then she stands and tells me to get ready for lunch at Nan and Pop's.

'Jane, get changed into that nice dress your aunty gave you for your birthday. The one with the spots,' she says. 'Sal, wait here a moment.'

I stop at the door, turn back. Mum and Sal are on the bed. Mum is holding the book she'd hidden under her pillow. She wipes her eyes and without looking up, says, 'Now, Jane.'

'I have news too,' Mum says while we're eating lunch at Nan and Pop's. My aunt and uncle and cousins have come down from Springwood; we're all squashed around the table in Nan's kitchen eating roast chook, garden salad and buns. 'Everyone, shhh!' She taps her glass with her fork, and we all stop talking, even the little kids.

Nan and Pop swap looks. They've already heard about Sal and Robbie getting engaged and making a baby, and then my aunt said she was going to have another baby too. Dad has a strange look on his face, like he's scared of what Mum might say next.

Mum laughs. Her hair is all soft and fluffy around her face. She looks pretty. Has she had a trim? Is she wearing make-up? 'Not that kind of news.' The grown-ups burst out laughing, and I do too, even though I don't get it. 'I've got a job.'

What? Mum's been talking about it for ages, arguing with Dad about it, but I didn't think she'd really go through with it. Nor did Dad. He's staring at Mum in disbelief.

'What's this?'

'First you've heard of it, Trev?' Pop puts in.

Dad keeps staring at Mum, leaning away from her like he doesn't know her at all.

'Really, love?' That's Nan. 'What kind of job?'

'It's more volunteering, actually.' Mum's chin juts out. 'I only found out on Friday. It's at a refuge – a women's refuge. I'll be working there one day a week.'

'Friday? But you didn't say—'

'I was waiting for—'

'That's lovely, dear,' Nan says, with an encouraging nod. 'Anyone want some more rice salad? Trev? Paul? Come on, you know you do. Fill your plates, there you go.'

'A women's refuge?' It's Pop. He looks confused. 'What's that for?'

That's what I'm wondering.

'Oh, Dad,' my aunt says from across the table, 'it's a place for women who leave their husbands because ...' she hesitates, looking at my cousins who are playing with their food instead of eating, and lowers her voice, 'you know. It's not safe.' Her voice switches to happy-bright: 'Hey rascals, you look like you're finished. You can go and play outside now if you like.'

My younger cousins explode from the room like firecrackers on bonfire night. Mum doesn't tell me or Jim to leave the table. I think she wants us to listen this time.

'Hmph,' Pop grunts, gnawing at a chicken drumstick. 'In my day, marriage was forever. No matter what.'

Beside him, Nan nods. 'We were told to accept your lot. Get on with things.'

'Things are changing,' Mum says. 'Women can make different choices now.'

My aunt agrees. 'They are, that's true.'

'I'm setting an example for my girls.'

Pop shakes his head. 'Bleeding hearts, the two of you.' He looks at Dad and my uncle while he says this, as if expecting support. They look at their plates. 'You do-gooder bra-burners keep shaking things up that should be left alone.'

'For Chrissake, Dad! Women should have a place to go if they need it.' Mum's voice rises. My mouth falls open. So do Jim and Sal's. Who is this woman? This is not like Mum at all. Swearing in front of kids. Yelling in public. She is the most sensible of all of us.

Dad reaches for her arm. 'Barb ...' She shakes him away, gesturing at Pop with her fork.

'You know what I'm talking about, Pa. Don't put your head in the sand, don't pretend you've got no clue. You know what used to happen with the people across the road. And don't you dare tell me what goes on in a marriage is between a husband and a wife. "It's private. It's none of our business." God! I'm sick to death of hearing that.' Her eyes fix on Dad for a burning moment. 'It's *everyone's* business. No one, none of us here,' she sweeps her arm around the table, knocking over her glass, 'should be turning a blind eye to women and children getting hurt.' She slams her hand on the table. And then she bursts into tears, thrusts back her chair and runs from the room. A door slams.

I don't know what to do. Should I go after Mum? My eyes flick around the table. No one else seems to know what to do either. It's as if she waved a wand, freezing us in place and time. Stone statues around a stone table.

Dad thaws first. 'She's right, you know. She's bloody right. Excuse me.'

Throats clear and, in the blink of an eye, everyone carries on as if Mum's outburst was perfectly normal. Nan fetches a tea towel, dabs at the water puddle spreading over the table. Pop fills his plate with seconds, muttering *she's gone and lost her head*. My uncle and Robbie start talking about Greg Chappell scoring more than a century in the England–Australia Test series, while my aunt excuses herself to check on my cousins.

'Looking forward to the first day of school tomorrow?' Nan asks.

I can tell she's distracted. She keeps looking towards the front door, at the clock, at Pop. I shrug. 'Yeah, I guess.'

'That's nice, love.' Nan stands. 'I'll just go see B—'

Pushing his plate away, Pop booms, 'What's for dessert?'

CHAPTER FIFTY-SEVEN

1980

Mum barely speaks on the drive home. She stares out the passenger window, sniffing, dabbing her eyes with a scrunched-up tissue. Dad glances at her now and then, a worried look on his face; me and Jim watch them from the back seat. For twenty minutes, the only thing louder than the heavy silence is the hot wind whipping through the open windows. In the far distance, bubbling clouds tell me a storm is brewing.

Eventually Dad switches on the radio. Mum's favourite song 'I Will Survive' blares out, and he taps his fingers on the steering wheel, making whistling sounds through his teeth. When the chorus comes on, he starts singing and after a moment, Mum joins in, then me, then Jim. After that, the car doesn't seem as hot or stuffy or heavy.

Acacia is waiting in her usual place, on the letterbox, when we pull up in front of our house. She waves but stays put instead of chasing our car down the driveway as usual.

'Can I go play with Acacia now? Mum?' I ask, unbuckling my seatbelt. There's still time to make the last day of the holidays one to remember.

'Sure, love,' she says. 'But try not to get your dress dirty.'

'Can I tell her about Sal and Robbie getting married and being a bridesmaid? And the baby? Is it still a secret?'

Mum and Dad exchange looks. 'Go right ahead, Jane,' she says. 'It'll all come out sooner or later. Everything does.'

As clouds build towering sky-castles and the muggy air smothers us, we spend the last few hours of the school holidays sprawled on towels under the wattle. Clouds breathe and puff and billow, while Rural Fire Service helicopters and an air tanker drone overhead. There's a bushfire somewhere. The air smells of smoke and coming rain.

Acacia is in one of her quiet moods, so I talk her ears off while she sucks on a pineapple Zooper Dooper. I tell her about Sal and the baby and how I'm going to be an eleven-year-old aunty. About being a bridesmaid, not a flower girl. About Mum's new job, leaving out the bit about it being a place where women went when they got hurt. She makes noises of approval but asks no questions. And then, I tell her all about our school. How most of the teachers are nice but Mr Phillips puts kids on rubbish duty for looking at him sideways and Mr Cartledge throws the blackboard duster at kids mucking up in class. And how Miss Sakuma uses her umbrella even when it isn't raining.

'I hope you're in my class. I'll be really upset if you're not.'

'Me too.'

'And I hope we get Miss Masters as Year 6 teacher because she's really nice. Jim reckons she plays music in class and teaches everyone the Nutbush dance.'

'We already know how to do that! I taught you at the street party, remember?'

I do. I wish I didn't. But there are things you can't unknow, you can't unsee, no matter how hard you wish them from existence.

'Promise to stay my best friend forever, even if we're in different classes?' A ray of sun pushes between the clouds, tracing a line of gold all the way to the ground. And like that, the clouds of doubt disappear. We've only known each other for seven short weeks, but our friendship is timeless.

Acacia crooks her little finger at me. Links it with mine. 'Promise.'

Behind us, lightning cracks the sky.

When Mum calls me in for dinner, the clouds are near-black. Sunlight shines through in patches, casting an eerie green-gold glow over the street. Now thunder and lightning play chasings across the sky, and the air has a strange, sweet smell. The birds are silent, the trees deathly still.

'Meet you in the morning. Out the front. Eight o'clock,' I call from the steps.

Under the wattle, Acacia's face is shadowed. When she steps out from under the tree, the clouds split. Sunlight paints her hair, brushing her with that same magical glow as the day we met. A wave, a smile, another promise.

A new portable telly is on in the kitchen; Dad is leaning against the bench, waiting for the weather report while Mum and Sal bring cold meats, buns, salad and sliced cheese to the table. Jim slides into the room, wiping wet hands on his shorts.

'What's for—'

'Shoosh.' Dad gestures at the telly. The weatherman says *brace yourselves for wild weather tonight.*

'A severe thunderstorm is predicted across the metropolitan area, with ten to twenty millimetres of rain. Some areas could cop up to forty millimetres and residents of the north-west could endure flash flooding …'

Newsreader Brian Henderson wraps up the news with a reminder for us kids to enjoy going back to school. Jim groans. So do I, but only half-heartedly.

Dad snaps off the telly. 'Come on, you lot. Jim, bring that water jug over, will you. Thanks, lad.'

'Might have to bring the dog in tonight,' he says, smearing margarine over his roll, loading it with salad and sandwich ham, grinding so much pepper on his tomato that it makes me sneeze. 'Nine News reckons that storm's going to hit here hard.'

'They've been saying that all summer.' Mum adds tomato to her roll. 'Pass the salt, Sal.'

A clap of thunder rattles the window. I count to thirty before lightning flashes, then do some fast maths. Ten kilometres. That's how far off this storm is.

'I reckon a good storm will clear everything out,' Mum says, switching on the overhead light. 'Bad things happen when it's hot for so long.'

The thunder-rumbles are increasing now; the clouds are black, bulging. The air smells wet and feels heavy, but the storm is playing games, teasing us. Looking out the window, I wish the storm would hurry up, be over and done with. The longer it takes, the more unsettled I feel. But it's not just the weather. I'm fidgety, nervy, worried, and I can't put my finger on it. Mum reckons I'm overexcited because of school starting.

'It's not school,' I tell her, packing my new pencil case and stickered schoolbooks into my school bag. Earlier, she'd laid out my school uniform and polished my school shoes. They're shiny like mirrors but won't stay that way for long. Aside from school photo day, the first day of school is the only one when everyone has shiny shoes. 'Something doesn't feel right.'

'Oh, love, you'll be fine tomorrow. Nothing to worry about. A big Year 6 girl like you has no need to be worried about school. Especially now that Mary Evans has moved away.' The soft expression on her face makes me wonder if she knows more about Mary Evans than I let on.

'No, not about me. About Acacia.'

Mum assumes I mean our friendship. Why wouldn't she? I've

been questioning it all summer. 'You girls are snug as a bug in a rug.' A quick hug. 'Don't you go worrying about that. Acacia is a loyal friend. She'll stick by you.'

'I know.' The pit in my stomach has me all confused.

'Early night tonight,' Mum says, standing up. 'Off you go, have a bath. Wash behind your ears and give those fingernails a good scrub. I'm off to sort out your brother.'

My eyes dart around the room, landing on Sal's vanilla-scented bubble bath. She raves about how relaxing it is, how delicious it smells, and hides it so I don't use it accidentally on purpose. Unscrewing the cap, I squeeze a little onto my pointer finger, rub it between finger and thumb, inhale the sweet smell of baking cakes. Will Sal notice if I use a blob or two?

My grip tightens on the bottle, but the storm starts before I make it to the bathroom. It's directly overhead, a spotlight from heaven. Wind gusts through the open bedroom window, jolting the screen and blowing the fragile seed pod Acacia had given me onto the floor. Dropping the bottle, I run in search of Mum. She's with Sal, peering out the living room window, which rattles as wind squalls shake the house.

But they aren't looking at the sky.

Daryl and Rose are facing each other on our driveway. His deep angry voice towers over her high-pitched shrieks, over the wind-howls. Like the storm clouds overhead, he looms over Rose, one hand raised. Acacia behind them, yelling. I hear the words: *You killed George.*

'Shut the door,' Dad barks, coming up behind us. 'It's not our business.' He says it like kids at school repeat times tables, words carved in memory. But then he stops. Looks. Swears.

Later, what happens next will replay in my dreams for years and years, but now I burst into action, the fighting kind that comes when someone you love is threatened. Pushing past Mum and Dad, I run to the front door, wrench it open, screaming, 'Stop it! Stop it! Stop it!' As if Daryl will listen to an eleven-year-

309

old girl. As if *I* can make a difference. Mum pries my hand off the handle. I shake her off. Lunge for it again.

All I know is this: I must get to my friend.

An earth-shaking rumble. Turdle barks, short and sharp. Lightning floods the street. It's perfectly timed, like a movie, as if this scene was written to happen at this precise moment.

'Crikey.' Jim joins us at the door. His voice cracks when Daryl grabs Rose by the throat. 'Dad. Dad! He's going to kill her!'

'Trev! Stop him! Sal! Call the police. Do it, Sal! Trev, do something!' Mum turns to Jim, pushing me towards him. 'Go! Stay in your rooms.' But Jim doesn't move and somehow through my angry, wet haze I understand that he is crying too.

'Leave my mum alone!'

Acacia! No!

With all the strength I have, I thrust myself away from Mum's hold and explode onto the verandah. Mum grabs at my dress; I yank against her hold while Acacia launches herself at Daryl, kicking and screaming like a wild animal. He slaps her face with a crack like a gunshot and I flinch against Mum as my best friend crumples in a pile of angry girl.

Dad bulldozes past us. 'You fucken gutless mongrel!'

Senses blur. Time warps. Speeds up. Slows down.

I see everything and nothing.

Hear everything and nothing.

Shreds.

Fragments.

A garbled emergency call. The push–pull on the verandah. Acacia on her feet, a lioness roar.

Voices yelling, imploring. Mine. Mum's. Rose's.

Stop it, Daryl! No, Acacia!

Thunder-slaps and lightning-cracks.

The thump of fists on flesh.

The war cries of Dad and other blokes who appear out of nowhere and charge like avenging angels.

Wind rushing against my face as I tear free.

'Acacia!'

Fat, warm raindrops falling on my head.

Someone, everyone calling my name.

'Acacia!'

But before the man-warriors can get there, before I can grab Acacia and pull her away, before the men pin Daryl down, Rose hurls herself at Daryl, screaming *bastard, don't touch my daughter, bastard* and he grabs her wrists yelling *look what you made me do* and then he punches her in the gut and Acacia charges again and Daryl shoves her away and she hits the letterbox with a thud and a snap and she doesn't move and the men grab Daryl and Rose slumps to the ground beside her, holding her stomach, screaming, crying, moaning: *look what you did, look what you did.*

The snap-crack of a wattle branch split by lightning; the thud as it crashes to the ground.

CHAPTER FIFTY-EIGHT

BLOSSOM

I used to be called Mary Evans. Well, I was until my name changed and now, I'm Mary someone else. I was a bully at primary school. A hurting person who hurt other people. I know now I was acting out my pain. Transferring it onto others. Using my size to intimidate, like my dad did with my mum. It's why it was so hard to believe that I deserved better.

I remember me and Mum laughing while watching a movie and Dad screamed at us: *Be quiet!* It was my fault when Dad got angry, Mum made that clear. When Dad left, one hot, angry afternoon, that was my fault too, and Mum took out her anger on me. If she came home and things were untidy, she would scream at me, then fall in a messy, sobbing heap. I carried that burden for years. I wanted my Mum to be stronger, but she couldn't or wouldn't, so I vowed not to be like her, while also vowing never to end up with someone like my dad. Instead, for a while, I turned into the same person my parents were. I married someone who was more like my dad than I realised until it was too late. And then, rather than dumping and running, I tried to fix *him*, to do better than my mum.

Poor Mum.

I had no idea what a healthy relationship looked like.

But there's still no excuse.

Some might say what happened to me was karma – what goes around comes around. Before I was slowly broken into pieces, I might have said the same. Like the song, the New Radicals one that got stuck in my head for months: 'You Get What You Give.' It's taken me years to accept that I didn't deserve what *he* gave me. But the day I saw the girl who used to be Jane Kelly, I knew *my* day of reckoning was coming.

Barbara Kelly's memorial was held at a new women's refuge named in her honour. When I reached the address, I wasn't sure it was the right place. There was no sign. Nothing that made it stand out. The kind of place you wouldn't notice because it blended in with every other house on the street. Just an ordinary brick-veneer house, with a brown wood-plank privacy fence. But it was the right place, according to the invitation Pat sent me. There were about a dozen cars parked up and down the street. Killing Heidi belted out the chorus of 'Weir' as I found a parking spot on a side street lined with old wattle trees, like the street I grew up on.

In a hidden car park down the driveway, about fifty people were gathered, mostly women, dressed in dark colours, smart casual. I looked down at the cheap skirt and blouse I'd found in the op shop near work, fighting the urge to make a hasty escape. Pat spotted me before I could retreat into invisibility, waved me over to a marquee where trestle tables sagged under the weight of steaming urns, cups, and trays of sandwiches and cakes. Help yourself, she said, hugging me before being swept away by a serious-faced woman with a notepad. A younger woman with a camera trotted after them. With a cup of tea in one hand, curried egg sandwich triangle in the other, I watched Pat pose self-consciously with a woman who had to be a politician. And then she was swept away once more.

Standing alone in a crowd of people, I shrunk back, into the shadows. Watched from the safety of a spreading shade tree, recognising familiar faces: refuge volunteers and staff, the police liaison officer from *that* day. The Kelly family. They formed a tight-knit group, like they always did. Twenty years older, but still recognisable. Mr Kelly, white haired and sixty-something now. Sal, the girl-next-door we all wanted to be, now in her late thirties, her hair streaked and tousled like a just-got-out-of-bed Meg Ryan. Beside her, a man, all receding hairline and Dad-paunch, and a lanky teenage boy in a Nirvana shirt and jeans that sagged around the hips. Jim Kelly, short-haired and well-built, with the upright, watchful bearing of an off-duty cop. And Jane. Taller than her sister, streaked blonde hair pulled back into a low ponytail, her face hidden by a sideswept fringe and big sunglasses. Pregnant, maybe seven months. Holding hands with a man I didn't recognise, cupping her belly with her free hand.

I felt the moment she noticed me all the way to my bones. Remembered long ago words I pretended not to hear, but oh, I did: *I hope I never see your face again*. Words that cut me to the bone. My just desserts. What would she say to me today?

The service was what you'd expect. Strangers said nice things about the woman I knew as Mrs Kelly, who had words with my mum about my behaviour at school more than once. I didn't like her in those days, resented her for sticking her nose in, punished Jane for being a dobber. God, I was so young, so self-absorbed, so cruel. Listening to the people speak, I finally understood what I'd been unable to as a hurting child – Mrs Kelly was the kind of person who stuck up for those who couldn't do it themselves. The kind of person you'd want in your corner. Way back in 1980, she started volunteering at the refuge I ended up at nearly twenty years later. From then on, she selflessly supported women in the community. No wonder Pat – everyone here – liked and respected her.

And then Mr Kelly spoke, flanked by his three adult children, his words burning onto my heart: *A long time ago, when my wife wanted to have difficult, challenging conversations about domestic violence, I told her to mind her own business. She ignored me, and I'm so glad she did. Because we cannot mind our business about this anymore.*

When he finished, the crowd applauded. The loudest of all was a woman in her fifties, with long pink and silver-streaked hair and twitching fingers the hallmark of a heavy smoker. Tears tracked down thin, prematurely aged cheeks as she clapped; she looked worn by life, but not worn down. Something about her was familiar, but I couldn't put my finger on it. A young woman with platinum-blonde hair and black fingernails stood by her side.

The moment finally came. Jane said something to her husband and approached me, lifting her sunglasses up onto her head. Her searching eyes whisked me back twenty years. Suddenly we were eleven again, kids at a suburban park, facing off near a seesaw.

You're nothing but a bully and I'm sick to death of the way you pick on people.

Only we were no longer kids, and it was time to say what I should have said to her years ago.

This is what I said: I'm sorry. I was a bully at school, and you copped the worst of it. I swallowed the 'but' that arose in my throat. I kept going: You deserved better. I can't change what I did, and I don't expect you to forgive me, but I am truly sorry for causing you pain.

My words trailed off, but really, what more was there to say?

Jane met my eyes and lifted her chin. I waited for the sucker punch of rejection I deserved, but instead she said, thank you for saying that. It means a lot.

A beat passed. I'm sorry too, she said. I slapped you, do you remember?

I shrugged. Yeah, I remember. I deserved it.

No, she said. No one does.

We stood in awkward silence, me grappling with inviting her for a coffee or something, anything to make up for past wrongs. Her, grappling with, well, me. I searched my mind for something to say, something to keep her there a little longer. From the corner of my eye, I noticed the pink-and-silver haired woman hug Sal, then Pat, and felt Jane pulling away from me, towards them. Someone said the name Rose. A memory surfaced: the girl who lived next door to the Kelly family that long, simmering summer. The girl with milk-white hair and too-big clothes whose mother's name was on everyone's lips. Who chose Jane Kelly over me.

Jane was opening her mouth to say goodbye or something polite, and I blurted out: What happened to your friend from that summer? I'm sorry, I can't remember her name. Something unusual.

Acacia. Acacia Miller. Yes, that's it.

She swallowed. Said, let me show you something.

Along the back fence at the Barbara Kelly Refuge, there's a garden filled entirely with different acacia species: Gold-dust Wattle, Sydney Golden Wattle, Spike Wattle, Sweet-scented Wattle, Fern-leaved Wattle. They weren't blossoming that day, but later that year, when I returned as a volunteer, they were in full glory. Golden balls of sunshine that made me sneeze. In the centre of the garden is a plaque with a tree of life engraved on it. It reads: *Remembering Acacia Miller. She protected her mother.*

That day, as Jane and I stood side-by-side, I could barely speak for the lump in my throat. What happened?

It's a long story. Not for today. She pointed at the pink-and-silver haired woman and said, that's her mum over there. Rose. She's going to volunteer here. And that's her sister – half-sister – Cassia. She's studying social work at the University of Western Sydney.

I nodded and said, thanks for meeting me. Turned to go.

She reached out and touched my shoulder and our eyes met again. There was a strength in hers – I wonder what she saw in mine – as she said, thank you for coming. And then she added, I forgave you a long time ago, want a cuppa one day?

This is something else I learnt at school. The wattle is resilient. It can be battered by wind, starved by drought, and burnt by fire, but still, it rises strong.

Just like me.

And you.

THE END

AFTERWORD

For the modern-day reader, the 'mind your business' and 'don't interfere' attitudes of some of characters in *Wildflower* are hard to swallow. But they weren't unusual. Back in 1979–80, when much of Wildflower is set, domestic violence was still not recognised by the law in Australia and police were dismissive of, and reluctant to, interfere in 'domestics'. With few options such as support by way of refuges, emergency housing and counselling, most women had little choice but to endure insidious 'private' abuse – leaving a husband was seen as a mark of disgrace.[1]

But things were changing and, increasingly, women were speaking out against violence against women. Refuges, beginning with the Elsie Women's Refuge in Glebe in 1974, opened their doors, with or without government assistance. By 1999, when the second *Wildflower* timeline begins, more than 300 similar refuges were operating nationwide.[2]

Much has changed since then. The shroud of silence over the issue of domestic violence continues to lift. Successive Australian Governments have been challenged to fund initiatives aimed at breaking the cycle of violence, as well as provide legal assistance services – to focus on reducing levels of this form of violence while also providing support. At the time of writing, violence against women was estimated to cost the Australian economy $22 billion a year.[3]

It's a complex and fraught issue, far beyond the scope of this novel. And there's more work to be done. Domestic violence against women – and men, although far less common[4] – continues. According to statistics summarised by White Ribbon Australia[5], on average one woman is murdered every week by a current or former partner, and domestic and family violence is the principal cause of homelessness for women and their children. In Australia, one in four children are exposed to family violence. If you are interested in digging deeper, I urge you to consider the statistics from the many sources available, including the White Ribbon Australia and Our Watch websites, and Jess Hill's powerful examination of the issue *See What You Made Me Do* (Black Inc., 2019).

For the most part, *Wildflower* examines the issue from the point of view of eleven-year-old Jane Kelly, who is compelled to speak up and out at a time when this was not deemed appropriate. My hope is that we, like Jane, continue to give voice and support to those affected by family and domestic violence.

If you or someone you know have been affected by domestic violence, the following organisation can offer support:

The National Sexual Assault, Family & Domestic Violence Counselling Line: 1800RESPECT or 1800 737 732

Visit au.reachout.com/articles/domestic-violence-support for a list of state-based organisations.

Remember, you deserve to feel safe, supported, and respected. Violence is never your fault.

1. https://dictionaryofsydney.org/entry/forty_years_of_the_elsie_refuge_for_-women_and_children
2. https://dictionaryofsydney.org/entry/forty_years_of_the_elsie_refuge_for_-women_and_children
3. https://www.whiteribbon.org.au/Learn-more/Get-the-facts/Facts-and-Statistics/Other-Facts-Statistics
4. https://www.whiteribbon.org.au/Primary-Preventatives/Understanding-The-Cause
5. https://www.whiteribbon.org.au/Learn-more/Get-the-facts/Facts-and-Statistics/Prevalence

ACKNOWLEDGEMENTS

Wildflower began as a short story that didn't win a competition but taught me about going deeper as a writer. After the competition, I contacted one of the judges for feedback so I could learn more about the craft. That judge and assessor was Laurie Steed. His warm and considered feedback and advice gave me the courage and motivation to stretch myself as a writer and stretch a short story into a novel. Laurie, the words 'thank you' don't seem enough, so let me say your guidance and support of authors is appreciated deeply by me, and so many others who have met you on their writing journey.

Thank you to the team at Bloodhound Books and my friends at Pilyara Press (especially Jennifer Scoullar for regular reminders that we are all magnificent). A special shout-out to editor Shelley Kenigsberg for your insightful advice.

Lily Malone, Teena Raffa-Mulligan, Maureen Eppen and Lorena Carrington all read early versions and convinced me not to leave *Wildflower* in the Drawer of Shattered Dreams. Once again, my husband read each version of the manuscript even though he'd much rather read French verbs and listened patiently when I mulled aloud about plot problems and word choices a million times. Blue Eyes, you are a one-in-a-million.

To Anne Moore, chief executive officer at the Lucy Saw Association – we met when I was a journalist for the local newspaper, and I have admired you and the work ever since. Thank you for pointing me in the right direction when I needed it. And to C, M and S – thank you for sharing your experiences of going to a women's refuge. Keep rising strong.

To Tabitha Ann Bird and Lyn Yeowart for your whole-hearted endorsements and support. It's more than I imagined, and I appreciate it from the depths of my heart.

To my readers. From the bottom of my heart, thank you for reading my story. Hearing that you've connected with it makes all the hard work worthwhile.

And finally, to women all over – you too can rise strong.

ABOUT THE AUTHOR

A former journalist and news editor, Monique Mulligan juggles creative writing with a marketing job in a busy arts centre. When she's not working you will usually find her a) writing b) reading c) cooking or d) taking photos for her cat's Instagram page. When she's socialising, she's usually behind a camera or in a corner hanging out with other introverts and making mental notes for stories. Monique is also a keen amateur photographer who loves taking close-up shots of flowers, and a passionate but messy cook, who believes love is the best ingredient in food. Her husband, adult children and cat agree.

Monique has had essays and short stories published in several anthologies, most recently *Reflections on Our Relationships with Anne of Green Gables: Kindred Spirits*, published by Cambridge Scholars Publishing, and *South of the Sun: Australian Fairy Tales for the 21st Century*. Her novel *Wherever You Go* will be published by Bloodhound Books in 2023.

Visit Monique's website for *Wildflower* Book Club Notes and a Spotify playlist, or to sign up for Monique's e-newsletter.

If you've enjoyed this book and have a moment or two, please leave an online rating or review. Reviews are of great help to authors.

www.moniquemulligan.com

A NOTE FROM THE PUBLISHER

Thank you for reading this book. If you enjoyed it please do consider leaving a review on Amazon to help others find it too.

We hate typos. All of our books have been rigorously edited and proofread, but sometimes mistakes do slip through. If you have spotted a typo, please do let us know and we can get it amended within hours.

info@bloodhoundbooks.com

Printed in Great Britain
by Amazon